About the Authors

Jennie Lucas' parents owned a bookstore and she grew up surrounded by books, dreaming about faraway lands. At twenty-two she met her future husband and after their marriage, she graduated from university with a degree in English. She started writing books a year later. Jennie won the Romance Writers of America's Golden Heart contest in 2005 and hasn't looked back since. Visit Jennie's website at: www.jennielucas.com

Addicted to daydreaming and romance from a young age, **Angela Bissell** suspects she was destined to become a writer although she did travel a convoluted career path on her way to authordom. Like many an intrepid Kiwi she also travelled the world, backpacking through Europe, Egypt, Israel, Turkey and the Greek Islands before settling for a time in London. Now she lives back home in New Zealand, never taking a day in her beautiful country for granted and loving the challenge of pursuing her writerly dreams.

The day **Maggie Cox** saw the film version of *Wuthering Heights*, was the day she became hooked on romance. From that day onwards she spent a lot of time dreaming up her own romances, hoping that one day she might become published. Now that her dream is being realised, she wakes up every morning and counts her blessings. She is married to a gorgeous man, and is the mother of two wonderful sons. Her other passions in life – besides her family and reading/writing – are music and films.

D0550907

Spanish Scandals

July 2020
Risking It All

October 2020
Secrets at Sunset

August 2020
Heat of the Night

November 2020
A Private Affair

September 2020
Ultimate Temptation

December 2020
Dangerous Liaisons

Spanish Scandals:
Dangerous
Liaisons

JENNIE LUCAS

ANGELA BISSELL

MAGGIE COX

MILLS & BOON

First Published in Great Britain 2020
By Mills & Boon, an imprint of HarperCollins*Publishers*
1 London Bridge Street, London, SE1 9GF

www.harpercollins.co.uk

HarperCollins *Publishers*
1st Floor, Watermarque Building, Ringsend Road
Dublin 4, Ireland

SPANISH SCANDALS: DANGEROUS LIAISONS
© 2020 HARLEQUIN BOOKS S.A.

Uncovering Her Nine Month Secret © 2014 Jennie Lucas
A Night, A Consequence, A Vow © 2017 Angela Bissell
Surrender to Her Spanish Husband © 2010 Maggie Cox

ISBN: 978-0-263-29868-0

MIX
Paper from
responsible sources
FSC® C007454

This book is produced from independently certified FSC™ paper to ensure responsible forest management.

For more information visit: www.harpercollins.co.uk/green

Printed and bound in Great Britain
by CPI Group (UK) Ltd, Croydon, CR0 4YY

UNCOVERING HER
NINE MONTH
SECRET

JENNIE LUCAS

To Pete

PROLOGUE

HE SEDUCED ME EASILY. He broke down my defenses as if they were paper. You wouldn't have been able to resist, either, believe me.

After so many years of feeling like a ghost in my own home, invisible, unloved, I think I would have fallen into his arms for one dark glance—one husky word. But Alejandro gave me so much more than that. He looked at me as if I were the most beautiful woman on earth. Listened to me as if every word on my lips was poetry. He pulled me into his arms, made me burst into flame, kissed my grief and cares away. After so many years of living in a cold gray world, my life exploded into color—because of him.

There was no reason why the Duque de Alzacar, one of the richest men in Spain, would want someone like me— plain, poor—rather than my beautiful, wealthy cousin. I thought it was a miracle.

It was only later that I realized why Alejandro had chosen me. He hadn't seduced me out of love—or even lust. It was many months before I realized the selfish reason that had caused him to overwhelm me with his charm, to dazzle me, to make me love him.

But by then, it was too late.

CHAPTER ONE

THE GRAY, LOWERING sky was falling like a shroud across the old colonial city of San Miguel de Allende when I heard the words I'd feared in nightmares for the past year.

"A man was here looking for you, Señora Lena."

Looking up at my neighbor, I staggered back, clutching my five-month-old son in my arms. "What?"

The woman smiled, reaching out to chuck the cooing baby's pudgy chin. "*Gracias* for letting me watch Miguelito for an hour. Such a pleasure…"

"But the man?" I croaked, my mouth dry. "What did he look like?"

"*Muy guapo,*" she sighed. "So handsome. Dark-haired and tall."

It could be anyone, I told myself desperately. The old silver mining town in central Mexico was filled with American expatriates who'd moved here to enjoy the lovely architecture and take classes at the famous Instituto. Many single women had come here to start new lives, pursuing new businesses as artists and sculptors and jewelry makers.

Like me. A year ago, I'd arrived pregnant and full of grief, but I'd still managed to start a wonderful new life. Perhaps this dark stranger was looking for a portrait of his sweetheart, nothing more.

But I didn't believe it. Fear was cold inside me. "Did he give his name?"

Dolores shook her head. "The baby was fussing in my arms when I answered the door. But the man was well dressed, with a Rolls-Royce. A chauffeur. Bodyguards, even." Her smile spread to a grin. "Do you have a rich new boyfriend, Lena?"

My knees went weak.

"No," I whispered.

It could be only one man. Alejandro Guillermo Valentín Navaro y Albra, the powerful Duke of Alzacar. The man I'd once loved with all my innocent heart. The man who'd seduced and betrayed me.

No. It was worse than that.

"He's not your boyfriend, eh?" My neighbor's voice was regretful. "Pity. Such a handsome man. Why did he come looking for you, then? Do you know him?"

Beads of sweat broke out on my forehead. "When was he here?"

She shrugged, looking bemused. "A half hour ago. Maybe more."

"Did you say anything about—about Miguel being my son?"

Dolores shook her head. "He didn't give me the chance. He just asked if you lived in the house two doors down. I said yes. He pulled out his wallet and asked me not to mention his visit, because he wanted to surprise you. Can you imagine?" She flourished some bills from her apron pocket in delight. "He paid me a thousand pesos for my silence!"

Yes. I could imagine. I briefly closed my eyes. "But you told me anyway," I whispered. "Bless you."

She snorted. "Men always want to arrive with a flourish of trumpets. I thought it better for you to be prepared." She looked at my shapeless white sundress and plain sandals with a moue of disapproval, then at my long, casual ponytail and makeup-free face. She sighed. "You have a good figure, but in that dress you look like a marshmallow. You don't make the most of yourself. It's almost like you don't *want* to be noticed!" She shook her head. "But tonight you must be at your most irresistible, your most sexy, *sí?* You want him to want you!"

No. I really didn't. Not that he would want me anyway, now his evil plan had succeeded. "He's not my boyfriend."

"So picky!" She made a *tsk* sound. "You don't want *this* billionaire, you don't want *that* one—I tell you, wealthy, handsome men are not so thick upon the ground as you seem to think!" Dolores glared at me. "Your son needs a father. *You* need a husband. Both of you deserve every happiness." Her expression turned suddenly sly. "And the man at my door looked like he would bring a *lot* of happiness to a wife. Every night."

"No doubt," I said over the razor blade in my throat. It was true. Alejandro had brought me intense joy for one summer. And a lifetime's worth of anguish since. "I should go."

"*Sí.* It's almost Miguel's nap time, isn't it, *pequeño?*" she crooned.

My baby yawned, his fat cheeks vying with his sleepy dark eyes for cuteness. Those eyes just like his father's.

I exhaled, running a hand over my forehead. I'd allowed myself to think we were safe. That Alejandro had given up looking for me. *I should have known.* I should have known better than to start sleeping at night, to start making friends, to start making a real home for myself and my son. *I should have known they would someday find me....*

"Lena?" My neighbor frowned. "Is something wrong? You do not seem happy."

"Did you tell him when I'd be back?"

"I wasn't sure when you'd be done, so to be safe I said four o'clock."

I glanced at the clock in her brightly painted front room. It was only three. I had one hour. "Thank you." In a burst of emotion, I hugged her, knowing that she'd been kind to me—to both of us—but I would never see her again after today. *"Gracias,* Dolores."

She patted my back. "I know you've had a hard year, but that's in the past. Your life is about to change for the better. I can always feel these things."

Better? I choked back a laugh, then turned away before she could see my face. *"Adios...."*

"He'll be your boyfriend, just wait and see," she called after me gleefully. "He'll be your husband someday!"

My *husband.* A bitter thought. I wasn't the one Alejandro had wished to marry. He wanted my wealthy, beautiful cousin, Claudie. It was the whole reason he'd seduced me, the poor relation living in the shadows of Claudie's London mansion. If he and Claudie wed, together they'd have everything: a dukedom, half of Andalucía, political connections across the world, billions in the bank. They'd have almost limitless power.

There was just one thing they could never have.

My eyes fell on my baby's dark, downy head. I clutched Miguel tightly against me, and he gave an indignant cry. Loosening my grip, I smoothed back his soft hair.

"Sorry, I'm so sorry," I choked out, and I didn't know whether I was begging my son's forgiveness for holding him too tightly, for tearing him away from his home or for choosing his father so poorly.

How could I have been so stupid? How?

Hurrying down the small street, I glanced up at the heavy gray sky. August was the rainy season, and a downpour was threatening. Cuddling Miguel against my hip, I punched in the security-alarm code and pushed open the heavy oak door of my brightly painted home.

The rooms inside were dark. I'd fallen in love with this old colonial house, with its tall ceilings, its privacy, its scarcity of windows on the street. I could not have afforded the rent in a million years, but I'd been helped by a friend who'd allowed me to live here rent-free. Well—I thought of Edward St. Cyr as a friend. Until a week ago, when he'd—

But no. I wouldn't think of that now, or how betrayed I'd felt when the friendship I'd come to rely upon had been revealed for what it was.

I'm tired of waiting for you to forget that Spanish bastard. It's time for you to belong to me.

I shuddered at the memory. My answer had sent Edward scowling from this house, back on his private jet to London. There was no way I could remain in this house, living rent-free, after that, so for the past week, I'd looked for a cheaper place to live. But it was hard to find any place cheap enough for the income of a new, self-employed artist. Even here.

San Miguel de Allende had become my home. I would miss the city's cobblestoned streets, growing flowers in my garden and selling portraits in the open-air *mercados*. I'd miss the friends I'd made, Mexicans and expats who'd welcomed an unmarried, heartbroken woman and her baby, who'd taped me up and put me back together.

Now I took a deep breath, trying to steady my shaking nerves. "I can do this," I whispered aloud, trying to make myself believe it. I knew how to grab passports, money and clothes and be out of here in five minutes. I'd done it before, in Tokyo, Berlin, Istanbul, São Paulo and Mumbai.

But then, I'd had Edward to help me. Now I had no one.

Don't think about it, I ordered myself, wiping my eyes. I'd go on foot and hail a taxi on the street. Once at the station, my baby and I would take the next bus to Mexico City. I'd use the emergency credit card Edward had left and fly to the United States, where I was born. I'd head west. Disappear. Once I found a job, I'd pay back Edward every penny.

I'd raise my child in peace, in some small town in Arizona or Alaska, and this time, I'd make sure Alejandro would never, ever find me....

A lamp flicked on in the foyer.

Alejandro was sitting in a chair across the room, staring at me with eyes that burned like fire.

I halted, choking out a gasp.

"Lena Carlisle," he said in a low voice. "At last."

"Alejandro," I breathed as terror racked through me. My hands instinctively tightened on my baby in my arms. "What are you— How did you..."

"How did I find you?" He rose to his feet, tall and broad-shouldered. "Or how did I get in to your house?" His voice was low and husky, with only the slightest accent, blurred from growing up in Spain, followed by years of running a billion-dollar business conglomerate from New York and London. "Do you really think any *security system,* no matter how expensive, could keep me from being where I wanted to be?"

He was even more handsome than I remembered. Seeing him in the flesh, after a year of being tormented by sensual dreams, made my knees tremble. I clutched Miguel closer, willing myself not to faint.

Alejandro's cold eyes never left mine as he walked toward me. He was dressed in black from his well-cut coat to his glossy Italian shoes, draped in *power*.

"What do you want?" I choked out.

He looked from me to my yawning, drowsy-eyed baby.

"Is it true?" His voice was deadly quiet, but the words burned through my heart. His face was grim. "Is this my baby?"

His baby. Oh, God. Please, no. I stumbled back in blind panic.

"My men are outside. You won't even make it to the street...."

I ignored him. Grabbing the wrought-iron handle, I

pulled open the heavy, weathered oak door and started to run. I stopped.

Six hulking bodyguards stood outside my house, in a semicircle, in front of the expensive sedan and black SUV now jamming the slender residential lane.

"Did you think," Alejandro said softly behind me, "that when I finally found you, I would leave anything to chance?"

He stood close behind me, so close I caught the scent of his cologne. So close I could feel the heat emanating from his powerful body. Briefly closing my eyes, I shivered at being so close to the man who had once possessed me, body and soul.

Unwillingly, I turned back to face the ghost who still haunted my heart. His hot black gaze held mine, and in the dark embers of that fire, I was lashed by memories I'd tried so hard to forget. I'd loved him hopelessly from the moment he'd first come to call on my beautiful, wealthy cousin. I'd watched from hallways, made them tea, organized their dinner parties. I'd done it all with a smile, any and all work my cousin required, ignoring the ache of my heart when she bragged after he left that she was going to catch the uncatchable Spanish duke. "He's nearly in my grasp!" Claudie had crowed. "I'll be a duchess before the year is out!"

Then, to everyone's shock, he'd suddenly jilted her.

For me.

He was the first man who'd ever noticed me—really noticed me—and I'd fallen like a stone beneath the sensual onslaught of his power and glamour and dangerous, sexy charm. For six reckless, miraculous weeks in London last summer, Alejandro had held me in his arms, and I felt as if I owned the world.

Memories of the hopes I'd had, the naive girl I'd been, ripped through me now like a torrent of blows. Alejandro's expression was stark, but I could remember his playful smile. The intensity of his dark gaze. The sound of his husky voice whispering sweet words in the night. I could remember hot kisses, and the feel of our naked bodies intertwined in his London hotel suite. In the back of his limo. And once, against the wall in the back stairs of the Carlisle mansion.

Our affair had seemed as infinite as the stars in the sky. But on that bright summer day when I finally gathered the courage to tell him I was in love with him, his smiling face had changed in front of my eyes.

"*Love me?*" Alejandro had repeated scornfully. "You do not even *know* me."

Two minutes later, he was gone, leaving me bereft and bewildered. But the broken, truly broken, came later...

Now, Alejandro took my hand, glancing up and down the quiet Mexican street.

"Come back inside, Lena. We have much to talk about."

Feeling the electricity of his hand wrapped around mine, I looked up with an intake of breath.

He was so close now. Touching me. My lips parted. He was somehow even more devastatingly handsome than I'd remembered. He had the kind of face that could break a woman's heart into a million pieces, to little shimmering fragments of gray dust, leaving you too dazed with his power and beauty to feel anything but gratitude as he lazily destroyed you.

Without my notice, he led me back into the foyer. Reaching over my head, he towered over me, his arm brushing against my hair, his body pressing against mine. I shivered, clutching my baby close. But he merely closed the heavy door with a sonorous bang behind me.

The hard-edged billionaire duke, in his sharply tailored clothes, stood out starkly against my comfortable, bohemian home, with its warm tile floors and walls I'd decorated with homemade paper flowers and my own paintings, one of the Parroquia de San Miguel, but the rest of my baby, the first from when he was just six days old.

Looking down at me, Alejandro said softly, "Is what Claudie told me true? This baby in your arms—it is mine?"

Trembling, I pulled away. Gathering my wits, I glared at him. "Do you really expect me to answer that?"

"It's an easy enough question. There are only two possible answers." Reaching out, he stroked my cheek, but there was no tenderness in his gaze. "Yes. Or no."

"You'd be a horrible father! I won't let my sweet boy be turned into a heartless bastard like—"

"Like me?" His voice was dangerously low. His dark eyes gleamed in the shadowy foyer. "Is that what you really think of me—after all we once shared?"

Caught in his gaze, I trembled. Once, I might have believed so differently. I'd managed to convince myself that beneath his wealth and power and aristocratic title, Alejandro was decent and good. Like generations of women before me, I had seen what I wanted to see. I'd been blind to the truth, until, against my will, the blindfold had been torn from my eyes.

"Yes. That's what I think of you."

A strange expression flickered across the chiseled planes of his face, an emotion I couldn't identify before it swiftly disappeared. He gave me a sardonic smile.

"You are right, of course. I care for nothing and no one. Least of all you, especially after you and your cousin have gone to such lengths to blackmail me over this child."

"Blackmail you?" I gasped. "You're the one who deliberately seduced me, and got me pregnant, intending to steal my baby away so you could raise him with Claudie!"

He grew very still.

"What are you talking about?" he ground out.

My body was shaking with emotion. "You think I didn't

know? When I found out I was pregnant, you'd already left me and gone back to Spain. You wouldn't return my calls. But fool that I was, I was still desperate to share the news, because I hoped you might care! So I begged Claudie for enough money to fly to Madrid. I was scared to tell her why I needed the money. She'd planned so long to marry you. But when I told her I was pregnant, she did something I never imagined."

"What?"

I took a deep breath.

"She laughed," I whispered. "She laughed and laughed. Then she told me to wait. She went into the hallway, but she left the door open and I heard her call you. I heard her congratulate you on your brilliant plan! *Thanking* you, even! How brilliant you were, how clever, to seduce her lowly cousin, the poor relation, to provide the heir you knew she could never give you! Now the two of you could get married immediately." My voice turned acid. "Just as soon as her lawyer forced me to sign papers terminating all my parental rights."

"Yes. She called me." His eyes narrowed. "But I never…"

"'Don't worry, I'll get Lena to sign her baby away,' she said!" My voice trembled as I remembered the terror I'd felt that day. "She asked you to send over a few security guards from your London office, just in case I tried to fight!" My voice choked and I looked away. "So I ran. Before either of you could lock me away somewhere for the duration of my pregnancy and try to steal my child!"

Silence fell. His eyes narrowed.

"From the day, from the *hour* Claudie told me you were pregnant, I've had investigators trying to track you down, chasing you around the world. Yes, she had some crazy idea that it was her inability to have children that kept me from marrying her. She was wrong." He came closer. "I raced to London, but you were already gone. And ever since, you've always managed to disappear in a puff of smoke whenever I got close. That, *querida,* is expensive. And so is this." He motioned at the high ceilings of the two-hundred-year-old colonial house. "This house is owned by a shell company run out of the Caymans. My investigators checked. So why don't you just admit who's helping you? Admit the truth!"

Something told me not to mention Edward St. Cyr. "And what's that?"

"Once you found out you were pregnant, you knew I would never marry you." His voice softened, his dark eyes almost caressing me. "So you came up with a different plan to cash in, didn't you? You struck a deal…with your cousin."

Whatever I'd expected, it wasn't that. I stared at him. "Are you crazy? Why would Claudie help me? She wants to marry you!"

"I know. After you disappeared, Claudie told me she knew exactly where you were, but that you refused to let me see the child until we could guarantee a stable home. Until I married her."

My lips parted in shock. "But I haven't spoken to Claudie for a year. She has no idea where I am!" I shook my head. "Did she really try to blackmail you into marriage?"

"Women always want to marry me," he said grimly. "They think nothing of stealing or cheating or lying for it."

I snorted. "Your ego is incredible!"

"It's not ego. Every woman wants to be the wife of a billionaire duke. It's not personal."

Of course it is, I thought unwillingly, my heart twisting in my chest. How could any woman not fall in love with Alejandro, and not want him for her own?

"But what I want to know is…" His voice became dangerously low. "Is this baby in your arms truly mine? Or is it just part of some elaborate plot you've set up with Claudie?"

My head snapped back. "Are you asking me if my son is some kind of *stunt baby?*"

"You would be surprised," he said tightly, "how often in life someone pretends to be something they are not."

"You think I'd lie about this—for money?"

"Perhaps not. Perhaps for some other reason." He paused. "If you were not working for Claudie, perhaps you were working for yourself."

"Meaning what?"

"You hoped that playing hard to get, disappearing with my child, would make me want to pin you down. To marry you." He lifted a dark eyebrow. "Not a bad calculation."

My mouth had fallen open. Then I glared at him. "I would never want to be your wife!"

"Right."

His single small word was like a grenade of sarcasm exploding all over me. For an instant my pride made me blind with anger. Then I remembered the dreams I'd once had and my throat went tight. I took a deep, miserable breath.

"Maybe that was what I wanted once," I whispered. "But that was long ago. Before I found out you'd coldheartedly seduced me so you could marry Claudie and steal my baby."

"You must know now that was never true."

"How can I be sure?"

He shook his head. "I never intended to marry Claudie or anyone."

"Yes, you said that. You also told me once that you never intended to have children. And yet here you are, fighting for a DNA test for Miguel!"

"I do not have a choice." His expression changed as he said sharply, "You named the baby Miguel?"

"So?"

"Why?" he demanded, staring at me with a sudden suspicious glitter in his eyes that I did not understand.

"After the beautiful city that took me in—San Miguel became our home!"

He relaxed imperceptibly. "Ah."

Now I was the one to frown. His reaction to our baby's name had been so fierce, almost violent. Had he wondered if I'd named him after another man? "Why do you care so much?"

"I don't," he said coldly.

My baby whimpered in my arms. Fiercely, I shook my head as I hugged him close, breathing in Miguel's sweet baby scent, feeling his tiny warm body against me. I nuzzled his head and saw tears fall onto his soft dark hair. "If you didn't get me pregnant on purpose, if it happened by accident and you don't want a child…just let us go!"

His jaw tightened. "I have an obligation…."

"Obligation!" I cried. "To you, he's just someone to carry on your title and name. To me, he's everything. I carried him for nine months, felt him kick inside me, heard his first cry when he was born. He's my baby, my precious child, my only reason for living." I was crying openly now, and so was my baby, either in sympathy or in alarm or just because it was past his nap time and all the adults arguing wouldn't let him sleep. Miguel's chubby cheeks were red, his eyes swimming with piteous tears. I tried to comfort him as I wept.

Alejandro's expression was stone. "If he's my son, I will bring both of you to live with me in Spain. Neither of you will ever want for anything, ever again. You will live in my castle."

"I'd never marry you, not for any price!"

"Marriage? Who said anything about that?" His lips twisted. "Though we both know you'd marry me in a second if I asked."

Stung, I shook my head furiously. "What could you offer

me, Alejandro? Money? A castle? A title? I don't need those things!"

He moved closer to me, his eyes dark.

"Don't forget sex," he said softly. "Hot, deep, incredible sex."

In the shadowy hacienda, Alejandro looked at me over the downy head of the baby that we had created. My breasts suddenly felt heavy, my nipples tightening. My body felt taut and liquid at once.

"I know you remember what it was like between us," he said in a low voice. "Just as I do."

I lifted my gaze to his.

"Yes," I whispered. "But what use are any of those things really, Alejandro? Without love, it's empty." I shook my head. "You must know this. Because the money, the palaces, the title—and yes, even the sex... Have those things ever made *you* happy?"

He stared at me. For a long moment, there was only the soft patter of the rain against the roof, our baby's low whimper, and the loud beat of my aching heart.

Then abruptly, for the first time, Alejandro looked, really looked, at our son. Reaching out, he stroked Miguel's soft dark hair gently with a large, powerful hand.

As if by magic, our baby's crying abruptly subsided. Big-eyed, Miguel hiccupped his last tears away as father and son took measure of each other, each with the same frown, the same eyes, the same expression. It would have been enough to make me grin, if my heart hadn't been hurting so much.

Suddenly our baby flopped out a tiny, unsteady hand against Alejandro's nose. Looking down at him in surprise, Alejandro snorted a laugh. He seemed to catch his breath, looking at Miguel with amazement, even wonder.

Then he straightened, giving me a cold glare.

"There will be a DNA test. Immediately."

"You expect me to allow a doctor to prick my baby's skin for a blood test, to prove something I don't want to be proved? Forget it! Either believe he's your son, or—better yet—don't! And leave us in peace!"

Alejandro's face looked cold and ruthless. "Enough."

He must have pressed a button or something—or else he had some freaky bodyguard alert, like a dog whistle I couldn't hear—because suddenly two bodyguards came in through the front door. Without even looking at me, they kept walking through the foyer, headed across the court-yard toward the bedroom I shared with Miguel.

I whirled on Alejandro. "Where are they going?"

"To pack," he replied coolly.

"Pack for whom?"

A third bodyguard who'd come up silently behind me suddenly lifted Miguel out of my arms.

"No!" I cried. I started for him, arms outstretched, but Alejandro held me back.

"If the DNA test proves he is not my son," he said calmly, "I will bring your son back to you, safe and sound, and I'll never bother either of you again."

"Let me go!" I shrieked, fighting him—uselessly, for with his greater power and strength, his grip was impla-cable. "You bastard! You bastard! I will *kill* you! You can't take him from me—Miguel! *Miguel!*"

"You are so sure he is mine?"

"Of course he is yours! You know you were my only lover!"

"I know I was your first...."

"My only! *Ever!* Damn you! *Miguel!*"

Something flickered in Alejandro's eyes. But I was no longer looking at him. I was watching as the bodyguard disappeared through the door, my baby wailing in the man's beefy arms. I struggled in Alejandro's grip. "Let me go!"

"Promise to behave, Lena," he said quietly, "and I will."

How I wished I could fight him. If only I had the same power he did—then we'd see who gave orders! If I had his physical strength, I would punch him in the face! If only I had a fortune, a private jet, my own bodyguard army...

My lips parted on an intake of breath.

Edward.

Would he help me? Even now?

That wasn't the question.

Would I be willing to pay the price?

"I don't want to separate you from the baby," Alejandro said, "but I must have the DNA test. And if you're going to fight and scream..."

I abruptly stopped struggling. Nodding, I wiped my eyes. "I'll come quietly. But please," I said softly, looking up at his face, "before you take him to Spain, could we stop in London?"

He frowned. "London?"

I nodded, trying to hide my eagerness—my desperation. "I left something at Claudie's house. Something precious. I need it back."

"What is it?"

"My baby's legacy."

He lifted a dark eyebrow. "Money?"

"And also," I said on a wave of inspiration, "if we could talk to Claudie, together, we could force her to admit how she played us both. Then maybe we could actually trust each other, going forward...."

Alejandro rubbed the back of his head, then nodded. "That would be better. And to be honest, there are a few things I'd like to discuss with your cousin myself."

His voice was grim. I believed him now when he said he didn't want to marry Claudie. Maybe Alejandro hadn't deliberately planned to get me pregnant after all.

But I'd been right about one thing. He still planned to steal my baby. He intended to keep Miguel at his side, to raise him as his heir in some cold Spanish castle, until he turned him into some heartless, unfeeling bastard like himself.

And Alejandro didn't intend to marry me. So I'd be powerless. Expendable.

"So we have a deal?" Alejandro said. "You'll allow the DNA test, and if he is my son, you'll come with us to Spain?"

"With a stop in London first."

"Yes. London. But after that, Spain. I have your word?"

"I honestly hate you," I whispered with feeling.

"I honestly do not care. Do I have your word?"

I glared at him. "Yes."

He looked down at me in the shadows. For a moment, there was a current of electricity between us, sparking in the shadows of the room. His fingers tightened. Then he abruptly released me.

"Thank you," he said coldly, "for being so reasonable."

Hiding the cold determination in my heart, I left him without a word, and nearly sprinted toward my baby.

Alejandro thought he owned me now. But I wasn't as helpless as he thought. I had one card left to play, if I was willing to pay for it.

Was I?

For my son?

Yes. I was.

CHAPTER TWO

THE FIRST TIME I saw London, I was a grief-stricken fourteen-year-old, newly orphaned, just arrived from New York. My grandmother, whom I'd never met, sent her driver to collect me from Heathrow. The sky was weeping and gray. I remembered trembling as I walked up the steps of the tall white mansion in Kensington, a house roughly the same size as my entire apartment building in Brooklyn.

Brought in by the butler, I'd found my grandmother sitting at her antique desk in the morning room. I stood in front of the fireplace for some moments, my eyes stinging and my heart aching, before she finally looked up.

"So you're Lena," she'd said, looking me up and down, from the lumpy coat my mother had made before her hands grew frail in illness, wasting away like her heart since my father's death six months previously, down to my feet crammed into cheap, too-small shoes that had been all my loving but sadly unskilled father had been able to afford. "Not much of a beauty," she'd said crisply, with some regret.

It was raining in London today, too.

As Alejandro's driver waited, holding open my door, I shivered, looking up at the white mansion. I felt suddenly fourteen again. Except now I was going to face my cousin.

Claudie and I were the same age, but she was so different in looks and manner that we could have been born on opposite sides of not just the Atlantic, but the universe.

When I'd first come to the house—devastated by the loss of both my mother and my father within six short months—I'd tried so hard to make my beautiful, spoiled cousin like me, but she'd scorned me on sight. She'd been determined to drive me from the house. Especially once grandmother died and she saw the terms of the will. And she'd finally gotten her wish. She'd won....

"What are you waiting for?" Alejandro said impatiently. "Get out of the car."

"I changed my mind. I don't need to go in."

"Too bad. You're going."

He looked far too handsome and rested. He'd slept and showered on his private jet. He was in a fresh suit. I, on the other hand, hadn't slept at all since yesterday. After an interminable visit to a private hospital in San Miguel de Allende, where he'd paid a small fortune for the DNA test, we'd gotten on his private 747 and I'd spent the long flight walking back and forth in the cabin, trying to calm Miguel enough to sleep. But the cabin pressure hurt his ears, and only my continual walking soothed him. So I'd gotten exercise, at least, using the aisle of Alejandro's jet as my own private treadmill.

But there'd been no shower for me. I felt groggy, sweaty and dirty, and I was still wearing the same white cotton sundress I'd worn in Mexico. There was no way I was going to face my cousin like this.

It was bad enough letting Alejandro see me.

He'd barely said ten words to me on the plane; in fact, he'd said just five: "Want me to hold him?" Of course, I refused. I hadn't wanted to give up possession of my baby, even for a moment. Even thirty thousand feet in the air, when there was no way for him to run off. The DNA test had proved the obvious—that Alejandro was Miguel's father—but I was fighting his emotional and legal claim with every cell and pore.

Now, as Alejandro looked at me in the backseat, the difference between his sleek gorgeousness and my chubby unattractiveness was so extreme I imagined he must be asking himself what he could ever have seen in me. Which begged the question: If he hadn't deliberately seduced me last summer to create an heir, then why on earth had he?

I licked my lips. "Alejandro," I said hesitantly. "I…"

"Enough delay," he growled. "We're going in."

I looked at my baby, tucked into a baby seat beside me in the back of the limo, now sleeping in blessed silence. "You go. I'll stay here with Miguel." Which would also be the perfect way for me to sneak to Edward's house, at the end of the street.

"Dowell can watch him."

I glanced at the driver doubtfully. "No."

"Then bring Miguel with us."

"Wake him up?" I whispered, scandalized. I narrowed my eyes. "Of course *you* wouldn't worry about that. You're not the one who spent the whole flight walking in circles trying to make him sleep."

Alejandro set his jaw. "I offered to take him…."

"You could have offered again." I was dimly aware that I sounded irrational. There was no way he could have taken Miguel from me on the jet except by force, which wouldn't exactly have gone over well, either. My cheeks got hot. "It doesn't matter."

He lifted a dark eyebrow. "You do know how to take care of Miguel better than I do."

His tone told me whom he blamed for that. "I had no choice. I thought you were going to steal him from me."

"So you stole him first?"

I blinked. I hadn't thought of it that way before.

"You could at least have called me directly," he ground out.

Now, that was unfair! "I tried! You wouldn't take my phone calls!"

"If I'd known you were pregnant, I would have." His jaw tightened. "You could have left a message with Mrs. Allen...."

"Leave a *message* with some faceless secretary at your London office to let you know, oh, hey, I'm pregnant with your baby? Seriously?" I lifted my chin. "You should have just taken my damn call!"

Alejandro stared at me, his lips pressed in a thin line. "This argument is over." He turned away. "Unlatch the baby carrier and lift it out of the seat. That won't wake him up, as you know perfectly well."

My cheeks burned slightly. Yes, I'd known that. I'd just been hoping *he* wouldn't.

When I didn't move, Alejandro started to reach around me. With a huff I turned and unlatched the seat. Miguel continued softly snoring in sweet baby dreams, tucked snugly in the carrier with a soft blanket against his cheek.

As the driver closed the door behind us with a snap, I stood on the sidewalk, staring up at the cold white mansion.

I'd never wanted to return to this house. But there was one silver lining. I hadn't been lying when I'd told Alejandro I wanted to come back for Miguel's legacy. Something I'd been forced to leave behind that had nothing to do with the inheritance I'd lost.

As I looked up, the soft drizzle felt like cobwebs against my skin. Like memories. Like ghosts.

"What now?" Alejandro was glaring at me as if I wasn't his favorite person. I couldn't blame him. He wasn't my favorite person right now, either.

Although at this moment there was one person I liked even less. I swallowed.

"I'm scared," I whispered.

He stared at me. "Of Claudie?"

I nodded, not trusting my voice.

"You don't need to be scared," he said gruffly. "I'm here

with you now." Reaching out, he took the baby carrier from my trembling hands. "Come on."

Alejandro carried our sleeping baby up the stone steps and knocked on the imposing front door.

Mr. Corgan, the longtime butler, opened the door. His jowly face was dignified as he greeted Alejandro.

"Good morning, Your Excellency." Then he glanced at me and his eyes went wide. "Miss Lena!" He saw the sleeping baby in the carrier, and the usually unflappable Mr. Corgan's jaw fell open. "It's true?" He breathed, then glanced at Alejandro, and the mask slipped back into place. Holding open the door, he said sonorously, "Won't you both please come in?"

He led us into the elegant front salon, with high ceilings and gilded furniture. Everything looked just as I remembered—vintage, French and expensive. I'd been allowed in this room only a handful of times, the last being when I'd begged Claudie for money to fly to Spain. The day my life had fallen apart.

Mr. Corgan said, "I regret that Miss Carlisle is…out…at the moment, but she has a standing order to welcome you at any time, Your Excellency, if you care to wait."

"Sí," Alejandro said coldly. "We will wait."

"Of course. She will be so pleased to see you when she returns. May I offer refreshments? Tea?"

Alejandro shook his head. He sat down on the pink striped couch near the window. He seemed incongruous there, this dark, masculine Spaniard with severely tailored black clothes, in a salon that looked like a giant powder puff, with the powder made of diamond dust.

He set down the baby carrier on the white polished marble floor beside the sofa. I swiftly scooped it up, and exhaled in relief now that my sleeping baby was safely back in my possession. I followed Mr. Corgan out of the salon and into the hallway.

Once we were alone, the butler's mask dropped and he turned to face me with a happy exclamation.

"We missed you, girl." He hugged me warmly. I closed my eyes, smelling pipe smoke and brass polish. Then I heard a crash and pulled back to see Mrs. Morris, the house-keeper, had just broken a china plate in the hallway. But she left it there, coming forward with a cry.

A minute later, both of them, along with Hildy, the maid, were hugging me and crying and exclaiming over Miguel's beauty, his dark hair, his fat cheeks.

"And such a good sleeper, too," Mrs. Morris said approvingly. Then they all looked at each other. I saw the delicate pause.

Then Hildy blurted out, "Who's his father, then?"

I glanced back at the salon, biting my lip. "Um…"

Hildy's eyes got huge when she saw who was in the salon. Then she turned to Mr. Corgan. "You were right. I owe you a fiver."

His cheeks went faintly pink as he cleared his throat with a *harrumph.* "I might have heard some of your conversation with Miss Carlisle the day you left, Miss Lena." He shook his jowly head with a glare. "It wasn't right what she did. Driving you from the house a year before you would have got your grandmother's inheritance."

I was surprised for only a second. Then I gave a wry smile. Of course they knew. Household staff knew everything, sometimes even before their employers did. "It doesn't matter."

"But it does," Mrs. Morris said indignantly. "Miss Carl-isle wanted your inheritance and the moment she convinced you to move out of the house, she got it by default. Just a year before it would have finally been yours!"

I pressed my hand against my temple as emotions I had spent the past year trying to forget churned up in me.

When I turned eighteen, I could have left for college,

or gotten a real job. Instead, I'd remained living in this house, working as a sort of house manager/personal assistant for my cousin beneath her unrelenting criticism as she tried her best to drive me away. I'd had a small salary at first, but even that had disappeared when she'd lazily announced one day that she was cutting the salaries of the staff by twenty percent. "They don't need it," she sniffed. "They are lucky, working all day in my beautiful house. They should be paying *me!*"

Mr. Corgan and Mrs. Morris and the rest had become my friends, and I knew they had families to support. So I'd given up my salary rather than see them suffer. Leaving me virtually destitute for years, in spite of working eighteen-hour days.

But I hadn't minded, not really, because I'd known all I had to do was remain in this house until I was twenty-five, just a few months from now, and I would have gotten the huge inheritance once destined for my father, before he'd been cut out of the will for the crime of marrying my mother.

Eight years ago, when my grandmother lay dying, she'd clutched his old teddy bear and dissolved in tears I'd never seen before as she remembered the youngest son she'd once loved best. She'd called for her lawyer.

If Robert's child proves herself worthy of the Carlisle name, my grandmother's will had read, *and she still lives in the house at the age of twenty-five, she may claim the bequest that would have been his.*

But now it had all reverted to Claudie. I hadn't cared a whit about the money last year, when I'd feared my baby would be stolen from me. But now...

"The house hasn't been the same without you, Miss Lena," Mr. Corgan said.

"Half the staff resigned after you left," Mrs. Morris said.

"She's been intolerable without you to run interference."

Mr. Corgan shook his head grimly. "I've worked for this family for forty years, Miss Lena, but even I fear my time here is nearing an end." Leaning closer, he confided, "Miss Carlisle still insists she'll marry your duke."

"He's not my duke…."

"Well. He's the only man rich and handsome enough for *her,* though she says she'd marry any rich idiot who'd make her a duchess…." Glancing back over his shoulder, he coughed, turning red.

Turning, I saw Alejandro standing in the doorway of the salon. I wondered how much he'd heard. His face was half hidden in shadow, his expression inscrutable.

"Did you change your mind about the tea, Your Excellency?" Mr. Corgan gasped, his face beet red.

Alejandro shook his head. His eyes were dark, but his lips quirked at the edges. "We rich idiots prefer coffee."

The butler looked as if he wished the earth would swallow him up whole. "I'll get it right away, sir…."

"Don't bother." He looked at me. "Did you get what you came for?"

He'd heard everything, I realized. He thought I'd come for my inheritance. He thought that was the precious thing that had brought me here. It wasn't.

I turned to Mrs. Morris urgently. "Did she throw out my things?"

"She wanted to," she said darkly. "She told me to burn it all. But I boxed it all up and left it in your attic room. I knew she'd never bother to go all the way up there to check."

"Bless you," I whispered, and hugged her. "Stay and have coffee," I called to Alejandro. "I'll be back in a few minutes." I started up the stairs, carrying my sleeping baby with me.

Climbing three floors, I reached the attic. It looked even more desolate than I remembered, with only one grimy window, an ancient metal bed frame and stacks of boxes. Setting down the baby, I went straight for the boxes.

"What are you looking for?"

Hearing Alejandro's husky voice behind me, I turned. "These boxes hold everything from my childhood."

He stepped inside the attic room, knocking his head against the slanted roof. He rubbed it ruefully. "I can see why Claudie wouldn't come up here. This place is like a prison cell."

"This was my home for over ten years."

His dark eyes widened. "This room?" He slowly looked around the attic, at the rough wood floors, at the naked lightbulb hanging from the ceiling. "You lived here?"

I gave a wistful laugh. "From the time my parents died when I was fourteen, until I left last year when…well. It looked nicer then, though. I made decorations, paper flowers." A lump rose in my throat as I looked around the bare room where I'd spent so many years. The bare mattress on the metal bed frame where I'd slept so many nights. I gently touched the bare lightbulb and swung it on the cord. "I had a bright red lampshade I bought from the charity shop on Church Street."

"A charity shop?" he said sharply. "But you're Claudie's cousin. A poor relation, I know, but I'd assumed you were well paid for all your work…."

This time my laugh was not so wistful. "I was paid a salary after I turned eighteen, but that money had to go to—other things. So I started earning a little money doing portraits at street fairs. But Claudie allowed me so little time away from the house…"

"*Allowed* you?" he said incredulously.

I looked at him. "You heard about my inheritance."

"How much would it have been?"

"If I was still living in this house on my twenty-fifth

birthday, a few months from now, I would have inherited thirty million pounds."

His jaw dropped.

"Thirty…"

"Yes."

"And you left it all?"

"To protect my baby. Yes."

"To protect our baby, you sacrificed more money than most people see in a lifetime."

He sounded so amazed. I shook my head. "Any mother would have done the same. Money is just money." I glanced down at Miguel, and a smile lifted my cheeks as I said softly, "He is my life."

When I finally looked up, his dark, soulful eyes were looking at me as if he'd never seen me before. My cheeks went hot. "I expect you think I'm an idiot."

"Far from it," he said in a low voice.

He was looking at me with such intensity. Awkwardly, I turned away and started digging through the top box. Pushing it aside, I opened the one beneath it.

"What are you looking for?" he said curiously.

Not answering, I pulled out old sweaters, old ragtag copies of books I'd read and reread as a teenager, *Rebecca, A Little Princess, Jane Eyre*. Finally, at the bottom of the box, I found the three oversize, flat photo albums. "Thank you," I whispered aloud when I saw they hadn't been burned, or warped from being left to rot in the rain or scribbled on with a venomous black marker, or any of the other images I'd tormented myself with. Pressing the albums against my chest, I closed my eyes in pure gratitude.

"Photo albums?" Alejandro said in disbelief. "You begged me to come to London for *photo albums?*"

"I told you," I said sharply. "I came for my baby's legacy."

"But I never thought…" Frowning, Alejandro held out his hand. "Let me see."

Reluctantly, I handed them over, then watched as he turned through the pages of the top album, at old photographs pressed against yellowing adhesive pages beneath the clear plastic cover.

"It nearly killed me to leave them behind," I said. "It's all I have left of my parents. My home." I pointed to a picture of a tenement building where the ground floor was a butcher's shop. "That was our apartment in Brooklyn."

He turned the page. "And this?"

My heart twisted when I saw my mother, young and laughing, holding a ragtag bouquet of flowers, sitting in my father's lap. "My parents' wedding day. My dad was a student in London. He fell in love with a waitress, an immigrant newly arrived from Puerto Rico. He married her against his family's wishes, when she was pregnant with me…."

Alejandro looked at me for a long moment, then silently turned more pages. My babyhood flashed before my eyes, pictures of me as a tiny baby, getting bathed in the sink, sitting on a towel on the kitchen floor, banging wooden spoons against a pot and beaming with the same chubby cheeks that Miguel had now.

Finishing the first album, Alejandro handed it to me without a word, and thumbed through the second book, then the third. My childhood passed swiftly—learning to ride a bike…my first day at school…

"Why are you interested?" I said haltingly. "Is it—to make fun of me?"

"To make fun?" He looked at me with a scowl. "You think I would taunt you about having a happy childhood?" He shook his head. "If anything, I envy you," he said softly, looking back at the pages that my tenderhearted mother had made for me when I was a child. Right up to the very last photo, of my father at Christmas, sitting beneath the tree wearing a Santa hat, smiling lovingly at the camera as he held my mother's homemade gift of a sweater. Two months later, he was dead. There were no more photos. The last few pages of the album were blank. Alejandro said softly, "I have no pictures of myself with my mother. None."

I blinked. "How is that possible? I mean, I'd think you'd have a million pictures taken...."

He abruptly looked at me. Without answering, he closed the photo album and handed it to me.

"Perhaps you're not who I thought you were."

"Who did you think I was?"

"Exactly like all the other women I've ever dated. In love with the idea of being a rich duchess." He looked down at me, his dark eyes infinite and deep as the night sky. "But I'm starting to think you're different. A woman who would willingly leave thirty million pounds... You were actually in love with me, weren't you?"

My breath got knocked out of me.

"That was a long time ago."

Our eyes met, and I suddenly had to get out of the attic. I picked up Miguel's baby carrier with one arm and carried the albums with the other. "I'll be downstairs."

Without looking back, I fled, rushing down the flights of stairs. My teeth were chattering, and I was shaking with strange emotion. *Edward,* I reminded myself. The other reason I'd come to London. I had to get his help before Alejandro could bully me into going to Spain. Although it actually wasn't going to Spain that frightened me. It was never being able to leave again. It was being separated from my baby. It was being completely under the control of a man who'd almost destroyed me once, just by making me love him.

As I reached the bottom of the staircase, I heard a car door slam outside. Through the windows, I saw a flash of purple.

Claudie had come home.

I turned to where Hildy was loitering at the bottom of the stairs. "Hildy!"

"Oh, hello," she said, blushing when she saw me. "I was just dusting the banister, Miss—"

"My cousin is here. Please." Grabbing Hildy's arm, I whispered, "I need you to take a message to Edward St. Cyr."

"Edward St. Cyr?" Hildy's eyes nearly popped out of her head. "Mr. St. Cyr himself? Are you serious?"

"Tell him I need to see him," I said with more assurance than I felt.

"Here, miss? You know he and Miss Carlisle hate each other...."

Hearing my cousin fumbling at the door, I shook my head. "Tell him...the Princess Diana Playground in thirty minutes."

With a quick, troubled nod, Hildy hurried toward the back door. Just in time, too. The front door slammed.

"Well. Look who's back."

My cousin's voice was a sneer. Warily, I turned to face her for the first time in a year.

"Hello, Claudie." She was wearing a tight, extremely short bandage dress, the kind you might wear to a club if you wanted a lot of attention, in a vivid shade of purple that almost matched the hollows beneath her eyes. "Late night?" I said mildly.

She glared at me.

"If you came to beg for your inheritance, forget it. My solicitors went through the will with a fine-tooth comb," she ground out. "You'll never..." Then she saw the baby and gasped in triumph. "You brought the brat here? I knew you'd see reason." She rubbed her hands together in glee. "Now I'll either make him marry me, or else I'll—"

"You'll what, Claudie?" Alejandro said coolly from the top of the stairs.

My cousin looked up, speechless for the first time in her life. But she recovered almost instantly. Smiling up at him, she put her hand on her hip, setting a pose that showed her figure to advantage, wearing her six-inch heels and skin-tight purple dress, trailing a cloud of expensive perfume. Her gorgeous, long blond hair tumbled over her shoulders, emphasizing the bone structure of her sharp cheekbones.

But as she licked her big lips, beneath her smile, her eyes were afraid. "Alejandro. I didn't know you were here."

He came down the stairs, looking down at her. He stopped in front of her. Even though she wore such high heels, he was still taller.

"You lied to me, Claudie," he said pleasantly. "Lena wasn't holding my baby hostage. You were."

She visibly trembled, then tried to laugh. Reaching into her crystal-encrusted bag, she got out a pack of cigarettes. "Darling, I don't know what kind of lies my precious cousin might have told you, but…"

He grabbed her wrist almost violently.

"Do not," he said coldly, "smoke near my son."

"*Your* son," she breathed, searching his gaze, then ripped her arm away. "Are you so sure of that?" Her beautiful blue eyes hardened. "How do you know he's yours? You should have seen all the men who used to come through here, Alejandro—trooping up to Lena's bedroom every single night—"

A little gasp escaped me, like an enraged squeak.

Alejandro lifted an eyebrow. "Then they must have been lost, on their way to *your* room, Claudie."

Her eyes narrowed. "I don't like what you're implying—"

"We did a DNA test," he said, cutting her off. "The baby is mine."

For a moment, she stared at him. But you could almost

see her gather her forces. "He doesn't have to be." She looked from him to me. "If you don't treat him like your son, no one else will."

"You think I would abandon my own child?"

"Fine," she said impatiently. She flung a skeletal finger toward my sweetly sleeping son. "We can take her baby. She's nobody, Alejandro. She won't be able to stop us...."

With a gasp, I protected the baby carrier with my body.

"Just think." Claudie swayed her hips as she walked toward Alejandro with her hypnotic red smile. "Just think how perfect our future could be." She started to wrap her arms around him. "With your money and title, and my money and connections...the two of us could rule the world."

He looked down at her coldly. "Do you really think I'd want to rule the world, if the price would be marriage to you?"

Shocked, she let her arms fall to her sides.

"You used Lena for years as an unpaid slave," he said, "then threatened to take her baby, for the sake of stealing what you wanted—her inheritance. And then you tried to blackmail me into marrying you!"

She licked her lips. "I..."

He held up his hand sharply, cutting her off. His voice was deep and harsh. "For the past year, you've lied to me, saying if I ever wanted to see my child, I had to marry you. Blaming Lena, making me think she was the one to blame. For that, you deserve to go to hell. Which I hope you will find— " he gave her a sudden, pleasant smile "—very soon. *Adios,* Claudie." Scooping up the baby carrier, he turned to me gravely. "Shall we go?" Without another word, he walked out the front door.

"Alejandro, wait," Claudie gasped, but I was the only one left to hear. *"You."* Her face as she turned to look at me really did look like a snake's. Or maybe a dragon's—I could almost see the smoke coming out of her nostrils as her blue, reptilian eyes hardened. "You did this!"

For the past decade, I'd dreamed of what I would say to her if given the chance, after all my lonely years, crying alone in my attic. All the subtle and not so subtle ways she'd insulted me, used me, made me feel worthless and invisible for the past ten years. But in this moment, all those things fled from my mind. Instead, the real question came from my heart.

"Why did you hate me, Claudie?" I whispered, lifting my tearful gaze to hers. "I loved you. You were my only family. Why couldn't you love me? Why wouldn't you let me love you?"

My cousin drew herself up, all thin gorgeousness.

"Why?" She lit her cigarette with shaking hands. "Because you're not my real family." Taking a long draw on her cigarette, she said in a low, venomous hiss, "And you're not good enough for Alejandro. Blood always tells. Sooner or later, he will be embarrassed by you, just as I was. He'll take your child and toss you in the gutter, like you deserve."

My mouth fell open as her poisoned dart hit me, square in the heart.

"It didn't have to be this way," I choked out, and I turned and fled, still holding my photo albums against my chest, like a shield.

Outside, a sliver of sun had split through the dark clouds, through the rain. Stopping on the sidewalk, I turned back and looked up at the Carlisle mansion for one last time.

"Goodbye," I whispered.

Then I climbed into the limo, where the driver waited with my door open, and he closed it behind me.

"Enjoy a tender farewell?" Alejandro was already in the backseat, on the other side of Miguel, who had woken and was starting to whimper.

"Something like that," I muttered, trying to surreptitiously wipe my tears.

"I was surprised. It's not like you to let me walk off with—" His voice cut off as he saw my face. "What's wrong?"

"Nothing," I said. Turning to my baby, I pressed his favorite blanket against his cheek and tried to comfort him. Tried to comfort myself. My baby's tears quieted and so did his quivering little body, as he felt the hum and vibration of the car's engine beneath him. His eyelids started to grow heavy again.

"What did she say?" Alejandro said. Frowning, he looked closer at my face. "Did she…"

There was a sudden hard knock on his window. Miguel's little body jerked back awake, and his whimpers turned to full-on crying. Alejandro turned with a growl.

Claudie stood by the limo, her eyes like fire. "Open this window!" she yelled through the glass.

Alejandro's expression was like ice as he rolled it down a grudging two inches. She leaned forward, her face raw with emotion.

"We could have ruled the world together, Alejandro, and you're throwing it all away—for that little whore and her brat!"

Alejandro said softly, his face dangerous, "If you ever insult either my son or his mother again, you will regret it."

Claudie looked bewildered. To be fair, she'd insulted me for so long she'd probably forgotten it wasn't nice.

"But Alejandro…" Her voice had a strange begging sound I'd never heard from her. "You'll never find someone with my breeding, my beauty, my billions. I love you.…"

"You love my title."

Her cheeks flushed red. "All right. But you can't choose her over me. She's…nothing. No one."

I swallowed, blinking fast.

"Blood always tells," she said. "She's not good enough for you."

Alejandro looked quickly at my miserable face. Then he turned back to Claudie with a deliberate smile.

"Thank you for your fascinating opinion. Now move, won't you? I need to take Lena shopping for an engagement ring."

"You're—what?" Claudie staggered back. I gasped. Miguel was crying.

The only one who looked absolutely calm was Alejandro. Turning away from her, he sat back in the plush leather seat, and said to Dowell, "Drive on."

Claudie stared after us, looking stupefied on the sidewalk, and almost forlorn in her tight club dress and bedraggled mascara. Looking back at her through the car window, I felt a strange wave of sympathy.

Because I, too, knew what it felt like to be left by Alejandro Navaro y Albra.

"You didn't have to be so cruel," I whispered.

"Cruel?" he said incredulously. "You defend her, after the way she treated you?"

"She's still my cousin. I feel sorry for her...."

"Then you're a fool," he said harshly.

I stroked my crying baby's cheek. My lips creased sadly. "Love makes us all fools."

"She doesn't love me. She doesn't even know me."

"That's what you said to me, too," I said softly. I met his gaze. "I wonder if any woman will ever truly know you."

For an instant, I thought I saw hunger, even yearning in his dark eyes as he stared down at me. Then the expression shuttered, leaving me to decide I'd imagined it. But even then, he continued to look at me, as if he couldn't look away.

"What are you staring at?" I put my hand to my messy ponytail, feeling suddenly self-conscious. "I must look a mess."

"You look…" His eyes slowly traced over my hand, up my arm, to my neck, to my lips. "You look like a woman who cares more about her baby than a fortune. Like a woman who works so hard and so well—for free—that she's beloved by the entire household staff. You look," he said softly, "like a woman who feels sympathy, even for the coldhearted creature who tried to destroy her."

"Are you—complimenting me?"

He gave a low laugh. "If you're not sure, I must be losing my touch."

I flushed. Turning away, I took a deep breath. And changed the subject. "Thank you for bringing me back to London. For these." I motioned toward the photo albums. "And for giving me the chance to finally ask Claudie something I've wanted to know all my life. I always wondered why nothing I did was good enough to make her love me." I looked out the window at the passing shops of Kensington High Street. "Now I know."

Silence fell.

"Are you all right?" he asked.

I nodded over the lump in my throat.

"I know how it feels," he said in a low voice, "to be alone."

"You?" I looked at him sharply, then gave a disbelieving snort. "No, you don't."

His dark eyes were veiled. "When I was young, I was good friends with…our housekeeper's son. We were only six months apart in age, and we studied under the same governess. Friend? He was more like a brother to me," he said softly. "People said we looked so much alike, acted so much alike, we could have been twins."

"Are you still friends?"

He blinked, focusing on me, and his jaw tightened. "He died in the same crash that took the duke, the duchess. The housekeeper. Twenty-three years ago."

"They all died in the same crash?" I said, horrified.

He looked down. "I was the only one to survive."

I thought of a young boy being the only survivor of a car accident that took his parents, his best friend. That made him a duke at the tender age of twelve. I couldn't even imagine the loneliness. The pain. Reaching out, I took his hand and whispered, "I'm sorry."

Alejandro drew away. "It was a long time ago." I saw tension in his jaw, heard it in his voice. "But I do know how it feels."

I swallowed, feeling guilty, and embarrassed, too, for all my complaining when he'd suffered worse, and in silence. "What was his name? Your friend?"

He stared at me, then his lips lifted slightly. "Miguel."

"Oh." I gave a shy smile. "So that's why you don't mind that I named our baby Miguel—"

"No." He seemed to hide his own private smile. "I don't mind at all."

I frowned, looking at him more closely.

His expression shuttered, and his dark eyebrows came down into a scowl. "His surname, however…"

I sighed. "I thought you might want to change that. But don't worry." I gave an awkward smile. "I won't hold you to your marriage proposal."

His eyes were dark and intense. "What if I want you to hold me to it?"

My lips parted in shock.

"What?" I said faintly.

His dark eyes challenged mine. "What if I want you to marry me?"

"You don't want to get married. You went on and on about all the women who tried to drag you to the altar. I'm not one of them!"

"I know that now." Leaning his arm across the baby seat,

he cupped my cheek. "But for our son's sake, I'm starting to think you and I should be…together."

"Why?"

"Why not?" He gave a sensual smile. "As you said, I already broke one rule. Why not break the other?"

"But what has changed?"

"I'm starting to think…perhaps I can trust you." His eyes met mine. "And I can't forget how it felt to have you in my bed."

Something changed in the air between us. Something primal, dangerous. I felt the warmth of his palm against my skin and held my breath. As the limo drove through the streets of London, memories crackled through me like fire.

I remembered the night we'd conceived Miguel, and all the other hot days of summer, when I'd surrendered to him, body and soul. I trembled, feeling him so close in the backseat of the limo, on the other side of our baby. Every inch of my skin suddenly remembered the hot stroke of Alejandro's fingertips. My mouth was tingling, aching….

"That's not a good reason to marry someone. Especially for you. If I said yes, you'd regret it. You'd blame me. Claim that I'd only done it to be a rich duchess."

He slowly shook his head. "I think," he said quietly, "you might be the one woman who truly doesn't care about that. And it would be best for our son. So what is your answer?"

My answer?

I remembered the darkness I'd fallen into the last time Alejandro wanted me—then stopped wanting me. I'd never let myself be vulnerable to him ever again. I couldn't. He'd almost destroyed me once. I could never live through that again.

Sooner or later…he'll take your child and toss you in the gutter, like you deserve.

I couldn't give him control over me, ever again. I

couldn't be tempted. My only hope was to get away. My only hope was...

Oh, heaven...what time was it?

"I need to..." As I saw the time on the dashboard of the limo, my heart nearly burst in panic. "Stop the car!" I leaned forward desperately toward the driver. "Let me out!"

Looking confused, Dowell pulled over on the side of the busy road.

"What are you doing?" Alejandro demanded, looking at me as if I was crazy. I felt crazy.

I unbuckled our baby, who'd just stopped crying and was looking drowsy. "Miguel needs a walk to help him sleep...."

"Is that a joke?"

I didn't answer. Cradling our baby, I stepped out on the sidewalk in front of Kensington Palace, and started running into the park, toward the playground. Toward Edward.

CHAPTER THREE

THE PRINCESS DIANA PLAYGROUND was in the corner of Kensington Gardens, just north of the palace. It was still early, and the playground had just opened, but in the midst of August holidays it was already starting to fill with children of every age, laughing and whooping as they raced toward the teepees and leaped on the ropes of the life-size pirate ship. It was a magical place, as you might expect of a children's playground, near a palace, based around a Peter Pan theme and named after a lost princess.

But I was here desperate for a different kind of magic. Protection.

Edward St. Cyr had protected me more than once. We'd first properly met three years earlier, when I'd been walking up from the Tube late at night and I'd passed a group of rowdy teenagers on Kensington High Street. I'd been weighed down with groceries, and tried to keep my head down as they passed. But some of the boys had followed me up the dark street, taunting me crudely. As one started to knock the grocery bags out of my hand, there'd been a flash of headlights on the street and the slam of a car door, and suddenly a tall man in a dark coat was there, his face a threatening scowl, and the young men who'd scared me fled like rabbits into the snow. Then he'd turned to me.

"Are you all right, miss…?" Then his expression had

changed. "But wait. I know you. You're Claudie Carlisle's cousin."

"Yes, I…"

"You're all right now." He'd gently taken my trembling hand. "I'm Edward St. Cyr. I live a few streets from here. May I give you a ride home?"

"No, I couldn't possibly. I…"

"I wouldn't mind a walk myself," he said briskly, and with a nod to the driver of his Rolls-Royce, he'd insisted on walking me home, though it took ten minutes.

"Thank you," I'd said at the door. "I never meant to impose…."

"You didn't." He'd paused. "I remember what it's like to feel alone and afraid. Will you let me check on you in the morning?"

I'd shaken my head. "It's truly not necessary."

"But you must." He'd lifted a dark eyebrow. "If for no other reason than it will annoy your cousin, whom I've despised for years. I insist."

Now, as I looked out at Kensington Gardens in the distance, I saw the paths where we'd once walked together, he and I. He'd been kind to me. We'd been—friends.

Or had we? Had he always wanted more?

I'm tired of waiting for you to forget that Spanish bastard. It's time for you to belong to me.

I shivered. When we left Mexico yesterday, I had been prepared to make any sacrifice to save my baby from Alejandro. Even if the price would have been going to bed with a man I did not love.

But now I was starting to wonder if that was truly necessary. Perhaps Alejandro was not entirely the heartless monster I'd once feared him to be….

"You shouldn't have run."

Hearing Alejandro's dark voice behind me, I whirled around. "How did you catch up so fast?"

He was scowling. "Did you think I'd let you disappear with Miguel?"

"I didn't disappear. I…"

"Had some kind of baby emergency?" He folded his arms. "You ran for a reason. And we both know what it is."

Could he have somehow found out about Edward St. Cyr? The two men were slightly acquainted. And far from being friends. I didn't think he would take it well. I bit my lip, breathing, "I…"

"You panicked because I asked you to marry me," he accused.

Oh. I exhaled. "We both know you weren't serious."

"We both know I was."

"You won't be, once you have a chance to think about it. You don't want to get married. You said so a million times."

"I never intended to have a child, either," he pointed out, "so there was no reason to marry. But now… You heard what Claudie said. Marrying you will make clear to the whole world that he's my son. That he's my heir. Right or wrong," he said tightly.

Right or wrong? Meaning I wasn't good enough? That Miguel wasn't? My eyes narrowed. "I don't love you."

"I can live with that," he said sardonically. "We both love our son. That is the only love that matters."

"You're wrong," I said stubbornly. "My parents loved me, but they also loved each other, till the day they died. I remember how they looked at each other…."

"Most people are not so fortunate," he said harshly. "I've spent a year pursuing you, Lena. I don't want to fight over custody now. I don't want to worry, anytime you take him for a walk, that you might try to run away with him. I want this matter settled between us, once and for all."

Ah. Now we were getting down to it. "You mean I should give you total control over me, body and soul, so you can avoid the inconvenience of a custody battle?" I said incredulously, then shook my head. "This idea of marriage is just a momentary madness with you—it will pass...."

My voice trailed off as I saw Hildy on the edge of the playground, frantically signaling.

Alejandro frowned. "What is it?" He started to turn his head. "What are you..."

"On second thought, let me think it over," I said quickly. Touching his arm, I gave him a weak smile. "So much has happened since yesterday. Maybe I'm too exhausted to think straight." I pointed toward the outdoor café at the front of the playground. "Could you...please...get me some coffee?"

Alejandro's dark gaze flickered over my bedraggled dress, the dark circles under my eyes. "Of course, *querida*," he murmured courteously. Turning away, he started toward the outdoor café.

The instant he was gone, I rushed to meet Hildy.

"Where's Edward?" I said desperately.

She was already shaking her head. "Mr. St. Cyr wasn't home. They said he's in Tokyo."

Of all the bad luck! "Can I borrow your phone?"

"Yes...." She reached into her pocket, then looked up, her mouth a round *O*. "I didn't bring it! It's still at home!"

Alejandro was already handing over money at the café. I saw him pick up two coffees from the counter. No time.

My shoulders fell. "Thanks anyway. You'd better go."

"Good luck, miss...."

Defeated, I looked out across the green park, deep emerald beneath the lowering gray London sky. I suddenly wondered what the weather was like in Spain. Warm. Sunny. Blue skies. With the chance of a hot, seductive Spaniard demanding that I share his bed.

No! I couldn't let myself think about it! Just sharing custody of Miguel would be bad enough. I would never, ever be Alejandro's lover! And certainly not his wife!

"Here." Alejandro handed me a white paper cup that warmed my hands. The coffee smelled like heaven. I took a sip, then sighed with appreciation as I felt the heat melt me from the inside. It was sweet, and creamy.

"You remembered how I liked it," I said in surprise.

He took a sip of his own black coffee, and gave a wicked grin. "That's how all women like it."

"That's not true!"

He shrugged. "It's mostly true. Cream and sugar will calm a woman down every time."

I glared at him. "You are such a—"

"A heartless bastard?" He paused, then tilted his head. "Do you still think I'll be such a disaster as a father?"

He sounded wistful, even—hurt? No. Impossible. A man like Alejandro had no heart to injure. But still, guilt rose in me, making my cheeks burn. "Maybe you're not *completely* evil." I looked down at the cup. "You did get my coffee right. Even though you're completely wrong with your stereotype about women liking cream and sugar."

"Obviously," he agreed. He tilted his head. "Your arms must be getting tired from holding Miguel all this time."

"A bit," I admitted sheepishly. "He's starting to get too heavy to carry like this for long."

Finishing off his coffee, he threw the empty cup in the trash and reached out. "Give him to me."

I hesitated, then handed him over. I watched anxiously, but Alejandro was careful, holding him, even turning Miguel around so he could see the world around him. Alejandro caught my look. "How am I doing?"

"Not bad," I said grudgingly.

"Would you care to walk?" He lifted a dark eyebrow. "Since he needed a walk so badly that you almost jumped out of a moving car. This taking babies on walks must be a serious business. Or else you had some other reason for coming here that you don't want me to know about."

I looked at him sharply. Did he know something? Or was he just fishing?

He gave me a bland smile.

I shrugged. "It was what you said. Pure panic at your marriage proposal." I took a sip of coffee. "Kind of like how you reacted last year when I told you I loved you. Instant disappearance." For a moment, we stared at each other. Then I turned away. "Yes. Let's walk."

The rain had eased up, and though gray skies were hovering, eager children of all ages, speaking many different languages, were now playing everywhere as we strolled past the pirate ship.

"So what is your answer?" he said casually, as if he'd been asking me out for a movie.

"About what?"

He looked at me.

"Oh." I licked my lips. "That."

"That."

"Be serious."

"I'm trying to be. But I've never asked any woman to marry me before. I'm starting to think I must be doing it wrong. Do I need to get down on one knee?"

"Don't you dare."

"Then what is it?"

I'm afraid you'd make me love you again. The cold knot near my heart, which had started to warm on the edges, returned to ice. "Come on," I mumbled, looking at the ground. "We both know that I'm not exactly duchess material."

"Are you trying to let me down gently?" he demanded. He stopped, leaning our baby against his hip as he looked at me. "Is there someone else? Perhaps the person who helped you flee London last year, and travel around the world?"

"It's not like that."

"When a man protects a woman," he said grimly, "it is exactly like that."

"How do you know it's a man?"

"By looking at your face," he said softly. "Right now."

I looked away. My throat hurt as I took another sip of the rich, sweet coffee, watching all the mothers and fathers and smiling nannies hovering on the edge of their children's delighted play. Some of them looked back at me. They probably imagined we were a family, too.

But we weren't.

I would have given anything if Alejandro could have been a man I could trust with my heart. A regular guy, a hardworking, loving man, who could have been my real partner. Instead of a selfish playboy duke who didn't know the meaning of love, and if married would plainly expect me to remain a dutiful wife imprisoned in his castle, raising our child, while he enjoyed himself elsewhere. Why shouldn't he? If love didn't exist, I could only imagine what he thought of fidelity.

"Why did you seduce me, Alejandro?" I blurted out.

He blinked. "What?"

My voice trembled as I looked up at him. "If you weren't trying to get me pregnant to provide an heir for you and Claudie, why did you seduce me? Why did you even notice me?"

"I don't understand."

"Are you really going to make me spell it out? Fine. You're—you—" I waved my half-full coffee toward him "—and I'm…" I indicated my white dress I'd worn for thirty-six hours now, wrinkled and possibly stained with baby sick I didn't know about, and I shivered in the cool morning air. "I believed Claudie's story last year because, for the first time, everything made sense. There was no other reason for you to… I mean, why else would a man like you, who could have any woman in the world, choose a woman like…"

Reaching out his hand, he cupped my cheek. "Because I wanted you, Lena. Pure and simple. I wanted you." Looking down at me, he said in a low voice, "I've never stopped wanting you."

My lips parted. I trembled, fighting the desire to lean into his touch. The paper cup fell from my hand, splashing coffee across the grass. But I barely noticed. Craning back my head, I blinked back tears as I whispered, "Then why did you break up with me like that, so coldly and completely? Just for telling you I loved you?"

Alejandro stared at me, then dropped his hand. "Because I didn't want to lead you on. I'd promised myself I'd never have either wife or child…."

"But why?" I said, bewildered. "Why wouldn't you want those things? You're the last of your line, aren't you? If you died without an heir…you would be the last Duke of Alzacar."

"That was my intention," he said grimly.

"But why?"

"It doesn't matter anymore." He looked down at Miguel in his arms. "Fate chose differently. I have a son." His dark eyes blazed at me, filled with heat and anger and something else…something I couldn't understand. "And I will protect his future. Right or wrong."

"You keep saying *right or wrong*. What is wrong about it?" I narrowed my eyes. "If you're trying to imply that he's not good enough—"

"Of course not," he bit out.

"Then it's me—"

He shook his head impatiently, his jaw tight. "I'm talking about me."

The great Duque de Alzacar, admitting some kind of fault? I blinked. I breathed, "I don't understand…."

"What is there to understand?" he said evasively. "Now that I am a parent, my priorities have changed. Wasn't it the same for you, when Miguel was born?"

I hesitated. It was true what he said, but I still had the sense he was hiding something from me. "Yes-s...."

"We have a child. So we will do what is best for him. We will marry."

"You didn't want to marry me in Mexico."

"That was when I thought you were a liar, a thief and probably a gold digger. Now my opinion of you has improved."

"Thanks," I said wryly.

"Why are you fighting me? Unless—" He gave me a sharp, searching gaze. "Are you in love with someone else?"

The image of Edward flashed in front of my eyes. I wondered if Alejandro would still keep his improved opinion of me if he knew I'd been living in another man's house. It would look sordid, even if the truth had been so innocent. At least—innocent on my side. Swallowing, I looked away.

"I'm not in love with anyone." My voice was barely audible over the noisy children at play.

His shoulders relaxed imperceptibly. "Then why not marry me?" His tone turned almost playful. "You really should consider it for the jewels alone...."

I gave a rueful laugh, then looked at him. "I'd never fit into your world, Alejandro. If I took you at your word and became your wife, we'd both be miserable."

"I wouldn't be."

I shook my head. "Your expectations of marriage are lower than mine. It would never work. I want—" I looked down as my cheeks turned hot "— to be loved. I want what my parents had."

Alejandro abruptly stopped. We were in the far back of the playground now, in a quiet overgrown place of bushes and trees. "But what about our son? Doesn't he have some rights, as well? Doesn't he deserve a stable home?"

"You mean a cold, drafty castle?"

"It's neither drafty nor cold." He set his jaw. "I want my son, my heir, to live in Spain. To know his people. His family."

I frowned at him. "I thought you had no family."

"My grandmother who raised me. All the people on my estate. They are like family to me. Don't you think he deserves to know them, and they should know him? Shouldn't he know his country? Where else would you take him— back to Mexico?"

"I loved it there!" I said, stung.

"We will buy a vacation house there," he said impatiently. "But his home is with his land. With his people. With his parents. You of all people," he said softly, "know what it means to have a happy, settled childhood, surrounded by love."

I sucked in my breath. I felt myself wavering. Of course I wanted all those things for my son.

"You'll be a duchess, honored, wealthy beyond imagining."

"I'd be the poor stupid wife sitting at home in the castle," I whispered, hardly daring to meet his gaze, "while you were out having a good time with other, more glamorous women...."

His dark eyes narrowed. "I have many faults, but disloyalty is not one of them. Still, I can understand why you'd immediately think of cheating. Tell me—" he moved closer, his sardonic gaze sweeping over me "—did you enjoy having the use of Edward St. Cyr's house? His jet?"

My eyes went wide. My mouth suddenly went dry.

"How did you find out?" I said weakly.

"Before my jet left Mexico, I told my investigators to dig into the layer of the shell company that owned the house in

San Miguel. If it wasn't Claudie who helped you," he said grimly, "I intended to find out who it really was."

Well. That explained why he'd stopped asking. "Why have you pretended all day you didn't know?"

His handsome face looked chiseled and hard as marble beneath the gray sky. "I wanted to give you the chance to tell me."

"A test?" I whispered.

"If you like." His eyes glittered. "Women always find the quality of danger so attractive. Until they find out what *danger* really means. Tell me. Did you enjoy using St. Cyr's possessions? His money? His jet? How about his bed? Did you enjoy sharing that?"

"I never shared his bed!" I tried not to remember the husky sound of Edward's voice. *It's time for you to belong to me.* Or the way he'd flinched at my reaction—an incredulous, unwilling laugh. He'd taken a deep breath. *You'll see,* he'd whispered, then turned and left. Pushing the memory away, I lifted my chin. "We've never even kissed!"

"I see." Lifting an eyebrow, Alejandro said scornfully, "He helped you out of the goodness of his heart."

That might be pushing it. I bit my lip. "Um…yes?"

"Is that a statement or a question?"

"He's a friend to me," I whispered. "Just a friend."

Alejandro looked at me more closely. "But he wants more, doesn't he?" The sweep of his dark lashes left a shadow against his olive skin, his taut cheekbones, as he looked down at our baby in his arms. After all this time, he still carried Miguel as if he were no weight at all. He said in a low voice, "I won't let my son keep such company. Because I, at least, have clear eyes about what *danger* means."

"And I understand at last," I choked out, "why you suddenly want to marry me."

He narrowed his eyes at me. "Lena—"

"You say he is dangerous? Maybe he is. But if it weren't

for Edward St. Cyr, I don't think I could have survived the darkness and fear of the past year. He was there for me when you deserted me. When you left me pregnant and alone and afraid."

His face turned white, then red. "If you'd given me the chance—"

"I did give you a chance. You never called me back." I took a deep breath. "I know now you weren't the monster I thought you were. But I'll never be able to trust you like I did. It's lost. Along with the way I loved you."

Silence fell, the only sound the children playing on the other side of the trees. I heard their shrieks of joy.

When Alejandro spoke, his voice was low, even grim. "Love me or not, trust me or not, but you will marry me. Miguel will have a stable family. A real home."

I shook my head. He moved closer.

"You promised to come to Spain, Lena," he said. "You gave your word."

I threw him a panicked glance. "That was when—"

"Ah. You hoped you could break your promise, didn't you? Perhaps with St. Cyr's help?"

My silence spoke volumes. His dark eyes hardened. "You gave me your word that if I brought you to London, you would come with me to Spain."

He was right. I had. Now, I felt so alone and forlorn. Alejandro was starting to wear me down. To break my will. To remind me of a promise I'd never wanted to keep.

"It will only lead to misery," I whispered.

"Wherever it leads," he said softly, "whatever we'd once planned for our lives…you are part of my family now."

"Your family. You mean your grandmother?" I shivered, imagining a coldly imperious grande dame in pearls and head-to-toe vintage Chanel. A little like my own grandmother, in fact. "She will hate me. She'll never think I'm good enough."

He gave a low laugh. "You think you know what to expect? A cold, proud dowager in a cold, drafty castle?"

"Am I wrong?"

"My grandmother was born in the United States. In Idaho. The daughter of Basque sheep ranchers."

"Idaho?" My mouth fell open. "How did she...?"

"How did she end up married to my grandfather? It is an interesting story. Perhaps you can ask her when you meet her." His lips twisted grimly. "Unless you intend to break your promise, and refuse to go to Spain after all."

I swallowed, afraid of what it would mean to go to his castle. Surrounded by his family and friends. Surrounded by his *power*. How long could I resist his marriage demand then?

"Enough. You always spend too long in your mind, going back and forth on decisions that have already been made. End it now." Reaching into his pocket, Alejandro pulled out a phone and dialed a number. He pushed it into my hand. "It's ringing."

"What?" I stammered, staring down at the phone. "Whom did you call?"

"My grandmother. If you are breaking your promise to me, if you are truly not willing to bring Miguel to Spain to meet her, tell her now."

"Me? I can't talk to your grandmother!"

"No. *I* can't," he said coldly, "because I love her. *You* have no feelings for her whatsoever, so you should have no trouble being cruel."

"You think I'm cruel?" I whispered as the phone rang.

His eyes met mine. "Tell her she has a great-grandchild. Introduce yourself. Tell her I've asked you to marry me. Go on."

I stared at him numbly, then heard a tremulous voice at the other end of the line.

"*¿Hola?* Alejandro?"

It was a warm, sweet, kindly voice, the sort of voice that a grandmother would have in a movie, the grandmother who bakes cookies and is plump and white-haired and gives you hugs and tells you to eat more pie—or in this case, more paella?—because food is love, and she loves you so much that you're her whole existence, her light, her star. It was the type of voice I had not heard since my parents had died.

"Alejandro?" The woman sounded worried now. "Are you there?"

"It's not Alejandro," I replied, my voice unsteady. "But he asked me to call you. I'm a…friend."

"A friend?" The sweet tremulous voice gasped, her accent definitely American. "Has he fallen sick? Was he in an accident?"

"No, he's fine…."

"If he were fine, he'd be calling me himself, as he always does." A sob choked her voice. "You're trying to break it to me gently. But you can't. First I lost my children, then my…." Her voice broke. "Alejandro was all I had left. I always knew I would lose him someday. That sooner or later—" another sob "—fate would catch up with me and…"

"Oh, for heaven's sake!" I cried in exasperation. "Alejandro's fine! He's standing right by me!"

She sucked in her breath. Her tone changed, became curious. "Then why are you calling me on his phone?"

"He…wanted me to tell you the happy news." Glaring at Alejandro, I kept my voice gentle as I said, "You're a great-grandmother."

"A—" her voice ended in a gasp. A happy gasp. "Alejandro has a child?"

"We have a five-month-old son. I'm the baby's mother."

"You're American? Canadian?"

"Born in Brooklyn."

"Why didn't he tell me before? What's your name? Have we met?" She didn't seem like the snooty duchess I'd imagined. She continued eagerly, "Did you elope? Oh, I'll never forgive Alejandro for getting married without me—"

"He didn't tell you because—well, he wasn't sure about it. For your other question, we're not married." I gritted my teeth. "And we have no plans to be."

"You have no—" She cut herself off with an intake of breath. Then changing the subject with forced cheer, she said, "So when can I meet my great-grandson? I can hardly wait to tell my friends you're coming to live in the castle. The pitter-patter of little feet at Rohares Castle at last!"

"I'm sorry. We're not going to live in Spain."

"Oh." I heard the soft whoosh of her whimper. "That's… all right." She took a deep breath. "So when are you coming to visit so I can meet him?"

I bit my lip. "I don't know if we can…."

"I understand," she sniffled. "It's fine. Just send me a Christmas card with the baby's picture, and…it's fine. I've had a good life. I don't need to meet my only great-grandchild…."

My own fear of spending time with Alejandro, of allowing him more power over me, suddenly felt small and selfish compared with letting her meet Miguel—and even more important, allowing my son to have the family I myself had yearned for. What did I have, a heart of stone?

"All right." With a sigh, I accepted the inevitable. "We'll come to Spain in the next day or two. Just for a visit, mind!"

But even with that warning, her cries of joy exploded from the phone. I held it away from my ear, glaring all the while at Alejandro. "I'll let you talk to Alejandro," I told her, then covering the mouthpiece, I handed him the phone and grumbled, "I hate you."

"No, you don't." He took it from my hand, looking down at me seriously. "I'll win your trust, Lena. And then…"

"Then?"

He gave me a sensual smile. "You'll be my wife within the week."

There are many different kinds of seduction.

There's the traditional kind, with flowers, chocolates, dinner by candlelight. That's the way Alejandro had seduced me last summer. He called the Kensington mansion, asked for me, invited me to dinner. He showed up at the door dressed in a tux, his arms full of roses—to Claudie's rage—and greeted me with a chaste kiss on the cheek.

"You look beautiful," he'd murmured, and took me to the best restaurant in London. He asked me questions, listened aptly and physically grew closer and closer, with the innocent touch of his hand, the casual brush of his body against mine. He held my hand across the dinner table in the candlelight, in full view of the other patrons, looking at me with deep soulful eyes, as if no other woman had ever existed. Afterward, he took me to a club. We danced, and he pulled me into his arms, against his hard, powerful body. Closer. Closer still, until my heart was in my throat and I started to feel dizzy. In the middle of the dance floor, he lowered his head and kissed me for the first time.

It was my first kiss, and as I closed my eyes I felt the whole world whirling around me. Around us.

When he finally pulled away, he whispered against my skin, "I want you." I'd trembled, my heart beating violently, like a deer in a wolf's jaws. He'd looked down at me and smiled. Then took me back to his rooftop terrace suite at the Dorchester Hotel.

There had been no question of resistance. I was a virgin in the hands of a master. He'd had me from the moment he kissed me. From the moment he showed up at my door in a sleek tuxedo, with his arms full of roses, and told me he wanted me in his low, husky voice. He'd had me from the moment he'd seared me with the intensity of his full attention.

That was the traditional way of seduction. It had worked once, worked with utterly ruthless efficiency against my unprepared heart. But I knew the moves now—that is to say, I knew how they ended. With pleasure that was all too brief, and agony that was all too long.

But there are many different kinds of seduction.

Alejandro had decided we wouldn't leave immediately for Madrid, but would spend one night in London, resting at his usual suite of rooms at the Dorchester. He told me it was because the baby and I both looked tired. I was immediately suspicious, but as we left the park, he did not try to kiss me. Even after we'd arrived at the luxurious hotel, he did not look deeply into my eyes and tell me I was the most beautiful woman on earth, or pull me out onto the rooftop terrace, overlooking Hyde Park and all the wide gray sky, to take me in his arms.

Instead, he just ordered us lunch via room service, then afterward, he smiled at me. "We need to go shopping."

I frowned at him, suspecting a trick. "No, we don't."

"We do need a stroller," he said innocently. "A pushcart. For the baby."

I could hardly argue with that, since we'd left the umbrella stroller back in San Miguel. "Fine," I grumbled. "A stroller. That's it."

"You're very boring."

"I'm broke."

"I'm not."

"Lucky you."

"I can buy you things, you know."

"I don't want you to."

"Why?"

I set my jaw. "I'm afraid what they'd cost me."

He just answered with an innocent smile, and had his

driver take us to the best shops in Knightsbridge, Mayfair and Sloane Street. He bought the most expensive pushcart he could find for Miguel, then pushed it himself, leaving the bodyguards trailing behind us to hold only shopping bags full of clothes and toys for the baby.

"You said just a stroller!"

"Surely you wouldn't begrudge me the chance to buy a few small items for my son?"

"No," I sighed. But Alejandro kept pushing the boundaries. All the bodyguards who trailed us were soon weighed down with shopping bags.

"Now we must get you some clothes, as well," Alejandro said, smiling as he caught me looking wistfully at the lovely, expensive dresses. I jumped, then blushed guiltily.

"No. Absolutely not."

"It's the least I can do," Alejandro replied firmly, "considering it was because of me that you lost your inheritance."

"That wasn't your fault…" I protested. He looked down at me with his big, dark, Spanish eyes.

"Please let me do this, *querida*. I must," he said softly. "Such a small thing. You cannot deny me my desire."

I shivered. That was exactly what I was afraid of. That if I couldn't deny him this, I wouldn't be able to deny him anything. And soon I'd be putty in his hands again, like a spaniel waiting for her master with slippers in her mouth.

I'd end up married to a man who didn't love me. Who would ignore me. And I'd spend the rest of my life like a ghost, haunting his stupid castle.

Wordlessly, I shook my head. He sighed, looking sad.

I was proud of myself for sticking to my guns. But as we walked through the expensive shops, Alejandro saw me looking at a pretty dress a second too long. He gave one of his bodyguards a glance, and the man snatched it up in my size.

"What!" I exclaimed. "No. I don't want that!"

"Too bad," he said smugly. "I just bought it for you."

Irritated, I tried to foil Alejandro's plan by carefully *not* looking at any of the beautiful clothes, shoes or bags as we walked through the luxury department store and designer boutiques. But that didn't work, either. He simply started picking things out for me, items far more expensive and flashy than I would have picked out for myself. Instead of the black leather quilted handbag I might have chosen, I found myself suddenly the owner of a handbag in crocodile skin with fourteen-karat-gold fittings and diamonds woven into the chain.

"I can't wear that!" I protested. "I'd look a proper fool!"

He grinned. "If you don't like me choosing for you, you have to tell me what you want."

So I did. I had no choice.

"Dirty blackmailer," I grumbled as I picked out a simple cotton sweater from Prada, but his smile only widened.

The salespeople, sensing blood in the water, left their previous customers to follow eagerly in our wake. The size of our entourage quickly exploded, with salespeople, bodyguards, Alejandro, me and our baby in a stroller so expensive that it, too, might as well have been made of rare leathers and solid gold. Other people turned their heads to watch as we went by, their eyes big as they whispered to each other beneath their hands.

"I feel conspicuous," I complained to Alejandro.

"You deserve to be looked at," he said. "You deserve everyone's attention."

I was relieved to return to his suite of rooms at the Dorchester, even though it was so fancy, the same suite Elizabeth Taylor had once lived in. I was happy to be alone with him.

And yet not happy.

It took a long time for the bodyguards to bring up all the packages. Even with help from the hotel staff.

"I didn't realize we bought so much," I said, blushing.

Alejandro gave a low laugh as he tipped the staff then turned back. "You hardly bought anything. I would have given you far more." He looked down at me. Running his hand beneath my jaw, he said softly, "I want to give you more."

We stood together, alone in the living room of the suite, and I held my breath. Praying he wouldn't kiss me. Wishing desperately that he would.

But with a low laugh, he released me. "Are you hungry?"

After I fed Miguel and tucked him to bed in the second bedroom, we had an early dinner in the dining room, beneath a crystal chandelier, on an elegant table that would seat eight, with a view not just of London, but of the exact place where, last summer, he'd pressed me against the silver wallpaper and made love to me, hot and fast and fierce against the wall.

All through dinner, I tried not to look at that wall. Or think about the bed next door.

I told myself he wasn't trying to seduce me. Maybe he wasn't. Maybe it was just my delusion, reading desire in his dark, hot glances. It had to be me. He wouldn't actually be intending to…

Alejandro suddenly smiled at me. "You are tired. It has been a long day for you."

"All that shopping," I grumbled. He grinned, taking an innocent sip of his after-dinner coffee.

"I meant before that. Mexico. Claudie. Your sleepless night on the plane…"

"Oh." I yawned, as if on cue. "I am a little tired."

"So go take some time for yourself. Take a nap. A shower. Go to bed. I will take over."

"Take over?"

"With Miguel." As I blinked at him in confusion, he lifted a dark eyebrow and added mildly, "Surely you can trust me that far—as far as the next room? If there is any problem, I will wake you. But there won't be. Go rest."

I took a long, hot shower, and it was heaven. Putting on a soft new nightgown straight from the designer bag, I fell into the large bed, knowing that someone else was watching our child as I slept, and I wasn't on call. That was the most deliciously luxurious thing of all.

When I woke, early-morning sunlight was streaking across the large bed, where I'd clearly slept alone. Looking at the clock, I saw to my shock I'd slept twelve hours straight—my best night's sleep in a year. I stretched in bed, yawning, feeling fantastic. Feeling grateful. Alejandro...

Alejandro!

He couldn't possibly have stayed up all night with the baby! He must have left. Jumping out of bed in panic, I flung open the bedroom door, terrified that Alejandro had spirited away our baby and left me behind.

But Alejandro was in the living room, walking our baby back and forth, singing a Spanish song in his low, deep voice, as Miguel's eyes grew heavy. Then Alejandro saw me, and he gave me a brilliant smile, even though his eyes, too, looked tired.

"*Buenos días, querida.* Did you sleep?"

"Beautifully," I said, running my hands through my hair, suddenly self-conscious of my nightgown, which in this bright morning light looked like a slinky silk negligee. I tried to casually cover the outline of my breasts with my arms. "And you?"

"Ah," he said, smiling tenderly down at his son. "For us, it is still a work in progress. But by the time we are on the plane to Madrid, after breakfast, I think our little man will sleep. He's worn himself out, haven't you?"

I stared at the two of them together, the strong-shouldered

Spaniard holding his tiny son so lovingly, with such infinite care and patience, though he'd clearly kept Alejandro up most of the night.

Miguel looked up with big eyes at his father. They had the same face, though one was smaller and chubby, the other larger and chiseled at the cheekbones and jaw. But I could not deny the look of love that glowed from Alejandro's eyes as he looked into the face of his son.

I'd been wrong, I realized. Alejandro did know how to love.

He just didn't know how to love *me*.

Turning back, Alejandro gave me a big grin, filled with joy and pride. Our eyes locked.

The smile slowly slid from his face. I felt his gaze from my head to my toes and everywhere in between. His soulful dark eyes seemed to last forever, like those starlit summer nights.

I looked at Alejandro in this moment, and I was suddenly afraid. Seeing him as a father, as a true partner in caring for the tiny person I loved so much, I trembled.

I could handle his gifts. I might even be able to handle the sensual awareness that electrified the air between us. I could keep my heart on ice. I could resist.

But this?

There are many different kinds of seduction. Some are of the body. Some are of the mind.

But others, the most powerful, are of the heart.

CHAPTER FOUR

I'M NOT GOING to lie. A private jet makes travel easier. Especially with a baby. We had a quick flight from London to Madrid. No standing in lines, no fighting for overhead space. And I felt much better than I had on the last flight. I was well slept, showered. My hair was brushed until it tumbled over my shoulders. I'd even put on a little mascara. Arriving in Madrid in my new soft pink blouse and form-fitting jeans, I felt almost pretty.

"Where's your diamond handbag?" Alejandro teased as we left the jet, going down the steps to the tarmac of the private airport, followed by his men carrying our luggage. "Don't you like it?"

I bit my lip. "Well…"

He put his hand on his heart, as if it had been stabbed with grief. "You don't!"

"Don't worry," I assured him. "I'll still use it. I was needing a new diaper bag."

He gave a low laugh, then sobered, his dark eyes resting on mine as he said softly, "I'll have to see if I can find some other gift to please you more."

I shivered at his glance, then looked out the window of the SUV. *He's not trying to seduce me,* I repeated silently to myself. *He's not. He's just trying to lure me into a loveless marriage of convenience—don't fall for it, don't…*

Madrid was beautiful, an elegant, formal city with its

nineteenth-century architecture, spreading regally across the banks of the Manzanares River. All the gray clouds of San Miguel and London seemed a million miles away. Here, the August sky was bright blue, and the Spanish sun burning hot.

Alejandro's driver took us to his penthouse apartment near the Prado, the bodyguards and luggage following in the car behind. We arrived at the flat, which took the entire top floor, and were answered at the door by a middle-aged woman who seemed far too young to be his grandmother. He quickly introduced her as his longtime housekeeper, the only paid staff at the penthouse, Mrs. Gutierrez, who lived on a floor below.

Alejandro walked us around the enormous apartment, with its stark contemporary furnishings and enormous windows overlooking the city. "What do you think?"

"It's beautiful," I said slowly, "but so cold. You can hardly tell anyone lives here." Shivering, I cuddled my warm baby close. "You must not stay here much."

He blinked. "More blunt honesty."

"Was I rude?"

"I can take it." He shifted his weight, then clawed back his thick, dark hair. I wondered what it would feel like to... No! I stopped the thought cold. Oblivious of my inner struggle, he continued with a sigh, "My company is head-quartered here. I am in Madrid all the time."

"Oh," I said, looking at all the sharp edges of the furniture, all the glass and chrome. "Um. Well. It's very—masculine."

He lifted a dark eyebrow. "Perhaps it needs a woman's touch."

In my current frame of mind, I wondered if he was talking about more than his apartment. My cheeks went hot and I cleared my throat. "I'm surprised your grandmother isn't here. She sounded so keen to meet her great-grandson."

"You'll meet her tomorrow. I have an event tonight in Madrid, and Abuela doesn't like to leave her roses, or all the people who count on her at the castle."

"The castle?"

"Rohares, near Seville. Where the Dukes of Alzacar have lived for four hundred years."

"Cold and drafty," I sighed.

"Exactamente." He gave me a sideways glance, seeming to hide a smile. "I can hardly wait for you to see it."

"Yeah," I grumbled. "How many rooms?"

"I lose count," he said, and I couldn't tell if he was joking. But at least such a large building would create more space between us. Even this large penthouse felt too...close, when we were together. Every glance, every word, made me more attracted. It was dangerous.

As soon as his grandmother met the baby, I told myself firmly, I'd be out of this country and away from Alejandro. We'd come to some agreement over custody. Preferably one that involved Miguel living with me in Mexico.

Although it would be a shame to separate my son from a father who loved him, just because I was afraid of being hurt....

I pushed the thought away. "You said something about an event tonight?"

"A celebration—a ball, really. Hosted by my company. Starts in—" he glanced at his platinum watch and said calmly "—twenty minutes."

Thank heavens! I wouldn't have to spend the evening with him, trying desperately not to feel tempted! With real relief, I said, "Go and have a good time. We'll be fine. I'll tuck Miguel into bed and maybe read a book until..."

But he was already shaking his head. "Leave you alone with our son, giving you the opportunity to run away again? No."

"Why do you think I'd run away?"

"Why would I think you wouldn't?"

"You could post your bodyguards at the door," I suggested.

"You'd charm them and escape."

He thought I was charming? For an instant I felt flattered. Then I folded my arms. "You could just decide to trust me."

"I will trust you." He tilted his head, looking down at me with amusement. "As soon as you marry me."

"Never going to happen, and believe me, after this momentary madness—or whatever it is—passes, you'll thank me."

"Fine," he sighed, plunking down on the soft sofa in front of a wide-screen TV and a window with a view of the city. He reached for the remote control. "Shall we see if there are any good movies on tonight? Maybe order takeaway?"

I stared at him, my lips parted. "You can't miss your own party."

He shrugged. "Yes. It's a pity. Especially since it was to celebrate my company's upcoming IPO on the stock exchange. But I can miss it to watch a TV movie with you. No problem."

"Are you crazy? You can't miss something like that. You're the host! If you don't even bother showing up, what do you think it will do to your stock price?"

"It's fine. Really." He shrugged. "I don't have a date to the ball anyway."

"You honestly expect me to believe you don't have a date—*you?*"

"You have to admit it's kind of your fault."

Now we were getting down to it.

"How is it my fault?" I said suspiciously.

Tilting his head, he looked at me from the sofa. "I *did* have a date for tonight." He stroked his chin thoughtfully.

"A beautiful Swedish swimsuit model, in fact. But when I called her yesterday and explained I wouldn't be picking her up in my jet because I'd just discovered a former mistress had my baby and I had to spend the day buying you presents instead of flying to Stockholm to collect her, well—for some reason, Elsa wasn't interested in flying coach to Madrid to be my date tonight."

I hid a laugh, tried to look mad. "Too bad for you. But it's really not my problem."

He nodded sagely. "You're scared."

"Scared? Of what?"

"Of spending time with me. You're scared you'll be overwhelmed with desire and say yes to everything, and wake up tomorrow morning, in my bed, with a ring on your finger."

In his *bed?* My mouth went dry.

"It's all right. I understand." He fluttered his dark eyelashes outrageously. "You don't trust yourself, because you want me so badly."

It was so true. "That's so not true!"

He lifted his eyebrows. "Then you'll be my date?"

I thought about the type of people I'd be likely to meet at his party. A bunch of wealthy, beautiful, *mean* people. Just like Claudie. "No, thanks."

"Why?" he demanded.

"The baby will wake up at midnight for a feeding…" I said weakly.

"I'll have you back by midnight. Via pumpkin coach if necessary."

"There's no one I can trust as his babysitter!"

"Mrs. Gutierrez raised four children, and has ten grandchildren. She's very trustworthy and experienced, and she's agreed to stay."

"You thought of everything," I grumbled.

"So say yes."

"I won't fit in with your friends, okay?"

"Always so afraid," he sighed. "Of me. Of them. Of your own shadow."

He was clearly taunting me, but I couldn't help but bristle. "Even if I wanted to go with you, it's too late. Your party starts in twenty minutes, and unless you bought a ball gown in London yesterday without me noticing, I have nothing to wear!"

Alejandro smiled. "Did I ever show you our bedroom?"

I shook my head with a scowl. "It's either yours or mine. Not *ours*."

"That's what I meant," he said innocently. Walking ahead in the hallway, he pushed open a door.

The bedroom was enormous, with an amazing view of Madrid, but sparsely furnished, with only an expensive, masculine bed. And, incongruously, a crib beside it.

But when I looked closer at the bed, I saw a flash of pink. Coming closer, I gasped when I saw a pale pink gown, a delicious confection of flowers and silk, spread across his plain white bedspread. I picked it up with one hand, then dropped it when I saw the tag peeking at me. Oscar de la Renta.

A pumpkin coach, indeed! I whirled to face him. "You bought this yesterday. You always intended to bring me as your date tonight," I accused.

His lips were curved in a sensual smile, then his hands went up in mock surrender. "I admit it." Then he put down his hands, and his expression changed. His dark eyes became intent. Sensual. "I always get what I want," he said softly, searching my gaze. "And I don't give up. When something is difficult to possess, that only makes me want it more."

For a long heartbeat, we stared at each other in his bedroom.

Then I tossed my head, hoping he couldn't see how my

body was trembling. "Fine. Have it your way. I'll come with you tonight, since it means so much to you. I'll do it for Miguel's sake, so your friends will know he wasn't just the result of some cheap one-night stand. But that's it."

His dark eyes burned into mine. "A cheap one-night stand? That is the last thing you were to me. You should know that by now."

A shiver went down my spine and through my soul. I straightened, locking my knees, and I handed him the baby. "I'll get dressed as quickly as I can."

Thirty minutes later, Alejandro helped me out of the limo, holding my hand as we walked up a red carpet, past the flashbulbs of the paparazzi.

"I thought your company was a metals and real estate conglomerate," I murmured beneath all of the attention.

"It is," he said innocently, "among other things. We recently bought a movie studio. Look." I followed his gaze to see a beautiful movie star whom I'd admired for years just ahead of us in a tight sequined gown. "That's the reason for the paparazzi."

"She is beautiful," I said.

He looked down at me. "You're more beautiful than her on your worst day. Even when you are wearing a dress like a sack and barely brush your hair."

I snorted, expecting mockery. "You are so full of—"

Then I saw his expression, the frank hunger in his eyes as he looked at me, and my mouth went dry.

"Come on," he said roughly. "The sooner we get this done, the sooner we can go home."

I licked my lips, tasting lipstick, which was foreign to me. But in this pale pink ball gown, I didn't feel like myself at all. I might as well have been wearing glass slippers....

Alejandro led me into a large ballroom, filled with people dancing and drinking champagne beneath enormous crystal chandeliers high overhead. I watched as, ten minutes after we arrived, he went to the elevated dais and made a short speech into a microphone, congratulating the staff of his company, and thanking all their investors and friends, which was met by a roar of applause. When he left the microphone, he returned to my side.

"Now the work is done," he whispered, nuzzling my ear. "Let's have some fun."

He took me out on the dance floor, and I trembled, remembering the last time he'd held me in his arms on a dance floor, the way he'd slowly seduced me, until I surrendered in my first kiss. Now, I felt his arms around me, and I shuddered from deep within, feeling his warmth and strength beneath the tuxedo, breathing in his cologne and the scent that was uniquely him. When the music ended after the first dance, I pulled away.

"I—I need some champagne," I said unsteadily.

"Of course," he said huskily, his dark eyes intent, as if he saw through me, every inch and pore, down to my heart and soul.

For the rest of the night, Alejandro was the perfect gentleman, solicitous, getting me champagne, even cheerfully introducing me to the acquaintances who quickly surrounded us.

One of his friends, a German tycoon of some kind, looked me over appreciatively. "Where did you keep this beautiful creature hidden, Your Excellency?"

"Yes, you should have introduced us," a handsome Japanese millionaire said.

"You sure you want this guy, Miss Carlisle?" An actor I recognized from a big summer movie, where he'd gotten revenge against aliens who blew up Paris, gave me a big shiny grin. "You haven't given the rest of us a chance yet."

I blushed. The whole night seemed unreal, as if I were playing a part, with my hair pulled back into a high ballerina bun, wearing the petal-pink ball gown with tiny flowers embroidered over it. Remembering the part I was to play, I glanced at Alejandro. "Sorry. I only want Alejandro."

His relief was palpable. He smiled back at me.

"Awww, so sweet," the movie star said, somewhat ironically. "Well. Whenever the romance is over, feel free to…"

"It's not a romance," a man said behind us. "It's extortion."

Turning, I sucked in my breath. A man stood behind us, dressed exactly like the others, in a sharp black tuxedo. The man I'd been so desperate to see—and yet, oddly, he seemed out of place here. Handsome. But malevolent.

"Edward," I breathed. "I thought you were in Tokyo—"

His eyes softened. "My staff called me. I was glad to hear you'd gone to London to see me. But not so glad to hear who was with you." He glared at Alejandro, his jaw tight, even as he continued to speak to me. "Are you all right?"

"Of course I'm all right," I said, suddenly nervous.

The two men were glaring at each other, both of them straining the size of the ballroom between their shoulders and masculine pride. I had a sudden dismaying flash of two predators, growling over the same female—or the same prey.

Alejandro's eyes narrowed, but with a swift glance at me, he politely put out his hand. "Edward St. Cyr. I know you by reputation, of course."

The words were courteous and cool. Edward took them as the insult they were no doubt intended. Without taking the offered hand, he bared his teeth in a smile. "How gracious of you to say so. I know of you not just from reputation, but also from more…personal sources." He looked down dismissively at Alejandro's hand. "It does seem a little…tacky?…that after dragging Lena to Europe, you'd force her to pose as your date."

"I didn't force her."

"Of course you did," he said roughly. "What is it, some

feeble attempt to project stability for the benefit of future shareholders? Or—no, don't tell me—some attempt to make her love you again?" Smiling his shark's smile, Edward held up his glass of champagne in salute. "You'd think destroying her once would be enough for you. But if anyone would be selfish enough to try for twice, it's you, Navaro."

No respectful *Your Excellency*. Just Alejandro's surname, tossed out with scorn. The entire group, including me, stared wide-eyed as Edward drank down the entire contents of his champagne glass. We looked at Alejandro.

He had dropped his hand, his eyelids now narrowed to slits. "Whatever you might have heard about me, it was a mistake." He glanced at me. "Lena now knows the truth."

Edward lifted an eyebrow. "Convinced her of that, have you?"

"What are you even doing here?" Alejandro's face hardened. "I don't recall sending you an invitation."

Setting his empty glass down on a nearby tray, Edward looked over the ballroom with a small smile. "I have plenty of friends. One was happy to bring me along."

"Who?"

"The Bulgarian ambassador." Edward turned back with lifted eyebrows and said mildly, "Surely you're not going to throw us out and risk an international incident?"

Alejandro looked at a gray-haired, distinguished-looking man across the ballroom, who appeared deep in conversation with someone I recognized from newspaper photos, who'd recently won the Nobel Peace Prize. He turned back with gritted teeth. "What do you want, St. Cyr?"

"I want Lena, since she's asked for me," he said softly. He turned to me, holding out his arm. "Shall we go, love?"

I heard a low, almost barbaric growl, and suddenly Alejandro was in front of me, blocking me from Edward's outstretched arm.

"So it's like that, is it?" Edward said. "She's your prisoner?"

"She's here with me of her own free will."

"Free will." Edward's lips pulled back, revealing white, sharp teeth. "Meaning you probably blackmailed her over that baby. You have no real claim on her."

"I have every claim."

"Because she had your child?" He snorted, jerking his chin. "Keep it," he said derisively. "If I'm the man she wants, I will give her more."

I gasped aloud at his cold reference to Miguel. *It?*

Edward couldn't have referred to my precious baby as "it." He couldn't have implied that he could get me pregnant and replace Miguel in my arms, in my life, as easily as someone might replace a new shoe.

Could he?

The black slash of Alejandro's eyebrows lowered. Every line of his hard-muscled body was taut, as if he were barely holding back from attack. He reminded me of a lion, or a wolf, coiled to spring, with only a thin veneer of civilized reason holding him in check—but not for much longer.

The two of them were about to start a brawl. Right here, in this elegant gilded ballroom, surrounded by the glitterati of Spain and all the world. The crowd around us was already growing, and so were the whispers. I wished I'd never started this by trying to contact Edward. Desperately, I yanked on his sleeve. "Please. Don't..."

Edward looked down at me condescendingly. "It's all right, Lena. I'm here now. I won't let him bully you." His eyes were hard, and his broad shoulders were square, like a rugby player's. And the condescending smile he gave me, after the cold, contemptuous stare he'd just given Alejandro, made me wish he was a million miles away. "You're safe. I'll take over."

"Take over?" I repeated incredulously.

Just yesterday, I'd wished so ardently for Edward's help. I'd remembered only that a year ago, when I'd needed to escape London, when I'd felt desperate and terrified and alone, I'd been grateful for his strength. But now...

I'd forgotten what Edward was really like.

Forgotten the times he'd visited his house in Mexico after Miguel was born, when he'd seemed irritated by Miguel's cries when my son's tummy hurt or he was unable to sleep. Edward had made several dark hints about adoption, or sending the baby back to Claudie and Alejandro. I'd thought Edward's jokes were in poor taste, but I'd let it go, because I owed him so much.

But now—

Edward was no longer even looking at me. He was smiling at Alejandro, utterly confident—like a dog who couldn't wait to test out his slashing claws and snarling teeth, to prove who was the stronger, meaner dog, in the pretext for a brawl of fighting over a bone—me.

Alejandro's dark eyes met mine. For a moment, they held. Something changed in his expression. He seemed to relax slightly. He drew himself up, looking almost amused.

"Yes, Lena is the mother of my child," he drawled. "And because of that I have a claim on her that you never will. But that's not the only claim. I have one deeper even than that." He glanced at me. "We intended to keep it private for a few days more, as a family matter, but we might as well let everyone know, shall we not, *querida?*"

"Um, yes?" I said, as mystified as everyone else.

Still smiling that pleasant smile, Alejandro turned and grabbed a crystal flute and solid silver knife off a waiter's passing tray. For a moment I froze in fear. Even with a butter knife—heck, even with his bare hands—I knew Alejandro could be dangerous. Boxing and mixed martial arts were hobbies in his downtime, the way he kept in shape and worked out the tension from a hard day making billion-dollar deals.

I exhaled when he didn't turn back to attack Edward. In fact, he rather insultingly turned his back on him, striding through the ballroom, to the dais, as the crowds parted like magic. He climbed the steps to the same microphone where he'd given the speech before. Most of the guests, seeing him, immediately fell silent. A few continued to whisper amongst themselves, staring between him and Edward—and me.

Alejandro chimed his knife against the crystal flute, so hard and loud that I feared the delicate glass might break in his hand. The entire ballroom fell so quiet that I could hear my own breath.

"I know this is a business gathering," he said, "but I must beg your indulgence for a moment. I am, after all, amongst friends…." His eyes abruptly focused on me across the crowd. "I have some happy news to announce. My engagement."

No. My face turned red and my body itched in an attack of nervous fear beneath my pale pink ball gown as a thousand people turned to stare at me. The whispering increased, building like the roll of distant thunder.

"Many of you probably wondered if I'd *ever* get married." Alejandro rubbed the back of his dark hair then looked up with a smile that was equal parts charming and sheepish. "I confess I wondered that myself." His low, sexy voice reverberated across the gilded ballroom. "But sometimes fate chooses better for us than we could ever have chosen for ourselves."

No, no, no, I pleaded desperately with my eyes.

He smiled.

He lifted his champagne flute toward me. "A toast. To Miss Lena Carlisle. The most beautiful woman on earth, and the mother of my baby son…"

The whispers exploded to a sharp roar.

"...to the future Duchess of Alzacar!"

There were gasps across the crowd, the largest of which was probably mine. But Alejandro continued to hold up his flute, so everyone else did, too. He drank deeply, and a thousand guests drank, too. Toasting to our engagement.

Only two people continued to stare at him blankly.

Edward.

And me.

My body trembled. All I wanted to do was turn and flee through the crowd, to disappear, to never come back. To be free of him—the man who'd once destroyed me. Who could, if he tried, so easily do it again—and more, since now our child could be used against me.

But that child also meant, in a very real way, that I was bound to Alejandro for the rest of my life. We both loved Miguel. We both wished to raise him.

Which meant, no matter how fiercely I wished otherwise, and no matter how I'd tried to deny it, I would never be truly free of Alejandro—ever.

Cheers, some supportive, some envious and some by bewildered drunken people who'd missed what all the fuss was about but were happy to cheer anyway, rang across the ballroom, along with a smattering of applause. Alejandro left the dais, where he was stopped by crowds of well-wishers, including the glamorous movie star I'd recognized and two heads of state.

Behind me, Edward seethed with disappointment and fury, "He doesn't own you."

"You're wrong," I whispered. I turned to Edward with tears in my eyes. "He owned me from the moment I became pregnant with his baby."

Edward's face went wild.

"No," he breathed. He started to reach toward my face, then he stiffened as he became aware of all the people watching us, the strangers starting to hover, no doubt awaiting their chance to congratulate me on snagging a billionaire duke into illustrious matrimony. Gorgeous, beautiful women in designer clothes, thin and glossy like Claudie, were already staring at me incredulously, clearly in shock that someone like me could possibly have captured the heart of a man like Alejandro.

The answer was simple. I hadn't.

This was my future. Everything I thought I'd left behind me in London, all the pity and dismissive insults. Except it would be even worse. Being described as a poor relation was practically a compliment, compared with the epithet that strangers would soon use to describe me: *gold digger*.

It would have been different if Alejandro and I had actually loved each other. Thinking of it, my heart ached. If he'd loved me, and I'd loved him, I wouldn't have given two hoots what anyone else thought. But as it was…

"You agreed to marry him?" Edward said incredulously.

"Not exactly." Swallowing over the ache in my throat, I breathed, "It doesn't matter. Now he has proof he's Miguel's father, he'll never let him go. And I will never leave my son. So we might as well be married…."

"Like hell."

Edward grabbed my arm, his eyes like fire. Without warning, he pulled me through the crowd. I had one single image of Alejandro's shocked face across the ballroom, watching us, before I was out the side door and down the hall, pushed into a dark, quiet corner of the empty coatroom.

Edward turned to me, his face contorted by shadows.

"Run away with me," he said urgently.

I drew back in shock. "What?"

"Navaro has no hold on you."

"He's Miguel's father!"

"Share custody of the kid if you must," he said through

gritted teeth. His hand gripped my forearm. "But don't throw yourself away on a man who will never deserve you."

"What are you saying?" I tried to pull away my arm, but his grip was tight.

"He terrified you for a year—got you pregnant just to steal your baby—"

"I was wrong—he didn't! It was all Claudie! She's the one who said it, and I believed her."

"So he's innocent? No way," he said grimly. "But even if he is—even if he didn't do that one awful thing, what about the rest?"

"What do you mean?"

"He made you love him, then he *abandoned* you. Don't you remember how gray your face was for months afterward? How your eyes were hollow and you barely spoke? I do."

I swallowed. "I…"

"Where was he when you wanted to give him everything? When you tried to tell him you were pregnant? He *changed his phone number.* How can you marry him now? How can you forget?"

I flashed hot, then cold. Yes. I remembered.

"And after all that, he gets you back?" Edward pulled me closer, looking down at me in the shadowy cloakroom with a strange light in his eyes. "No. I was there for you. I took care of you. I'm the one who—"

"Get your hands off my woman."

The low voice was ice-cold behind us. With a gasp that must have sounded guilty, I whirled to face him. "Alejandro!"

His eyes were dark with fury as he looked at me. "So this is why you were so reluctant to marry me?"

"No, you—"

"Be silent!"

I winced.

"Don't talk to her that way," Edward said.

Alejandro didn't look away from me. He held his body in a dangerous stillness as he ground out, "You have nothing to do with us, St. Cyr."

Either Edward didn't see the warning, or he didn't care. "Don't I? Who do you think was supporting her this past year? Who held her together after you blew her apart?" Coming closer to Alejandro, he said softly, with a malicious look in his eyes, "Who was at Lena's side at the hospital, when she gave birth to your child? Where were you then, Navaro?"

Alejandro slowly turned to look at him. I saw the hard set of his shoulders, the rapid rise and fall of his breath. I saw his hands tighten at his sides, and knew Edward was about to lose half of his face.

"Stop!" I cried, stepping between them in real fear. "Stop this at once!" I pressed on Edward's chest. "Just go."

He lifted his eyebrows in shock. "You can't honestly choose him over me?"

"Go. And don't come back." I glanced back at Alejandro and knew only the fact that I stood between them kept him from attack. I took a deep breath. "Thank you for everything you did for me, Edward. I'll never forget how you helped me." My jaw hardened. "But it's over."

Edward's face contorted. "You're throwing yourself away on *him*? Just because of some *stupid baby*?"

My sympathy disintegrated.

"That *stupid baby* is my son."

"Dammit, you know I didn't mean…"

But my heart had iced over. Releasing him, I stepped back, closer to Alejandro. "Yes, I choose him. Over you."

"You heard her," Alejandro said roughly. "You have thirty seconds to be out of my building, before security throws you out."

"Sending in your goons, eh?" he sneered. "Can't be bothered to do it yourself?"

"Happy to," Alejandro said grimly, pushing up the sleeves of his tuxedo jacket as he took a step forward, fists raised.

"No!" I grabbed his arm. My hand couldn't even fully wrap around the full extent of the hard, huge biceps beneath his tuxedo. "Please, Alejandro," I whispered. "Don't hurt him. He was good to me, when I had no one else. I never would have survived without him. Neither would Miguel. Please. For my sake."

Jaw taut, Alejandro slowly lowered his fist. "For your sake." His voice was low and cold as he turned to Edward. "Thank you. For protecting what I love."

Love? For a moment I stared at Alejandro, then I realized he was speaking of Miguel.

Edward glared at him. Obviously not realizing he'd just narrowly escaped death, he sneered, "Go to hell." At the door, he turned back and said, "I'll be back for you, Lena."

Then he was gone. And Alejandro and I were suddenly alone in the cloakroom. But my relief was short-lived.

"No wonder he loaned you his house," he said. "No wonder he protected you. He sees you as his. Why does he believe that?"

I whirled to face him. The cold fury in his eyes was like a wave. But there was something else there, too. Hurt.

"He tried to kiss me last week," I admitted in a low voice, then shook my head. "But I just gave a shocked laugh and he left. Whatever he might have hoped, all he ever was to me was a friend—"

"*Friend,*" he said scornfully. "You knew what he wanted."

I shook my head fiercely. "Not until last week, I never—"

"Then you were willfully blind. He's in love with you."

"You're wrong there." Shivering, I crossed my bare arms over my pink strapless ball gown. "If he'd really loved me, he would have loved Miguel, too. But he was always getting annoyed about him. Suggesting things…like I should send him away, farm him out for adoption…"

Alejandro's eyes darkened. "And you were willing to call him a friend? To let him near our son?"

I wanted to lash back at him. To tell him he was being unreasonable, or that I hadn't had a choice. Instead, I said the only thing that mattered. The only thing that was true.

"I'm sorry," I said in a low voice. "I was wrong."

He'd been opening his mouth to say more, no doubt cutting, angry accusations. But my humble, simple words cut him off at the knees. For a long moment, he stared at me in the shadowy cloakroom. Down the hall, we could distantly hear music playing, people laughing. Then he turned away, clawing back his dark hair.

"*Bien.* I wasn't exactly perfect, either," he muttered. Lifting his head, he glared at me. "But you're never to see him again. Or let him near Miguel."

"Fine," I said.

"Fine?"

"He stopped being my friend the moment he called my baby 'it.'"

"So," he said with a casual tone that belied the tension in his shoulders, "did you let him kiss you?"

I gaped at him. "Oh—for heaven's sake!" I stomped my foot against the plush carpet. "I'm not going to say it again!"

"I found the two of you here, talking…"

"And I just saw you talking to an actress in the ballroom. I didn't accuse you of making out! He made a pass at me last week. I refused. End of story."

"Once we are married…"

My cheeks went hot. "Married!" I stared at him, shocked. "Who said anything about marriage?"

Now Alejandro was the one to look shocked.

"I just asked you to marry me!"

"*Asked?*" My voice was acid. "When you asked, I said no. Tonight, you just *announced* it! In front of everyone! You may have asked—I never said yes!"

"We are going to be wed. Accept it."

"I will accept *an engagement*," I retorted. "I will accept that we need to live in the same town, perhaps even the same house, for our son. A public front, a pretense for Miguel's sake, to make it appear we are actually a couple—that he wasn't just some *mistake!* But nothing more. There's no way I'm actually going to *marry* you. Do you think I would ever give you my body again? Or my heart?"

"I told you," he ground out. "I'm not asking for your heart."

"Then you can forget anything else—I won't give you my body, or take your name! I owe you respect as Miguel's father, but that's it," I said through gritted teeth. "Whatever you might believe, you don't own me, any more than Edward did!"

"I'm not Edward. I'm the father of your child." He grabbed my wrist, looking down at me. "I'm the man you will wed. I don't need your heart. But your body, at least, will be mine."

"No!" But even as I gasped with fury, heat flashed from his possessive grip on my wrist. Electricity crackled up my arm, to my throat, to my lips, to my breasts, down, down, down to my core. Pushing me back roughly against the coats, he looked down at me in the shadows.

"Did you really think," he said softly, "once I found you, I would ever let you go? I gave you up once for the sake of a promise. I gave you up to *do the right thing*. But fate has thrown you back into my arms. Now you will be entirely mine—"

Lowering his head, Alejandro kissed me fiercely, his lips hot and hard against mine, plundering, demanding. I tried to resist. I couldn't let myself feel—I couldn't—

Then I melted as the banked embers inside me, beneath the cold ash of the past lonely year, roared to a blazing fire. My body shuddered beneath his ruthless, almost violent embrace, and I wrapped my arms tightly around him, holding him to me, lost in the sweet forbidden ecstasy of surrender.

CHAPTER FIVE

HIS LIPS SAVAGED MINE, his tongue hot and salty and sweet. I clutched his shoulders, desperate to sate my desire. I'd hungered for him every night, even when I hated him, against all reason, against my will.

Alejandro's hands ran along my bare arms then moved to the tangle in my hair, tilting my chin so he could plunder my mouth more deeply. Long tendrils of hair had pulled free from my chignon. I felt them brush against my naked shoulders as his hard, muscular body strained against me, towering over mine, overpowering me. But it wasn't enough. Not nearly enough...

His hot kisses moved slowly down my neck, as he murmured husky endearments in Spanish against my skin. My head fell back against the wall of coats, and I closed my eyes, feeling tight and dizzy. He nuzzled my bare skin over the neckline of my gown. His hands cupped my breasts straining against the pink silk of the bodice.

So sweet. So hot. My breath came at a gasp, and as my eyelids flickered, the world seemed to spin in whirling patterns of shadows and light, echoes of past love and longing. For over a year I'd longed for him. For all my life, I'd longed for this. And it was even better than I remembered, a powerful drug beyond imagining. Wrapped in his embrace, I forgot myself, forgot my own name, and knew only that I had to have him or die....

A low deliberate cough came behind us. Startled, I turned my head, and Alejandro straightened. The Bulgarian ambassador stood at the cloakroom door, with his wife draped in pearls behind him.

"Excuse us," he said gravely, and stepping forward, he took a black fur coat off the hanger behind us.

I heard his wife titter as they left, "See, Vasil? I told you it was a love match!"

"Poor devil deserves some pleasure, at least," the man's reply echoed back to us, "after the grasping creature tricked him into marriage with a pregnancy."

Shamefaced, I looked up at Alejandro. The air in the cloakroom suddenly felt thin and cold.

"Let me go," I said.

His hold on me only tightened. "Who cares what they say?"

"I care," I whispered.

"Bull," he cut me off ruthlessly. "You're too strong to be ruled by gossip." His hands moved slowly down the bare skin of my upper back, and I shivered, fighting my own desire. "It's this you're afraid of. This." He stroked my arms to my breast, then abruptly pulled me up to stand, hard against his body. "This is all that matters...."

"It's not," I choked out. "There's love. And trust...."

"Love for our son. And trust for your husband. Your partner."

For a second, I trembled. I did want those things. A real home. I'd already accepted that we would need to live in the same town, or better yet, the same house. Why not accept a partnership? We could share a life, a son, even a bed. Would it be enough, without romantic love? Could I live without that? Could I?

For Miguel's sake?

"Maybe I could accept a marriage without love," I said in a small voice. I took a deep breath and raised my gaze to his. "But there is no partnership without trust. Can you promise you've never lied to me? And that you never will?"

I watched as the brief triumph in his eyes went out. "No."

My lips parted in a silent gasp. I hadn't expected that. My heart twisted as I thought how, with just a few hot kisses and the dream of giving Miguel a real home and family, I'd been perilously close to giving up my dreams.

"Well, which is it, Alejandro?" I choked out. "Did you lie to me in the past? Or will you lie to me in the future?"

His jawline tightened. For a moment, his face seemed tortured. Then, as I'd seen happen before, his expression shuttered, becoming expressionless, leaving me to wonder if I'd imagined the whole thing. "Take your pick."

I stiffened. Hating him—no. Hating *myself* for letting him kiss me. Letting him? All he'd had to do was touch me and I'd flung myself into his kiss with the hunger of a starving woman at a piece of bread. "What have you lied to me about?"

"You expect me to tell you the truth about that?"

"Other women?"

He glared at me. "I told you. I believe in honor. Fidelity. No. My lie is about—something else."

"What?"

"Me," he ground out through gritted teeth. "Only me."

Which didn't tell me anything at all! "Fine. Whatever." I glared at him. "You shouldn't have kissed me."

He relaxed imperceptibly now that we were no longer talking about his secrets.

"This isn't the place," he agreed.

"I didn't just mean the cloakroom. I mean anywhere."

"I can think of many places I'd like to kiss you."

"Too bad." My cheeks flamed, but I wouldn't let him distract me. "Take your kisses, and your lies, somewhere else."

"A marriage in name only?" He sounded almost amused. "Do you really think that will work?"

"Since I can't even trust you, let alone love you, there will be no marriage of any kind," I snapped. "And if you keep asking, even our engagement will be remarkably short."

"Why are you trying to fight me, when it's so obvious that you will give in?" he said. "You want to raise Miguel. So do I. What do you expect to do—live next door? In my stable?"

"Better that than your bed."

His dark eyes glittered. "That wasn't how you kissed me."

Heat pulsed through me. I could hardly deny it. I looked away. "Sex is different for women. It involves love!"

He snorted. "Right."

"Or at least caring and trust!" I cried, stung.

"Who is speaking in generalities now?" he said harshly. A cynical light rose in his eyes. "Many women have sex with strangers. Just—as you said—as many women prefer to drink their coffee black, without the niceties of sugar and cream!"

My cheeks flushed. "Fine for them, but—"

"Lust is just an appetite, a craving, such as one might have for *ensaladilla rusa*. No one says that you must be deeply committed to the mayonnaise in order to enjoy the taste of the potato salad!"

I lifted my chin. "Go seduce one of those salad women, then! I don't want you in my bed, I don't want you as my husband and I just regret I'm stuck with you as Miguel's father!"

"Enough." His voice was deadly cold. "You have made enough of a fool of me, making me beg—for the truth about Miguel, for the DNA test, for access to him. I even had to beg you to keep your promise to come to Spain. There will be no more begging, at least—" his eyes glittered "—no more begging from me."

Alejandro had begged me for stuff? I must have missed that. "I never—"

"You will marry me. Tonight."

"Don't be ridiculous!"

"Right now. Choose." His expression had hardened. "A priest. Or a lawyer."

"Are you threatening me?"

"Call it what you want."

I licked my lips, then tried, "Edward would help me. He has money and power to match even yours...."

"Ah." Alejandro came closer, softly tucking back a long tendril of hair that had escaped when he'd crushed me a few moments ago in his passionate embrace. "I wondered how long it would be before Mr. St. Cyr's name made an appearance. That was even quicker than I expected."

My cheeks went hot, but I lifted my chin. "He would still help me if I asked."

"Oh, I'm sure he would," he said softly. "But are you willing to accept the cost of his help?"

I swallowed.

"And the price to Miguel. Think of it." He tilted his head. "A custody war, when each side has infinite resources to pay lawyers for years, decades, to come." He gave a brief, humorless smile. "Miguel's first words after *mamá* and *papá* might be *restraining order*."

I sucked in my breath.

"And the scandal... The press will have a field day." Pressing his advantage, he stroked my cheek almost tenderly. "Miguel will grow so accustomed to paparazzi he'll start to think of them as members of his family. With good reason, for he'll see them more frequently than he sees either of us." He dropped his hand. His voice became harsh. "Is that really what you want?"

"Why are you doing this, Alejandro?" I choked out.

"I won't risk having Edward St. Cyr as my son's future stepfather."

I shook my head. "It will never happen!"

"I'm supposed to believe that? A few minutes ago, you promised you'd never see him again. Now you're threatening to use his wealth and power in a custody battle against me."

He looked at me with scorn, and I didn't blame him. I wiped my eyes. "You're right. I shouldn't have done that— but you're forcing my back against the wall! I have no choice!"

"Neither do I." His sensual lips curved downward. "You think you can control him. You cannot. He's selfish. Ruthless. Dangerous."

I flashed him a glare full of hate. "Are you talking about him," I said bitterly, "or yourself?"

"Yes, I could be dangerous," he said softly. "If anyone tried to hurt someone I cared about. I would die—or kill— to protect someone I loved."

"But you don't love anyone!"

"You're wrong." His voice was low. His lips pressed together in a thin line. "So will it be marriage between us—or war?"

"I hate you!"

"Is that your final answer?"

Tears of hopeless rage filled my eyes, but I'd told Edward the truth. Alejandro had owned me from the moment I'd become pregnant with his child. I would give anything, sacrifice any part of myself, for my son. My heart. My dreams. My soul. What were those, compared with Miguel's heart, his dreams, his soul?

My baby would not spend his childhood in and out of divorce courts, surrounded by pushy paparazzi, bewildered by the internecine battles of his parents. Instead, he would be safe and warm and surrounded by love. He would be happy.

It was all I had to cling to. All I had to live for.

My shoulders fell.

"No," I whispered. "You win. I will marry you."

"Now."

"Fine! I hate you!"

He looked down at me, his expression sardonic. "Hate me, then. At least that I can believe. Far more than your so-called *love.* But you will be my wife. In every way."

Yanking me into his arms, he kissed me, hard. But this time, there was nothing of tenderness, or even passion. Just a ruthless act of possession, showing me he owned me, a savage kiss hard enough to bruise.

Pulling me out of the cloakroom and outside into the warm Spanish night, he called for his driver. The paparazzi were long gone, and the street was quiet, even lonely.

Alejandro took me to the house of a local official, where with a quiet word a certificate of permission to marry was produced in record time. Then to a priest, in a large, empty church, so old and full of shadows it seemed half-haunted with the lost dreams of the dead.

And so Alejandro and I were wed, in that wan, barren church, with only flickers of candlelight and ghostly moonlight from the upper windows lighting the cold, pale marble. My pink ball gown of silk and embroidered flowers, which once seemed so beautiful, now hung on me like a shroud.

There was no wedding dress. No cake. No flowers. And no one, except the priest and his assistant called as witness, to wish us happiness.

Which was just as well, because as I looked at the savage face of my new husband as we left the church into the dark of night, I knew happiness was the one thing we'd never have.

* * *

Alejandro looked across the front seat of the car. "You're going to have to talk to me at some point."

I looked out the window at the passing scenery as we drove south into Andalucía. "No, I don't, actually."

"So you intend to ignore me forever?" he said drily.

I shrugged, still not looking at him. "Lots of married couples stop talking eventually. We might as well start now."

We'd been alone in the car together for hours, but it felt like days. Alejandro was driving the expensive sports sedan, with Miguel in the baby seat behind us, cooing and batting at plush dangling toys. Three bodyguards and his usual driver were in the SUV following us. "I want some private time with my new bride," Alejandro had told them with a wink, and they'd grinned.

But the reason he'd desired privacy wasn't exactly the usual one for newlyweds. I'd given Alejandro the silent treatment since our ghastly wedding ceremony last night. Seething. It wasn't natural for me to bite my tongue. I think he was waiting for me to explode.

He'd gotten me home by midnight as promised. The instant we returned to his Madrid penthouse I'd stalked into the bedroom where my baby slept, and though I couldn't slam the door—too noisy—I'd locked it solidly behind me. Very childish, but I'd been afraid that once Mrs. Gutierrez left, he might demand his rights of the wedding night. Pulling on flannel pajamas, I'd stared at the door, just daring him to try.

But he hadn't. About three in the morning, feeling foolish, I'd unlocked the door. But he never came, not even to apologize for his brutish behavior. There was no way I would have let him seduce me...but my nose was slightly out of joint that he hadn't even bothered to try. Our marriage was only a few hours old, and he was already ignoring me?

I didn't see him until this morning, when he was coming out of the guest bathroom next door, looking well rested and obviously straight out of the shower. His dark hair was wet, a low-slung towel wrapped around his bare hips and another towel hanging over his broad, naked shoulders.

I'd stopped flat in the hallway, unable to look away from the muscular planes of his bare chest, laced with dark hair, or the powerful lines of his body, to the slim hips barely covered by the clinging white terry cloth.

Alejandro had greeted me with a sensual smile. "Good morning, *querida*," he'd purred, then lifting a wicked eyebrow as if he already knew the answer, he'd inquired, "I trust you slept well?"

But I was starting to get my revenge. His lips were now set in an annoyed line as he kept his eyes on the road, pressing on the gas of his very expensive, very fast sedan. "We are husband and wife now, Lena. You must accept that."

"Oh, I do," I assured him. "But we're a husband and wife who happen to hate each other. So perhaps just not talking is best."

Alejandro exhaled in irritation, his hands tightening on the steering wheel. I turned away, staring out wistfully at the scenery of Spain flying past us. In any other circumstance I would have been in awe at the magnificent view. The farmland and soft hills of central Spain were turning to a drier landscape. Lovely thick bushes of pink and white oleander flowers separated the highway, a vivid, wild, unexpected beauty, much like Spain itself.

Oleander. I shivered a little. So beautiful to the eyes. But so poisonous to the heart.

Just like Alejandro, I thought. I wouldn't let him in. Husband or not, I'd never let him close to me. In any way.

We'd stopped only once since we left Madrid, to feed

and change the baby, and to put gas in both cars. Alejandro offered to take a small detour and stop for lunch in Córdoba, to show me the famous cathedral that had once been a Great Mosque. But I'd refused. I didn't want him doing me any favors. Though later I regretted it, because I heard a lot about the famous Mezquita.

As the car flew south, turning on a new road, I blinked in the bright sun flooding the windows. After weeks of rain in San Miguel, and London's drizzle and overcast skies, the Spanish sun had come as advertised, with a wide blue horizon that held not a single cloud. The arid landscape suddenly reminded me of Mexico. Which reminded me of the freedom and independence I'd had so briefly.

And Edward.

I'll be back for you, Lena.

"Stop it," Alejandro growled.

I nearly jumped in the smooth leather seat. "What?"

"I can hear you. Thinking about him."

"You can hear me thinking?"

"Stop," he said quietly, giving me a hard sideways glance. "Or I will make you stop."

"*Make* me—" I snorted derisively, then I looked at him, remembering his last ruthless kiss in the cloakroom. And the one before it, which had been even more dangerous. I remembered how it had felt, surrendering to his embrace, how it had made my whole body tremble with need.

"You're such a jerk," I muttered, folding my arms mutinously. "My thoughts are my own."

"Not if they are of a man like St. Cyr. Thoughts lead to actions."

"I told you, I don't even like him anymore!"

He snorted. "And that is supposed to inspire trust? You've made it plain you did not wish to marry me. Perhaps you're wishing now you took the other choice."

I looked at him. "What other choice?"

"A war between us," he said grimly. He was staring forward at the road, his jaw tight. "St. Cyr would be eager to help you with that."

My arms unfolded. "No." I frowned. "I don't want war. I'd never deliberately hurt you, Alejandro. Not now."

"Really," he said in clear disbelief.

"Hurting you would hurt Miguel." I looked out the window and said softly, "We both love him. I realized the truth last night, even before your marriage ultimatum—neither of us wants to be apart from him." Blinking fast, I faced him. "You're right. We're married now. So let's make the best of it."

"Do you mean it?" he said evenly. I nodded.

"Let's make sure Miguel has a wonderful childhood and a real home, where he'll always feel safe and warm and loved."

His hands seemed to relax a little around the steering wheel. He looked at me. There was something strange in his eyes, something almost like—yearning—that made my heart twist.

"If it's really true you'd never deliberately hurt me…" He seemed to be speaking to himself. "I wish I could…"

"What?"

He shook his head, and his jaw went hard. "Nothing."

What had he been about to say? I looked down, blinking as my eyes burned. Telling myself I shouldn't care. Willing myself *not* to care.

My lie is about something else.

What?

I remembered the stark look in his eyes. *Me. Only me.*

Stop it, I told my heart fiercely. *Don't get sucked in! Keep your distance!*

Silently, Alejandro stared forward at the road. For long minutes, the only sound was Miguel cooing to himself in the backseat, chortling triumphantly as he grasped a soft toy hanging from the top of his baby seat, and making it squeak. I smiled back at my son. He was the reason. The only reason.

"I'm glad you feel that way. The truth is I don't want to hurt you, either." Alejandro tightened his hands on the steering wheel. He glanced at me out of the corner of his eye. "Our son is what matters. We'll focus on him. I'll never leave you or Miguel. Together we'll make sure our son is always well cared for."

Our eyes locked, and an ache lifted to my throat. Turning away, I tried to block the emotion out with a laugh. "Miguel will be a duke someday. That's crazy, isn't it?"

Alejandro turned his eyes back to the road.

"Sí," he said grimly. "Crazy."

I'd been trying to lighten the mood. But his voice sounded darker than ever. "Did I say something wrong?"

"No. You are correct. Miguel will be Duque de Alzacar." I frowned. But before I could figure out what lay behind the odd tension in his voice, he turned to me. "So you forgive me for forcing you to marry me against your will?"

I exhaled.

"It's a very complicated question."

"No. It is not."

Something broke inside me. And words came pouring out.

"You think I was silly and selfish to want to marry for love. But for the past ten years, that dream was all I've held on to." I looked at my hands in my lap. "Ever since I was fourteen years old, I've felt so alone. So unwanted. But then, last year, when I met you..." I lifted agonized eyes to his. "All my dreams seemed to be coming true. It was as if...I'd gone back in time. To the world I once knew. The one filled with love. The world where I was good enough. Wanted. Even cherished."

Alejandro's expression darkened. "Lena..."

"Then you abandoned me," I whispered. "You told me you didn't love me, that you never would." I looked at him. "But I still married you yesterday, Alejandro, knowing that. Knowing you've lied to me in the past and will lie in the future. I married you knowing that the loneliness I tried to leave behind me in London will now follow me for the rest of my life. Only now, instead of being a poor relation, I'm the gold digger who got pregnant to ensnare a rich duke. And everyone will say, weren't you so good and noble to marry me? Wasn't it an amazing sacrifice for you to make me your wife? How generous of you! How kind!"

He glowered. "No one will say that."

I cut him off with a low laugh. "*Everyone* will. And I know there will be days when I'll feel that marrying you was the biggest mistake of my life." I drew a deep, shuddering breath, then met his gaze. "And yet I can't regret it," I whispered. "Because it will make Miguel's life better to have you in his life. Every single day. He will know you. Really know you."

"I wish he could." Alejandro stared at me. His dark eyes were liquid and deep. "I wish I could tell you…"

I held my breath. "Yes?"

His face suddenly turned cold, like a statue. He looked away. "Forget it."

I exhaled, wishing I hadn't said so much.

He drove the car off the main road, then took a smaller one, then turned on a private lane that was smaller still, nothing but a ribbon twisting across the broad-swept lands. Alejandro stopped briefly at a tall iron gate, then entered a code into the electronic keypad. We proceeded inside the estate, which looked so endless and wide, I wondered how anyone had wrapped a fence around it, and if the fence was visible from space, like the Great Wall of China.

Then I saw the castle, high on a distant hill, and I sucked

in my breath. It was like a fairy-tale castle, rising with ramparts of stone and turrets stretching into the sky.

"Is that…?" I breathed.

"Sí," Alejandro said quietly. "My home. The Castillo de Rohares. The home of the Dukes of Alzacar for four hundred years."

It took another fifteen minutes to climb the hill, past the groves of olive trees and orange trees. When we reached the castle at last, past the ramparts into a courtyard surrounding a stone fountain, he stopped the car at the grand entrance on the circular driveway. He turned off the engine, and I could hear the bodyguards climbing out of the SUV behind us, talking noisily about lunch, slamming doors. But as I started to turn for the passenger-side door, Alejandro grabbed my wrist. I turned to face him, and he dropped my arm.

"I am sorry I hurt you, Lena. When I left you last summer, when I refused to return any of your phone calls—I did that for good reason. At least—" his jaw tightened "—it seemed like good reason."

"No, I get it," I said. "You didn't want me to love you."

"No. That's not it at all." He lifted his dark eyes to mine. "I didn't leave because you loved me. I left because I was falling in love with you."

CHAPTER SIX

I STARED AT him in shock.

"What?" I breathed.

A hard knock banged against the car window behind me, making me jump. Turning my head, I saw a plump smiling woman, standing on the driveway outside, dressed in an apron and holding a spoon. She waved at us merrily. I saw the bodyguards greeting her with obvious affection as they went into the grand stone entrance of the castle.

"Another housekeeper?" I said faintly.

"My grandmother," he said.

"Your—" I whirled to face him, but he had already opened his door and was getting out of the car, gently lifting Miguel out of his baby seat. Nervously, I got out of the car, too, wondering what the dowager Duchess of Alzacar would make of me.

"Come in, come in," she said to the bodyguards, shooing them inside. She kept switching from English to Spanish as if she couldn't quite make up her mind. "Knowing Alejandro, I'm sure you didn't stop for any lunch, so everything is ready if you'll just go straight to the banqueting hall..."

"Abuela," Alejandro said, smiling, "I'd like you to meet my son. His name is Miguel."

"Miguel?" she gasped, looking from him to Alejandro.

He blinked with a slight frown, shaking his head. "And this is my new wife. Lena."

"I'm so happy to meet you." Smoothing one hand over her apron, she turned to me with a warm smile, lifting the wooden spoon high, like a benign domestic fairy about to grant a really good wish. "And your sweet baby! I can hardly wait to…" Her eyes suddenly narrowed. "Your new what?"

Coming over to me, Alejandro put his free arm around my shoulders. "My wife."

She lowered her spoon and looked me over, from my long hair to my soft white blouse with the Peter Pan collar, to my slim-cut jeans and ballet flats. I braced myself for criticism.

Instead, she beamed at me, spreading her arms wide.

"Oh, my dear," she cried, "welcome to the family. Welcome to your new home!"

And she threw her arms around me in a big, fierce, welcoming hug.

Shocked, I stiffened. Then I patted her awkwardly on the back.

"But I'm being silly," she said, drawing back, wiping her eyes with her brightly colored apron. "My name is Maurine. But please call me Abuela, if you like, as Alejandro does. Or Grandma. Or Nana. Whatever. I'm just so happy you're here!"

"Thank you," I said, unsure how to handle such immediate warmth and kindness.

"But you—" she whirled on her grandson with a scowl "—you should have known better than to elope!"

Alejandro looked abashed. It was a funny, boyish expression on his masculine face. "We would have waited and had a proper wedding," he said, rubbing his neck sheepishly, "but Abuela, it happened so quickly…."

"Huh. Don't think you're getting off that easy. We'll talk about it later. Now—" her plump face softened as her eyes lit up "—let me hold that baby."

Ten minutes later, Maurine was giving me a speed tour of the castle, on the way to the dining hall. "The foundations of Rohares date from the times of the sultan," she said happily. "But most of the building dates from the early seventeenth century. It was bombed in the war, then when we came back we had no money and it fell into disrepair." She looked sad, then brightened, smiling up at her grandson. "But Alejandro made his fortune in Madrid, then restored every part of it, made Rohares better than it had ever been before! And here's where we'll have lunch...."

I stopped in the huge doorway of an enormous dining hall that looked as if it came from the late Renaissance, complete with soaring frescoed ceilings, suits of armor beside the ancient tapestries and a stone fireplace tall enough to fit a person inside. And at the center of the huge, gymnasium-size room, there was a long wooden dining table, large enough to seat forty or fifty people, and groaning beneath the weight of the luncheon spread, flower arrangements, and place settings carefully designed with fine china and the brightest decor.

My mouth dropped as I stared at it.

"Cold and drafty, *si?*" Alejandro said smugly, grabbing a marinated green olive and piece of cheese off the platter on the table. "Just as you said."

"I've never seen anything like this," I breathed. "And the food..."

He gave a low chuckle. "Abuela believes food is love."

"I can see that," I said faintly, staring up at his face.

I left because I was falling in love with you.

My knees were still weak at what he'd said in the car. It was so far from everything I'd ever imagined, I couldn't believe I'd heard him right. "Alejandro..."

"Abuela can be bossy about it, but she loves nothing more than taking care of people, along with her garden and home." He grinned, shaking his head ruefully. "She now has an unlimited budget, a clear schedule—now she's given up her charity work—and infinite time. When it comes to the domestic arts, she is unstoppable."

"Amazing." I looked at him hesitantly. "But Alejandro…"

"Yes?"

"Did you mean what you said?"

His dark eyes met mine. He knew what I was talking about. "Don't be afraid. As you said—much has changed in this past year."

I hadn't realized I'd been holding my breath, but at that, I exhaled, like air fizzing out of a tire. "You're right," I said, keeping my voice steady. "Everything is different now."

"The past is past. Now we are partners, parents to our son."

"Exactly." I looked away. The bodyguards, apparently accustomed to being fed lunch like this by the dowager duchess, were already at the table, filling their plates and murmuring their appreciation.

Maurine suddenly reappeared in the solid-oak doorway, holding Miguel with one hand, a small card in the other. Going to the table, she snatched a card off a place setting, then replaced it with the new card. Turning back, she patted the chair, beaming at me. "You're to sit here, dear."

"Oh. Thank you, Maurine."

Smiling, she looked at Miguel in her arms, and started another peekaboo game. She'd been lost in baby joy from the instant she'd picked him up in her arms, and the love appeared to be mutual. I watched, smiling, as Maurine hid her face with her hand, before revealing it so Miguel could reach out to bat her nose triumphantly, leaving them both in hopeless squeals of laughter. Alejandro watched them, too.

"Thank you," he said quietly.

"For what?"

His dark eyes met mine. "For coming to Spain like you promised."

"Oh." My cheeks flooded with shame to remember how I'd initially refused. "It's, um, nothing."

He turned away, watching his grandmother play with his son. "It's everything to me."

My blush deepened, then I sighed. "I was wrong to fight it," I admitted.

"You? Wrong?" Alejandro shook his head. "Impossible."

I scowled at his teasing tone. "Yes, wrong. I'm woman enough to admit it. After all, Maurine is Miguel's family, too." I looked around the huge banqueting hall, filled with antiques that seemed hundreds of years old. I had to crane my head back to see the wood-timbered ceiling, with its faded paintings of the ducal coat of arms. "And this is his legacy," I said softly. "This will all belong to him some-day...."

Alejandro was no longer smiling.

"Yes," he said. "It will."

For some reason I didn't understand, the lightness of the mood had fled. I frowned.

He abruptly held out his arm. "Let's have lunch, shall we?"

Even through his long-sleeved shirt, I could feel the warmth of his arm. The strength of it. From the end of the long table, I saw the bodyguards looking at us, saw one of them nudge the other with a sly grin. To outward appearance, we must have looked like goofy-in-love newlyweds.

Alejandro pulled out the chair Maurine had chosen for me, waited, then after I sat down, he pushed it in and sat beside me.

Looking down at the table, I saw three different plates of different sizes stacked on top of each other in alternating colors. At the top of the place setting, there was a home-made paper flower of red-and-purple tissue paper, very

similar to the paper flowers my mother had made for me
when I was young. Beside it was a card that held a small
handwritten name, with elegant black-ink calligraphy.

The Duchess of Alzacar
my darling new granddaughter

Looking at it, a lump rose in my throat. "Look what
she wrote."

Alejandro looked at the card, and smiled. "Yes."

"She's already accepted me in the family. Just like that?"

"Just like that." He made me a plate with a little of everything, and poured me a glass of sparkling water, then
red wine.

"Wine for lunch?" I said doubtfully.

"It's from my vineyard by the coast. You should try it."

"All right," I sighed. I took a sip, then said in amazement, "It's delicious."

"You sound surprised."

"Is there anything you're not good at?" I said a little
sulkily. He smiled.

Then the smile fled from his handsome face. His dark
eyes turned hollow, even bleak.

"Keeping promises," he said.

The blow was so sudden and unexpected that it felt like
an anvil hitting the softest part of my belly. The moment I'd
let my defenses down, he'd spoken with such unprovoked
cruelty it took my breath away. Reminding me.

*Did you lie to me in the past? Or will you lie to me in
the future?*

Take your pick.

"Oh," I breathed, dropping my fork with a clang against
the twenty-four-karat-gold-rimmed china plate.

He'd done me a favor reminding me, I told myself sav-
agely. I couldn't start believing the pretense. I couldn't start

thinking we were actually a family. That we were actually in love. I couldn't surrender!

And yet…

"Are you enjoying yourself, dear?" I looked up to see Maurine smiling down at me from the other side of the table, with chubby Miguel still smiling in her arms. "I hope you see something you like!"

"I do," I replied automatically, then realized to my horror that the exact moment I'd spoken the words I'd been looking at Alejandro. Quickly, I looked down at my plate. "What's this?" I asked, looking at one of the dishes, some kind of meat with leeks and carrots.

"Pato a la Sevillana, a specialty of the area. Slow-cooked duck roasted in sherry and vegetables."

I took a bite. It was delicious. "And this?"

"Rabo de toro. Another classic dish of Andalucía. Vegetables, slowly braised with sherry and bay leaf."

Bull's tail? I tasted it. Not bad. I tried the fresh papayas and mangoes, the *albóndigas,* the fried-potato-and-ham *croquetas.* I smiled. *"Delicioso!"*

"Muy bien," Maurine sighed happily, then turned on her grandson, tossing her chic, white hair. "Though *you* don't deserve lunch. I should let you get fast food at a drive-through in Seville!" She hitched her great-grandbaby higher on her hip against her pinafore apron. "I cannot believe you got married without inviting me to the wedding! My only family! After I waited thirty-five years to see you get married! After the way you used to make me bite my nails over those wretched skinny, self-centered women you used to cavort with!"

"At least I didn't marry one of them, eh, Abuela? Do I not get credit for that?"

"Yes," she sighed. "On that, you did well."

The two of them smiled at each other, and I had the sudden image of what it must have been like for him to be raised by Maurine in this enormous castle. Alejandro had lost his parents even younger than I'd lost mine. My father had died of a stroke, my mother six months later of illness. But Alejandro had lost both parents in a car crash when he was only twelve. He'd also lost his best friend, Miguel, whom he'd thought of as a brother, and even their housekeeper.

My smile suddenly faltered. All this time, I'd moaned and whimpered so much about my own difficult childhood. But Alejandro had barely hinted aloud about his. A very masculine reticence, but enough to make me writhe with shame. No wonder Alejandro had been so determined that our Miguel, his only child, should come back to Spain, his home, and meet his grandmother, his only family, who'd raised him and loved him.

Even though she didn't seem to be one hundred percent loving him right now.

"But still." His grandmother's chin was wobbling. "All I asked was that you let me attend the wedding. It was my one and only chance to see you get married and I…"

"It was the worst wedding ever," I heard myself blurt out.

Both of them turned to face me. She looked amazed. He looked faintly strangled, as if he were afraid of what I might say next.

"It was just the two of us—" I shook my head "—along with the priest and some stranger as witness. There was no cake. No flowers. You didn't miss anything, Maurine!"

"Call me Abuela, dear," she said faintly. Her gaze softened as she looked at me. Whatever anger she was now lavishing on Alejandro clearly did not extend to me. She blinked with a frown, tilting her head. "You didn't have any flowers? Not one?"

"It's not entirely his fault," I said apologetically. "We felt we should get married immediately, without too much fuss, because of…" I glanced at our baby in her arms.

"Ah." A look of understanding filled her eyes. "Yes, of course."

"The legal part is done, but Alejandro was just saying on the drive that he wished we could have a reception, a party of some kind, to introduce me to his neighbors and friends. I mean, he did tell a few people in Madrid that we were engaged—" I looked at Alejandro beneath my lashes "—but that's not the same as celebrating with neighbors and family."

"No, it's not," she said thoughtfully.

Taking a bite of juicy ripe papaya, I sighed. "But we just don't know what to do. I mean, Alejandro is so busy with his company, and of course I have my hands full with Miguel. I wouldn't have a clue how to organize a party anyway, not a big one. So we were thinking we could maybe hire a party planner, maybe from Madrid…."

"A *party planner!*" Maurine gasped indignantly. "My new granddaughter—and my great-grandson, this little angel—introduced to all my neighbors and friends with some dreary, chic party arranged by a paid *Madrileño!*" She put a dramatic hand over her fulsome chest. "I would turn over in my grave!"

Alejandro's eyes met mine. His lips quirked as he said, "But Abuela, you're not dead."

"You're right, I'm not," she snapped. "Which is why *I* will be planning your wedding reception. Oh, there's no time to waste." Turning away with Miguel still in her arms, she hurried from the dining hall, calling, "María! Carmen! Josefa! Hurry! We have a new project—the most important party I've ever done!"

I turned back to my lunch, only to find Alejandro looking at me. He said in a low voice, "Why did you do that?"

The intense way he was looking at me made me feel nervous and fluttery inside. "Do what?"

"You could have told her the real reason for our quick

marriage. That I forced you to marry me, against your will. That I threatened a custody battle."

"Oh." Awkwardly, I looked back at my plate. I took another bite of the *Pato a la Sevillana.* He just waited. Finally, I said in a small voice, "I didn't want to tell her that."

Alejandro came closer, the hard edges of his jaw and cheekbones leaving shadows across his face. "Why?"

My cheeks felt hot. I couldn't meet his eyes.

"Were you trying to protect her?" He was so close now that I could almost feel the heat through his black tailored shirt. My gaze remained down, resting on his shirt just below his ribcage. Just below his heart. His voice was so quiet I could barely hear as he said, "Or were you trying to protect me?"

"You," I whispered.

The only noise in the cavernous dining hall was the distant murmured conversation of the bodyguards sitting at the far end of the table, the clink of silverware against china, the thunk of wineglasses against the wood.

Alejandro leaned forward, his elbow against the long oak table, bringing his face very close to mine. It was almost painful to be that close to so much masculine beauty. Unwillingly, my eyes traced the hard slant of his cheekbones, the rough edge of his jawline. His darkly intent eyes.

And his sensual mouth. That most of all. I watched, unable to look away, as his lips moved to shape a single word.

"Why?"

I swallowed, sweeping my hand to indicate the elaborate decorations and luncheon spread down the long table.

"She loves you. And you love her." I shook my head and blurted out, "All this time I've been moaning about my family in London. I feel so stupid for complaining about my childhood—while all the time, you yourself—"

He put his hand on my cheek. "It doesn't matter now."

Our eyes locked. I caught my breath, feeling the warmth

of his fingertips brushing my skin. Feeling how much, deep inside, I wanted him to touch me. On my cheek. Down my neck. Everywhere. Unwillingly, I licked my lips.

But I couldn't give in. I couldn't surrender. If I ever gave him my body, as I'd done the year before, my heart would follow. And I didn't think my shattered heart could survive when he betrayed me as he inevitably would—hadn't he told me as much himself?

Is there anything you're not good at?

Keeping promises.

I pulled back, suddenly desperate to get away from the dangerous energy sizzling between us.

"You love each other. You're a family." My voice trembled, betraying me. "I want you to be happy."

He suddenly leaned forward, his eyes dark.

"What would make me happy," he said huskily, "is having you in my bed. Right now."

I sucked in my breath. My body trembled.

"No," I whispered.

His dark eyes met mine. "We both know how this will end."

He was right. *He was right.*

"Thank Maurine for me…." Setting down my silverware, I stumbled to my feet, tossing my napkin over my half-empty plate. "I'm done…."

And I ran.

Tears blurred my eyes as I fled the dining hall, into the shadowy hallway. I dodged antique chests and an old suit of armor, only to run straight into Maurine.

"My dear, whatever is the matter?" she said, looking astonished.

"I just need some—some fresh air," I choked out.

"Of course." Looking bewildered, with my baby still smiling and happy in her arms, she pointed to a door down the hall. "That leads to the gardens…."

I ran down the dark hallway, beneath the cool, thick stone walls of the *castillo*. Flinging open the door, I found myself beneath the bright, hot Spanish sun and the softly waving palm trees. I kept going, almost blindly—wanting only to be away from the castle. From the man who owned it.

Just as he now owned me.

But he would not own my heart, I vowed to myself, wiping my eyes. Not my heart and not my body...no matter how he might tempt me otherwise. I couldn't give in. I couldn't....

I ran down the stone path, past green hedges and huge oak trees with soft, full greenery, past a pond and a picturesque gazebo in an English-style garden, past something that looked like a hedge maze straight out of *Alice in Wonderland*. Choking out a sob, I abruptly stopped. I found myself in a rose garden, surrounded by a profusion of colorful blooms, gentle yellow, soft pink, innocent white and a blaze of red like heart's blood.

"Lena."

His voice was low behind me. Shocked, I whirled around.

"How did you...?"

Alejandro stood in front of me, dark and tall and powerful. Colorful roses and the primal green of the garden hemmed us in on every side, like a riotous jungle. "I know this garden. It's been my home since I was a child."

The sun left a frost of golden light against his dark hair, like a halo, tracing down the length of his body, his tanned, olive-toned skin, his sharp cheekbones, his hard-muscled body that moved with such sensual grace.

"I won't sleep with you," I breathed. "I won't!"

His cruel, sensual lips curved.

"We both know you will." I watched, mesmerized, as the words caused his tongue to flick against the edges of his lips, into the warm, dark honey of his mouth. I remembered how it had felt when he'd kissed me last night. My lips still felt bruised, from the sweet remnants of that fire. "You want me. As I want you."

"I won't let you take me because I am *convenient*." I shook my head fiercely. "You can't have me now, Alejandro!"

He came closer, towering above me, our bodies so near they almost touched.

"Can't I?" he said huskily.

I stared up at him, shivering. Sunshine shimmered in the greenery around Alejandro, making the flowers gleam like colorful lights, the roses like tumbled scarlet against the deep forest green, the leaves and thorns and tangling vines.

Reaching out, he stroked a long tendril of my hair. "I wanted you from the moment I saw you in the hallways of that London mansion, watching me with such longing in your eyes." He lifted his gaze. "I wanted you then. I want you now. And I will have you."

His dark eyes were like deep pools, illuminated by streaks of amber in the sunlight. The kind of eyes that make you lose your breath, the kind a woman could drown in.

The kind of eyes that could make a woman forget a whole lifetime of grief and everything she should have learned from it.

He wanted me. The thought was like a flower. Like one of those beautiful, hardy, deeply poisonous oleander flowers I'd seen growing along the Spanish highway.

He wanted me.

"We are married now," he said.

"For Miguel's sake."

"*Sí.* We married for the sake of our son." He followed me, his powerful body intent, with his dark hair and his dark clothes, like a stalking panther. "But that is not why I want you in my bed."

"But I can't trust you—"

He straightened, his face dangerous. "Why do you think that?"

"You said you lied to me and will lie again. You said you're no good at keeping promises...."

Alejandro looked away. "That was about...something else." He looked back at me. "I will always keep my promises to you."

"But how can I believe that?" I whispered, my heart running like a scared deer.

"Because it's true." He moved closer, running his hand down my long, loose hair, down my back. I shivered beneath the soft, seductive touch. Lifting his hand, he stroked my cheek as he whispered, "Be with me. Be my wife."

My whole body trembled, leaning toward him.

"And if you still think you can't trust me..." His fingers gently stroked my cheeks, lifting my chin as he said softly, "Trust this."

Lowering his head, he pressed his lips against mine. I felt his warmth, his power, the strength of his body. I closed my eyes, lost, dizzy with desire. When he finally pulled away, I stared up at him, trembling.

"Please," I choked out. I lifted my gaze to his. *Please don't make me love you.* "Please don't make me want you...."

He rubbed the pads of his thumbs along my swollen lower lip, and gave me a smile that was breathtaking in its masculine triumph. "Too late."

In the distance, I heard Maurine calling from the castle. I twisted my head, listening, and so did he.

Alejandro suddenly cupped my face in his hands. His eyes were dark. Merciless. "Tonight," he whispered. "You will be in my bed. Tonight..." He ran his fingertips down my shoulders, cupping my breasts. I gave a soft gasp, and he returned a sensual smile. "You will be my wife."

CHAPTER SEVEN

TONIGHT, YOU WILL be in my bed.

Tonight, you will be my wife.

The day raced by. I could not hold the hours back. The clock was ticking and when night fell, I knew he would take me, if not against my will, then at least against my heart.

The dinner table was busy and crowded and happy, because apparently Maurine, the daughter of American-Basque sheep ranchers, had gotten into the habit of eating with her entire household staff, many of whom lived in cottages on the edge of the Rohares estate, and their wives and children were always welcome, as well. Freshly made breads, fruit and cheese were spread across the table in a feast that also included meats, stews and seafood paella, and all kinds of desserts, *tortas* to *galletas*.

"You should see it on holidays," Maurine said to me with a smile, when she saw my eyes widen at the crowd that completely filled all the chairs at the table in the dining hall. "Then, everyone invites their extended families as well, and they come from all over Andalucía."

"Where on earth do they sit?"

Maurine's smile lifted to a grin. "We have to bring all the tables out of the attic and extra rooms, and bring in every antique chair we've got, and the old benches and chests."

"Nice," I murmured. I exhaled. "This place is amazing."

"Because of Alejandro." She looked a few places down the table, to where he was holding court with our baby son in his lap, introducing him to the families of household staff. The women were clustered around him, as if to offer obeisance to a visiting pasha. "He is my whole world. I owe him everything."

"I bet he'd say he owes everything to you. And looking at all this—" I looked at the food, at the decorations, at the care taken with all the details "—I'd have to agree."

"Oh, no." She shook her head vehemently. "If not for him, I never would have survived the aftermath of that car crash, when I lost my whole family...."

"I'm so sorry," I murmured. "I heard about that. Losing your son and daughter-in-law, and even the housekeeper and her son.... I can't imagine how awful. But Alejandro lived."

"That's right. Yes." Shuddering, she closed her eyes. "He saved me. I can still see him in the hospital, his little, injured face covered with bandages, his eyes so bright. Bones in his face had been broken, and he'd never look the same, but he was worried about me, not himself. 'It'll be all right, Abuela,' he told me. 'I'm your family now.'" She blinked fast, her eyes sparkling with tears. "He gave me something to live for, when I wanted to die. And more." She shook her head. "He saved this castle. Even at twelve years old, he was determined to win back our family's lost fortune. He knew he could do it. And he wasn't afraid."

"No." Alejandro wasn't afraid of anything. And he always got what he wanted. I shivered, remembering the dark promise in his eyes in the garden. *Tonight, you will be in my bed. Tonight, you will be my wife....* I pushed the memory away. "How did he build a fortune out of nothing?"

"He went to Madrid at seventeen," Maurine said. "Worked eighteen-hour days, three different jobs. He took all the money he earned and poured it into risky investments that somehow paid off. He wasn't afraid to gamble. Or work. It just goes to show that nobility is in the heart," she said softly, almost as if she were talking to herself, "not the blood."

I snorted. "What are you talking about? He's the son of a duke. It doesn't get more noble than that."

Maurine abruptly focused her gaze on me. "Of course. That's what I meant. He's noble by birth."

Was she confused, or was she just confusing me? "Did people give you a hard time because of your background? I mean—" I shook my head awkwardly "—Alejandro said you grew up in the U.S., the daughter of sheep ranchers…"

"Shepherds, actually," she said, with a twinkle in her eye.

"Exactly. You were a regular girl—then you married a duke." I paused, trying to form the right words. "Did all the other aristocrats treat you badly? Did they call you a gold digger?"

"Me? No." She blinked, and her expression abruptly changed. "Oh, my dear. Is that what's been happening to you?"

I felt the color drain from my cheeks. "No, I…"

"Oh, you poor child." Her plump, wrinkled face was sympathetic, her blue eyes kind. She reached over and patted my hand. "Don't worry. You'll triumph over all the ugly, silly words that people can say. Alejandro loves you. And you love him. That's what matters."

Now my cheeks went hot. "Uh…"

"And I'm so happy you're part of our family." She gave my hand a little squeeze, then chuckled. "I was a little worried. You should have seen the women he dated before you. He didn't bring a single one home. For good reason. He knew I'd skewer them."

"I'm the first woman he ever brought home?" I said faintly.

She nodded. Her gaze became shadowed as she looked at Alejandro farther down the table. "I was starting to think he'd never let any woman into his heart. That he'd never let anyone know who he truly is." She gave me a sudden sharp look. "But you know. Don't you?"

I furrowed my brow. Was she talking about a biblical knowing? Otherwise I didn't really understand. "Um, yes?"

She stared at me, then releasing my hand, abruptly turned away. "How did you like the rose garden?"

I shivered in spite of myself. "It is...very beautiful," I managed. "Like paradise. But what were you saying about Alejandro...?"

Maurine's eyes shadowed. She bit her lip. "I can't believe you don't know. But if you don't, he has to be the one to..."

"Querida," I heard Alejandro say behind me. "It is time for bed."

Seriously? He was announcing this in front of his grand-mother and the whole table? I turned with a scowl, then saw him holding up our sleepy-eyed son. Oh. He meant Miguel. With dinner served so late in Spain, it *was* past our baby's bedtime, and he was yawning in Alejandro's arms, caus-ing dimples in his fat little cheeks. "Right." I held out my arms. "I need to give him a bath first...."

But Alejandro shook his head. He wasn't letting me es-cape so easily. "I'll help you. It's time I learned to do these things as well, don't you think?"

The gleam in his black eyes told me he knew I was scrambling to think of a way to avoid being alone with him tonight. Wondering if I could find a door with a lock. Surely there had to be one in this castle, with its choice of approximately five million rooms. I shook my head with an awkward laugh. "*You* don't want to learn how to give a baby his bath and put him to bed, Your Excellency!"

He snorted at that last bit. "A man needs to know how

to take care of his own son." He lifted a dark eyebrow. "Don't you agree?"

"Yes," I grumbled.

"Such a good father," Maurine sighed.

I narrowed my eyes, then gave him a smile. "I'll show you how to change his diaper, too," I said sweetly.

He gave me a crooked grin. *"Excelente."*

A moment later, we were walking down the dark hallways, the noise of the happy dinner party receding behind us, beneath the thick inner walls of the castle.

"This way," he said, placing his fingertips innocently on the base of my spine to guide me. I trembled.

Tonight, you will be in my bed.

Tonight, you will be my wife.

"Our bedroom is in the new wing...."

"New wing?"

"This castle might have been home to this family for four hundred years, but antiques are—how shall I say this?—not my style."

Going up another flight of stairs, still holding our baby protectively with his muscled arm, he pushed open the door at the end of that hall. I followed him inside, and saw an enormous, high-ceilinged room with floor-to-ceiling windows overlooking a balcony. Modern, masculine, stark. With only one real piece of furniture.

An enormous bed.

I stopped. "But where's the crib?"

"I've had the room next door turned into a nursery." To my relief, Alejandro didn't even glance at the big bed, but just kept walking straight into the connecting door that led to the nursery, and its en-suite bathroom.

The bathroom connected to the nursery was as severe and cold as the master bedroom had been, all white marble and gleaming chrome. But it did have an amazing view. Wide windows overlooked the dark vistas of his estate, lit only by moonlight and distant twinkling lights on the horizon.

He stopped, frowning at the marble bathtub. "On second thought, I don't think this is going to work," he said tersely, looking from the enormous tub to the baby in his arms. "He's too small. We need to get a special baby-size tub...."

It was endearing, really, to see how worried he was. "Tomorrow, if you like, we can go get one. For today, it's no problem." Smiling, I took Miguel in my arms. "Since he can't sit up on his own yet, we'll just hold him up. And be careful." Leaning over, I turned on the water. "Having an extra pair of hands will help."

His eyes met mine. "So you don't...mind that I'm helping you?"

"No," I said softly, "I'm glad."

His expression changed. He started to speak, then turned away, sticking his hand in the water. When the temperature was Goldilocks-acceptable—neither too hot nor too cold— he plugged the drain so the bathtub could fill.

Sitting the baby on the marble counter, I started to pull off his clothes and the clean diaper beneath. "Can you grab his baby shampoo? It's in my bag. Oh." I turned. "It's still in the car—"

With a grin, Alejandro held up the baby shampoo from a nearby drawer, along with a white, fluffy towel. "You mean this?"

"Oh," I said. My cheeks went hot. "It was nice of your staff to unpack everything for me, but..."

"But?"

"It's just strange to have someone going through my stuff."

"You'll get used to it. You'll never have to lift a finger again, unless you want to. Especially with Abuela to oversee everything. She enjoys cooking, cleaning, shopping..."

He paused, suddenly looking uncertain. "That is, if you wish that."

I lifted my eyebrows. "If I?"

Alejandro came closer to me.

"You are the duchess now," he said. "As far as the *castillo* is concerned, your rule is now law."

My cheeks went hot. I licked my lips, tried to laugh as I sat on the edge of the bathtub and checked the water with my elbow. "So you mean I could fire everyone, throw out your tenants, buy Maurine a condo in Barcelona, get rid of all the furniture and paint the walls pink?"

But he didn't laugh.

"If you like," he said in a low voice. "Though I'd prefer we keep the staff and tenants. If you decided otherwise, I would need to take care of them some other way."

"Give them all houses and jobs in Madrid?"

"Something like that."

This kind of thinking surprised me. Most of the high-powered CEO types I'd seen in New York and London seemed to constantly need to resole their expensive shoes, due to the wear caused by stepping on all the little people. I looked at Alejandro curiously. "You really feel responsible for them, don't you?"

"Of course. They—" Tightening his jaw, he looked away. "They're my people."

"Oh." I bit my lip. "Maybe you're not entirely the bastard I thought you were."

"But I am," he said in a low voice. He lifted his gaze to mine. "I can't change who I am."

Something about the expression of the chiseled lines of his handsome face made me feel all confused and jumbled inside. For a moment, the only sound between us was the water running into the bathtub, and the soft yawns of our baby.

"All right, fine. The staff can stay." I sighed. "It would probably be easier to just get rid of me, then."

His lips quirked upward. "Never. Sorry."

"Miguel is your responsibility. Not me," I pointed out. "You don't have to worry about me. I'm not...one of your people." I looked away. "I can support myself. Just so you know."

"I do know. I've seen your paintings."

I stiffened. Edward had often patronized my *little hobby*. "What is that supposed to mean?"

"Isn't it obvious? I think you're talented," he said softly. He pointed toward the nursery. "Or didn't you notice?"

Frowning, I went to the door. And I sucked in my breath as I looked around the dark nursery, at the paintings lining the walls.

"You brought them," I whispered. "All the paintings from Mexico...all the pictures I did of Miguel since he was born."

"I wanted them here. With him." He looked at me. "With us."

A shiver went through me from deep inside.

"You are welcome to paint, or do any work you want," he said gravely, "but only if it nourishes your soul. And any money you make is exclusively your own."

"But that's not right. I don't expect you to support me, to support all of us—"

"That is my job," he said firmly, "to financially support you and Miguel and, God willing, other children."

Other children!

I swallowed, breathing hard. It was as if he were offering me everything I'd never dreamed I could ask for. After growing up an only child, an orphan, I'd always secretly yearned to have a large family. Now Alejandro didn't just want to be a father for Miguel. He wasn't offering just financial stability for us both. He wanted to give me more children, too.

And create those children inside me....

No! I had to get ahold of myself. No matter how Alejandro looked at me in the shadows, or how the husky sound of his voice made me tremble. No matter if he seemed to be offering me my dreams. Without love, without honesty, *it wouldn't work*.

I shook my head. "You don't need to do these things out of duty."

"Not duty." His hand cupped my cheek. "It is my honor. And more." His eyes met mine as he said huskily, "It is my pleasure."

My cheeks flamed with heat. Sparks of need crackled down my body from that single point of contact. My lips went dry, and tension coiled hot, deep inside.

Nervously, I pulled away, looking down at the enormous marble bathtub. "Water's ready."

I carried Miguel to the tub, and Alejandro was suddenly beside me, rolling up his long sleeves to reveal his powerful forearms, dusted with dark hair. "Allow me."

Together, we propped him up to sit in the few inches of water. Alejandro held him upright as I lathered up Miguel's soft, wispy dark hair. The baby was already yawning as we toweled him off, and got him into his blue footsie pajamas decorated with baby animals. He was half-asleep as I took him into the nursery, to cuddle him in a rocking chair and feed him before bed. Alejandro sat beside us in a cushioned window seat. His face was in silhouette as he watched us, with the wide view of the moon-swept valley and the distant lights of Seville.

I cuddled our baby close, until his eyes were heavy and his mouth fell off the nipple, though his plump mouth still pursed, drinking imaginary milk as he slept sweet baby dreams.

I finally rose to my feet.

"Can I put him to bed?" Alejandro said. "At least try...."

"Sure," I said softly. I handed him the burping cloth, then the fuzzy cuddle blanket. "But you'll need to burp him first."

"Um...I'm not so sure that's a..."

"You'll be fine." I lifted a sleepy Miguel against his shoulder, over the burping cloth, and showed him how to gently pat his small back. Hesitantly, Alejandro followed suit, until our baby came up with a huge burp, before he softly sighed, and his eyes became heavy again.

Alejandro flashed me a look of triumph. "Ha!"

Seeing him that way, this handsome, ruthless, broad-shouldered man holding his tiny sleeping son—our son—my heart twisted. I smiled, and hoped the dim light of the nursery wouldn't let him see how I was fighting tears.

Against everything I'd once believed, everything I'd once feared, Alejandro was an amazing father. I knew he would take care of Miguel and love him and always be there to catch him if he fell.

"Now what?" he whispered.

"Tuck him into the crib, on his back," I answered over the lump in my throat.

Alejandro moved slowly, careful not to wake Miguel, careful to hold his head. He looked as if he were sweating bullets, like a man under the pressure of disarming a nuclear weapon, as he gently set our baby down into his crib. Leaning over beside him, I placed Miguel's favorite baby blanket, the fuzzy one decorated with elephants, softly by his cheek.

For a long moment, we stood over the crib, watching our son slumber, listening to his quiet, even breathing. Then Alejandro lifted his head to look at me.

Our eyes locked. And what I saw in his face left me shivering beneath the open weight of his hunger. Wordlessly, he pulled me from the room, closing the door behind us.

We were alone. In his bedroom.

I stared at him, my heart pounding. "You have to know—what happened in the garden today was a mistake."

"Sí," he agreed. "It was."

He was taking it a lot better than I'd thought he would. I exhaled. "So we won't…"

My voice trailed off as, for the first time, I realized someone had been in this bedroom while we'd been bathing Miguel. My eyes went wide.

A fire now crackled in the fireplace. Candles glowed from the marble mantle. And…no, surely it couldn't be…

Going toward the king-size bed at the center of the room, I picked up one of the scarlet, fragrant petals that had been scattered over the white bedspread.

"Rose petals?" I said dumbly. Turning, I held it up. "I don't understand…."

He gave a low, sensual smile. "Don't you?"

I exhaled. "You arranged this."

"Yes."

"But you just agreed that our kiss was a mistake—"

"It shouldn't have happened in the garden. Or the kiss in the coatroom in Madrid, either. I wanted you. I lost control. That was the mistake." Coming close to me, he shook his head. "But this won't be."

"Don't look at me like that," I whispered.

"Like what?"

"Like…" I licked my lips. "Like it's all you can do to keep yourself from ripping off my clothes and sliding me beneath you…"

"Because, *querida,*" he said, cupping my face, "it is. I've dreamed of you for so long…."

"You dreamed of me?" I breathed, remembering all the

nights I'd yearned for him, in hot dreams that had made me ache, only to wake up bereft and cold in the morning.

"Yes. But tonight, *querida,* tonight," he whispered, lowering his head toward mine, "my dreams come true. Not for duty. Not for convenience. But for pleasure. For need." He slowly traced his hand down the side of my body. "There's been no one for me since you, Lena. Did you know that? No other woman I've wanted in my bed. Just you. And now you are mine at last—as I am yours...."

As the fire crackled in the fireplace, I saw the shadows of red and orange move across the hard edges and planes of his handsome, saturnine face.

"It can't be true."

He pulled me into his arms.

"Tonight," he said softly, "will be the first night of forever."

Trembling, I looked up into his dark eyes. I tried to think of something, anything, to send him away from me. I tried to make my body move away, to run. But it was no longer obeying me. My body knew what it wanted. What it had always wanted.

I felt his hands tighten on my back, over the fabric of my blouse, as he pulled me close.

And he lowered his head to mine. I felt the warmth of his breath against my skin. A hard, reckless shiver went up and down my body. Of need. Of desire so great it made me shake.

Because what I wanted now, though beautiful as flowers, could poison my soul, and kill my heart. Just like the oleander...

"Please," I breathed as I felt the roughness of his jawline brush against my cheek. It was all I could do, to keep from leaning into him, kissing him, pulling him hard and tight against me. I wanted him so badly, I could almost have wept from it.

He traced his fingertip very gently from my earlobe, along my cheek, to my full, aching lower lip. "Please?"

"Please…" I tried to remember what I wanted. *Please kiss me. Please don't.*

But he didn't give me time to gather my senses. Lowering his mouth to my ear, he whispered, "You are mine. Forever and always. My pleasure. My duchess. My wife. My lover…"

"No," I whispered. "I can't be…."

"I forgot." He drew back, his eyebrows an amused slash over his heavy-lidded eyes. "You said you do not want me."

"I don't," I said, praying he would believe such a lie.

"I see." He ran his hand down the bare skin to my throat. "So you feel nothing when I do this…."

Trembling, I shook my head.

"And this…" His large hand cupped my breast over my blouse, the tip of his thumb rubbing over my nipple, which pebbled, aching and taut beneath the fabric.

I couldn't speak. I looked up at him, my lips parted, my heart pounding.

"Give in. To me."

"But I don't love you," I choked out, but what that really meant was *Don't make me love you.*

"I do not ask for your heart. But your body—*sí.* Tonight… your body will be mine."

And he lowered his mouth to mine.

His lips were gentle, even tender. One touch, and I was proved a liar. Of course I wanted him. Of course I did.

I sighed, as his kiss deepened, became demanding, hungry. My arms wrapped around his shoulders, pulling him close.

He slowly lowered me back against the enormous bed covered with rose petals. I gloried in the heavy weight of his body over mine, pressing me deep into the soft mattress.

He pulled off my blouse, kissing down my body as

each opened button revealed more of my skin. He lifted me against him, to pull off my shirt. I felt the warmth of his fingertips trailing down my naked arms, down my back. With expert precision, he unlatched my bra with a single flick of his fingers, and my breasts hung free, full and heavy and aching for his touch.

I heard the hoarseness of his breath as he pushed me back against the bed. Cupping my breasts with his hands, he nuzzled between them, lowering his head to one taut nipple, then the other, pulling it gently into his mouth as I gasped with pleasure.

"Wait," I choked out. "I want to feel you—"

Reaching for his shirt, I yanked it hard from his body. I was definitely not as careful as he'd been about the buttons. At least one ripped off entirely and scattered noisily against the floor in my desperation to feel the warmth of his skin. I exhaled when I could at last run my hands over his naked chest, feeling his hard sculpted muscles beneath the light dusting of dark hair. A low groan came from his lips, and he fell against me on the bed, ravishing my lips with his own.

Ohhhh… Deeper, deeper. The pleasure of his tongue against mine, his lips hard and so sweet, made me burn all over, made me lose my mind….

He kissed slowly down my bare skin, working his way to my belly button, which he flicked with his tongue. Unbuttoning my jeans, he rolled them with my panties down my hips, peeling the fabric inch by inch down my legs, kissing and licking and nibbling as he went, until I was naked and gasping for breath.

He kissed the hollow of my foot, then gently pushed my legs wide. From the base of the bed, he looked up at me, spread-eagled across the bed, naked for his pleasure. I quivered with need. If he tried to leave me now—my lips parted. In that moment, I would have done anything—begged, even—to get him to stay.

But no begging was necessary. With a low growl, he removed his own trousers and then fell hard and naked upon me. I felt the length of him, like steel, pressing between my legs. Looking up at his face in the flickering shadows of the firelight, I realized that he wasn't in nearly as much control of himself as I'd imagined. In fact, he was barely keeping himself in check.

"You don't have to hold back," I choked out, pulling him down against me, my hips lifting of their own volition against his. "Please…"

And this time, there was no question what I wanted. But he would not let me control him or set the pace. Shrugging off my grasp, he slid down my body, then parted my legs with his shoulders at my knees. I felt the heat of his breath against my inner thighs. I gasped, reaching my hands out to grip the white comforter beneath me.

Pressing his large hands against my thighs, he spread me wide. He lowered his head and took a long, languorous taste.

My hips bucked beneath his tongue. The pleasure was almost too much to bear. I tried to move away. But he held me fast. He stroked me, licked me, leaving me wet and in the agony of almost unbearable pleasure. His sensual tongue flicked against my taut core, and I held my breath, tilting my head back, my eyes rolling back in my head as I lifted higher, and tighter.

The moment before I would have exploded, he pulled back. I whimpered. I heard his low laugh as he changed position, returning his mouth to where it had been, but pressing his hands beneath my backside to hold me hard against him. Spreading his mouth wide, he worked me with his tongue, going wide, then deep, then wide again. I felt his tongue thrust inside me, and cried out. My back arched against the mattress as he forced me to accept the pleasure, and as he proved to me, against my will, how much more of it my body could endure.

With a single ragged breath, I lifted higher, and higher, but again, just as I was about to explode, he lifted his mouth. He smiled down at me.

By this point I was starting to turn to a mindless mess, somewhere between blubbering and wanting to resort to physical violence, because I knew he was teasing me, forcing me to soar, to coast, then soar higher still.

Abruptly, he lifted my legs to wrap around his tight, trim hips. Rose petals flew up from the bed as he moved me, the flowers leaving a sensual, heady fragrance as they fell back to earth, sliding first against his body, then mine. I felt him pressing hard and stiff and huge between my legs. I exhaled, pressing my fingers into his back, nearly weeping with need.

Again, he started to pull away, but this time, I wouldn't let him go. My fingernails dug into the skin of his back, and I gave a low growl. *"Bien, querida,"* he panted. *"Bien."*

He positioned his hips, and in one rough movement, he shoved himself inside me, hard and thick and enormous, ramming himself to the hilt. That very first thrust made me explode from the inside out. I saw stars as waves of bliss shook through me. I heard a rising animal cry and realized to my shame that it came from my mouth. I fell back against the soft mattress, as if from a far distance, landing a limp heap on his bed.

He froze, still deep inside me in that first thrust.

"You can go on…" I panted, trying to catch my breath. "I already…"

"More," he said, eyeing my face hungrily. "Do it again." Again? Was he crazy? I shook my head. "I can't…"

"Again," he said grimly.

He slowly pushed inside me, this time letting me feel

every inch. He made me stretch for him, as I felt him deep inside. It felt good. But he was holding himself back for no reason. I knew there was no way I could…

Drawing back, he slowly filled me again, and then again. Gripping my shoulders tight with his hands, he rode me. To my amazement, a new tension began to build deep inside me. Different this time. Even deeper. With a gasp, I wrapped my hands around him, feeling the clench and unclench of the muscled cheeks of his backside, feeling the sweat on his skin as he fiercely held himself in check.

His thrusts became rougher as he rode me harder, faster, our sweaty naked bodies sliding against each other. He held my shoulders tight enough to bruise, as he pounded me hard, hard, hard. Deep, deep, deep. My back started to arch again. Seeing that, he sucked in his breath and lowered his lips to mine, kissing me. I felt the flick of his tongue against mine as he rammed into me so deep, and that was it—the brutality and force and lust shook me into an explosion so great I screamed into his mouth.

His self-control evaporated. With a low guttural growl, he shoved into me one last time, and with a gasp and groan, he spent himself inside me.

He collapsed, his body heavy over mine on the bed.

It took long moments for me to return back to earth. When I did, my eyes flew open.

"We forgot to use a condom," I blurted out. I expected him to look horrified. He did not.

"I forgot nothing." He gave me a heavy-lidded smile. "I want to get you pregnant, Lena."

Shock went through me as I stared at him with wide eyes. "But we…"

"I will fill you with my child, *mi esposa*. Try to fight me if you must," he whispered, then his smile lifted to a grin. "It is always a pleasure to battle with you."

CHAPTER EIGHT

SUNSHINE WAS SPILLING from the windows, across our naked, intertwined bodies spread across the bed, the white cotton sheets twisted and tangled at our feet. My first thought when I woke was to think it all had been a dream. Then I saw Alejandro, still sleeping in my arms, a soft smile on his chiseled face.

I caught my breath. My heart beat faster, in a rhythm like music, because joy—pleasure—everything I'd ever wanted had all come true at once.

Slowly, Alejandro opened his eyes, and his smile widened. His expression was open, and young, and he, too, seemed to be shining with happiness. *"Buenos días,"* he whispered, leaning forward to kiss me tenderly on the forehead, *"mi corazon."*

"Good morning." I blushed, looking away, feeling oddly shy.

Reaching out, he lifted my chin and kissed me, until all thoughts of shyness disappeared beneath the mutual hunger building anew between us.

How was it possible? We'd made love three times last night—three times!—and yet he was still brand new. I gloried in his touch, in the feel of his naked, hard-muscled body against mine, his arms holding me as if I were truly the precious names he'd called me. *My pleasure, my duchess, my wife. My lover.*

And now something more. Something new he'd called me for the first time.

My heart...

We made love once more, hot, hard and fast—and good thing about that last bit, because thirty seconds after we'd both collapsed in a sweaty, gasping heap on top of each other, I heard an indignant cry from the nursery.

We looked at each other and laughed.

"I'll get him," I said, starting to rise from the bed.

"No." He put his hand on my shoulder, pressing me back against the soft sheets, and rose from the bed, pulling on a white terry-cloth robe over his hard-muscled body. "You got up last time. Relax. Go take a shower. Take your time."

I came out, hot and clean and pink-cheeked and happy. I got dressed in a soft pink shirt and skirt, and fed the baby as my husband had a shower in his turn.

This was just as I'd always dreamed. No. It was better. Just the three of us...

For now.

My hand slowly fell on my belly. *I want to fill you with my child.* Was I afraid? Yes. But did I also want, desperately want, another baby? Also yes.

So much had changed since the last time I was pregnant. Instead of being a fearful fugitive, I was married now. Settled. With a home.

Would it be so wrong to just let myself be happy? Alejandro was a good father. He was proving to be a good husband. He wanted to take care of me forever. He wanted us to be a family. And the way he made love to me... I shuddered at the memory of ecstasy.

Would it be so forbidden, so foolish, to trust my husband with my heart?

If only I knew the lie he was telling me, or had told, or would tell. He said he'd been faithful to me for a year, that he'd never be disloyal.

Of course, that could be the lie....

My lips pressed together, and I grimly pushed the thought away. I told myself that, since he'd shared so much of his body, surely he'd soon find it irresistible to share the secrets of his heart. And then I forced myself not to think about it.

Denial is a beautiful thing. A woman in love can be very good at focusing on the rose and ignoring the thorn—at least until it draws blood. Over breakfast, I kept smiling at Alejandro over my plate of eggs and *jamón,* my coffee diluted with tons of cream and sugar. And instead of treating me like a lovesick fool, as I no doubt looked like, Alejandro, the dark, dangerous, ruthless duke, did the unthinkable.

He kept smiling back.

"I'd like to take you around the estate today," he said, sipping his black coffee and reading the morning newspaper, "to meet my tenants."

"What?" I nearly dropped the baby rattle I'd been holding out for Miguel, who was sitting in my lap. Chortling, the baby grabbed it in his fat little fist and triumphantly began to shake. "I thought I'd meet them at the wedding reception."

"Abuela told me it will take her two months to plan the reception. We cannot wait that long." His eyes met mine. He seemed to sense my fear, because he gave me an encouraging smile. "You are my wife. It is right that I introduce you to the tenants on the estate. That is the merest good manners."

"But..."

"Besides. Knowing Abuela, the reception will be a lavish affair, to impress acquaintances and friends. I want the first introduction to be private. Personal." He paused. "Many of them have been farming this land for generations. They might have heard rumors. They might think that having a baby first, and getting married second, is a little..."

"Modern?" I supplied.

"Yes. Modern. I don't want them to wonder if this is a real marriage, or if we'll stand the test of time."

"Will we?" I whispered.

"We will," he said seriously, looking straight into my eyes. "And I want them to have no doubt you are here to stay." Leaning forward, he took my hand in his own. "I want them to think well of you, as I do." He looked at me. "Will you meet them?"

Having Alejandro look at me with his deep dark eyes, and hold my hand, and ask me something, in his husky voice, there was no possibility of resistance. No matter how the thought of trying to impress a bunch of strangers and convince them I would make an excellent *duquesa* filled me with dread. What if they thought I wasn't good enough? What if they had such deep doubts, Alejandro changed his mind about me and decided to find some other wife more worthy? "All right," I said hesitantly. "If you think it truly necessary."

"I do." Alejandro's eyes softened as he looked at our baby. "I'd like Miguel to come, as well. Because he is their future. And they are his."

I bit my lip, trying my best not to look nervous. "Right. Four hundred years on this land, right? So it's in Miguel's blood."

"Something like that." Alejandro put down his napkin and rose to his feet. "We'll see the Widow Ramirez first. She was my governess, once."

The thought warmed my heart. "She taught you as a child?"

"Both me and the…housekeeper's son."

"You mean Miguel," I said softly. "Your friend."

"Yes. We played together as children, studied together, fought. It didn't matter that one of us was a future duke and the other just the housekeeper's son. We studied the same subjects, lived in the same house. We both loved Abuela. We were friends. Until Miguel died that day."

"And you survived," I said gently, touching his shoulder.

"Yes. I survived." He turned away. "I'll get the keys."

I finished my breakfast and my orange juice. When Alejandro returned, he said, "Señora Ramirez is no longer as sharp as she used to be, but she still has a lot of influence with the other tenants."

"No pressure," I muttered, my heart suddenly cold with fear. I looked down at my pink shirt and floppy cotton skirt. "Maybe I should change."

He barely glanced at me. "You're fine."

"I want them to like me...."

Alejandro laughed. "Fancy clothes won't make them like you. In fact, if you showed up in a designer dress and five-inch stiletto heels, they'd like you *less*. The farmers respect honesty, hard work and kindness when it's called for. Bluntness when it's not." His dark eyes gleamed. "You should get along just fine."

"Oh, all right," I sighed, sure he was wrong.

A half hour later, the three of us were in his estate vehicle, a black, open-air Jeep, headed over a dirt road that crossed the wide fields and hills belonging to the Castillo de Rohares.

The Widow Ramirez's house was a snug little cottage on the edge of the estate, where she grew organic peaches and persimmons, aubergines and artichokes, and raised goats that produced milk and cheese. Frail and wizened, barely as tall as my shoulder, when she answered her door she looked at me with critical, beady eyes. But by the end of the visit, she was smiling and pushing more of her homemade butter cookies toward me.

"Eat, eat," she pleaded. "You must keep up your strength if you are to give your husband more children."

I felt Alejandro looking at me, and blushed.

"Gracias, Pilar," he said, putting his hands on my shoulders. "We wish for more children very much."

"Of course you do," she said, pouring him tea. "I know it was always your desire to have a larger family, growing up so lonely, up in that huge castle, with your older sister off working in Granada. And your mother," she sniffed, "working night and day, when she wasn't distracted by the duke...."

"Sister? What sister? Alejandro is an only child," I added, frowning up at him. "Aren't you?"

He cleared his throat, glancing at his old governess. "You're confused, Pilar," he said gently. "You're thinking of Miguel. Not me."

Her rheumy eyes focused on him. Then she nearly jumped in her chair. "Yes. Yes, of course. That was Miguel. You are El Duque." She abruptly held out a plate to me. *"¿Más galletas?"*

"Yes, please."

She beamed at me. "It makes me so happy you like my cookies. Alejandro—" she looked at him severely "—barely ate one."

He laughed. "I had three."

"Hardly any," she sniffed. She smiled at me. "You should take the example of your wife, and eat four or more."

"Gracias," I said happily, and took another one, buttery and flaky and sweet. "I will need this recipe."

"I'll be delighted to send it to you!"

Shortly afterward, as we rose to leave, Alejandro hugged the widow's small frame gently and looked at her with real love. "Take care of yourself, Pilar. We'll see you soon."

"You, too, M—Alejandro." Shaking her head with a wry smile, she reached up and patted his cheek, then looked down and kissed the top of our baby's head. Looking among the three of us, she said, "I'm so happy for you, my dear. How it's all turned out. You deserve a happy life."

Leaving her cottage, we got back into his open Jeep, tucking Miguel into the baby seat in the backseat. As we drove across the bumpy road, I exhaled in pure relief. Closing my eyes, I turned my face up to the warm morning sun, feeling happy that I'd somehow—I had no idea how—passed the first test. Instead of her tossing me out, she'd fed me cookies. And I'd pretty much eaten all of them. What can I say? They were delicious. I really did need that recipe.

Smiling, I turned to look at my husband. "She was nice."

"I'm glad you think so." He was looking at me with a strange expression, as if he wanted to say something. I frowned, and I parted my lips to ask what he was thinking. Before I could, he looked away.

"We'll visit the Delgado family next."

For the rest of the day, as my confidence built, I spoke with all of the tenants on his estate. They seemed relieved and happy that I spoke Spanish, though they took pleasure in teasing me mercilessly about my accent. They adored the baby, and all of them praised my new husband to me, even when he was out of earshot. One after another, they told me stories of his noble character, his good heart.

"The land was neglected, and El Duque brought it back from the brink...."

"My roof was falling apart, but El Duque helped me fix it...."

"When the crop died, I thought I would have to leave. But El Duque gave me a loan, enough for seed and animals. He saved us, and he himself was only eighteen...."

"He gave my son a job in Madrid, when there were no jobs to be had. José would have left for Argentina." The old woman wiped her eyes. "El Duque kept my son here in Spain, and I'm so grateful. I'll never forget...."

By the time we visited the last house in early evening, I was no longer even nervous. I was relaxed, holding our baby, laughing and chatting with the farmers, complimenting them on their well-cared-for fields and animals, complimenting their wives on their delicious *tartas*. And seeing how they admired Alejandro, how they treated him with such respect. His people did love him.

And by extension, I realized, they were willing to love me, for his sake. And for the sake of our child.

On the drive back home over the dusty road, back to the castle at the top of the hill, we didn't speak in the open-air Jeep. Miguel was sleeping in the back. Finally, I smiled at Alejandro. "That went well, don't you think?"

"Yes," he said shortly.

What could he possibly be mad about now? Biting my lip, I looked at the passing scenery. I was already starting to love Spain, especially Andalucía. The air was warm, dusty from our tires on the dirt road. The sun was starting to fade to the west, leaving a soft golden glow across the fields. I felt the warm breeze against my skin, the air scented by honeysuckle and bougainvillea and the jacaranda trees in bloom.

But Alejandro didn't say a word. He pulled the truck in front of the garage. Getting out, he opened my door. When I stepped out of the Jeep, he pulled me into his arms. I looked up at him, biting my lip. "Alejandro, didn't I do—all right?"

"All right?" he said huskily. I saw the warmth in his deep brown eyes. They held the same glow as the soft Andalucían morning. "I am proud of you beyond words, *mi corazon.* You made them love you. As…"

He cut himself off, but as I looked up at his face, my heart started to pound. "They loved me for your sake."

"No." He shook his head. "They loved you only for yourself. Your warmth, your smile, your…" Reaching down, he stroked my cheek. Something seemed to stretch tight between us, making me hold my breath. His hand trailed down my hair, down my back. "Come upstairs with me," he whispered. "Right now…"

"But dinner…"

He lowered his head to mine in a deep, passionate kiss, taut and tender, slow and sweet. I clutched his shoulders, lost in his embrace.

Miguel gave a plaintive whine from the back of the Jeep, and Alejandro released me with a rueful laugh. "But Abuela will be expecting us for dinner."

"Yes." I shook my head with a snort. We'd been fed at literally every house we visited. "I won't be able to eat a bite. I'm not the least bit hungry."

"Funny. I'm starving." He gave me a dark look that made my body burn, and I knew he wasn't talking about food. He sighed grumpily. "But you're right. Dinner has been arranged. We wouldn't want to disappoint Abuela…."

"No. We wouldn't." I took our baby out of the truck, and we went upstairs to give Miguel his bath. Alejandro left to dress for dinner tonight, as Maurine had requested. I fed our baby, cuddling him in the rocking chair as he drifted off to sleep, plump and adorable in his footsie pajamas, holding his soft blanket against his cheek. I finally tucked him into his crib, then went to the master suite next door.

I felt dusty from the road, and was tempted to take a shower, but feared that would make me late, which would be rude. Especially since Maurine had insisted tonight's dinner was special somehow. So I just brushed out my hair and put on a long slinky dress and high heels. She'd asked us to dress up for dinner tonight, though what made tonight different from the other nights, I had no idea. I put on some red lipstick and looked at myself in the mirror. I looked so different, I thought. I barely recognized myself. I tossed my hair, seeing the bold new gleam in my eye—and liking it.

Smiling, I went downstairs. But as I walked down the sweeping stairs, voices echoed from the shadows of the stairwell below.

"You should tell her the truth." Maurine's voice was uncharacteristically sharp.

"No," Alejandro answered coldly.

"She's your wife—"

"She cannot know. Not yet. Perhaps not ever. I don't know if I can trust her."

"But this is your life we're talking about!"

"Not just my life. Also yours. And Miguel's. She could destroy us all if she—"

Then they looked up and saw me. I shaped my mouth into a bright smile, as if I hadn't heard anything, as if my heart wasn't pounding.

"You look spectacular, *mi esposa*," Alejandro murmured, and held out his arm. He was dressed in a dark tailored shirt and trousers. "May I escort you to dinner?"

I nodded. But as we walked down the hallway toward the banqueting hall, the happiness that had been building inside me all day had suddenly gone *pfffft* like a balloon.

What was he hiding?

It was growing harder to push the question from my mind. Even denial will carry you only so far. My recent happiness suddenly felt like a house of cards waiting to fall.

I'd felt such incandescent joy, being in his arms last night. Being by his side today, meeting his neighbors and the people who mattered to him. Being introduced, with pride, as his wife.

Every moment I spent with him, I was falling deeper and deeper into an emotion I'd sworn I'd never feel for him again. Especially since I knew he was lying to my face. I was walking straight into heartbreak, only this time, I'd have no one to blame but myself.

Abruptly, I stopped in the middle of the hallway.

He frowned down at me. "What, *querida?*"

I looked at him, my heart aching. "I need to know what you're hiding from me."

Setting his jaw, he shook his head.

"I wish I'd never told you," he said harshly. Dropping my hand, he looked at me with cold eyes. "Should we spend dinner apart?"

He was ruthlessly ending the conversation. Swallowing back tears, I shook my head. He held out his arm again.

We walked, the only sound our footsteps against the flagstones. "I wonder why Maurine insisted that we dress up for dinner tonight," I said over the awkward silence. "I just saw her wearing an old cardigan and jeans...."

We entered the banqueting hall, and my voice cut off.

It was completely empty of other people. The only light came from the blazing fire in the enormous stone fireplace. Tall tapered candles lit the table. Beneath the high, timbered ceilings, the shadows and fire made the room breathlessly romantic.

I blinked, bewildered. "This is why Maurine wanted us to dress for dinner...?" Then Alejandro gave me a sensual smile, and it all clicked into place. "You arranged this," I breathed.

He shrugged. "I spoke with her before we left this morning, and she agreed newlyweds need time alone."

"But what about dinner for everyone else?"

"They already ate." He came closer, his dark eyes intent. "And I'm glad," he said huskily. "I want you to myself."

I stared at him, still conflicted about the way he'd coldly cut off my earlier question. Going to the table, he poured us each a glass of red wine that sparkled like a ruby in the firelight.

"Manzanilla wine. From my vineyard."

As we sat next to each other at the end of the long table, near the fire, I felt my anger starting to be melted by his nearness. The dinner was probably delicious, but I ate mechanically, barely tasting it. Alejandro moved his chair closer. He did not try to touch me. He started asking me questions, asking what I thought of Spain, how I liked the estate, how I liked the baby's nursery. He asked me how I'd first started painting.

"My father taught me," I said softly. "He always wanted to be an artist. But once he got married and had a family, he had to try to earn a living...." I gave a rueful laugh. "He was never good at earning money. But we loved him, just as he was."

Alejandro leaned forward, his elbow on the table, his chin resting on his hand, listening to every word. He focused his attention on me, as if nothing and no one else existed.

I knew how this worked. I'd seen it before. And yet I still could not resist. With every breath I felt him seducing me, drawing me in closer. Against my will, my heart started to warm.

The enormous banqueting hall, usually chilly inside the castle even on a hot summer day, was growing increasingly hot. I found myself leaning forward, asking him questions in my turn, and all the while wishing he would kiss me, and hating myself for wanting it. Finally, I could bear it no longer.

"Why can't you tell me your secret?"

"Put it from your mind," he said harshly. "Or go."

"Fine," I said tearfully. I stood, turning away.

He grabbed me by the wrist.

Slowly, Alejandro rose from the chair, his body grazing mine as he fully stood, towering over me. My head tilted back to look at his face. He was bigger than me, stronger by far. But it wasn't his strength that overwhelmed me, but the stark vulnerability I suddenly saw in his hard, handsome face.

"This is all you need to know," he whispered.

He pushed me against the edge of the stone fireplace, holding my wrists above me, kissing my lips, my throat.

Closing my eyes, I tilted back my head as waves of desire crashed over me.

"I want you, Lena," he whispered, his voice husky, his lips brushing my earlobe. *"Te deseo."*

I shivered. Then remembered why I was mad at him and tried to pull away. "I—I am dusty and sweaty from the road." I gave a casual laugh that no one would believe, least of all me. "I rushed downstairs because I didn't want to be late." He continued to kiss my face, and I closed my eyes, breathing, "But I should...really...go take a bath...."

"Bien," he purred. "I'll join you."

My eyes flew open. "A shower, I mean, not a bath," I stammered. "There's not much room in the shower for two...."

He ran his hands down my back, holding me against him. "Just enough."

He kissed me, and beneath the sensuality of his embrace, I sighed, and my lips parted. My body melted into his, my soft curves pressing into his hard angles as if his body had been made for mine.

Lifting me into his arms as if I weighed nothing at all, he carried me upstairs to our private, luxurious bathroom, where he gently set me on my feet. His dark eyes never left mine as he slowly pulled off my dress, then my bra, then my panties.

When I was completely naked in front of him, he wrenched me hard against him and kissed me deeply, hungrily. I desperately began to unbutton his shirt, then his trousers, until he, too, was naked.

Pulling away, he turned on the water in the shower. I glanced back longingly at the bed, but it was in the next room and seemed a million miles away. He kissed me again, and I gasped against his lips, his naked body hard against mine. Steam lifted from the hot water of the shower, making the luxurious bathroom of white marble and silver a magical, otherworldly place of ice and snow.

Except for the heat. Every inch of me felt warm, bursting with fire.

Alejandro pulled me into the shower. He pushed me away from him firmly, and I whimpered.

"Patience," he said, and I could almost hear his smile. He was still in control. Unlike me…

With agonizing slowness, he washed me in the shower, tangling shampoo in my hair, rubbing soap over my body, scrubbing every inch of me. I felt him stroke my full, naked breasts, my waist, my hips, the soft hair between my legs. I closed my eyes, swaying on my feet. I felt hot and unsteady as he caressed my hair, down my earlobes, my neck. I left handprints in the glass wall of the shower, against the white steam.

Turning me around to face him, he ran his hands down my breasts, over my belly, over my hips and thighs. Hot shooting streams of water poured over us both.

And he knelt before me. Gently parting my thighs, he pressed his face between my legs.

I gasped. His lips were tender and sensual and warm. His tongue slid against me, inside me, the merest breath of a stroke, hot and wet beneath the warm water.

I closed my eyes, pressing my hands against the glass wall behind me.

His hands slid around me, holding me firmly against his mouth. He teased me with the tip of his tongue, soft and light against the most sensitive part of me, then spread me wide and lapped me, until I tossed back my head, slapping my long wet hair against the glass as I shook all over. The hot, steamy water poured over us both as I felt his hands—his tongue—slide over my wet, pink skin.

For an intoxicating eternity, he teased me, bringing me almost to an explosion of pleasure beneath the steamy pulse of the shower, then backing away the very second before I would have exploded into bliss. It might have been seconds or hours, that he seduced me with this sweet torment....

When my need was too much to bear, and I was shaking so hard I could barely breathe with desire, Alejandro turned me around, pressing me against the glass, my bottom resting against his hard, thick length.

"You're mine," he growled in my ear. "Say it."

"I'm yours," I breathed, pressing my arms against the glass.

"Again."

"I'm yours!"

"Forever."

"Forever," I whispered.

He thrust inside me roughly, deep and hard, and I gasped.

I forgot everything in the overwhelming pleasure of having him inside me. *Pleasure* was not a big enough word for it. I melted, lost myself, found myself, until he exploded inside me, and I soared.

Afterward, both of us were panting and spent, and he abruptly turned off the water. He opened the shower door and toweled me off. Without a word, he lifted me in his arms and carried me to our enormous bed. Looking back, I saw the trail of water he'd left across his stark floor.

Clinging to my husband's naked chest as he carried me, I felt as if I were in another time or place. I wondered dreamily about other lovers who'd done this, hundreds of years ago, in this very castle, when the sultan ruled.

Setting me down naked on our bed, he looked down at me. I smiled up at him, blinking tears of emotion, of anger and joy all mixed up together.

Climbing beside me, he held me, kissing my temple tenderly. Our bodies intertwined, his wet skin sliding against mine. My hand stroked the hardness of his chest, laced with dark hair. He held me tight. My eyes were heavy, and started to close.

I'd told him the truth in the shower.

I was his.

Now and forever.

Because I love him....

The realization hit like a bolt of lightning, causing my eyes to fly open.

I was in love with him, and there was something he was keeping from me. A reason he was lying. A secret he thought would hurt me.

I was in love with my husband.

But if I knew the secret he hid from me, would that love be destroyed?

CHAPTER NINE

THE NEXT FEW weeks fled by in a blur. We spent our days doing the work of the estate, talking to tenants and managing the house. I started painting in the garden in the morning, and played with our baby on the floor of Alejandro's home office as he worked on the computer and spoke on the phone to employees around the world.

"I begrudge them every hour," he told me, stroking my cheek. "I would rather spend it with you."

My heart sang as the birds did, flying free through the lush green trees, across the wide blue Spanish sky. But eventually, Alejandro had to go on a business trip. "Madrid?" I pouted.

He laughed. "Granada."

"Isn't that where the Alhambra is?" I said eagerly, picturing the famous Moorish castle. "I'll come with you!"

He shook his head. "It will be a one-day trip, there and back. Very boring. Stay here with Miguel. Paint. Enjoy your day." He kissed my temple and said huskily, "I'll be back before bedtime."

Then he kissed me *adios* until my toes curled.

But after he'd gone, all the fears and shadows came back crashing around me, without Alejandro's warmth and strength to hide behind.

Was he really going to do business in Granada, as he'd said? Or was he there for some other reason?

Was this his lie?

Don't think about it, I ordered my trembling heart, but it was impossible, now that I loved him.

I feared knowing the truth.

I feared never knowing it.

"Dear?" I heard Maurine's tremulous voice. "I wonder if I could ask you a favor?"

"Of course," I said, desperate for distraction.

She smiled at me. "You are such a talented artist. I love the paintings you've done of my roses. You are the only one who's ever done them justice." As I blushed, she continued, "Alejandro's birthday is next month. Would you do a portrait of me and Miguel, in the rose garden…?"

"I'd love to!" I exclaimed, my mind immediately filled with painting materials, size and composition. I went into Seville for supplies, and by late afternoon, after Miguel's nap, the three of us were outside. I propped up an easel in front of where they sat on a bench, surrounded by greenery and red, yellow and pink roses.

The warm Spanish sun filtered golden light over the garden as I painted the portrait of the dowager Duchess of Alzacar and her great-grandbaby, the future duke.

Maurine's lovely white hair was like a soft cloud around her twinkling eyes and smiling face. I drew her outline in loose strokes. That was easy, compared with the challenge of the wiggling, giggling baby in her lap. But I'd painted and drawn my son so many times over the past six months, I knew his chubby face by heart. I could have done it blindfolded.

I smiled to myself, picturing how happy Alejandro would be at the gift, reaching up to adjust the floppy pink hat I was wearing to keep the sunlight out of my eyes. Maurine chattered nonstop, while entertaining the baby in her lap. She told me how she'd first fallen in love with her husband, who'd had a title, "though it seemed useless enough, with no hope of returning to Spain, with the political situation," and absolutely no money or marketable skills. "It's so much easier to know how to work when you've been raised to it. My husband had spent his adult life sleeping in the spare rooms of rich friends from his Eton days."

"Sounds like my father. He wanted to work, but didn't know how."

"It's the upbringing, I think. Even when we finally returned to Spain, with the Navaro fortune lost, Rodrigo had no idea how to pay for the upkeep of this castle. It's not like the old days, when a duke could simply demand peasants give him tribute." She gave a soft laugh. "He was desperate to keep the title and the land, for the sake of his family's history. I loved him, so I did my best to help." She looked away, blinking fast. "I sold oranges from the orchard and gave castle tours. Sadly, our son was no better with money—the earning of it, I mean, not the spending of it. By the time Alejandro became duke, the roof of the castle was caving in, we were mortgaged to the hilt, and I was beginning to think I'd spend my elderly years begging on the streets, or selling oranges at street corners."

I laughed. "As if Alejandro would ever allow that." I smiled, remembering his bossy ways when he'd informed me that taking financial care of us was his job. "He, at least, had no trouble figuring out how to make money."

"No." She smiled, playing patty-cake with the baby. "But of course, his background is so different. He didn't have an overbearing father constantly telling him how an aristocrat was supposed to behave. The small silver lining of having no father at all, I suppose...."

"No father?" Frowning, I lifted the brush off the canvas. I looked around the casel. "But Alejandro's father was the duke. Your son."

Maurine looked up at me sharply, her face oddly pale. "Oh, yes. Of course."

I gave a laugh. "Is the sun getting to you, Maurine?"

"I'm an old woman. I get confused." Her blue eyes suddenly wouldn't meet mine. "But you're right. I think I've been in the sun too long."

She rose to her feet, still holding Miguel, who looked happy to be moving at last after so long sitting still. "I'm a little tired. I'll have the staff bring you some lemonade. And maybe look for Alejandro's hairbrush. Yes, his hairbrush..."

She left the rose garden without waiting for a reply. I stared after her, frowning. What did lemonade have to do with Alejandro's hairbrush?

"I thought she would never leave."

With a gasp, I whirled around. The paintbrush fell from my limp hand, landing with a soft thud into the grass.

Edward St. Cyr stood in the rose garden, near the thick hedge on the edge of the forest. Brambles had ripped the sleeves of his dark tailored jacket.

"Edward," I breathed. "What are you doing here?"

He stopped five feet in front of me, looking down at me. His eyes were stark against his tanned face as he gazed at me hungrily. "You have no idea how I've wanted to see your face."

He reached out a hand, but I stumbled backward, my long skirt dragging against the grass. Holding my floppy pink hat against my head, I glanced uneasily to the left and right.

Having him here, in Maurine's rose garden—in Alejandro's castle—felt all kinds of wrong. Like finding a deadly snake amid the lush flowers. "How did you get in here?"

His lips twisted. "It wasn't easy."

"I told you I never wanted to see you again!" I narrowed my eyes. "You must get out of here! Alejandro will kill you if he finds you here!"

"Ah, but he's gone, isn't he?"

I sucked in my breath.

"And as for your precious duke…" A low, guttural curse came from Edward's lips. "I know you don't want him." He looked contemptuously around the lush, sunlit garden, to the stone walls of the castle just beyond the perfectly trimmed green hedges. "I've come to save you from this… prison."

"It's not a prison," I retorted. "It's my home! And Alejandro is no jailer. I…" I licked my lips, then whispered aloud, "I love him."

Edward's eyes narrowed, and his lips twisted downward, giving him an expression that was hard, even cruel.

"He seduced you, didn't he?" He took another step toward me, and I again backed away, knocking over the easel behind me. I gulped as Edward slowly looked me over, from my hat to my long cotton skirt covered with an artist's long smock. "He's got to you." He straightened, and this time his contemptuous glance was just for me, all for me. "You fell for his lines *again*."

I took a deep breath.

"I love him," I said quietly. "In a way I never loved you—and I never will."

His hands tightened at his sides.

"The charming Duque de Alzacar. Beloved by all." His lip curled. "Of course you're faithful to him. But is he faithful to you?"

I drew myself up coldly. "Of course."

"Are you sure?" He lifted a dark eyebrow. "You know, you must know, about the woman he visits in Granada?"

My lips parted. "Woman?"

"Ah," Edward said, smiling. "You didn't know. They have dinner together. Often. He bought her a tavern in the Albaicín district. Sometimes he even plays his guitar there. Singing old Spanish love songs. In front of everyone."

My mouth went dry.

Alejandro hadn't played his guitar for me. Not once.

Licking my lips, I croaked, "There are all kinds of reasons for…"

Edward moved in for the kill. "Sometimes he stays the night in the residence above her tavern. But sometimes," he said softly, "he just goes for a quick visit. For the day." His lips curled. "A bit of love in the afternoon."

The chill turned to ice. I desperately tried to think of a reasonable explanation for why Alejandro hadn't wanted me to come with him today.

I'll come with you!

It will be a one-day trip, there and back. Very boring. Stay here with Miguel.

It was the nightmare I'd imagined when I'd refused to marry Alejandro. Except this was a million times worse.

Because I'd let myself love him.

"Lying to your face." Edward came closer. "He has no shame. He thinks, in his arrogance, that he can have you, as well. He's out enjoying himself—keeping you prisoner…."

"I'm not a prisoner," I choked out.

He lifted a condescending eyebrow. "No?" He slowly looked around the rose garden. "I could make him pay," he whispered. "I could make him regret."

I gasped—not in fear, but in fury. "If you dare hurt him, I'll…"

"*Hurt* him?" His blue eyes suddenly blazed. "*He* is the one you are worried about? Where was his concern for *you* when he left your heart in ashes?" He took another step toward me, his expression changing as he reached toward me almost wistfully. "Where is your love for me, for saving you…?"

I turned away, stepping back out of his reach. My voice was very cold. "I appreciated your friendship—until the moment I realized you had no time for my baby."

"Lena, you can't…"

"If you touch me, I'll scream. And Alejandro will come running...."

Edward moved closer.

"He's not here, though, is he?"

This time, the expression in his face scared me. For a moment, I stared at him, heart pounding. But as I opened my mouth to scream, like a miracle, I heard Alejandro's voice from the other side of the garden.

"Lena? Are you out here?"

I nearly wept with relief.

"I'm here!" I shouted. "I'm here, Alejandro! In the rose garden!"

Shaking, I turned back to face Edward, but he was already gone, melted back into the forest.

"And don't ever come back," I whispered aloud. I prayed I'd never see him again. But I still heard his ugly words.

You know, you must know, about the woman he visits in Granada?

He was *lying,* I told myself. Alejandro told me he'd be loyal, that he'd been faithful for the past year, wanting only me....

But then, I remembered, he'd also told me he was a liar.

When I saw my husband's strong, powerful body push through the trees to me, I nearly wept.

"Querida," Alejandro murmured, kissing my forehead as he pulled me into his arms. "I came back early. I couldn't bear to be away for...but what's this?" He drew back, his handsome face the picture of concern. "You're shaking."

"It's nothing," I said. My teeth chattered. "M-my easel fell."

"Ah." He smiled at me, his dark eyes warm. "Let me take care of that."

"Don't look at the painting!" I cried. "It's supposed to be a surprise. For your birthday."

Good-naturedly covering his eyes, he handed me the canvas. "I didn't see a thing."

I took the painting, slightly smeared from the fall and half-finished, with Maurine and Miguel looking like ghosts. And I wished I'd covered my ears and not heard a thing when Edward had told me about the woman in Granada.

"It has occurred to me," Alejandro murmured a week later, leaning over the sofa where I sat feeding Miguel, "that we never had a honeymoon."

"Honeymoon?" I said, twisting my head to look back at him. I shook my head. "You mean, without Miguel?"

"Don't worry." He brushed the back of my neck with his fingertips, making me shiver. "I'm not thinking Tahiti. That will have to wait. But a single night, just a two-hour drive away, surely you could manage that?"

I hesitated. "I don't know…"

"I promise you'll enjoy it." He stroked my hair, then gently kissed the crook of my neck, the edge between my shoulder and my neck. My shiver turned harder. "We will get a nice hotel. Go out for dinner. I'm thinking Granada…."

"Granada?" I stared at him, and the color must have drained from my cheeks, because he frowned.

"I thought you wanted to see the Alhambra."

I'd dreamed of seeing the famous Moorish castle since I was a child. But I'd spent the past week guarding my heart. Trying to stay distant and cold. Trying not to think about what I didn't want to know. Granada was the last place on earth I wanted to go.

Or was it?

"Maybe," I said.

He smiled, really smiled, for the first time in a week. Since I'd started keeping my distance, even when we were as close as a man and woman could be. "Is that a yes?"

He tilted his head, looking over me slowly with a sensual, heavy-lidded gaze. "I'd be happy to spend time persuading you…."

My body immediately clamored for him to persuade me, hot and sweet and long. But sex wasn't our problem. We made love every night. Physically, we were closer than ever.

Emotionally, the weight of secrets had caused an ocean between us.

You know, you must know, about the woman he visits in Granada?

My smile faded. Like my courage. I shook my head. "On second thought…forget it."

"Why?" His eyes narrowed, and he moved around the sofa with lightning speed. He cupped my face, looking down at me fiercely. "I am trying to make it up to you!"

"What?" I breathed, searching his gaze. "What are you trying to make up for, Alejandro?"

"Whatever has made you so angry at me." His fingertips tightened infinitesimally. "I want you to look at me like you used to."

"And I want to trust you," I choked out, "like I used to."

He stared at me. He'd never heard that tone from me before. "When I was in Granada…"

I held my breath.

He continued, "You were alone with my grandmother. Did she…" He hesitated. "Did she say something?"

"Did she tell me your secret, you mean?" I said bitterly. "No. She is loyal to you."

He abruptly released me and rose from the sofa, his face hard. "Enough. We are taking a one-night honeymoon. You will come with me. You will have a good time."

I lifted my chin defiantly. "Is that a command, Your Excellency?"

"Take it as you wish." He glared back at me, his eyes cold. "I will tell the staff to pack your things immediately."

The drive to Granada was short, especially after Alejandro stepped on the gas of his yellow Lamborghini. But with just the two of us trapped in the small space, it still took far too long. The tension between us was boiling, about to explode.

I forced myself to look at the guidebook he'd bought me about Granada. I tried to distract myself with its history. To choke back my frustration, my hurt, my rage. Because if I let out my feelings, I feared our marriage would end, and so would any chance at happiness. Forever.

I desperately wanted to ask him about the woman.

I desperately was afraid of the answer.

Alejandro did not speak to me. He drove us to a small hotel, a *parador* amidst the gardens of the Alhambra itself, in a building that was once a fifteenth-century convent, and a royal chapel to the kings of Spain, and before that, a palace and mosque of the Moorish emirs. Once there, he seemed angry at everyone. He glowered at the hotel staff. The moment we were alone in the simple, starkly furnished bedroom, he turned on me, and pressed me to the large four-poster bed in a ruthless, unyielding embrace.

All the women's magazines tell you to do one thing. To have self-esteem. To turn away from any man you cannot completely trust. Especially one who has broken your heart before. They say the past predicts the future.

I knew all this, but when I felt his hand stroke my cheek, the sweet satin stroke of his touch sent liquid fire through my veins. I saw the dark gleam of his eyes as he slowly lowered his head to mine, and I could not resist.

He kissed me, and I felt my heart explode in my chest. Felt my taped-together soul shatter again into a million pieces, even tinier than before, in infinite chiming shards that I would never be able to put together again.

I had to ask him. I had to be brave enough to ask, and

be brave enough to listen to his answer—whether he answered with words, or with silence.

I suddenly realized this might be the very last time we'd ever make love....

"Maravillosa," Alejandro whispered against my skin. As he pulled off my clothes, as I pulled off his, as I kissed him, tasting the salt of his skin, I knew that even amid the pleasure, I was tasting the salt of my own tears.

I loved him.

So much.

And I knew—I'd always known, really—how this would someday end.

Through my tears, I kissed him back desperately, letting him pull me into the whirlwind of mingled anguish and pleasure.

But when the heat between us was satisfied, coldness was all that was left. Both of us still naked, he held me against him on the bed. His voice was low.

"Why do you not look at me like you used to? What has changed? What do you—know?"

I looked at him. His face shimmered through my tears.

"Edward came to see me last week. At Rohares."

"What!" he exploded, sitting up.

I held his hand. "I didn't ask him to come. He snuck in. I only spoke with him for a moment. He wanted me to run away with him. When I refused, he told me...you had a woman here. In Granada. That you visited her. That you bought her a tavern. That you even sing to her...."

For a long moment, we stared at each other in the slanted bars of sunlight coming through the window blinds. I could almost hear the pounding of my heart.

Then Alejandro's lip slowly curled.

"I will kill him," he said, and with cold menace, started to rise from the bed.

"No!" Grabbing his arm, I looked up at him pleadingly.

"It's not about Edward anymore. It's about us. You and me." I swallowed, blinking fast as I whispered, "Do you love her?"

He looked down at me.

"Yes," he said dully.

My lips parted in a silent, heartsick gasp. Numbly, I let him go.

"So that is your big secret. The thing I expected from the beginning." I tried to laugh, wiping my eyes. "How very boring."

"It's not like that." Sitting on the edge of the bed, he scowled at me. "You think so little of my loyalty, even after all the time we've spent together?"

"But you said you love her," I whispered. "You've never said that to me. Not once."

I heard his intake of breath. "It's not like that," he repeated, setting his jaw. "Theresa is not my mistress."

"Then what?" I choked out. "What secret could you possibly be keeping, that would hurt me worse than that?"

"I protect the people I love. At any cost." His voice was bleak. I looked at him sharply, and saw the vulnerability in his eyes. The yearning. He took a deep, shuddering breath. "How I wish I could tell you everything."

Our eyes locked. Held. I opened my lips to plead—

He shook his head and rose to his feet. The yearning in his expression shuttered. His face returned to the handsome mask I knew so well—powerful, ruthless and cold.

"Come," he said. "Our time is short."

After a silent luncheon on the lovely terrace of the *parador,* we walked through the gardens of the Alhambra, with their flowers and trees and wide lush pools. As beautiful and varied and wide as they were, they didn't hold a candle to the gardens of Rohares, in my opinion. Though perhaps I was biased. Because the castle had become my home.

Alejandro held my hand tightly as we walked. I didn't

even try to resist. The truth was I wanted the comfort of his hand. It felt warm and strong in mine. Was it wrong of me to still want to believe? To trust him?

Yes. I was a fool. Any of the women's magazines would have called me an idiot for not already being on my way to a lawyer's office. And yet...

We met a guide who took us on a private tour. We walked through the graceful arcades of the Alhambra complex, through the lush terraces with their views of Granada in the valley below, past the blue pools hedged by myrtle, reflecting the wide blue sky. But in spite of the fact that I'd dreamed of visiting the Alhambra all my life, I barely noticed the beauty. As we walked through cavernous rooms, decorated with tile and geometric patterns and arabesques of Arabic calligraphy in plaster, beneath jaw-dropping ceilings soaring high above, of the sun and stars, my mind was scrambling, trying to put the clues together.

Why would Alejandro need to protect Maurine and Miguel? What could the secret be?

We had our picture taken together in the famous stone Court of the Lions, from the fourteenth century.

"No," the guide laughed. "You are newlyweds. Stand closer."

And so Alejandro put his arm around me. I looked up at his face, and again, I saw the yearning in his eyes. The yearning that matched my own.

"*¡Perfecto!* Now you look like lovers!"

As we left the Alhambra, I turned back to look at it one last time. It had been neglected over the years, vandalized, nearly blown up by Napoleon's soldiers. But after all that, it stood tall and proud over Granada. Unbowed. Unbroken. And so beautiful now. So loved.

"We don't need to see any more," I whispered over the ache in my throat.

"You're here. See it all." Silently, Alejandro drove us

down the mountain to the city. We visited the Capilla Real, the royal chapel, getting special permission for a private tour that took us immediately past the long line of tourists outside, past the gypsies begging on the streets and musicians busking along the crowded edges.

In the dark, quiet interior of the enormous stone chapel, I saw the tomb of Ferdinand and Isabella, who together had practically ruled the medieval world in their day, even before they'd sent Columbus in ships to the New World. Together, they'd finally ended seven hundred years of Moorish rule, laying siege to Granada and driving the last sultan, called Boabdil, from the city.

It was said that the reason he gave up without a fight was to prevent the destruction of his beloved Alhambra. And so he spent the rest of his life mocked, and in poverty, a sultan without a throne....

Alejandro came to stand beside me in the cool shadows of the royal crypt. "What are you thinking?"

I looked at him. "How loving the wrong thing—or the wrong person—can ruin your life," I whispered.

"Sí," he said quietly. He turned away. "Come. This place leaves me cold."

Outside the echoes of the shadow-filled chapel, we were hit by the brilliant Spanish sunlight, the noise of tourists laughing and talking, the distant sound of music. Life.

"Enough history," Alejandro said, shaking his head ruefully. "There's an ice-cream shop down the street, the most famous in Granada. The American first lady visited here recently and said it was the best ice cream in all of Spain...."

But I wasn't listening. I was too busy trying to think things through. Eating the ice-cream cone some time later as we walked, I looked at Alejandro sideways beneath my lashes. He was so handsome, so dark-haired and broadshouldered. The man of my dreams, come to life.

What was the secret? What was it he couldn't tell me, for fear of endangering his grandmother and his son?

We walked through the narrow streets of Granada, and I bought some chocolates and a garden ornament for Maurine, and a small stuffed toy for Miguel, plus a wooden sword and shield he wouldn't be able to play with for at least a year.

I couldn't stop thinking of that last sultan, Boabdil, who'd sacrificed everything, his honor, his fortune, his pride, rather than see the palace he loved blown up into ash.

What would I sacrifice for love?

What would you?

Love me? Alejandro's words floated back to me. *You do not even know me.*

Maybe he'd been right. A year ago, maybe I'd just fallen for his power, his wealth, his influence. His beauty.

But now, as I looked at his face, I loved him for who he really was. The man who took care of everyone. Who was willing to sacrifice himself for those he cared about. As a father. A grandson. A neighbor. A boss.

A husband.

My heart caught in my chest. What was I missing?

Twilight was falling when Alejandro suggested we go out for dinner and drinks. "A…friend of mine owns a restaurant in the Albaicín district."

I looked at him sharply. He nodded.

"Yes," he said quietly, watching me in the deepening dusk. "I want you to meet her."

I was shaking when we walked up the cobblestoned alleys of the Albaicín, the old Moorish quarter on the hillside beneath the Alhambra. We reached a prosperous-looking tavern, filled with people and music. I froze.

"Come on," Alejandro said gently. "It'll be all right." Pulling me inside, he brought me through the crowds to the bar, where he was greeted eagerly by the other patrons.

"Are you going to play tonight, *señor?*"

With a slight smile, he shook his head. "Where is Theresa?"

The man motioned toward the end of the bar with his glass of sangria. With a quick nod, Alejandro pulled me down toward a dark-haired woman.

"Theresa," he said, kissing her on each cheek.

"Alejandro," she exclaimed, returning the embrace. "I didn't expect you so soon!"

I stared at the woman. She wasn't what I'd expected. She had dark eyes and a round, friendly face, and she seemed at least ten years older than Alejandro. She smiled as she turned to me. "And this must be your wife." A big smile lit up her face. "Your Lena?"

My lips parted. *His* Lena?

"Sí." Alejandro put his arm around me. "My Lena."

"I'm so happy to meet you at last!" she said with clear delight. "I told him he had to bring you here. Wait until you hear him play!"

"Play?" I echoed, looking at him.

He blushed. I swear he did. "Yes. I play a little guitar sometimes. No one cares I'm a duke here. They only care how well I play the guitar...."

"Are you that good?"

"Let him show you." Theresa gave me a wink. "Drink orders always go up thirty percent when you sing, Alejandro." She turned to me with a smile. "Go grab a table, if you can find one.... And what will you have?"

"Bourbon," he said. "Rocks."

"Right. Lena?"

"Something light...sangria?"

She chuckled. "Light?"

"Isn't it mostly juice with a bit of red wine?"

She gave a hearty guffaw and glanced at Alejandro affectionately. "Innocent little thing, isn't she?"

"Very," he said quietly.

She sighed, looking back at me, she suggested, "I'll make you a *tinto de verano*. Dash of wine, sugar and a little lime with sparkling water. Trust me. It won't go to your head."

She was right. The delicious concoction was a mixture of tart and sweet and bubbles, with lemon and limes floating beside the ice. I had one glass, then another, then a third, then looked down at my empty plate and realized I'd ordered and eaten a whole plate of dinner without paying the slightest attention.

"What time is it?" My head was swimming. I put my hands to my temples. "She said this drink wouldn't go to my head," I said accusingly.

Alejandro gave a low laugh. "It wouldn't, but you had four of them."

"Four?" I looked with amazement at my empty glass. "They just taste so light. The most delicious wine cooler ever invented."

"You should stop."

I looked at him brazenly. "You should tell me who you really are."

Time suddenly stood still.

"Don't you know?" he said hoarsely. "Haven't you guessed?"

"Don't tell me you're already having your first fight." Theresa was holding out a guitar. "Fix it, *pequeño*. Play."

"Sí!" the people around us clamored, pounding on their tables. "Play!"

Alejandro shook his head. "We're leaving."

But I didn't want to leave. I wanted to see what everyone else apparently already knew. The other side of my husband. The one he'd never let me see. "Will you play?" I whispered. "For me?"

He whirled to look at me. Then he gave a slow nod.

"For you, *mi amor.*" He slowly took the guitar in his hand, and there was a burst of cheers and applause. "This is just for you."

Walking across the crowded tavern, past all the tables to the tiny stage, Alejandro sat on a stool. With his guitar in his lap, he said simply into the microphone, "This is for my bride. The mother of my child." He looked at me. "The woman I love."

My lips parted in a silent gasp.

Could he have said…

Surely he couldn't have said…

How strong were those *tinto de verano* drinks anyway?

Exhaling, Alejandro strummed his guitar, and in a low, husky voice began to sing. It sounded very old, and Spanish. He was a good musician, I thought in amazement, really good, far better than any tycoon-slash-duke had a right to be. The music was so heartbreaking and pure that at first, I didn't bother to listen to the words.

Then I did.

Alejandro stared at me from across the room, and sang about a young peasant boy who'd dared to put on the clothes of a prince. He'd gone through life as an imposter, until he died heartbroken, wishing he could see, just one last time, the peasant girl he'd left behind.

Love me? My whole body flashed hot, then cold as his words took on new significance. *You do not even know me.*

I dimly heard the whispers hissing through the room. "That's the Duke of Alzacar—and she must be his new wife—they're obviously in love…." But I just listened to the music, and suddenly, it all fell into place.

Maurine's shaky words. *If not for him, I never would have survived the aftermath of that car crash, when I lost my whole family…. I can still see him in the hospital, his little injured face covered with bandages, his eyes so bright….*

He was worried about me, not himself. "It'll be all right, Abuela," *he told me.* "I'm your family now."

Pilar's voice. *I know it was always your desire to have a larger family, growing up so lonely, up in that huge castle, with your older sister off working in Granada. And your mother working night and day, when she wasn't distracted by the duke....*

I couldn't breathe. I felt as if I was choking. The walls of the tavern were pressing in. Rising unsteadily to my feet, I pushed through the tables and headed for the door. I saw Theresa's surprised face as I flung it open and headed outside.

In the quiet night, in the empty, cobblestoned alley, I fell back against the rough stone wall and looked up at the moonlight, shaking. I jumped when I heard the slam of the door behind me.

"So now you understand," Alejandro said quietly behind me.

"You're not the duke at all," I choked out, hardly able to believe it even as I said it. "The real Alejandro died in that crash, didn't he? Along with his parents. And your mother—the housekeeper."

"I had to do it." The only sign of emotion was the slight tightening of his jaw, the low tone of his voice. "Maurine had lost everything. And I loved her. Growing up in the castle, she'd always treated me like a grandson. And on that terrible day, the day of the crash, she lost everyone. When she came to see me at the hospital, she seemed to have aged ten years. She was so alone. I couldn't leave her to die in the dilapidated castle, with no one to take care of her...." Swallowing, he looked down at the cobblestoned street. Moonlight left a trail of silver on his dark silhouette as he said quietly, "So I told Maurine I would be her family from now on. Her grandson."

"How is it possible no one knew?"

"Alejandro and I looked very much alike. We were the same age, same build. And after the accident, my face was injured. We used that to explain the difference. Not that anyone asked. People had long since stopped coming to the castle. The duke and his family had chased most of the tenants away by harassing them over rents. Even their old society friends shunned them, since they were always asking to borrow money. Alejandro's parents felt ashamed of how far they'd fallen. Just not ashamed enough to work for something better." He looked up. "My mother was the only servant left, and she hadn't been paid in a year." Taking a deep breath, he said simply, "When Abuela claimed I was her grandson, and pawned the last of her jewelry to pay the transfer-of-title fees, no one questioned it."

"But a few people knew."

He nodded. "Pilar, our governess." He glanced at the restaurant door. "My older sister. Theresa."

My lips parted. "Your sister?"

"Half sister. She's eight years older. She was working in Granada when the accident happened. She rushed to the hospital as soon as she heard, but Abuela convinced her to keep the secret. They have all kept it. Because they love me. And they love Abuela." He looked away. "As I grew older, it felt wrong, stealing Alejandro's title and name. I promised myself that I would never marry, never have a child. The family line, and the family lie, would end with me. I convinced myself that was redemption."

I stared at him, tears now falling down my cheeks in the moonlight. "That was why you said you're no good at keeping promises," I whispered. "Because you had a child. And then you married me. I thought…" I shook my head. "I thought you meant you could never keep your promises of fidelity…."

"That I would cheat on you?" he said incredulously. He came closer, his face blazing with emotion as he reached out to cup my cheek. "From the moment we met, you've been the only woman I wanted. Even for the year we were apart—there was no one else for me. No one."

"But…when I told you I loved you…"

He gave a low, humorless laugh. He shook his head. "You really don't understand, do you? When I promised myself I'd never marry or have a child, I made sure I would keep that promise by only allowing myself to date women like Claudie…cold, sophisticated, heartless women I'd never be tempted to love. You were different. You were the woman I could not resist," he said softly. "You made me break every promise I'd made to myself. I wanted to tell you everything. Where you were concerned, I had no self-control."

I stared up at him, my lips parted.

"When I heard you were pregnant with my child, I was desperate to find you. But once I did, and we were wed, I suddenly knew I'd never be able to tell you the truth. At first, because I was afraid you'd use the information to blackmail me, and try to take my son away. Then because I owed it to Miguel. You were so proud our son would some-day be a duke.…"

"I never cared about that!" I said fiercely. "All I care about is you. And Miguel…" I looked up at him with an intake of breath. "Your real name is Miguel."

He gave me a wicked grin. "You can see why I didn't mind our son's name."

My knees shook, because my world was spinning. "But after we were married—surely then you knew you could trust me?"

"You have such an honest heart." He sobered. "I didn't want you to have the burden."

"Burden? Are you kidding?" I gave a laugh that was giddy, almost hysterical. "If you knew what I'd imagined…"

"It's worse than you think." His face had turned deadly

serious. "My grandmother and I both broke laws with our lies. We could be charged with fraud and possibly sent to prison. For myself, I would have been willing to take the risk, to tell you the truth. But Maurine..." He looked down. "I was afraid to take the risk, for her sake. The idea of her in jail..."

A sudden noise down the quiet street, perhaps a cat knocking over a trash can in a nearby alley, caused us both to jump. I looked at him.

"You can trust me. No one will ever know." I swallowed and whispered. "Did you really mean what you said in the tavern?"

"The song?"

"That you—" I blushed a little "—actually—love me?"

His eyes went wide. Then, with a low laugh, he pulled me in his arms.

"Oh, *querida*. I have loved you from almost the first moment we met. Your sweetness, your nobility, your honesty."

"I was so afraid.... I believed all the wrong things...."

Alejandro wrapped his hands around mine. "And now you hold my heart, my life, in your hands," he said quietly. "You have the power to take Miguel from me, to go back to Mexico, to walk away." He lifted his dark gaze to mine in the moonlight. "You own me completely. What will you do?"

"What will I do?" I whispered, tears in my eyes. Putting my arms around him, I pulled him close and pressed my forehead against his heart. "I will love you, Alejandro. Forever."

CHAPTER TEN

WE ROSE FOR a late breakfast the next morning, after a night in our hotel room with much giggling and even more love-making. As eager as I was to see our baby after a whole night away from him, I was also lingering, enjoying every last moment of this brief, perfect honeymoon.

No one would ever be able to part us again.

"I think," Alejandro said thoughtfully as we left the hotel, "that was the best honeymoon I've ever had."

"Best and only," I said.

"No, surely not only. Our marriage will be nothing but one long honeymoon," he said huskily, then to prove it, he kissed me. The kiss soon became so intense and deep that Alejandro muttered something about renting the room for another night, and started to pull me back toward the hotel.

"But we can't!" I protested with a laugh. "Miguel…"

"All right," he grumbled, then his eyes smoldered. "But I'm taking you back to our bedroom as fast as the car will go."

But at my request, we returned to Rohares the long way. He took me to the spot where legend said Boabdil, the last sultan of Spain, took his very last look at Granada, after he was forced to cede it to Spanish King Ferdinand and Queen Isabella.

"Oh, no. I left the guidebook at the hotel," I said sadly,

then brightened. "But I left my name in it. Hopefully they'll find it and call."

"A guidebook? Get another one!"

"It's a souvenir," I whispered, "of the happiest night of my life."

He kissed me, then standing on the hill, we looked back at Granada. "They say Boabdil wept when he looked his last upon his city," I said wistfully. "And his mother mocked his tears. She sneered that he was weeping like a woman for what he could not fight for as a man. Can you believe that?"

"People can say hurtful things to those they love," Alejandro said quietly. "Especially when they're backed into a corner and their own hearts are breaking."

As we drove back home, I suddenly realized Alejandro was right. I thought of all my anguished years feeling lonely in London, wishing hopelessly for my grandmother, my uncle and Claudie to love me. But they could not, because they did not know how. Instead, they'd relentlessly pursued the wrong things, luxury and status and appearance. They'd never known that the only way to gain happiness was not only to follow your heart, but to give it away.

Leaning over, Alejandro took my hand. Bringing it to his lips, he fervently kissed it. My eyes blurred with tears as I smiled at him, thinking how lucky I was.

And that was the moment I forgave my family for not loving me. Sometimes, I thought, you have to make your own family.

Blushing, I said shyly, "So what do I call you now?"

He looked at me. "I've grown fond of Alejandro. I'll let my son keep Miguel." He turned away, facing the road. His hands tightened on the steering wheel. "After we get back, I'm going to talk to a lawyer. I'll see if there's any way to renounce the title without causing risk to Maurine." He looked at me. "But it seems so much to ask of you."

"What?"

"Would you be heartbroken to give up the title of duchess—and know Miguel would never be a duke?"

"Are you kidding?" I gave a low laugh. "I'm happy to give it up. Do you really think I'm duchess material?"

He looked at me seriously. "Yes, *mi amor*. Yes."

"I'm happy as your wife," I whispered. "However that may be." And he squeezed my hand in his.

When we arrived at Rohares Castle, we hugged our baby and Maurine, who immediately started telling us every small detail of their extremely uneventful night, which mostly involved patty-cake and Miguel dozing as his great-grandmother read him Washington Irving's *Tales of the Alhambra*. "So Miguel felt part of the experience, too. It seemed appropriate...."

"Like his name," I said. Smiling, I glanced back at Alejandro. "It turns out I named him after his father."

With an intake of breath, Maurine looked between us. Then she gave a whoop of joy. "Took you long enough," she cried, then hugged us, telling us we were silly to be so emotional as she wiped her own eyes. "So. I, too, have news. The best news of all." Maurine looked between us, beaming. "While the two of you were on your honeymoon, I did something with your hairbrush...."

The house phone rang loudly from across the great room. Wondering if it might be the hotel calling about my guide-book, I said hurriedly, "Just a minute." Rushing across the room, I answered breathlessly, "Hello?"

"Don't say my name."

Edward?! I gritted my teeth and rasped, "I'm hanging up now."

"If you do, you'll be sorry."

Something about the cool confidence of his voice made me hesitate. "Why?"

"Because I know."

"What?"

"Everything."

A chill went down my spine. I tried to bluff. "Everything about what?"

"About your husband. And the lie he told twenty-three years ago."

The chill turned to ice. "I don't know what you're talking about."

He snorted, then said quietly, "I followed you to Granada. I was in the shadows on the street. When you came out alone from the restaurant, I was going to comfort you. Then your husband followed you out. And gave me all the ammunition I would ever need to destroy him. And that so-called grandmother of his."

Turning, I stared wide-eyed at Alejandro and Maurine across the great hall, where they were laughing together. I gripped the phone. "What do you want?"

"What I've always wanted. You."

"I don't love you—"

"Yes. I know. You love him. So if you want to protect him, this choice should be easy for you. I'm waiting in a car at the castle gate. Call the guard. Tell him to let me in."

"If I tell Alejandro how you're trying to blackmail me, he will kill you."

"I'm sure you're right. Which is why you won't tell him."

"You don't understand! That's not just an expression. He will literally kill you!"

"Let him try," he said flatly. "Tell him, if that's how you want this to go. I'm not afraid. I have nothing to lose." He paused. "Do you?"

I shuddered, trembling, afraid that Alejandro would really kill him, and he'd end up in jail not just for fraud, but for murder. "What do you want me to do?"

His voice was smooth and slick. "Tell him you've changed your mind about your marriage. Tell him you only wanted him when you thought he was a real duke, but now…you're in love with me."

Horror filled my heart. "He'll never believe it—"

"He *will*. That's what frightens you." He gave a low laugh. "Tell him you're going to spend tonight with me, and your lawyers will be in touch about divorce—and custody. That bit about custody is just for you, by the way. I'll let your baby live with us. Doesn't that show how much I care?"

"You never cared about me," I whispered. "If you did, you couldn't do this."

"I took care of you. I saved you. I earned you. Not him."

"I'm a human soul—not some trophy to be won!"

"You should be mine," he said coldly. "Let him watch you leave with me. Make him believe I'm the one you want. And I'll forget what I know. Do it for his sake. And the old woman's."

"Edward, please…"

"Three minutes. Then I'm calling a press conference."

"And he'll kill you!"

"Then Navaro will be in jail for the rest of his life. And your kid will have no father. Or great-grandmother. Make your choice. You say you really love them? Prove it."

The line clicked off.

My whole body shook as I hung up.

"Who was it?" Alejandro said behind me.

"N-nothing. I mean, no one."

"Which is it? Is something wrong?" His eyes were sharp. Of course he knew something was wrong. He saw right through me. Saw my anguished heart.

So how could I break his—with a lie?

And yet—how could I not?

Wide-eyed, I looked across the great hall toward Maurine, who at her age would likely never come back from the shock of a scandal and trial for fraud, much less being sent to prison. I looked at my sweet baby in his baby swing, who would endure the experience I'd feared most—being surrounded by paparazzi—before he lost his father. And Alejandro. I looked at him, hardly able to breathe. If he really did attack Edward as I feared...

I remembered the look in his eyes in Granada when I'd told him that Edward had visited me. I remembered the cold menace in his face.

I will kill him.

"Lena?" Alejandro frowned, coming closer. "Who was on the phone?"

The phone suddenly rang again. I picked it up.

"Your Excellency?" It was the security guard at the gate. "There's an Edward St. Cyr here. He has no appointment. Should I let him inside?"

I took a deep breath.

"Let him in," I said faintly, then hung up the phone. I picked up my handbag. I walked slowly toward my family, feeling as if I was going to die.

But I would die for them. I looked at those three beloved faces, in this beautiful old castle I'd already come to love. My family. My home. Would I do it? To save them?

Yes.

"Where are you going?" Alejandro said.

"I'm sorry." My teeth were chattering. My words were faint. "Our marriage is over. I'll be back tomorrow. So we can discuss c-custody...."

I stopped at the door. Alejandro was staring at me with open-mouthed shock. I was trembling so hard it was all I could do not to black out.

But it was the only way to save him. To save all of them.

I was the one who'd allowed Edward into our lives. I was the one who should pay for that. Not them.

But as I looked into Alejandro's face, I knew that he, too, would suffer. Squeezing my eyes shut, I turned away.

"Edward's come for me," I choked out. "I'm leaving with him now. We both know it never would have worked out with us, Alejandro. Not for long…"

"What are you saying?" he breathed, searching my gaze. "I don't believe you!"

"I'll be back with a lawyer—tomorrow.…" My voice ended on a sob. Whirling around, I fled for the door. Outside, I saw Edward waiting in an expensive SUV. The windows were all rolled down, the engine still running. Sobbing, I climbed in beside him. He gave me a triumphant, cruel smile.

"Wise choice," he said coldly. "Very smart."

"I don't feel smart," I whispered, hating myself, hating this choice already, wanting to do nothing more than jump out of the vehicle. And suddenly, that's just what I needed to do. "No. NO. I can't do this—"

Reaching over me, Edward put on my seat belt. It felt like a restraint.

"You'll soon be free of his influence," he said softly, reaching toward me. "I promise you."

I shuddered at his touch. "Don't!"

With a low laugh, he put down his hand. "Have it your way. I am a patient man.…"

But as he turned the steering wheel and started to drive down the circular courtyard, Alejandro was suddenly there, standing ahead of us, blocking the way to the road.

He wasn't looking at Edward. He was looking only at me. I saw his lips form my name.

"Make him believe you love me," Edward growled in a low voice. "Make him believe."

I licked my lips. I looked at Alejandro's stark face. The anguish in his dark eyes.

And I couldn't go through with it.

"I can't." My voice trembled as I started fumbling with my seat belt. "I can't do this. Let me out of here!"

"Too late," Edward said grimly, holding on to the latch as I tried to fight him.

Alejandro saw us struggling through the front window. Hands clenched at his sides, he started walking toward the SUV, now staring at Edward with narrowed eyes, his powerful warrior's body threatening his murder.

Edward's mouth twisted as their eyes met. He glared back, the same expression of murder in his face.

They both intended to kill or be killed today.

Over me.

With a low, cruel growl, Edward stomped on the gas, increasing speed as he drove the SUV straight at Alejandro, who was unprotected and alone in the castle courtyard.

But my husband didn't turn and run. He didn't back down. Instead, he started running straight at the car—as if a man could play chicken against seven thousand pounds of steel!

I screamed. Grabbing the steering wheel, I twisted it hard to the left. Veering off balance, Edward's SUV crashed into the stone fountain and twisted, then flew, high into the air.

As if in slow motion, I felt us fly up, up, up, at the same time we flipped in sickening circles, around and around. We hit the ground with a bone-jarring crunch and rolled down the long hill, all the way down. Then, with a shudder and metallic groan, the SUV was still.

I wasn't dead. I was upside down, held into the passenger seat by the taut seat belt that had knocked the air out of me, leaving a streak of pain where it crossed my chest.

Panting, I looked over at the driver's seat. It was empty. Edward was gone.

"Lena!" Alejandro cried. A moment later, my door was wrenched open, and suddenly he was there. He yanked open the seat belt, and caught me in his strong arms as I fell.

Cradling me desperately, my husband sank to the ground,

still holding me against his chest. He ran his hands over my body, found no life-ending injury and exhaled, holding me tight against him, rocking me in his lap. "Oh, my love," he choked out. "You're safe. You're safe. For a moment I thought..." He looked at me fiercely. "Don't ever do that to me again!"

"I'm sorry," I wept, pressing my head against his chest. "He learned the truth and said if I didn't come with him, he would ruin your life and Maurine's and even Miguel's. I couldn't risk you going to jail for the rest of your life—"

"I'd rather be sent to jail for a million years," he said hoarsely, "than lose you." I felt his body trembling beneath me. Reaching up in amazement, I brushed away a single tear trailing down his tanned, hard-edged cheek.

Pressing my forehead to his, I whispered, "Thank you for not letting me go."

He cupped my face, looked me straight in the eyes. "Never. We are forever...."

A low growl made us both turn.

"You'll be sorry." We turned to see Edward collapsed on the grass, where he'd been flung from the vehicle, across the hill. "Both of you," he panted, "will be sorry."

Alejandro's hands tightened on me. I looked up at him in terror. "Don't kill him. It's not worth it. Remember you promised you'd never leave me...."

"Kill him?" He looked at me incredulously. "Why should I? Look at him...."

For the first time, I noticed the odd way Edward's arms and legs were stretched out in unnatural directions on the grass. But even his body wasn't as contorted as his face.

"I'll tell the world," Edward panted, "how you all committed fraud. I'll ruin your lives both of you—the old woman and that baby, too...."

Alejandro glared at Edward, parting his lips to answer. But someone else beat him to it.

"Calm down, dear. You're acting crazy."

Maurine stepped calmly between us on the hill. She peered down at Edward benignly, as if about to offer him cookies at a party, and the upside-down SUV behind us, with its crushed steel doors and a wheel still spinning, was just a decoration, like fairy lights or balloons. "Whatever you think is wrong, Alejandro is my grandson."

Edward gave a hard laugh. "It's a lie." He coughed. "I'll prove it when I get the court order for a blood test...."

"You know, I always wondered." She smiled, then looked at Alejandro, who was still on the ground, holding me protectively in his lap. She gave a brisk nod. "I was about to tell you, before all the fuss broke out. The hairbrush. You're my grandson, Alejandro. Really and truly. The grandson of my heart." She gave us a broad, self-satisfied smile. "Also a grandson of a DNA test."

I felt Alejandro jump. His face was pale.

"What...?" he breathed.

"The silly secret was just causing such a problem between you two." She looked between us severely. "And the way you were botching things. It just was ridiculous. Honestly, I'd always wondered why your mother stayed on as housekeeper for all those years, even when my son wasn't paying her. And then there was that family resemblance.... Anyway. It never mattered to me one way or the other. Until it started to interfere with your happiness." She grinned. "So I took your hairbrush and had a DNA test. You are my grandson, Alejandro. By heart, as you always were. But also by blood."

"No!" Edward screamed. Then he was suddenly quiet. I think he had fainted from pain.

Rather vengefully, I hoped he had. Although I didn't want him to die, of course. I didn't. Really, I didn't.

Alejandro's eyes were wide. "Is this true, Abuela?"

She nodded. "Remain the Duke of Alzacar, and if anyone wants to check if you are my grandson, let them." She looked at him and said quietly, "There is no one left in the family to inherit, if not you. No one you're cheating of his rightful due. And let me tell you something more. You're the finest duke of them all."

I saw him blinking suspiciously fast. He rose to his feet, helping me to rise, as well. He hugged his grandmother, then pulled me into the embrace. When we finally pulled away, I wiped my eyes, then glanced over at Edward, still unconscious.

"We should call an ambulance, do you think?"

"I can see him breathing," Maurine said with a dismissive wave of her hand. "He's fine." She sighed. "But I'll call." She glanced at Alejandro. "And I expect the *policia* will want to come, as well...."

She went toward the castle, and Alejandro looked at me.

"She's right. We have only a few moments before the police arrive," he said quietly. "A choice must be made."

"So make it," I said, trusting whatever he'd decide.

He clawed back his hair. "I am tired of secrets. Tired of lies." He turned to me. "I never want another secret to shadow the light between us."

I nodded, unable to speak over the lump in my throat.

"So." He smiled at me, blinking fast, then gave a decisive nod. He walked over to Edward, who was still unconscious, his legs stretched out at a painful angle. He put his fingertips to the other man's neck, then straightened.

"Is he—dead?" I said. Not hopefully. Really.

He shook his head. "His pulse is strong. He will recover."

"Too bad," I said.

Alejandro looked at me in amazement. Coming back, he wrapped his arms around me. "It's not like you to be bloodthirsty, *mi amor*," he murmured.

"I can be dangerous—" I reached up my hand to caress his cheek "—when it comes to protecting those I love."

"Yes." The corners of his sensual mouth quirked. Then his expression became serious. "But are you brave enough to face what lies ahead? There will be scandal. Or worse. Though perhaps I can protect Maurine...."

"How?"

"I will say that she was distraught over her family's death, and that I tricked her into believing I was her grandson."

"Oh, she won't like that at all."

"No," he agreed. He looked at me, emotion in his dark eyes. "Can you bear it, Lena? The storm that might come? Miguel will lose his legacy...."

"You're wrong." I put my hand on his cheek. My eyes were watery. "His legacy is more than some title. It's doing the right thing, even when it's hard."

"And love," Alejandro whispered, pressing my hands together as he kissed them fervently. "Loving for all your life, with all your heart."

"It's family, always and forever." Looking up at my husband, I smiled through my tears. "And whatever may come—our forever has already begun."

There are all kinds of ways to make a family.

Some ways are big, such as the way Maurine took in an orphaned twelve-year-old boy and insisted on claiming him as her grandson.

Some ways are small, such as when I sent an invitation to my wedding reception to my cousin Claudie.

Autumn had arrived at Rohares Castle, and with it harvest season for our tenants. The summer heat had subsided, leaving a gorgeous swath of vivid colors, of morning mists and early twilight, full of excuses to sip oceans of hot tea with milk in the morning and go to bed early with my husband with a bottle of ruby-red wine. Every night, we lit a fire in the fireplace—and in our bed. And that fire, as months passed, seemed only to get bigger and brighter.

Just that morning, Maurine had caught us kissing in the breakfast room. She'd laughed. "I don't think the honeymoon will really ever end for you two," she said affectionately. Then the doorbell rang, and she'd hurried from the room with a desperate cry: "The florist! Finally!" And we were alone.

I'd given Alejandro a sensual smile.

"Could I interest you in a little more honeymoon?" I said, batting my eyes coyly, to which my husband whispered, "All day, every day," before he kissed me senseless, then picked me up like a Neanderthal and carried me upstairs, back to bed.

Now, the crowded banqueting hall was lit up for evening, bedecked gloriously in autumn flowers in the most beautiful wedding reception I'd ever imagined. Across the crowds of our guests, I caught Alejandro's eye. He smiled back at me hungrily, as if it had been a year since he'd last taken me to bed, instead of just a few hours. His hot glance almost made me forget we were surrounded by family and friends.

"I told you he would be your husband," a voice crowed behind me. "I always can tell!"

"You were right." Turning, I smiled at Dolores, my neighbor from San Miguel de Allende who'd been whisked here from Mexico for the reception. She'd been equal parts impressed and triumphant when Alejandro had sent a private jet to collect her.

I'd sent Mr. Corgan, Mrs. Morris and Hildy a first-class ticket here from London. They were still working for Claudie. "But she's mellowed a great deal since she became Mrs. Crosby," the butler informed me. "He's rich, and that has made her very happy."

But I could see that for myself. Claudie had arrived at

my door swathed in fur, with her brand-new husband at her side.

"I'm going to give you your inheritance back," was the first thing she announced to me. "David said it's the right thing to do. And besides—" she grinned "—we can afford it."

Same old Claudie, I thought. And yet not exactly the same. "Thank you," I said in surprise. I paused, then smiled. "Donate it to charity. Introduce me to your husband?"

She beamed. "I'd love to."

David Crosby was fat, short and bald, but he was indeed very rich, a king of Wall Street. They looked totally wrong together. Until you saw the way they looked at each other.

Claudie told me they'd met through a matchmaking service just for rich people.

"Trophy wives for billionaires?" I guessed.

"After all, Lena," she sniffed, "not everyone can manage to randomly fall pregnant by the love of their lives."

"No, indeed," I said.

"And I'm so happy…" she said wistfully, and I thought that she, too, must have been very lonely in London.

"I'm happy for you, truly," I said, and impulsively hugged her. My cousin stiffened, then let me hug her. I was encouraged. We weren't exactly best friends, but it was a start. And after all, we *were* family.…

Pulling away, she wiped her eyes. "At least you dress better now. Your style used to make me physically ill."

Distant family, thankfully.

But Alejandro and I were surrounded by people who cared about us. I looked around at all the people who were here, celebrating our marriage. Thinking with relief about the one who was not.

I still woke up in a cold sweat occasionally, thinking how I'd almost lost everything by getting into Edward St. Cyr's SUV that day.

Edward, sadly, had lived.

Oops, did I say that out loud?

Yes, he lived. From what I'd heard, he'd had an easier time than he deserved. A punctured lung and five broken bones. When the ambulance and police arrived, he'd refused to press charges against anyone, or even talk about the accident. But as he'd been lifted into the ambulance, our eyes had met, and he'd coldly and silently turned his face to the wall. He was done with me. A fact that left me profoundly grateful.

I tried to wish him well, because he had once been my friend.

Okay, but seriously. He'd tried to run over my husband with his Range Rover. That's not the kind of thing I could ever forgive, or forget. So mostly I just tried not to think of it.

Because we had so many other things to be grateful for. As I stood in the banqueting hall of our castle, wearing flowers in my hair and a blue silk gown, I caught Alejandro's eyes across the crowd. And I suddenly didn't see all the princes and farmers, starlets and secretaries, or the happy mix of our neighbors and friends. I didn't see the champagne, or the amazing food, or the flowers hung joyously across the rafters amid a profusion of music and laughter. When I met my husband's gaze, I shivered, and no one else existed.

Alejandro had contacted a lawyer and confessed everything. With the lawyer's advice, he'd thrown himself on the mercy of the court. As Maurine's DNA test had proved, he was the duke's heir, and his only heir at that, and so the group of nobles who oversaw this type of thing decided to allow him to keep his title. He'd also kept the name. Apparently the combination of money and being a direct blood descendant made a big difference. Suddenly, no one was using the word *fraud*.

The scandal was intense, though. For weeks, our castle had been under siege, with crowds of reporters shaking our gates, clamoring for a picture or an interview. But since no one on the estate or in the nearby town would talk, even the scandal died eventually, especially when the Hollywood star I'd seen at Alejandro's party in Madrid had been discovered naked, drunk and belligerent at the base of the Eiffel Tower. Bless her heart. The paparazzi eventually melted away, as our story was old news. Just in time for our reception today, too.

Tomorrow was Alejandro's birthday. His *real* birthday. I would give him the painting of Miguel and Maurine, and show him the brand-new photo album I'd begun for our family. On the back page, I'd tucked in a picture of a sonogram. We were going to have another baby sometime next summer, when the jacaranda trees were in bloom.

I could hardly wait to give Alejandro his gift....

I heard a clank of silverware against crystal. "Everyone. Could I have your attention?" Looking up, I saw Alejandro holding up his champagne glass. "I'd like to thank all our family and friends for coming today...."

"Any time you want to send your private jet," someone shouted.

"Or first-class tickets!"

"Or help me pave my garden path—how's Wednesday?"

There was scattered laughter, and a few tipsy cheers.

Alejandro grinned. "I'd also like to thank my grandmother for doing such a wonderful job designing this party...."

"Darn straight," Maurine said stoutly, holding our smiling baby in her arms. Miguel, though barefoot as he did not like shoes, was suitably dressed in a baby tuxedo.

"I'd like to thank our baby son for sleeping so well at night...."

Darn straight, I echoed, but didn't say aloud.

"But most of all—" Alejandro's dark eyes glowed with tenderness that took my breath away as he looked at me "—I'd like to thank my beautiful wife. Lena. You gave me the family I never dreamed I could have. Just waking up in your arms every morning is a heaven beyond what any mortal man should deserve. But I will spend the rest of my life trying." He held up the flute. "To family. Forever."

"Family forever," everyone cried, with the greatest cheer of all.

"Thank you," I said to them. I blinked fast, smiling with tears in my eyes. "I love you all." I looked at my husband. "Especially you."

Coming through the crowd, Alejandro took me in his arms, and kissed me soundly in front of everyone. And I kissed him back. Oh, boy, you bet I did.

It was crazy. Just a year ago, I'd been so scared and alone. I'd hated Alejandro. I'd thought I would remain a single mother forever.

The disastrous night we were married in Madrid, Alejandro said sometimes fate chooses better for us than we can choose for ourselves. But I think there's more to it.

It's not just fate. You create your own future, step by step, by being brave. By doing the right thing. By telling the truth. By trying your best.

By reaching for the man you love, and giving him the chance to reach back, pull you into his arms and finally show you the man he really is inside—the powerful, infuriating, sexy, compassionate man whom no one else will ever truly know.

Love, like trust, is earned. It is kept, day by day, night by night, as we reveal to each other who we were. Who we are. And most of all, who we hope to be.

* * * * *

A NIGHT,
A CONSEQUENCE,
A VOW

ANGELA BISSELL

For Bron – author, mentor and friend.
Your support and encouragement have
meant the world.

CHAPTER ONE

'YOU OWE ME for this, Xav.'

Ramon de la Vega dropped into a chair in front of his brother's desk and stretched out his legs.

Eight hours on a transatlantic commercial flight, another hour in the back of a company limo inching through endless queues of bumper-to-bumper traffic, and he felt as if he'd been straitjacketed for a week.

His mood carefully harnessed, he lounged back and perched his feet on the corner of his brother's desk. 'I had planned to spend the weekend in Vegas,' he added.

His brother, Xavier, sat in a high-backed chair on the other side of the massive oak desk—an antique heirloom their father had handed down along with the company reins to his eldest son. Behind him a thick pane of wall-to-wall glass framed a sweeping view of Barcelona that drew no more than a brief, disinterested glance from Ramon. Instead, he focused on his brother, who looked impossibly cool and immaculate in a dark tailored suit in spite of the mid-August heat. As always, Xav's features were stern, his posture stiff. Only his right hand moved, his fingertips drumming an incessant beat on the desktop's fine leather inlay.

The sound, amplified by the dearth of any other in the vast corner office, penetrated Ramon's eardrums like a blunt needle and reminded him that flying and alcohol made for an unwise mix.

'Doing what?' Xav's voice carried the hint of a sneer. 'Gambling or womanising?'

Ramon ignored the disdain in his brother's voice and unleashed his grin—the one he knew could fell a woman at fifty paces. Or tease the tension out of an uptight client in a matter of seconds. Against his only sibling, however, the impact was negligible. 'It is called recreation, brother.' He kept his tone light. 'You should try it some time.'

The deep plunge of Xav's eyebrows suggested he'd sooner lose an arm than indulge in such hedonistic pursuits. His fingers stopped drumming—*mercifully*—and curled into a loose fist. 'Get your feet off my desk.' His gaze raked over Ramon's jeans and shirt before snapping back to his feet. 'And where the hell are your shoes?'

Ramon dropped his feet to the floor. His loafers were… He squinted, trying to remember where he'd left them. *Ah, yes.* In the outer office. Under the desk of the pretty brunette whose name had already escaped him. He considered the rest of his appearance: stonewashed designer jeans; a loose open-necked white shirt, creased from travel; and a jaw darkened by eighteen-plus hours' worth of stubble. A far cry from his brother's impeccable attire and his own usual standard, but a man had to travel in comfort. Especially when his brother had had the nerve to issue an urgent summons and then deny him use of the company jet.

Ramon made a mental note.

Buy my own plane.

At least the curvy redheaded flight attendant in First Class who'd served him meals and refreshments during the flight from New York hadn't minded his attire. But, yes, for the Vega Corporation's head office in the heart of Barcelona's thriving business district, he was most definitely under-dressed.

Still, Xav needed to chill. Cut him some slack. He had ditched everything, including a weekend in Las Vegas with his old Harvard pals, and flown nearly four thousand miles across the North Atlantic—all because his brother had called out of the blue and told him he needed him.

Needed him, no less.

Words Ramon had once imagined would never tumble from his proud brother's mouth.

Yet, incredibly, they had.

Beyond that surprising entreaty, Xav had offered no more by way of explanation and Ramon had not demanded one. As CEO, Xav technically outranked him but it wasn't his seniority that commanded Ramon's loyalty. Xav was family. And when it came to family there was one truth Ramon could never escape.

He owed them.

Still, he allowed his grin to linger. Not because his mood leaned towards humour—nothing about being back in Spain tickled his funny bone—but rather because he knew it would irritate his brother. 'Flying makes my feet swell,' he said, 'and your secretary offered to massage them while you were wrapping up your meeting.'

A look of revulsion slid over Xav's face. 'Please tell me you are joking.'

'*Sí*, brother.' Ramon broadened his grin. 'I am.'

Though he *had* got the impression as he'd kicked off his shoes and settled in for a friendly chat with… Lola?… Lorda?…that she'd happily massage a lot more than his feet if he gave her half a chance. And maybe he would if she was willing. Because God knew he'd need a distraction while he was here. Some way to escape the toxic memories that sooner or later would defy his conscious mind and claw their way to the surface.

Xav pinched the bridge of his nose, a *Lord give me patience* gesture that reminded Ramon of their father, Vittorio. Not that any likeness could be attributed to genetics: Xav had been adopted at birth by their parents after two failed pregnancies. Four years later Ramon had come along—the miracle child the doctors had told his mother she'd never conceive let alone carry to term.

Miracle Child.

The moniker made Ramon's gut burn. He hated it. He was no heaven-sent miracle. Just ask the Castano family, or the Mendosas. No doubt they would all vehemently agree and then, for good measure, throw in a few fitting alternatives.

Ramon could think of one or two himself.

Like Angel of Death.

Or maybe Devil Incarnate.

He snapped his thoughts out of the dark mire of his past. This was why he gave Spain a wide berth whenever possible. Too many ghosts lurked here. Too many reminders. 'Tell me why I'm here,' he demanded, his patience dwindling.

'There's a board meeting tomorrow.'

He frowned. 'I thought the next quarterly meeting was six weeks from now.' He made a point of knowing when the board meetings were scheduled for so he could arrange to be elsewhere. In his experience, day-long gatherings with a bunch of pedantic, censorious old men were a special brand of torture to be studiously avoided. 'Since when does our board meet on a Saturday?'

'Since I decided to call an emergency meeting less than twenty-four hours ago.'

Ramon felt his mood start to unravel. 'Why the hell didn't you say over the phone it was a board meeting you were dragging me over here for?'

'Because you would have found an excuse not to come,' Xav snapped. 'You would rather waste your time at a poker table—or buried between the legs of some entirely unsuitable woman!'

Ramon's brows jerked down. 'That's out of order,' he growled.

Abruptly Xav stood up, stalked to the window behind him and stared out. Ramon glowered at his back. Xav *was* out of order. Yes, Ramon avoided the boardroom. Pandering to the board, keeping the old cronies happy, was his brother's responsibility. Not his. But no one could deny that he gave his pound of flesh to the Vega Corporation. He'd done so every year for the last five years, in fact. Ever since he'd accepted the vice-presidential role his father had offered him on his twenty-fifth birthday. He'd side-lined his architectural career. Gone from designing luxury hotels and upscale entertainment complexes to buying them and overseeing their management.

He'd excelled—and he'd realised in that first year of working hard to prove himself that this was how he could repay his family. How he could compensate in a tangible way for the pain he'd inflicted, the destruction his eighteen-year-old self had wrought and the shame he'd brought on his family. He could stamp his mark on the business. Contribute to its success.

It had been a tall order. The de la Vega empire was well-established. Successful. It spanned continents and industries, from construction and real estate to hospitality and entertainment. Any contribution Ramon made had to be significant.

He had risen to the challenge.

First with his acquisition of the Chastain Group—a collection of luxury resorts and boutique hotels which had doubled Vega Corporation's market share on the European continent, and then with the expansion of their portfolio of private members' clubs into a lucrative network of sophisticated high-end establishments.

Yes, he had made his mark.

And yet to his brother—and most of the board—the spectacular results he'd achieved year upon year seemed to matter far less than how he chose to conduct his personal life.

It rankled.

He didn't deliberately court the press but neither did he

waste his time trying to dodge the attention. Evade one paparazzo and ten more would materialise from the shadows. It was easier to give them what they wanted. Flash his trademark grin at the cameras, drape his arm around the waist of a beautiful woman and the tabloids and their gossip-hungry readers would be satisfied.

But dare to deny them and they'd stalk you like prey. Look for scandal where none existed. Or, worse, where it *did* exist. And the last thing he needed was someone digging into his past and shining a spotlight on his teenage transgressions. Nurturing his playboy reputation served a purpose. The tabloids saw what he wanted them to see. A successful, wealthy, aristocratic bachelor who pursued pleasure as doggedly as he pursued his next acquisition.

He reined in his anger. 'Why an emergency meeting?'

Xav turned, his expression grim. 'Hector is making a play for the chairman's role.'

Ramon narrowed his eyes. 'I thought you and Papá had earmarked Sanchez for the role,' he said, referring to their newest and most dynamic board member—an accomplished former leader of industry who Xav had persuaded the board to accept in an attempt to inject some fresh blood into the company's governance. Aside from Xav and their father, who was about to retire as Chairman, Sanchez was the only board member for whom Ramon had any genuine respect.

Hector, on the other hand, was a nightmare. Their father's second cousin, he craved power and status and resented anyone who possessed more than he did. The man was self-centred. Narrow-minded. Not figurehead material.

Ramon shook his head in disbelief. 'He'll never get the support he needs.'

'He already has it.' Xav dropped into his chair, nostrils flaring. 'He's been working behind my back, garnering support for a coup. Persuading the others that voting in Sanchez is a bad move.'

'Surely Papá can pull him into line?'

His brother threw him a look.

'Papá has already taken a step back. He's too unwell for such drama—something you would know if you made an effort to visit more often,' Xav said, the glint in his eyes hard. Accusatory.

A sharp jolt went through Ramon. He knew their father had high blood pressure, and had suffered from mild attacks of angina over the past two years, but he hadn't been aware of Vittorio's more recent decline. He tightened his jaw against the surge of guilt. He kept his distance from family gatherings for a reason. There was too much awkwardness there. Too many things left unsaid. No. Ramon would not let his brother guilt trip him. He did everyone a favour, himself included, by staying away.

'The board members respect you,' he pointed out, marshalling his thoughts back to the business at hand. 'Win them back.'

Xav's jaw clenched. He shook his head. 'Whatever diamond-studded carrot Hector is dangling to coerce their support, it's working. Lopez, Ruben, Anders and Ramirez have all avoided my calls this week.'

Ramon dragged a thumb over his bristled chin. 'So what's the purpose of the meeting?'

'To confront Hector out in the open. Force him to reveal his hand and compel the others to choose a side—show where their loyalties lie so we know what we're up against.'

'"We"?'

'I need your support. As does Sanchez, if we've any chance of seeing him voted in as Chairman. We need to provide a united front. A *strong* front. One that'll challenge Hector and test his alliances.'

A single bark of laughter escaped Ramon. 'I cannot see

how my presence will help your cause,' he said, and yet even as he spoke he could feel the sharp, addictive surge of adrenalin he always experienced in the face of a challenge.

Something else rose in him, too. A sense of familial duty he couldn't deny. A compulsion to help his brother.

He studied Xav's face for a moment. It wasn't only anger carving deep grooves around his brother's mouth.

'You're worried,' he observed. 'Why?'

'The Klein deal went belly up.'

Without thinking, Ramon pursed his lips and let out a low whistle. Xav's expression darkened.

'I'm sorry,' Ramon said, his sympathy genuine. He too had suffered the occasional business failure. Had experienced the disappointment and utter frustration that came after investing countless hours of manpower and resources into a potential deal only to see it fall over at the eleventh hour. 'You're concerned that your credibility with the board is damaged,' he surmised.

'Hector's already laid the failure squarely on my doorstep. Called my judgement into question.' Xav's voice grated with disgust. 'He'll use it to undermine the board's confidence in me. We need a win to regain the board's trust. Something that will make them forget about the Klein debacle and give us some leverage.' He sat forward, his grey eyes intense. 'Have you managed to secure a meeting with Royce yet?'

Ramon felt his spine tighten.

Speaking of failures.

'Not yet,' he said carefully.

Xav leaned back, the intensity in his eyes dimming. He breathed out heavily. 'It was always going to be a long shot.'

His tone was dismissive enough to needle under Ramon's skin. Setting his sights on The Royce—one of London's oldest, most prestigious and highly exclusive private clubs—was ambitious, but his brother shouldn't be so quick to underestimate him.

'Have a little faith, brother,' he said. 'I've hit a minor roadblock, that's all. Nothing I can't handle.'

'A roadblock?'

'Royce has a gatekeeper.' He downplayed the matter with a one-shoulder shrug. 'Getting access to him is proving…a challenge.'

Xav's frown deepened. 'Do they not know who you are?' His voice rang with a note of hauteur. 'Surely the de la Vega name is sufficient to grant you an audience with Royce?'

Ramon nearly barked out another derisory laugh.

The importance of the family name had always carried more weight in Xav's eyes than his. Their mother and her siblings were distant cousins of the King of Spain and directly descended from a centuries-old line of dukes. Marry that blue-blood lineage to the vast wealth and success of their father's industrialist family and the de la Vega name, since the early eighties when their parents had wedded, had been inextricably linked with affluence and status.

'Are you forgetting the clientele The Royce serves?' He watched Xav silently bristle over the fact that their family's power and influence, while not insignificant, did not merit any special recognition in this instance. Not from an establishment that catered to some of the wealthiest, most powerful men in the world.

'And yet if there is truth to the rumours you've heard, Maxwell Royce is not selective about the company he keeps. Surely a meeting with you is not beneath him?'

Ramon sensed a subtle insult in that statement. He gritted his teeth for a second before speaking. 'It's not rumour. The information I received comes from a trusted source. It's reliable.'

As reliable as it had been surprising, for the discreet disclosure had come from his friend Christophe completely out of the blue. 'Royce has a gambling problem and mounting debts,' he said. 'It came from the mouth of his own accountant.' Who apparently, after indulging in one too many Manhattans in a London cocktail bar with a pretty long-legged accountant—who happened to be Christophe's sister—had spilled the dirt on his employer. Christophe's sister had relayed the tale to her brother and Christophe, never one to sit idly on useful information, had called Ramon.

'Where trouble resides, so does opportunity,' he said, voicing a belief that had served him well over the years when scouting out potential acquisitions. People resistant to selling could quickly change their tune when faced with a financial crisis. A buyout offer or business proposal that had previously been rejected could suddenly seem an attractive option.

The Royce had been owned by the same family for over a hundred years, but it wasn't uncommon for third or fourth generation owners to opt to sell the family business. For legacies to be sacrificed expediently in favour of hard cash. And if Maxwell Royce needed cash… It was an opportunity too tempting not to pursue, long shot or not. Ramon's clubs were exclusive, sophisticated and world-class but The Royce was in a whole different league—one that only a dozen or so clubs on the planet could lay claim to. An establishment so revered would elevate his portfolio to a whole new level.

Xav sat forward again. 'I don't need to tell you how much an acquisition of this nature would impress the board.'

Ramon understood. It would be the win his brother was so desperately seeking. A way to cut Hector's critical narrative off at the knees, wrestle back control of the board and regain the directors' confidence.

'Deal with Royce's gatekeeper, whoever he is, and get that meeting,' Xav urged. *'Soon.'*

Ramon didn't care for his brother's imperious tone, but

he bit his tongue. Xav was under pressure. He'd asked for Ramon's support. How often did that happen?

Not often.

Besides, Ramon had as much desire as Xav to see Hector at the company's helm.

He thought of the obstacle in his path.

Not a *he*, as Xav had assumed, but a *she*.

A slender, blonde, not unattractive *she* who had, in recent weeks, proved something of a conundrum for Ramon.

He'd readily admit it was a rare occasion he came across a woman he couldn't charm into giving him what he wanted.

This woman would not be charmed.

Three times in two weeks she'd rejected him by phone, informing him in her very chilly, very proper, British accent that Mr Royce was too busy to receive unsolicited visitors.

Ramon had been undeterred. Confident he could net a far more desirable result in person, he'd flown to London and turned up at the club's understated front door on a quiet, dignified street in the heart of fashionable Mayfair.

As expected, security had been discreet but efficient. As soon as he'd been identified as a visitor and not a member, a dark-suited man had ushered him around the outside of the stately brick building to a side entrance. Like the simple, black front door with its decorative brass knocker, the black and white marble vestibule in which he'd been left to wait was further evidence of The Royce's quiet, restrained brand of elegance.

Ramon had got quite familiar with that vestibule. He'd found himself with enough time on his hands to count the marble squares on the floor fifty times over, plus make a detailed study of the individual mouldings on the ornate Georgian ceiling.

Because she had made him wait. Not for ten minutes. Not for twenty, or even forty. But for an *hour*.

Only through sheer determination and the freedom to stand up, stretch his legs and pace back and forth across the polished floor now and again had he waited her out.

After a while it felt like a grim little game between them, a challenge to see who'd relent first—him or her.

Ramon won, but his victory was limited to the brief surge of satisfaction that came when she finally appeared.

'You do not have an appointment, Mr de la Vega.' Grey eyes, so pale they possessed an extraordinary luminescence, flashed at him from out of a heart-shaped face, while the rest of her expression appeared carefully schooled.

Pretty, he thought upon first impression, but not his type. Too reserved. Too buttoned-up and prim. He preferred his women relaxed. Uninhibited. 'Because you would not give me one,' he responded easily.

'And you think I will now, just because you're here in person?'

'I think Mr Royce would benefit from the opportunity to meet with me,' he said smoothly. 'An opportunity you seem intent on denying him.'

The smile she bestowed on him then was unlike the smiles he was accustomed to receiving from women. Those smiles ranged from shy to seductive, and everything in between, but always they telegraphed some level of awareness and heat and, in many cases, a brazen invitation. But the tilt of her lips was neither warm nor inviting. It suggested sufferance, along with a hint of condescension.

'Let me tell you what *I* think, Mr de la Vega,' she said, her voice somehow sweet and icy at the same time—like a frozen dessert that gave you a painful case of brain freeze when you bit into it. 'I think I know Mr Royce better than you do and am therefore infinitely more qualified to determine what he will—and won't—find of benefit. I also think you underestimate my intelligence. I know who you are and I know there's only one reason you could want to meet with Mr Royce. So let me make something clear to you right now and save you some time. The Royce is *not* for sale.'

Colour had bloomed on her pale cheekbones, the streaks of pink an arresting contrast to her glittering grey eyes.

Interesting, he thought. Perhaps there was a bit of fire beneath that cool facade. He held out his business card and took a step towards her but she reared back, alarm flaring in her eyes as if he had crossed some invisible, inviolable boundary. *Huh*. Even more interesting. 'Ten minutes of Mr Royce's time,' he said. 'That is all I am asking for.'

'You're wasting your time. Mr Royce is not here.'

'Then perhaps you would call me when he is. I'll be in London for another forty-eight hours.'

He continued to hold out his card and finally she took it, exercising great care to ensure her fingers didn't brush against his. Then she gave him that smile again and this time it had the strangest effect, igniting a spark of irritation, followed by a rush of heat in the pit of his stomach. He imagined kissing that haughty little smile right off her pretty face. Backing her up against one of the hard marble pillars, taking her head in his hands and devouring her mouth under his until her lips softened, opened and she granted him entry.

Carefully he neutralised his expression, shocked by the direction of his thoughts. He'd never taken a woman with force. He had no aversion to boisterous sex, and he'd indulged more than one bed partner who demanded it rough and fast, but on the whole Ramon liked his lovers soft. Compliant. Willing.

She took another step back from him, the flush of pink in her cheeks growing more hectic, her eyes widening slightly. As if somehow she'd read his thoughts. 'Mr Royce will not be available this week,' she said, her smile replaced now by a thin, narrow-eyed stare. 'So unless you have extraor-

dinary lung capacity, Mr de la Vega, I suggest you don't
hold your breath.'

And she turned and walked away from him, high heels
clicking on the shiny chequered marble as she made for
the door across the small foyer from which she'd emerged.

She had a spectacular backside. Somehow Ramon's
brain had registered that fact, his gaze transfixed by the
movement of firm, shapely muscle under her navy blue
pencil skirt even as a wave of anger and frustration had
crashed through him.

The sound of Xav's desk phone ringing jolted him back
to the present. He shifted in his chair.

Xav placed his hand on the receiver and looked at him.
'Speak with Lucia on your way out,' he said. 'I told her to
make a dinner reservation for us this evening. Get the details off her and I'll see you at the restaurant. We'll talk
more then.'

Ah. Lucia. Yes, that was the name of his brother's secretary. Not Lola or Lorda. Ironic that he couldn't recall
the name of the attractive brunette he'd just met, and had
already considered sleeping with, yet he had no trouble
summoning the name of the English woman he'd rather
throttle than bed.

Her name, it seemed, was indelibly inked on his brain,
along with the enticing image of her tight, rounded pos-
terior.

Emily.

EMILY ROYCE SAT behind her desk and took a deep breath that somehow failed to fill her lungs. For a moment she thought she might be sick and the feeling sent a rising tide of disbelief through her.

This was not how she reacted to bad news. Emily had learnt how to handle disappointment a long time ago. She did not buckle under its weight. When bad news came, she received it with equanimity. Practicality. Calm.

And yet there was no denying the sudden stab of nausea in her belly. Or the cold, prickling sensation sweeping over her skin.

She dug her fingers into the arms of her chair, some dark corner of her mind imagining her father's neck beneath her clenched hands.

She was going to kill him.

At the very least she was going to hunt him down, drag him out of whichever opulent hotel suite or illicit den of pleasure he was currently holed up in and yell at him until she was hoarse.

Except she wouldn't.

Emily knew she wouldn't.

Because no matter how many times in her life she'd imagined venting her anger, letting loose even a bit of the hurt and disappointment she'd stored up and kept tightly lidded over the years, she never had.

And this time would be no different. She would do what she always did. What she had to do. She would shove her emotions aside and pour all her energy into limiting the damage. Into doing whatever was necessary to sweep Maxwell Royce's latest indiscretion under the rug and in so doing keep his reputation—and, by association, the reputation of The Royce—intact.

Only this time, if what she had just been told was true, Maxwell had outdone himself. He'd created a situation so dire she struggled to accept that even he could have done such a stupid, irresponsible, *selfish* thing.

And this would not be a mere matter of slipping a wad of cash to some unscrupulous opportunist to prevent embarrassing, compromising photos of her father from finding their way to the tabloids. Or of dipping into her personal savings and hastily rebalancing the club's books, with the help of their accountant, to cover up Maxwell's misappropriation of funds from one of their business accounts.

Not that any of her father's prior indiscretions could be labelled trivial, but this…*this*…

Her grandfather would turn in his grave. As would his father, and his father before him.

Edward Royce, Emily's great-great-grandfather and a wealthy, respected pillar of British high society at the turn of the twentieth century, had founded the club on which he'd bestowed his name in 1904. Since then ownership of the prestigious establishment had been proudly passed down through three generations of Royces, all male heirs—until Emily. More than a hundred years later, The Royce remained a traditional gentlemen's club and one of western Europe's last great bastions of male exclusivity and chauvinism. A society of powerful, influential men who between them controlled a good portion of the world's major industries, not forgetting those who presided over governments and ruled their own countries and principalities.

On occasion Emily amused herself with thoughts of how the majority of their members would react to learning that fifty per cent of their precious club was now owned by a woman.

She imagined there'd be deep rumblings of discontent

and much sputtering of cigar smoke and Scotch beneath the lighted chandeliers in the Great Salon. But she also knew her grandfather had acted with calculated intent when he'd bequeathed half of the club's ownership to his only grandchild. Gordon Royce had known his errant son could not be trusted with sole proprietorship. Rewriting his will to leave fifty per cent of the shares to Emily—the granddaughter he'd wished had been born a boy—had surely been an undesirable but necessary course of action in Gordon's mind.

Not that her grandfather had been able to overcome his misogynistic tendencies altogether. He'd gone to significant lengths to ensure the Royce name would live on through a male heir.

It was terribly ironic—that her grandfather should manipulate her life from beyond the grave when he'd shown scarcely a flicker of interest in her while he'd been alive.

Emily closed her eyes a moment. Her mind was wandering. She needed to harness her thoughts, to wrestle her brain around the problem and come up with a solution. She needed time to think. Alone. Without the sinister presence of the man who sat in the upholstered chair on the other side of her desk.

She stood slowly, her features composed, her legs steady only through sheer force of will.

'I think you should leave now, Mr Skinner.'

She spoke with all the authority she could muster but her cool directive failed to have any visible impact on her visitor.

His head tilted to the side, his thin lips stretching into a humourless smile that sent an icy ripple down Emily's spine. 'That's a pity,' he said. 'I was just starting to enjoy our conversation.'

Emily didn't like the way he looked at her. Carl Skinner—one of London's most notorious loan sharks—looked old enough to be her father, yet there was nothing paternal in the way his gaze crawled over her body. She fisted her hands by her sides. Her pinstriped skirt and white silk blouse were smart and conservative and not the least bit revealing. There was nothing for him to feast his filthy eyes on, she assured herself—except maybe for the angry colour rising in her cheeks.

'Our conversation is over.' She gestured towards the single sheet of paper he'd produced with a smug flourish when she'd questioned the veracity of his claim. It lay upon her desk now, the signature scrawled at the foot of the agreement unmistakably her father's. 'I'll be seeking a legal opinion on this.'

'You can have a hundred lawyers look over it, sweetheart.'

Emily tried not to flinch at the endearment.

'It was legally binding when Royce signed it seven days ago,' he continued. 'And it'll be legally binding in another seven days when I collect on the debt.' He leaned back, his gaze roving around the interior of her small but beautifully appointed office, with its view overlooking one of Mayfair's most elegant streets, before landing back on her. 'You know, I've always fancied myself as a member of one of these clubs.'

Emily almost snorted. The idea of this man rubbing shoulders with princes and presidents was ludicrous, but she endeavoured to keep the thought from showing on her face. Skinner's business suit and neatly cropped hair might afford him a civilised veneer but she sensed the danger emanating from him. Insulting this man would be far from wise.

'Mr Royce's debt will be settled in full by the end of the week.' She injected her voice with a confidence she prayed wasn't misplaced. If her father's gambling debt wasn't settled within the week, the alternative—Carl Skinner getting his hands on a fifty per cent shareholding of The Royce—

was an outcome far too horrendous to contemplate. *She would not let it happen.*

'You sound very certain about that, little lady.'

'I am.'

Skinner's lips pursed. 'You understand that assurance would carry more weight if I heard it straight from your boss?'

'My boss is not here,' she reminded him, instinct urging her now—as it had twenty minutes earlier when he'd turned up without an appointment demanding to see her father—not to reveal her surname. She'd introduced herself simply as Emily, Administration Manager and Mr Royce's assistant, and agreed to meet with Skinner in Maxwell's absence only because instinct urged her to hear what he had to say.

She coerced her cheek muscles to move, pulling the corners of her mouth into a rigid smile. 'I'm afraid you'll have to settle for *my* assurance, Mr Skinner,' she said, walking around her desk as she continued to speak. 'Thank you for your visit. I believe we have nothing more to discuss at this point. I do have another appointment,' she lied, 'so if you don't mind…'

Skinner rose and stepped in front of her and Emily's voice died, her vocal cords paralysed by the violent lunge of her heart into her throat. Her legs froze. He was standing in her space, two feet at most between them, and she wasn't used to such close physical proximity with another person. Especially someone she didn't know and had zero desire to. 'Mr Skinner—'

'Carl,' he said, and took a step towards her.

She stepped backwards, glancing to the right of his thick-set frame to her closed office door. Her palms grew clammy. *Why hadn't she thought to leave it open?*

His smile returned, the narrow slant of his lips ten times more unsettling than before. 'There's no need to stand on ceremony, Emily. This time next week I could be your boss...'

Her eyes widened.

'And I'm not big on formality. I prefer my working relationships to be a little more...relaxed.'

Nausea bloomed anew and she fought the instinct to recoil. She tried to tell herself his sleazy innuendo didn't intimidate her, but the truth was she felt horribly unnerved. She inhabited a world dominated by men but she wasn't familiar with this kind of unsolicited attention. For the most part she was used to being invisible. Unseen.

She straightened her shoulders. 'Let me offer you one more assurance, Mr Skinner,' she said, her heart hammering even as common sense told her he couldn't pose any physical threat to her person. Her admin assistant, Marsha, unless she'd gone for her morning tea break, would be sitting at her desk right outside Emily's door, and Security was no further away than one push of a pre-programmed button on her desk phone. 'Not only will you never be my boss,' she said, a sliver of disdain working its way into her voice now, 'But you will never, so long as I have any say in the matter, set foot on these premises again.'

No sooner had the final word leapt off Emily's tongue than she knew she had made a grave mistake.

Skinner's expression had turned thunderous.

Terrifyingly thunderous.

And he moved so fast—looming over her, his big hands clamping onto her waist like concrete mitts as he pinned her against her desk—that she had no time to react.

An onslaught of fragmented impressions assailed her: the sight of Skinner's lips peeling back from his teeth; the dampness of his breath on her skin as he thrust his face too close to hers; the overpowering reek of his aftershave which made the lining of her nose sting.

Panic flared, driving the beginnings of a scream up her

throat, but she gripped the edge of her desk behind her and smothered the sound before it could emerge. 'Take your hands off me,' she hissed. 'Or I will shout for Security and an entire team of men will be here in less than ten seconds.'

For a moment his grip tightened, his fingers biting painfully into her sides. Then, abruptly, he released her and stepped away, his sudden retreat setting off a wave of relief so powerful her legs threatened to buckle. He ran a hand over his hair and adjusted the knot of his tie—as if smoothing his appearance would somehow make him appear less brutish.

'Seven days, little lady.' His voice was gruff. Menacing. 'And then I collect.' He jutted his chin in the direction of the paper on her desk. 'That's a copy, of course. You can assure your lawyer that I have the original tucked away safe and sound.' He sent her a hard, chilling smile then showed himself out, leaving her office door standing open in the wake of his exit.

Emily sagged against her desk, just as Marsha rushed in.

'My God!' the younger woman exclaimed. 'What on earth happened in here? The look on that man's face—' She stopped, her eyes growing rounder as they took in Emily's slumped posture and the pallor she knew without the aid of a mirror had stripped the colour from her cheeks. 'Emily…?'

Rousing herself, she pointed a trembling finger over Marsha's shoulder. 'Call Security. Tell them to make absolutely certain that man leaves the building.'

Marsha hurried back out and Emily moved on shaky legs to the other side of her desk. She picked up her phone, pulled in a fortifying breath and dialled her father's mobile number.

The call went straight to voice mail.

Surprise…*not*.

She slammed the phone back down, frustration, fury

and a host of other feelings she didn't want to acknowledge building with hot, bitter force inside her.

Her eyes prickled and the threat of tears was as unfamiliar and unwelcome as the nausea had been.

What had Maxwell done?

Her lips trembled and she pressed them together, closed her eyes and pushed the heels of her hands against her lids.

She knew what he had done.

He'd borrowed a monstrous sum of money to enter a high-stakes poker game and put up his fifty per cent shareholding of The Royce as collateral.

And then he had lost. Spectacularly.

She wanted to scream.

How could he? How *could* he?

No wonder he'd been incommunicado this last week. He was hiding, the coward. Leaving Emily to clean up the mess, like he always did.

Bitterness welled up inside her.

Why shouldn't he? She was his fixer, after all. The person who made things go away. Who kept his image, and by extension the image of The Royce, as pristine and stain-free as possible. Oh, yes. Her father might be a selfish, irresponsible man but he wasn't stupid.

He'd finally discovered a use for the daughter he'd ignored for most of her life.

Emily dropped into her chair.

It wasn't unusual for Maxwell to disappear. As a child she'd grown to accept his fleeting, infrequent appearances in her life, sensing from a young age that she made him uncomfortable even though she hadn't understood why. As an adult she'd hoped maturity and a shared interest in The Royce's future would give them common ground—a foundation upon which to forge a relationship—but within the first year after her grandfather's death it'd become clear her hopes were misguided. The loss of his father had not changed Maxwell one bit. If anything he'd become more remote. More unpredictable. More absent.

It was Emily who had run the club during his absences, assuming more and more of the management responsibilities in recent years. Oh, Maxwell would breeze in when the mood took him, but he rarely stayed at his desk for more than a few token minutes. Why stare at spreadsheets and have tedious discussions about staffing issues and running costs when he could be circulating in the restaurant or the Great Salon, pressing the flesh of their members and employing his innate silver-tongued charm?

Emily didn't care that her job title didn't reflect the true extent of her responsibilities. Didn't care that for seven years her part-ownership of the club had remained, by mutual agreement with her father, a well-guarded secret. She knew The Royce's membership wasn't ready for such a revelation. The club was steeped in tradition and history, mired in values that were steadfastly old-fashioned. Its members didn't object to female employees, but the idea of accepting women as equals within their hallowed halls remained anathema to most.

Emily had a vision for the club's future, one that was far more evolved and liberal, but changes had to be implemented gradually. Anything fundamental, such as opening their doors to women... Well, those kinds of changes would happen only when the time was right.

Or they wouldn't happen at all.

Not if Carl Skinner got his grubby hands on her father's share of The Royce. There'd be no controlling Skinner, no keeping the outcome under wraps. It would be an unmitigated scandal, ruinous to the club's image. There'd be a mass exodus of members to rival establishments. In short, there would be no club. Not one she'd want to be associated with, at any rate. Skinner would turn it into a cheap, distasteful imitation.

Oh, Lord.

This was exactly why her grandfather had bequeathed half of the club to Emily. To keep his son from destroying the family legacy.

And now it was happening.

Under her watch.

She reached for the phone again, imagining Gordon Royce's coffin rocking violently in the ground now.

Her first call, to the bank, told her what she already knew—they were at the limit of their debt facility. Raising cash via a bank loan wasn't an option. Her second call, to The Royce's corporate lawyer, left her feeling even worse.

'I'm sorry, Emily. The contract with Mr Skinner is valid,' Ray Carter told her after she'd emailed a scanned copy to him. 'You could contest it, but unless we can prove that Maxwell was of unsound mind when he executed the agreement there's no legally justifiable reason to nullify the contract.'

'Is there nothing we can do?'

'Pay Mr Skinner what he's owed,' he said bluntly.

'We don't have the money.'

'Then find an investor.'

Emily's heart stopped. 'Dilute the club's equity?'

'Or convince your father to sell his shares and retain your fifty per cent. One or the other. But whatever you do, do it fast.'

Emily hung up the phone and sat for a long moment, too shell-shocked to move. Too speechless to utter more than a weak, distracted word of thanks when Marsha came in, placed a cup of tea in front of her and said she'd be right outside the office if Emily needed to talk.

Alone again, she absentmindedly fingered the smooth surface of the pearl that hung from a silver chain around her neck.

An investor.

Slowly the idea turned over in her mind. There had to be members of The Royce who would be interested in owning a piece of their beloved club. She could put some feelers out, make a few discreet enquiries... But the delicacy required for such approaches and any ensuing negotiations would take time—and time was something she didn't have.

Whatever you do, do it fast.

Ray's warning pounded through her head.

Abruptly, she swivelled her chair, dragged open the middle drawer of her desk and rummaged through an assortment of notepads and stationery until her fingers touched on the item she was seeking. She held her breath for a moment, then shoved the drawer closed and slapped the business card on her desk.

She glared at the name emblazoned in big, black letters across the card's white background, as bold as the man himself.

Ramon de la Vega.

A bloom of inexplicable heat crept beneath the collar of her blouse. She'd intended to throw the card away as soon as she returned to her office after her brief encounter with the man, but at the last second she'd changed her mind and tossed the card into a drawer.

He had unsettled her.

She didn't like to admit it, but he had.

Oh, she knew his type well enough. He was a charmer, endowed with good looks and a smooth tongue just like her father, except she had to concede that 'good looks' was a rather feeble description of Ramon de la Vega's God-given assets.

The man was gorgeous. Tall and dark. Golden-skinned. And he oozed confidence and vitality, the kind that shimmered around some people like a magnetic force field and pulled others in.

She had almost been sucked in herself. Had felt the irresistible pull of his bold, male charisma the instant he'd stepped into her zone—that minimum three feet of space she liked to maintain between others and herself. She'd taken a hasty step backwards, not because he had repelled her, but rather because she had, in spite of her anger, found herself disconcertingly drawn to him. Drawn by the palpable energy he gave off and, more shockingly, by the hint of recklessness she had sensed was lurking beneath.

They were qualities that didn't attract her, she'd reminded herself sharply. Not in the slightest. And not in a man whose audacity had already set her fuming.

She leaned back in her chair, her breathing shallow, her pulse feeling a little erratic. Was she mad even to consider this?

Or would she be mad *not* to consider it?

Forced to choose between Carl Skinner and Ramon de la Vega, she couldn't deny which man was the lesser of two evils. De la Vega had a pedigree, not to mention an impressive business acumen. She knew because she'd done an Internet search and, once she'd got past the dozens of tabloid articles and photos of him with beautiful women, the long list of accolades lauding his accomplishments as both an architect and a smart, driven businessman had made for interesting reading.

Before she could change her mind, she snatched up her phone and dialled the mobile number on his card.

Two seconds later, she almost hung up.

Maybe this needed more thought. Maybe she should rehearse what she was going to say…

'*Si?*'

The breath she'd unconsciously bottled in her lungs escaped on a little *whoosh* of surprise. For a second time that day, her vocal cords felt paralysed.

'Yes?' he said into the silence, his tone sharper. 'Who is this?'

Emily shook herself. 'Mr de la Vega?'

'Yes.'

'Good morning—I mean…' She paused as it occurred to her that he could be anywhere in the world—in a different time zone where it wasn't morning at all. She could have interrupted his evening meal. Or maybe it was the middle of the night wherever he was and he was in bed and… She froze, an unsettling thought flaring. Oh, no. Surely he wouldn't have answered the phone if…?

Before she could kill the thought, an X-rated image of entwined limbs and naked body parts—mostly naked *male* body parts—slammed into her mind.

She felt her cheeks flame. 'I'm sorry,' she said, mortified, even though he couldn't possibly know her thoughts. Where was her bulletproof composure? Skinner's visit must have unbalanced her more than she'd realised. 'I hope I'm not disturbing you. I'm—'

'Emily.'

Her breath locked in her throat for a moment.

'That's very impressive, Mr de la Vega.'

'Ramon. And you have a very memorable voice.'

Emily rolled her eyes. There was nothing special about her voice. There was nothing special about *her*. Ramon de la Vega was a silver-tongued fox, just like her father.

She sat straighter in her chair. 'Mr Royce would like to discuss a business proposition with you. Are you still interested in meeting with him?

'Of course.'

No hesitation. That was a good sign. She gripped the phone a little tighter. 'Nine o'clock tomorrow morning. Can you be here?'

'Yes.'

'Good.' She kept her voice professional. Courteous. 'We look forward to seeing you, Mr de la Vega.'

'Ramon,' he insisted. 'And I look forward to seeing you too, Emily.'

A flurry of goosebumps feathered over her skin. Had she imagined the sensual, lazy intonation to his voice that made her name sound almost…erotic? She cleared her throat. 'Actually,' she said, cooling her voice by several degrees. 'You may call me Ms Royce.'

Silence came down the line. In different circumstances, she might have allowed herself a smile.

Instead she hung up, before he could ruin her moment of satisfaction with a smooth comeback, and looked at her watch.

She had twenty-two hours to find her father.

CHAPTER THREE

RAMON DIDN'T BELIEVE in divine intervention.

Only once in his life had he prayed for help—with all the desperation of a young man facing his first lesson in mortality—and the silence in the wake of his plea on that disastrous day had been utterly, horrifyingly deafening.

These days he relied on no one but himself, and yet yesterday… Yesterday he had found himself wondering if some unseen hand was not indeed stacking the chips in his favour.

And today—today he felt as if he'd hit the jackpot.

Because the thing he wanted, the thing he needed after Saturday's volatile board meeting, had just dropped into his lap.

Almost.

'Fifty-one per cent,' he said.

The indrawn breaths of three people—two men and one woman—were clearly audible across the boardroom table.

Ramon zeroed in on the woman.

Ms Emily Royce.

Now, that was a surprise he hadn't seen coming.

Though admittedly it wasn't a patch on this morning's bombshell: Emily was not only the daughter of Maxwell Royce, she was a fifty per cent owner of the club.

Soon to be a forty-nine per cent owner, Ramon amended silently.

'Absolutely not,' she said, the incendiary flash of her silver-grey eyes telling him she wasn't the least bit impressed by his proposal.

His London-based lawyer leaned forward in the chair

beside him. 'We appreciate you're in a difficult situation, Ms Royce—'

'I don't think you *appreciate* our situation at all,' she cut in. 'I think Mr de la Vega wants to take advantage of it.'

'Emily.' Ray Carter, the grey-haired lawyer sitting on her left, touched her briefly on the arm. 'Let's hear what they have to say.'

Ramon watched her right hand curl into a delicate fist on the table-top. Knowing what he did now, he wouldn't have been surprised if she felt inclined to punch the man seated on her right, nor could he have blamed her. No one privy to the conversation that had just taken place could deny that Emily Royce had a right to be furious with her father.

Ramon and his lawyer had listened, incredulous, as Carter had laid out the facts, stating his clients were making full disclosure of the circumstances in the interests of trust and transparency.

And then Maxwell Royce had offered to sell his fifty per cent shareholding in The Royce in exchange for a swift and fair settlement.

It had taken less than an hour for both parties to agree on what constituted 'fair'. Royce's need for an expedient, unconventional deal had given Ramon leverage that he and his lawyer hadn't hesitated to use.

But it wasn't enough. Ramon wanted a majority shareholding. Wanted the control that additional one per cent would afford him.

Ms Royce mightn't like it, but if she and her father wanted a quick bailout she *was* going to sell him one per cent of her shares.

And if she didn't quit glaring at him as if he were the Antichrist, instead of the man about to save her from a far less desirable outcome, he was going to crush any sympathy he felt for her and damn well enjoy watching her yield.

He looked into those luminous, pale grey eyes.

'I am not unsympathetic to your situation,' he said, ensuring his gaze didn't encompass her father. For Maxwell Royce he felt not an iota of sympathy. The man had been reckless, irresponsible. Ramon was a risk-taker himself, and no saint, but he'd learned a long time ago the only kind of risk worth taking was a calculated one. You did not gamble with something—or some*one*—you weren't prepared to lose. 'But I think we can agree that your options are limited and what you need is a fast and effective solution to your problem.'

He leant his elbows on the table, his shoulders relaxed under the charcoal-grey suit jacket he'd donned over the matching waistcoat, white shirt and maroon tie that morning. He spread his hands, palms up in a gesture of conciliation. 'I believe that is what I am offering.'

'Demanding a majority shareholding is not a solution,' she said. 'It's a takeover.'

Angry colour rose in her face, the pink contrasting with her pale eyes and accentuating the elegant slant of her cheekbones. With her blonde hair scraped into a tight twist behind her head she looked as prim and buttoned up as she had the first time he'd met her. But now he found himself conceding that Emily Royce wasn't pretty...she was beautiful—despite the *back off* vibe she radiated with her prickly demeanour.

He dropped his gaze to her mouth. Remembered the swift, unexpected urge she'd aroused during their first encounter—the powerful desire to kiss her, to soften that condescending smile into something warmer, more inviting.

No smile adorned her mouth this morning but the tight moue of her lips did not diminish his appreciation of the fact they were lush and shapely.

Rather like her body, the generous curves of which he couldn't fail to notice. Not when the soft, pale blue top she wore moulded her ample breasts and slender midriff to utter perfection. He wasn't blind. He was a thirty-year-old red-blooded man who liked the opposite sex. A lot. When a desirable woman drifted into his orbit, his body was programmed to notice.

He clenched his jaw.

Lust had no place in this meeting. He was on the cusp of achieving what his brother had believed he couldn't. He wasn't about to lose focus.

He'd satisfy his libido later. Celebrate with a night out in London and find himself a woman who was warm and willing, not stiff and spiky, like the one sitting opposite.

'Correct me if I am wrong, Ms Royce,' he said. 'But my understanding from Mr Carter's summary of the situation is that you and Mr Royce have less than six days to raise the money required to settle his debt.'

Emily glanced at her father. Royce looked impeccable in a pinstriped navy suit but his clean-shaven face was noticeably drawn, his blue eyes underscored by dark shadows. In the moment his daughter looked at him, something that could have been regret, or shame, passed over his features.

Her gaze came back to Ramon. 'That is correct.'

'Then I will present you with two options. You can refuse my offer and watch me walk out of here—' he paused for a beat to let that threat sink in '—or you can sell one per cent of your shares to me in addition to your father's fifty and I will execute the deal and wire the money within the next forty-eight hours.'

Her eyes narrowed. 'Just like that?'

'We have established there is no time for prolonged negotiations, have we not?'

'What about due diligence?'

He waved a hand. 'Give us access to your books today and we'll satisfy ourselves there are no major issues for concern.'

She eyed him across the wide mahogany table, her head tilting to one side. 'I'm curious about your interest in The Royce, Mr de la Vega. Your own clubs seem to be doing rather well but they're hardly in the same league. This establishment is built on a foundation of prestige and tradition and we cater to an elite and very discerning clientele. We are not a playpen for the *nouveau riche.*'

She was baiting him and Ramon counselled himself not to bite. His clubs were not *doing rather well*, they were reaping the rewards of extraordinary success. Yes, they were luxurious—decadent, even—but every aspect of their design embodied taste and sophistication. And they were wildly popular. His newest club, launched in Paris just four weeks ago, had reached its full membership quota six months before opening night and now had a waiting list of hundreds.

'The Royce is an icon in the industry,' he said. 'I assure you I have no intention of doing anything that would undermine its reputation.'

Her mouth opened but her lawyer sat forward and spoke first.

'Naturally Ms Royce is passionate about the club and preserving both its reputation and heritage. As a traditional gentlemen's club, it embraces values that are very conservative and, since female members are still prohibited, Ms Royce's part-ownership is not common knowledge.' He put down his pen and folded his hands on top of his legal pad. 'That said, she is an integral part of the business. If she were to agree to become a minority shareholder, we would seek a guarantee that her job remains secure. In addition, she would expect a reasonable level of autonomy in managing the day-to-day operations.'

Ramon inclined his head. 'Of course.' He turned his gaze on her. 'I have no wish, nor reason, to oust you from your business.' He wrote a number on his lawyer's note-pad, locked his gaze onto those pale grey eyes again and slid the pad across the table.

She leaned forward to look, as did Carter. The two exchanged a glance, then she picked up her pen, slashed a line through the number Ramon had written and wrote down another. She pushed the pad back to him.

He glanced down at the number.

'Done,' he said, and ignored the small, wheezy cough that came from his lawyer.

Emily stared at him, wordless.

'I suggest we make an immediate start on reviewing the financials,' he said smoothly. 'That is, if we're all agreed…?'

A hush fell as all eyes looked to Emily. Ramon waited. Her features were composed but he knew she waged an internal battle.

Finally, she looked at Carter, gave the briefest of nods then stood and walked around the table. She extended her hand. 'Congratulations, Mr de la Vega.'

He rose, wrapped his much larger hand around hers and registered at once the warmth of her skin. Surprise flickered. For some reason he'd imagined her touch would feel cold. Clinical. But the heat filling his palm was intense, almost electric.

Her eyes widened as though she too had felt something unexpected. Abruptly, she pulled her hand out of his. 'If you'll excuse me, I'll talk to our accountant and arrange for our financial records to be made available to you.'

'Thank you.'

She started to turn away.

'Emily,' he said.

She paused. 'Yes?'

He flashed his trademark smile. 'You can call me Ramon.'

* * *

Emily locked the door of the powder room, turned on the cold tap over the basin and shoved her wrists under the water.

She felt flustered, unbearably hot, and she couldn't understand why. Couldn't understand why Ramon de la Vega should have this crazy, unbalancing effect on her. Just being in the same room as him somehow had elevated her body temperature. Made her lungs work twice as hard to get enough air into them. And when she'd touched his hand… Her nerve endings had reacted as if she'd grabbed an electrified wire.

She dried her hands and sank onto a stool.

Had she done the right thing?

She closed her eyes and rubbed her forehead.

What choice had she had?

Ramon de la Vega or Carl Skinner.

In the end she'd had no choice at all. Her hand had been forced. First by her father's irresponsible actions and then by Ramon de la Vega's ruthless, self-serving agenda.

In less than two days from now, the Vega Corporation would own fifty-one per cent of The Royce.

I'm so sorry, Grandfather.

She exhaled a shaky breath.

At least Maxwell had finally turned up, although she couldn't have said whether it was an attack of conscience or the four messages she'd left on his phone, ranging in tone from pleading, to furious, to coldly threatening, that had prompted his appearance.

He'd looked terrible, as if he hadn't slept in days, and part of her had hoped he hadn't.

Why should he get the luxury of sleep when she'd lain awake all night worrying?

And then he had agreed to sell his shares.

It had taken Emily a full minute to realise the tightness in her chest had been not only shock, but sadness.

The Royce was the one remaining connection she had to her father. Now that connection would be irreparably severed.

She stood up suddenly and smoothed her hands down the sides of her trousers. She wasn't going to do this. She wasn't going to get emotional. It would only make her feel worse.

Drawing a deep breath, she headed down the plush carpeted corridor and looked into the accounting office.

It was empty.

Further along, she stopped at Marsha's desk. 'Do you know where Jeremy is?'

'He called in sick this morning.'

She sighed. The news wasn't welcome, and not only because she needed financial data from Jeremy. He was one of the few people at The Royce she felt able to confide in—and the only other person aside from Ray Carter who knew about her father's gambling problem. It would have been nice to talk with him.

Marsha looked at her. 'Can I help with something?'

'Do you have access to the finance drive?'

Marsha nodded and Emily grabbed a pen and a piece of notepaper and scribbled out a list. 'Download these files onto a flash drive and take them to our guests in the boardroom.'

'Mr de la Vega?'

There was a gleam in Marsha's eyes that Emily tried not to notice. 'Yes. And please also arrange for refreshments and lunch for our visitors.' She moved towards her office. 'Thanks, Marsha. I'm going to keep my door closed for a while. If Mr de la Vega or his lawyer ask for anything more, let me know.'

So I can tell them to go jump.

Except she wouldn't, because she didn't have that luxury. But the thought was satisfying, if nothing else.

Sitting at her desk, she forced herself to focus. This morning's outcome was not what she'd anticipated but she still owned forty-nine per cent of The Royce. She still had a job to do. The staffing budgets had to be completed and she'd promised the executive chef she'd look at his proposed changes to the seasonal menu and give her stamp of approval.

Plus there was the small matter of drafting a discreet communication to the members. Maxwell had agreed to a carefully worded announcement in his name welcoming the Vega Corporation as a shareholder. The members already believed he was the sole owner. Armed with only selective facts, they'd assume her father had retained the balance of the shares, and he and Emily and the club's new shareholder would allow that assumption to go unchallenged.

It wasn't ideal, but discretion was necessary. The club's stability had to be her priority.

An hour later, despite her good intentions, Emily had abandoned her desk. She stood at her office window, her arms wrapped around her middle, her mind a tangle of thoughts as she stared sightlessly through the glass.

A knock at her office door jarred her out of her head. 'Come in,' she called over her shoulder, assuming it was Marsha.

It wasn't. It was her father.

She turned around and he closed the door, pushed his hands into his trouser pockets.

After an awkward silence, he said, 'The lawyers are fleshing out the terms. Ray will bring you a draft to review as soon as it's ready.'

'Fine,' she said, but it wasn't.

None of this was fine.

She wasn't fine.

Maxwell looked away first. He always did. 'If you don't need me—' he spoke to a point somewhere beyond her left shoulder '—I'll head off and come back when the agreement is ready for signing.'

If you don't need me.

Emily almost let out a bitter laugh.

Of course she didn't need him. She had needed him as a child, but he'd never been there, so she had taught herself to need no one.

'What will you do?' she asked, forcing the words past the sudden, silly lump in her throat.

He shrugged. 'I don't know,' he confessed, and Emily didn't think she'd ever seen Maxwell look quite so defeated.

'You still have the Knightsbridge apartment?'

Or had he gambled that away too? As he had everything else, including his father's stately mansion where Emily had lived at weekends and holidays when she wasn't at boarding school.

He nodded and, though she shouldn't care, she felt relieved that her father wouldn't be homeless.

He turned to go and all of a sudden Emily felt as if she were six years old and her daddy was abandoning her again. Walking out of the front door of the mansion and leaving her in that big, silent house with only her grandfather, his stern-faced housekeeper and her mother's ghost for company.

'Was it really so hard to love me?'

The words blurted from her mouth before the left side of her brain could censor them.

Maxwell paused, half turned. 'Excuse me?'

'Did you love *her*?'

She clasped the pearl at her throat and saw the tension grip her father's body. He had never talked about the woman who'd died giving birth to his only child.

'Your mother…' he began, and Emily's breath caught, her heart lurching against her ribs as she waited for him to go on.

But he simply shook his head.

'I'm sorry,' he muttered.

And then he left, closing the office door behind him.

Gone.

Just like all the times before.

Tightness gripped her throat and she blinked rapidly. *No tears*, she told herself fiercely. She returned to her desk, opened a spreadsheet on her computer and forced herself to concentrate. She hadn't allowed herself to cry in a very long time. She wouldn't start now.

Ramon draped his suit jacket over the back of the Chesterfield sofa in Maxwell Royce's soon-to-be ex-office and sat down. His briefcase, a sheaf of papers and his open laptop lay on the dark wood coffee table in front of him. He could have worked at the big hand-carved desk at the far end of the enormous office, but staking his claim before the deal was officially done felt a touch too arrogant, even for him.

He looked at his platinum wristwatch.

The lawyers had been hashing out terms in the boardroom for nearly two hours.

Trusting his own lawyer to nail down the finer details, he'd left them to it over an hour ago.

Several times since then he'd thought about seeking out Emily, but each time he'd curbed the impulse. This morning's meeting had been civil but tense. Allowing her a cooling-off period seemed sensible.

His phone buzzed and he pulled it from his pocket and checked the screen. Xav had sent a text:

Good work. Talk later.

He dropped the phone onto the table, annoyance flaring. After having sent his brother an update an hour and a half ago, he'd expected a more enthusiastic response.

He should have remembered Xav was not a man ruled by emotion.

The door to the office banged open. Jarred from his thoughts, Ramon looked up to see who had so abruptly intruded.

Emily.

Her fine features pinched into a scowl, she stood in the doorway with a sheet of paper clutched in one hand. She breathed hard, as though she had sprinted the length of the carpeted hall from the boardroom to the office. Her gaze found him and he felt the heat of her anger wash over him. Felt it reach into places he probably shouldn't have.

'Who said you could use this office?'

He rose to his feet. 'Your father,' he said, sliding his hands into his trouser pockets. 'Is that a problem?'

Stalking into the room, she raised the paper clenched in her fist. '*This* is a problem.'

He remained calm. 'Is my guessing what's on that paper part of the game?'

'This isn't a game, Mr de la Vega.' She threw the sheet of paper onto the coffee table and pointed a manicured finger at it. 'Care to explain?'

He glanced down. It was a page from the latest marked-up version of the agreement. He didn't need a closer look to guess which amendment had raised her ire.

He walked to the door and closed it. At her questioning frown, he said, 'We don't want the children overhearing our first argument, do we?'

Her eyes flashed, and the glimpse of a temper intrigued him. She grabbed the piece of paper off the table.

'We're not going to argue,' she said. 'You're going to take this to your lawyer—' she slapped the page against his chest, anchoring it there under her flattened hand '—and you're going to tell him to reinstate the bylaws under the list of matters that require shareholder unanimity.'

Ramon looked down at the slender hand splayed across his chest then back at Emily's upturned face. This close he could see the velvety texture of her long brown eyelashes and the rings of darker grey around the circumference of her irises.

When he breathed in, he caught a subtle fragrance that was musky and feminine.

For seconds neither of them moved.

Then, with her luminous eyes widening, she snatched her hand away, took a hasty step backwards and lost her balance.

Before she could fall, Ramon's reflexes kicked in and he caught her by the waist, hauling her against him. The paper fluttered to the floor and it took all of three seconds for his body to register the feel of her soft breasts against his chest, the shape of her delicate hips fitting to his.

His gaze went to her mouth. Her lips were no longer pursed in anger but slightly parted. A hot spark of appreciation ignited. When not taut with disapproval, those lips were sultry. Kissable…

'Stop.'

Emily's low, urgent command sent a jolt through Ramon. He realised he'd lowered his head—was millimetres away from satisfying his desire to know if she tasted as ripe and sweet as he imagined. He raised his head, noted the streaks of crimson over her cheekbones, the laboured quality of her breathing, and knew a rush of satisfaction.

The attraction was mutual.

She stiffened, even as she trembled. 'Let me go.'

His aroused body protested but his mind urged him to comply. He wasn't averse to mixing business with pleasure on occasion, but indulging his lust with the prickly

Ms Royce would be more complicated than a few hours or days of pleasure were worth.

Restored to his senses, he dropped his hands from her waist and stepped back.

She retrieved the paper from the floor and moved away, placing a good six feet of space between them. 'Is that how you settle disputes with your business partners?' Her face was flushed, her tone scathing. 'By kissing them?'

'Only the pretty ones,' he drawled.

She gave him a withering look. 'You're not funny, Mr de la Vega.'

'I thought I told you to call me Ramon.'

She flapped the paper in the air. 'And I thought you were serious about this deal.'

Her comeback sobered him. 'I am.'

'Then explain why you're proposing to curtail my voting rights.'

He pushed his hands back into his pockets. 'You want autonomy in the day-to-day operations,' he said. 'And I'm willing to grant you that. By the same token, as the majority shareholder I don't expect to need your agreement on minor policy changes.'

She sent him an incredulous look. 'Minor? The bylaws are hardly *minor*. They're the very foundation of the club. The rules and regulations that govern everything that's important to the members. Etiquette, dress code, membership—' She halted and, slowly, realisation dawned on her face. 'That's it, isn't it?' Her tone turned accusing. 'You want to push through a reciprocal membership arrangement with your own clubs.'

'No. But I do want to amend the membership protocols.'

Her eyes narrowed. 'Why?'

Because his brother needed leverage. Because it was an opportunity to counter Hector's underhanded power plays. Hector thought he could buy the loyalty of his fellow cronies, but what he failed to realise was that his supporters were no less duplicitous than he was. Offered the right incentive, they'd desert him in a heartbeat and give their allegiance to Xav.

And what better incentive than entry into a club where they'd rub shoulders with some of the most powerful, influential men in the world?

But first Ramon had to ensure there were no obstacles in the road.

'The approval process is archaic.' He went to the coffee table and picked up a bound copy of the club's rules and regulations. 'This says the protocol for accepting new members hasn't changed in more than sixty years.' He raised an eyebrow. 'Surely a review is overdue?'

She shook her head. 'You can't go changing the rules willy-nilly. The membership needs to be consulted. And the member who chairs the Admissions Committee is a stickler for tradition.' Her expression turned faintly smug. 'He won't be easily swayed.'

'Lord Hanover, you mean?' He smiled as the smugness slid from her face. 'A pleasant chap. At least, he seemed so when we spoke.'

Her mouth went slack. 'You…you spoke with Lord Hanover?'

'Briefly. Forty minutes ago. I've arranged to have lunch with him on Thursday.'

'You're *lunching* with Lord Hanover?' Her eyes narrowed. 'I don't believe you.'

He dropped the document, picked up his phone and started thumbing through his contacts. 'Would you like to ask his secretary?'

Emily snapped her mouth shut. 'Finc. I believe you. But aren't you jumping the gun? Our agreement isn't executed yet.'

He stilled. 'Are you suggesting it won't be?'

'Not in its present form.'

Tension clamped the back of Ramon's neck. 'There was a reason you called me yesterday,' he warned softly. 'Don't forget that.'

Her chin took on a mulish tilt. 'Are you saying this is a deal breaker?'

'Yes.'

Her head jerked back a little. Then she sucked in a sharp breath, crossed to the window and presented him with a perfect view of her long legs, graceful back and slender neck. Her blonde hair was still confined in a tight twist, but a few silky strands had escaped, and he was surprised to see how curly they were. He let his gaze slide lower. She wore black trousers that accentuated the gentle flare of her hips and, yes, her backside was spectacular.

She spun to face him. 'If I waive the unanimity requirement, I want something in return.'

He shifted his weight. 'Go on.'

'Grant my father an honorary position as chairman.'

He stared at her, his appreciation of her curves swiftly forgotten.

'Plus a modest monthly allowance.'

His disbelief ballooned. Sharp on its heels came a surge of anger. 'Your father's actions have jeopardised the future of this club, and you want to reward him with an honorary role and an *allowance*?'

Was the woman a complete fool? Or simply too forgiving? The latter possibility incensed him. Forgiveness had to be earned, and some deeds didn't deserve forgiveness. Some people didn't deserve forgiveness. Ramon knew that better than most.

She crossed her arms. 'My father can't disappear from the club altogether. It will raise questions. At worst, suspicion. For appearance's sake, he needs to maintain a presence, show his face occasionally.'

He gave her an assessing look. 'So this is about the club. Not your father?'

'Of course. The Royce needs stability. That's all I care about right now.'

He nearly bought the act, but her tone was too lofty, her body language defensive. The idea of Emily caring about her father's welfare after he'd risked her livelihood only deepened Ramon's anger. Royce didn't deserve his daughter's lenience.

Yet she made a good point. The stability of the club and its membership was paramount.

Abruptly, he said, 'An honorary position. No allowance.'

She pressed her lips together.

When she didn't respond after a moment he warned quietly, 'You need this deal, Emily.'

As did he.

She blew out a breath and closed her eyes. Finally, she looked at him again. 'Fine. Unless you have any more surprises to spring?'

He thought about the accountant and decided the issue could wait. 'No.'

To which she nodded wordlessly and strode from the room, giving him a very wide berth, he noted.

CHAPTER FOUR

THE DOCUMENT FORMALISING the sale of Maxwell Royce's fifty per cent shareholding in The Royce and a further one per cent of Emily Royce's shares to the Vega Corporation was signed by all three parties at six twenty p.m. on Tuesday night.

It would have happened sooner, but Maxwell had taken almost two hours to reappear after Emily had called him on his mobile to summon him back.

He hadn't been inebriated when he'd showed but the whisky fumes on his breath had been unmistakable. Ramon had snagged her eye as they'd congregated in the boardroom and she'd known from his hard expression that he too had detected the whiff of alcohol.

Emily's heart had pounded as she'd signed her name to the agreement, and once the deed had been done she'd escaped as quickly as she could.

Except Maxwell had followed her out of the room, and when he'd called her name it'd felt wrong to ignore him.

'The honorary role…' he'd said, examining his shoes. 'I don't know what to say.'

'"Thank you" will suffice,' she'd told him, mentally shredding the little vignette she'd created in her head—the one in which Maxwell wrapped his arms around her and expressed his gratitude with a hug.

Stupid, stupid girl.

When had her father ever hugged her?

She had turned her back on him then and walked away and now, a day later, that small act of rejection felt petty and mean.

A knock at the office door drew her gaze away from the

window. She swivelled her chair around and glanced un-
happily at the papers strewn across her desk. She'd arrived
into the office at seven a.m. and in the two hours since then
had achieved precisely nothing.

'Come in,' she called, then wished she hadn't, when the
man responsible for her lack of productivity opened the
door and strode in.

She wanted to hate Ramon de la Vega in that moment.
As much as she wanted to hate the uncontrollable way her
body reacted to him. Just his presence had the ability to
make her feel hot and unsettled, restless, in a way she'd
never experienced before.

He closed the door and she curled her hands over the
arms of her chair.

She wished she didn't know how hard and lean he was
underneath his swanky designer suit. But after yesterday,
when she'd stumbled in her haste to back away from him
and he'd caught her, she knew there wasn't an ounce of ex-
cess fat on his powerful frame. Every impressive inch of
him was hard, masculine muscle.

She pressed her thighs together, remembering the alarm-
ing flare of heat she'd felt between her legs, the tiny thrill
of illicit excitement when his mouth had descended towards
hers. The avalanche of sensations had been so unexpected,
so different from the revulsion Carl Skinner had evoked,
she'd barely returned to her senses in time to command
Ramon to stop.

She still reeled from the encounter. He'd almost kissed
her and for one crazy, reckless moment she'd wanted him
to. Had wanted to know how his mouth would feel against
hers and if he tasted the same as he smelled…earthy, with
a hint of spice and an undertone of sin…

Emily had tried hard to forget everything about that
moment, but not even last night's frenzied baking session
or the double helping of dark chocolate mousse cake she'd

devoured had helped. Afterwards, feeling slightly ill, she'd glared at the partly eaten cake as if it had failed her somehow. Baking treats in her kitchen and indulging her sweet tooth were her favourite forms of stress release, but last night neither had brought her comfort beyond the temporary sugar hit.

'Good morning,' he said, his deep voice, with its interesting mix of Spanish and American accents, as rich and decadent as the cake she'd gorged on last night.

He smiled and she ignored the way it made her stomach flutter. Reminded herself he was the kind of man who used his looks to flatter and seduce. It wouldn't surprise her if he practised that smile in front of the mirror every morning.

She said a brisk, 'Good morning,' then glanced at her watch. 'You're half an hour early.'

Last night, before leaving, she'd suggested an introductory meeting with the department heads at nine-thirty, followed by a tour of the club and, if he was interested, some one-on-one time with each manager for an overview of their respective areas.

It had only just gone nine.

Without asking, he took a seat on the other side of her desk—the same chair Skinner had sat in two days earlier—and scanned the room. 'You have a nice office,' he said, ignoring her comment about the time.

'Thank you,' she said, because her office *was* nice, and she liked it. It'd been her father's until her grandfather had died and Maxwell had taken the larger office further up the hall. After moving in, Emily had hung a piece of colourful artwork and applied a few feminine touches to the decor. The result was a professional but comfortable space that at times felt like a second home. 'I hope it remains that way.'

He raised an eyebrow. 'Nice?'

'Mine,' she said, and his dark brows angled into a frown. 'Your job is secure, Emily.'

Emily wanted to believe him, but having faith in people had never been her strong suit, and the last few days had tested her capacity for trust. She straightened a sheaf of papers on her desk. 'I've confirmed the meeting with the department heads for nine-thirty,' she told him, moving the conversation along so she could hasten his departure from her office. 'Is there something you need before then?'

He paused for a beat, his toffee-coloured eyes remaining serious, and a thread of tension pulled at Emily's insides.

'I need you to fire your accountant,' he said.

She went completely still. 'Excuse me?'

'Jeremy Turner.'

Feeling a flicker of something close to anger, she snapped, 'I know my accountant's name. What I don't know is why you're telling me to fire him.'

'He's a liability.'

She stiffened, everything in her rejecting that statement. 'Jeremy has been with The Royce for more than thirteen years. I trust him implicitly.'

'That's a mistake.'

The certainty in his voice sent a prickle of unease down her spine. 'How would you know that?'

'I know that Jeremy Turner got drunk in a cocktail bar several weeks ago and talked to someone about your father's financial problems.'

Shock stole the air from her lungs for a moment. Jeremy had been drunk? Had been talking about her father's private affairs *in a bar*? Divulging information she had shared with him in confidence? She leaned back. Her hands shook and she fisted them in her lap. 'To whom?'

'It doesn't matter.'

'It does to me.'

Ramon expelled a breath. 'To a woman with whom I'm acquainted.'

Acquainted? As in, lovers? For some reason the idea

turned the taste in her mouth bitter and she promptly redirected her thoughts. She tried to think of a reason Ramon would fabricate such an allegation and drew a blank. He had no reason to lie, and she had to admit it did make a horrible kind of sense. Why else would he have suddenly set his sights on The Royce, if not because he knew they were vulnerable?

A sense of betrayal knifed under Emily's ribs. She hadn't socialised with Jeremy beyond the occasional work-day lunch, but for the last few years she'd considered him a close colleague. A confidante, of sorts.

She rubbed her forehead. 'I'll talk to him.'

'No.' The hard edge in Ramon's voice brought her gaze sharply back to his. 'Turner goes,' he said. 'No compromise.'

Even as she nursed a sense of hurt over Jeremy's misdeed, Emily balked at such a merciless stance. 'He has a right to put his side of the story forward, surely?'

'It's irrelevant.'

'He exercised poor judgement—'

'He shared personal information about his employer with a stranger. That's indefensible.'

Jaw flexing, Ramon stood, the ruthless businessman emerging from behind the easy charm. The glimpse of arrogant intractability should have repelled her. Instead her pulse quickened, her heart pumping faster.

'I need to be able to trust the people who work for me,' he added. 'As should you. There's no room for soft hearts in business, Emily. Not everyone deserves a second chance.' There was a quiet ferocity in his voice that suggested he truly believed it. 'Cut him loose,' he finished. 'Or I will.'

His ultimatum delivered, he turned and walked out before she could articulate a protest.

Emily dropped her head in her hands.

She'd awoken this morning grimly resigned to yesterday's outcome and consoled herself with the thought that at least this week couldn't get any worse.

She laughed bitterly.

More fool her.

Emily didn't have to fire Jeremy in the end.

He resigned.

As soon as she walked into his office and confronted him, his face crumpled with guilt and he tendered his resignation with immediate effect.

Regret made her chest ache, but Jeremy's confession had tied her hands—made it impossible for her to plead his case with Ramon.

And, though it pained her to admit it, maybe Ramon was right. Maybe she was too soft. Too forgiving. How many times had she dug her father out of trouble, only for him to disappoint her and mess up again?

She paused outside his office. Or was it Ramon's now? She'd hoped it might be hers one day, but the future unfolding was very different from the one she had imagined. Was he even in there? She hadn't seen him since the meeting with the department heads and it was after three o'clock now. She took a deep breath, knocked twice and opened the door.

He looked up from behind the big mahogany desk that used to be her grandfather's.

So he had settled in.

The knot of resentment in Emily's stomach hardened. He looked perfectly at home, as if he had every right to be there, and she hated that he did.

She closed the door and he leaned back in the enormous leather chair as she crossed the office. He'd removed his suit jacket and tie—a liberty acceptable only in the privacy of the offices, given the strict formal dress code of the club—and he looked good in just a shirt, the tailored fit of the white fabric emphasising the breadth of his shoulders and a strong, well-proportioned physique that looked more suited to a rugby pitch than the office.

She stopped in front of the desk, squeezed all inappropriate thoughts of his body out of her head and placed her hand on a chair back for support. 'Jeremy's gone,' she said, intending to sound matter-of-fact, but to her horror a faint quaver hijacked her voice.

Ramon's eyes narrowed, telling her he hadn't missed it. He studied her until heat crawled around the back of her neck. 'Sit down,' he said.

'No. I only came to tell you—'

'Sit down, Emily,' he repeated, more firmly this time, and she closed her mouth and sat, even as she scorned herself for being so meek.

Rising, he turned to a shelf on the large bookcase behind him and picked up two crystal tumblers in one hand and a heavy vintage decanter in the other. He set the tumblers on the desk. 'First time firing someone?'

She watched him pull the stopper from the decanter and pour a shot of her father's whisky into each glass. 'I didn't fire him,' she said. 'He resigned.' But she knew that was just semantics. If Jeremy hadn't offered his resignation, she'd have been forced to terminate his employment.

Ramon slid one of the tumblers across to her.

'Why are we drinking?'

'Because you look as if you need it.'

She glanced at him sharply. Was he offering comfort? Or attempting to avert what he thought might be an emotional crisis?

Grabbing the tumbler, she swallowed the whisky and winced as it burned on the way down.

'Better?' he asked after a moment.

'Not really.' Although the warmth spreading through her stomach had a rather soothing effect. She met his gaze.

His eyes reminded her of hot, molten caramel—rich and tempting, but dangerous if you dipped your finger in too soon. She cleared her throat. 'I suppose you've fired plenty of people.'

'Three.' He sat, knocked back his whisky and put the glass down. 'Trust me, it's not something that brings me pleasure.'

So they had that in common at least. His words from this morning came back to her.

Not everyone deserves a second chance.

Did that harsh belief stem from personal experience?

'Emily.'

With a start, she realised he had spoken. 'I'm sorry?'

'I said you have a good team here,' he said. 'Dedicated. Professional. And they respect you.'

Warmth spread through her chest, though she told herself that was from the whisky, not his unexpected praise. 'Thank you,' she said. 'They're all extremely dedicated. Most of them have been here since my grandfather's time.'

And Emily had worked hard to earn their respect. She was young, but in the three years before her grandfather's death she had worked at ground level in every department including the kitchens to prove she was serious about learning the business. No one had been able to accuse her of looking for a free ride because her surname was Royce. Even her grandfather, who had rarely given praise, had remarked on her commitment. Of course, he had gone on to say her commitment to hard work would stand her in good stead for marriage and motherhood. In his mind, her greatest obligation to the family was to provide him with at least one great-grandson who would one day inherit his precious club and his wealth. He'd even rewritten his will in a sly effort to influence that outcome.

It'd been a wasted effort, of course. Emily had no intention of being ruled by a clause in a will.

Ramon spoke again and she tried to focus. What was wrong with her? One shot of whisky and her mind was all over the place. Or was it the effect of the man sitting opposite?

'My CFO will have one of his team pick up the slack until you've recruited a new accountant.'

'Oh…' She nodded slowly. 'Okay. Thank you.'

'I have a contact at a top recruitment firm here in London,' he said. 'I'll email his details to you. Once you start the process, keep me updated.'

Feeling off-kilter and not sure why, she simply nodded. 'All right.'

'And keep Friday night free for dinner.'

'Fine—' *Wait*. 'What?' she said.

'Dinner,' he repeated.

She blinked at him. 'With whom?'

'With me,' he said smoothly.

Emily opened her mouth and closed it again.

'Is that a problem?'

Yes. For too many reasons to list, not least of which was that she was smart enough to know she was out of her depth with this man. He had more sex appeal than anyone she'd ever met. Dealing with him in a professional setting required every ounce of composure she possessed. Outside of the office, she wouldn't stand a chance of remaining immune.

'I thought you'd be going back to New York by the end of the week,' she said.

He gave a slow smile that made her shift in the chair. 'Eager to be rid of me, Emily?'

'Of course not.' But a hot, incriminating blush burned her cheeks. 'I'm aware you have businesses all over the world, that's all. I assume you don't stay in one place for long.'

'Not unless something holds my interest.'

The heat in her face spread down her neck. He was talking about women. She didn't know how she knew that, she just did. Maybe it was the look in his eyes—the gleam that was making her feel as if *she* were the current object of his interest. Which was, she reminded herself, how every playboy operated. They were automatically programmed to flirt. To pull out their charm like a magic wand and zap a woman's defences. It was why men like Ramon—and her father—were never short of female companionship. Not that she'd seen her father in action with the ladies for herself. But the string of glittering, vacuous women who'd come and gone over the years spoke for itself.

'I'm not sure dinner is a good idea.' She shifted again, her skin feeling sticky under her blouse. 'Yesterday...' She trailed off, waiting awkwardly for him to catch her drift.

His brows rose. 'Yesterday...what?'

At the gleam in his eyes, she pressed her lips together. *He knew what.* She glared at him, her face growing hotter. 'You almost kissed me.'

As soon as the words came out she wished they hadn't. Mentioning it gave the impression she'd been thinking about it and that would only feed his ego. Of course, she *had* been thinking about it, which made everything—this conversation included—ten times more excruciating. She wanted to groan. How had they gone from the serious topic of firing people to this?

Unlike her, Ramon didn't appear at all discomfited. 'Which is why we should have dinner.'

She frowned. 'I don't understand.'

'We're business partners now.' His tone was patient. 'We have a relationship—'

'A professional one,' she cut in.

'Yes. Which would benefit from putting the tension—and events—of the last two days behind us and starting with a clean slate.'

Meaning, he wouldn't try to kiss her again? The thought provoked a sinking sensation she couldn't explain. Ignoring it, she raised her chin in challenge. 'By having dinner?'

He shrugged. 'It's a good way to relax and talk. To get to know one another.'

Put like that, it didn't sound completely unreasonable. But caution kept her wary. 'We can talk here. In the office.'

'Or we can enjoy a meal without work-day interruptions and you can give me an opportunity to show you one of my clubs.' His lips curved in a half-smile. 'Perhaps even improve your opinion of them.'

That made her pause—from guilt as much as anything. She'd not been very complimentary about his clubs.

In truth, she was intrigued.

His properties had a reputation for unrivalled luxury, and she'd read that A-list celebrities booked up to a year in advance to hold their private soirees in his West End club. His latest venture, in Paris, was meant to be even more glamorous and exclusive.

She puffed out a breath. She'd run out of arguments, or at least any that were valid. Telling him she couldn't have dinner with him because he made her feel hot and bothered was hardly an option. She stood up. 'Fine. A *business* dinner,' she said, putting a clear emphasis on 'business'.

One evening. She could grit her teeth and bear it, couldn't she? And, when it was over, he would disappear, to New York or Spain or Dubai or wherever, and Emily would get on with doing what she did best.

Running The Royce.

Two days later, standing in her bathroom, Emily applied a final coat of mascara to her lashes, stepped back from the mirror and gave her reflection a critical once-over.

She couldn't remember the last time she'd devoted this much effort to her appearance.

She smoothed the front of her dress with both hands. It was a safe choice. The scooped neckline revealed only a hint of cleavage and the hem stopped just above her knees. The midnight-blue fabric clung softly to her body and the subtle shimmer woven through it kept it from being boring. It was classy enough for an exclusive venue, but not attention-seeking.

She uncapped a tube of tinted gloss and slicked it over her lips. She'd gone for more make-up than usual, enhancing her grey eyes with soft, smoky colours, and lightly rouging her cheeks.

Recapping the gloss, she looked at her hair and felt a stab of uncertainty. Her curls were shiny, well-conditioned, but they were thick and unruly. She should have left them in the neat chignon she'd worn to work.

She pulled open a drawer filled with hair clips and bands as her doorbell chimed from the hallway.

With a fresh bout of nerves making her hands unsteady, she glanced at her watch.

Six-fifty p.m.

He was ten minutes early.

And standing at the front door of her flat, she thought with a flash of unaccountable panic.

Quickly, she slipped her bare feet into a pair of high-heeled navy sandals and went to the door.

Her renovated flat was on the top floor of a converted three-storey Victorian mansion. She had told Ramon to text her when he arrived and she would meet him on the street. She paused by the hall table and checked her phone. No message.

Maybe a neighbour was calling and it wasn't Ramon. How would he have gained access? Unless Mr Johnson, her elderly ground-floor neighbour, had forgotten to lock the main door again.

Taking a deep breath, she calmed her spinning thoughts and opened the door.

And forgot to breathe out.

Ramon stood there and he was…

Oh.

He was breathtaking…tall and powerful and a bit edgy-looking, dressed entirely in black. He wore a jacket, no tie, an open-necked silk shirt and he hadn't shaved, leaving a dark five o'clock shadow on his lean jaw that served only to magnify his sex appeal. He looked relaxed, yet lethal—a heady combination that turned her knees watery and her insides hot.

She steadied herself with one hand on the door, slowly growing aware of Ramon conducting his own appraisal—of her.

His gaze travelled all the way down to her coral-tipped toes and back up to her face.

Their gazes locked and Emily couldn't misinterpret the dark, appreciative smoulder in his hooded brown eyes.

Heat saturated her skin.

This was business, she reminded herself, not an evening of pleasure, but the electrifying hum of physical awareness didn't lessen.

And then his gaze shifted to her hair, moving over the wild mass of honey-blonde curls that more often than not defied her efforts to tame them. Which was why she always, always restrained her hair in a tight chignon for work.

Wishing again that she'd left it up, she tugged the end of a thick curl. 'It's a little wild.' She sounded almost apologetic. 'I was going to put it back up. If you wait a minute—'

Ramon caught her wrist before she could turn away. 'Don't.' His voice was deep, gruff. 'Your hair is beautiful.'

Her heart gave a little jolt, as if his touch had cranked up the voltage on her awareness and fired a tiny electric charge through her body. 'Actually, it's a nightmare,' she said, brushing off the compliment and ignoring the small dart of pleasure that pierced her.

He released her, and though it was fanciful she imagined she could still feel the warm imprint of his fingers on her skin.

'I like it.' His lips curved and she wondered how many women had fallen prey to that lazy, sensual smile. 'Are you ready?'

Because it was too late to back out, she made herself nod. 'I'll just grab my bag.'

Reluctant to invite him in, she left Ramon at the door while she slipped her phone and a few other essentials into a silver clutch and grabbed the velvet wrap she'd left on her bed when choosing her outfit.

On the landing, she stopped to lock the door and glanced at Ramon. 'This wasn't necessary, you know. I told you, I could have met you at your club.'

'Are those the kind of men you normally date?'

She looked at him sharply and felt heat creep into her cheeks. It had been a long time since any man had taken her on a date. 'Excuse me?'

'The kind who are happy to let you traipse across the city alone at night?'

Hearing his sharp tone, she turned to him. 'This isn't a date.' She slipped her keys into her clutch. 'And we might be business partners, but I don't think my personal safety falls under your purview.'

She headed towards the stairs and Ramon fell into step beside her.

'Perhaps not,' he said. 'But it would be very inconvenient if something happened to you.'

She shot him a sidelong glance. His profile looked stern, but there'd been a teasing lilt to his voice.

'I'm quite capable of looking after myself.' She had,

after all, been doing it for a long time. 'Believe it or not, I'm even rather good at it.'

'Yet you live in a building that isn't secure.'

As they started down the stairs, Ramon cupped her elbow and the brush of his fingers was warm, light and not entirely unwelcome. After six years she was familiar with the carpeted stairs that led to her beloved home, but she normally navigated them in the ballet flats that lived in her work bag for the specific purpose of her week-day commute. Descending in four-inch heels felt somewhat more precarious.

'The main door is usually locked,' she defended, and made a mental note to have another word with Mr Johnson. 'My downstairs neighbour is elderly. Sometimes he disables the self-locking handle if he's bringing in more than one load of shopping then forgets to unlatch it.'

'You should have an alarmed access system with an intercom for visitors.'

In spite of herself, Emily's mouth twitched. 'This is Wimbledon. Not the Bronx.' Something occurred to her then. 'How did you know which flat to come to?' The converted mansion housed five residences, two each on the ground and middle floors, and hers taking up the entirety of the top floor.

'You mentioned you lived at the top.'

She thought for a moment. Yes. She might have—when they'd had the conversation which had started with her telling him she'd make her own transport arrangements and ended with him overriding her. Ramon de la Vega, for all his easy charm, was not a man accustomed to hearing no.

Outside, a sleek, black sedan of European design waited by the kerb with its driver sitting patiently behind the wheel. Ramon guided Emily into the back and then joined her from the other side. His big frame made the enclosed space, with its tinted windows and luxurious leather, feel disconcertingly small.

Emily tugged at the hem of her dress, which had ridden up as she'd slid onto the soft leather, and cast around for a conversation starter. 'Tell me about your club,' she said, settling on a topic that felt safe.

'The London club?'

'Of course.' Wasn't that where they were going? 'I read somewhere that the waiting list for membership is estimated at five years long.'

'At least.' His tone wasn't boastful, just straightforward, matter-of-fact. 'We have a strict limit of a thousand members at any one time.' He went on to describe a range of high-end facilities, including restaurants and bars, a health spa and a grooming salon, fitness amenities and luxury accommodation for members who lived abroad.

Emily felt a touch of envy as she listened. Ramon had a clear vision for his clubs and the freedom to pursue it. She, on the other hand, was hamstrung by a conservative membership that was allergic to the very whiff of change and anything that might be remotely perceived as bucking tradition.

A short while later, when the car stopped and the purr of the engine ceased, Emily realised she'd lost track of time as well as their whereabouts. She glanced out through the tinted window beside her, expecting to see the night-time bustle of London's vibrant West End, and stilled.

She snapped her head back around to look at Ramon. Anger vibrated in her voice when she spoke. 'You have exactly three seconds to explain why we're sitting on a runway next to a plane.'

His expression was calm. 'I'm taking you to Saphir.'

Confusion blanked her mind for a moment, then understanding crashed in.

'We're having dinner in *Paris*?'

Three things seemed to converge on Emily at once. Shock, panic and a tiny, treacherous streak of excitement.

She shook her head. 'That's crazy. I... I can't.'

'Are you afraid of flying?'

'No.'

'Then what's the problem?'

She sent him a furious look. 'The problem is that travelling to another country for dinner is...is *insane*.'

'The flight is less than an hour.'

She gripped her clutch tightly in her lap. 'I don't care. You misled me. You said we were having dinner at your club.'

'I didn't say which one.'

'Lying by omission doesn't excuse you.' She set her jaw. 'Anyway, this is all pointless. I don't have my passport.'

He reached inside his jacket and withdrew something.

Eyes widening, heart pumping hard, she snatched the passport off him and checked inside it. She looked up, incredulous. 'How on earth did you get this?' It should have been sitting in a safe in her office.

'Marsha,' he said.

Emily threw him an appalled look. 'You should be ashamed of yourself.'

No doubt he had layered on the charm in order to coerce young Marsha's help. The poor girl wouldn't have stood a chance in the path of all that concentrated testosterone.

Emily shoved the passport into her clutch, snapped it closed and stared straight ahead. She could see the back of the driver's head through the glass partition, but if he'd overheard their conversation he gave no sign. 'Take me home.'

'After dinner.'

Ramon climbed out and walked around the car to her side. When he opened the door and stared down at her, she crossed her arms and refused to budge. He waited, and the seconds ticked by until she started to feel childish. Finally, muttering a curse under her breath, she got out. 'For the record, I don't like surprises.'

'Everyone likes surprises.'

The amusement in his tone grated. 'I don't. And I still think this is crazy.'

He closed the door and she leaned against the car for support, as if it were an anchor in a choppy sea—a safe, solid object that would keep her grounded, and stop her doing something stupid. Something she might regret. Like getting on that damned plane.

'It's just dinner, Emily.'

His voice had a deep, soothing quality, but it didn't help, because it wasn't just dinner. Not for her. Not when she stood there contemplating a giant leap out of her neatly ordered comfort zone. She eyed the plane. It was a small, sleek private jet. 'Is that yours or did you charter it for the evening?'

'I bought it yesterday.'

'Very funny.'

'I'm serious.'

She turned her head to look at him. There was no mockery on his face. She looked at the plane again. A uniformed male attendant stood at the foot of the steps, patiently waiting. 'This is very…spontaneous,' she said weakly.

'That's a bad thing?'

'Yes.' She held her wrap and her clutch against her chest in a death grip. 'I'm not very good at spontaneous.'

'Try it.' His deep, sinful voice coaxed. Enticed. 'You might like it.'

She might.

And where would that leave her?

Already she felt a gazillion miles out of her depth with this man, but it was everything else he made her feel that terrified her.

Never had she felt so physically attracted to someone before. The one intimate relationship she'd had had left her feeling deeply discontented, believing in the end she just wasn't that into sex, but Ramon…

He made her think about sex.

She, who guarded her space and preferred not to be touched, had caught herself more than once thinking about his big hands and his beautiful mouth and how they might feel on certain parts of her body.

She forced herself away from the car.

Thoughts were just thoughts, weren't they? Harmless unless translated into action, and that wasn't going to happen. Theirs was a professional relationship and she was too sensible to breach that boundary. She wasn't controlled by her desires. Not like her father.

It's just dinner.

She thought of all the women who would give their eye teeth to fly in a billionaire's private jet to Paris for dinner and then straightened her shoulders. 'Let's not stand around all evening, then.' She set off towards the plane. 'I'm famished.'

CHAPTER FIVE

RAMON HAD BEEN labelled 'reckless' from the day he'd been old enough to clamber out of his cot and send his mother and the entire household staff into a frenzied hour-long search of the house and grounds. As a fearless, rebellious child he'd become the bane of his parents' lives, unlike his brother, who'd never once defied authority or set a foot wrong.

As an adult, Ramon had learned to curb his impulses. The tabloids portrayed him as a playboy and his reputation wasn't entirely undeserved. But he didn't pursue pleasure with a careless disregard for the consequences, like some of his peers did. Risks, when taken, were calculated, impulses acted upon only if there was no potential for harm.

And he was no longer fearless. He understood the pain of loss. Understood that when you hurt people, when you took something precious from them, there were no words or actions that could undo the harm. No way of turning back the clock.

Tonight, as he took Emily's hand to help her from the limousine outside Saphir, Ramon understood something else. He understood that, for the first time in a long time, he had miscalculated.

Because he had believed he could keep his relationship with Emily professional. Had told himself that tonight was simply an elaborate attempt to break down her barriers and smooth the way for a more harmonious partnership. That, plus the opportunity to bring her to Saphir and showcase the best of his portfolio.

But he had failed to factor into his calculations the possibility that Emily would look the way she did tonight. Or that his body would end up humming with a raw, irrepressible desire he'd find impossible to quell.

He didn't want just to break down her barriers.

He wanted to rip off the dress that clung so seductively to every lush curve and dip of her body and haul her off to bed.

'Wow.'

She stood beside him, her face upturned, her gaze trained on the club's white stone entrance and the soaring, double-tiered archway bathed in subtle blue light. She'd loosened up in the last hour, maybe in part due to the champagne they'd consumed on the plane, along with canapés to tide them over, or maybe thanks to the small talk they'd settled into once her anger with him had subsided.

'Welcome to Saphir.' No sooner had he spoken than a pop of white light flashed in his periphery.

Blinking, Emily looked around, spotting the photographer a second after he did. 'Was he taking a photo of *us*?'

Ramon gestured to a security guard. 'Ignore it,' he said, guiding her inside with a hand pressed to the small of her elegant back. He nodded to the concierge as they entered the high-ceilinged granite and glass reception area. 'Security keeps the paparazzi at bay, but they're like flies. Swat one away and a dozen more appear. Unfortunately Saphir has become their new favourite haunt. This way.' He turned her down a hallway lined with contemporary art work and illuminated sculptures, many of which he'd handpicked in consultation with his designer. As they approached the restaurant, a willowy redheaded hostess whose name he couldn't remember greeted him with a deferential smile, relieved Emily of her wrap and escorted them through the restaurant's lively interior to a table in the private alcove he had specifically requested.

Emily took in their surroundings then looked out of the floor-to-ceiling window to an internal courtyard where sculptured water features and luxuriant plant life created an exotic, colourful haven. 'This is beautiful.'

Ramon signalled to the redhead, who pressed a button, and then the wall of glass beside them slid back.

A smile spread over Emily's face. 'I feel like I'm sitting in paradise!'

Her reaction was unguarded, her smile so beautiful, so real, that Ramon felt its impact like a burst of warmth in his chest. He was trying to process the feeling when a waiter materialised with menus, the champagne he'd pre-ordered and two *amuse-bouches* served in shot glasses with delicate glass spoons.

'*Foie gras*, figs and apricot,' the waiter explained. He uncorked the champagne, filled their flutes then melted away again.

After one mouthful of her *amuse-bouche*, Emily made an appreciative humming noise in her throat that Ramon was fairly sure he could feel in his groin.

'That is delicious.' She scraped the glass clean and savoured her last mouthful. 'Who's your executive chef?'

'Levi Klassen.'

Her grey eyes, which had a softer look about them tonight, rounded. 'The Dutch chef?'

'You know him?'

'I know of him. Our executive chef at The Royce speaks highly of him.'

He finished his own *amuse-bouche* and acknowledged it was exceptional. As he'd expected. He only hired the best. 'Perhaps we can have them collaborate on a menu some time.'

'Really? That would be amazing.' She turned her attention to the menu on the table. After a quick scan, she asked, 'Are the desserts on a separate menu?'

'Yes.'

'Oh.' She sounded disappointed.

He lifted an eyebrow. 'Problem?'

'I always check the desserts first.' She glanced up and must have seen the question on his face. 'So I know how much room to leave,' she elaborated.

Ramon tried to think of a time he'd taken a woman to dinner and watched her do more than pick at a lettuce leaf or a piece of white fish. He found himself smiling.

Her eyes narrowed. 'Have I amused you?'

'Surprised me,' he admitted. He caught the waiter's attention and sent the man for a dessert menu.

'Because I like to eat dessert?'

He shrugged. 'I don't often dine with women who admit to having a sweet tooth, let alone indulge it.'

'That's because supermodels live on diet pills and fresh air,' she said pertly and, given that a number of beautiful but rake-thin models had come and gone from his bed over the years, he was hard pressed to defend himself against that comment.

Fortunately, their waiter returned and saved him from having to. He sipped his champagne and watched as Emily studied the list of desserts, amusement mingling with a hot flare of curiosity. What other passions besides her sweet tooth did she hide beneath that beautiful, reserved exterior?

She put down the menu. 'Okay. I've made up my mind.'

The waiter noted their selections and then Emily settled back in her chair. 'The membership secretary put four new applications on my desk today.' She spoke quietly, her gaze fixed on her champagne, her long, slender fingers sliding idly along the delicate glass stem. 'I noted all four are board members of the Vega Corporation. I also saw that Lord Hanover has stamped his endorsement on all of them.' She glanced up, her expression difficult to read. 'How did you manage that?'

The same way he accomplished any major business win—by doing his homework, being prepared. 'In negotiations, there's a simple rule of thumb for getting what you want.'

She gave him a thoughtful look. 'Knowing what the other party wants?' she correctly guessed. She tilted her head, her magnificent honey-gold hair catching shards of reflected light from the modern chandelier above their heads. 'And Lord Hanover?' she asked. 'What does he want?'

His palms itched with a strong desire to bury his hands in those lustrous curls and explore their silken texture. He tightened his hand on his champagne glass. 'His son-in-law is chasing a major multi-billion-dollar construction contract in Saudi Arabia.'

Her gaze turned speculative. 'And…?'

'And he's hit a wall of red tape.'

'Ah. And you happen to have some connections that might smooth the way?'

He nodded, impressed. Emily was intelligent—he knew that—but she was also perceptive. Shrewd. 'My former Harvard roommate and friend to this day is a Saudi prince.'

Her eyes widened fractionally. 'Well…' After a moment, she lifted her champagne. 'Congratulations. Lord Hanover is very influential. Gaining his support is a smart move.'

He heard a trace of something in her voice. Not resentment—it was more wistful than bitter. Envy perhaps? 'Does it bother you that your shareholder status can't be revealed?'

She swallowed a mouthful of champagne and shrugged. 'Not really. It's just the way things are. There'd be an uproar if it was.'

'How can you be certain?'

She put her glass down. 'Because two years ago, three of our members proposed that women be permitted to join the club. It went to a ballot but things got very heated beforehand and some members threatened to leave if the proposal passed. It didn't…obviously.' She arched an eyebrow.

'That was their response to the idea of women joining their club. Can you imagine the reaction if they knew a woman *owned* their club?'

'And the proposers?'

'Ostracised. All three left within six months.'

It was outrageous but not surprising. Lord Hanover and his peers were prominent in the club and chauvinism was still rampant in their ranks. Ramon could imagine which way their votes had gone. 'So why did your grandfather leave half the business to you?' he asked. 'He must have known it could risk the club's stability.'

She took a moment to answer. 'Because my father has always been the way he is. Addicted to the high life, less so to responsibility. I guess my grandfather didn't trust his own son.'

'But he trusted you?'

Another shrug. 'He knew I was sensible. Devoted enough to do whatever was best for The Royce.'

'Including keeping your ownership secret.'

'Yes.'

So her grandfather had taken a calculated risk. Ramon could appreciate that strategy. And yet the old man had placed a tremendous burden on his granddaughter's shoulders. 'Surely people…the members…would expect that you'd eventually inherit the club from your father anyway?'

'Not necessarily. My father was only forty-six when his father died—fifty-three now. He could still remarry, have other children…other legitimate heirs.'

'Was that what your grandfather expected?'

'I think my grandfather stopped having expectations of my father a long time ago.'

'And you?'

She frowned. 'What do you mean?'

'What expectations did he have of you?'

Her lips twisted. 'My grandfather expected me to marry and start popping out babies—preferably boys—before the age of thirty. He only ever intended my ownership of The Royce to be a short-term guardianship.' She blinked and her mouth suddenly compressed in a tight line, as if she'd said more than she'd intended to and regretted the lapse. She shifted in her chair. 'I'm sure he turned in his grave many times this past week.'

'You think you've let your grandfather down?'

Her expression was tight. 'No offence, but the Vega Corporation owning fifty-one per cent of his precious club is not an outcome he would have endorsed.'

Ramon frowned. 'Would he have considered the alternative less desirable?'

Her gaze met his then slid away. 'Of course.'

'So the only person at fault is your father,' he said, but she looked unconvinced, and he wanted to reach across the table, grab her by the shoulders and give her a good shake. Either that, or drag her onto his lap and kiss the anguish from her face.

The latter held infinitely more appeal.

Her gaze came back to his, held for a moment, and awareness thickened the air between them. He saw the flicker of her eyelids, the surge of tell-tale colour in her cheeks, and knew she was just as conscious of their chemistry as he. Heat skated through him, but then the waiter arrived with their starters and Emily dropped her gaze. Lingering by the table, the waiter began to explain the different culinary elements on their plates. Ramon went to wave him off until he noticed that Emily was listening intently. He sat back and let the Frenchman finish, then watched her pick up her knife and fork and take a sample, sliding a sliver of beef carpaccio into her mouth. 'You're a foodie,' he observed, forcing his gaze away from those soft, perfectly shaped lips.

She glanced up. 'If that means I appreciate good food, then yes, I suppose I am.'

He picked up his own cutlery. 'Do you dine out often?'

She shook her head. 'Only occasionally.'

Her answer pleased Ramon more than it should have. He'd already learned from young Marsha—who had a talkative streak he'd shamelessly exploited—that Emily had no significant other and preferred working to socialising. But, workaholic or not, Emily Royce was too beautiful to escape male notice. If she'd said yes to his question, he would've imagined her being wined and dined by men with a great deal more than food on their minds, and that was sufficient to turn his thoughts inexplicably dark.

'I suppose you eat out all the time,' she said, 'With all the travelling that you do.'

'When the mood takes me.' Which, admittedly, was often. Dining alone rarely appealed and, no matter where in the world he was, he never wanted for a willing companion. Lately, however, his palate had become jaded, the abundance of food, wine and women failing to distract him.

This past week in London was a prime example. Twice he'd gone out with his friend Christophe only to return to his suite before midnight, alone. Not that he'd encountered a shortage of enthusiastic women, but none had held his interest. It'd left him restless and frustrated. Pursuing pleasure was a means of distraction. The alternative—boredom— was dangerous. It invited reflection, and looking too deeply inside himself never revealed anything good. That was why he never stood still for long. Why he always looked for his next challenge, whether in the boardroom or the bedroom.

Refocusing, he took a mouthful of rare, tender venison and, following Emily's lead, paused for a moment to savour the flavour and texture of the food. It was, he appreciated as he swallowed, outstanding.

'Good?'

Realising he'd closed his eyes, he opened them and looked straight into Emily's. 'Exceptional,' he said, dropping his gaze to her mouth, knowing he'd give up the rest of his meal in a flash for one taste of those luscious lips. There would be no boredom with Emily, he decided. Not with all those hidden depths to explore. She would challenge him in bed, just as she did in the office. Lust churned through his veins, hot and savage, triggering a flood of explicit thoughts as tempting as they were dangerous.

'May I ask what percentage of your revenue is generated by your food and beverage department?'

He looked at her, her question making a mockery of the desire raging through his body. She was talking business while he pictured her naked and spread beneath him. He wondered if he'd misread the signs of attraction and then he saw how tightly she gripped the handles of her cutlery. How short and shallow her breaths were and how the pulse in her throat flickered visibly. No. He hadn't misread anything. She was fighting for control of her body, just as he was doing. With brutal determination, he concentrated his thoughts and came up with a number that sounded correct.

And then she asked another question, something about the occupancy rate of Saphir's suites, and he understood that she was attempting to keep things impersonal. Preventing the undercurrent of sexual tension from pulling them under.

Right then his body wanted anything *but* impersonal. And yet his brain conceded that restraint was the wisest action. Emily didn't strike him as the kind of woman who indulged in casual affairs. If they slept together, and her expectations went beyond the physical side of things, she'd only end up disappointed. Or, worse, hurt.

Still, keeping his mind focused and his urges restrained proved a challenge throughout the rest of their meal. When Emily's dessert finally came, he sat with his double-shot espresso in front of him and watched her devour every last morsel of the rich, decadent dark chocolate soufflé. At the end she licked her spoon clean, the tip of her pink tongue catching one last smear of chocolate, and Ramon suppressed a groan. He could feel his body responding. Feel a stirring of the old, impulsive recklessness he knew better than to indulge.

Emily looked up and froze, the spoon in her hand suspended halfway between her mouth and the plate. 'Ramon...'

Hearing her say his forename for the first time—and in that husky, slightly breathless tone—sent a small shock-wave of heat through him that mingled explosively with the lust. He dragged his gaze from her mouth and locked onto those silver-grey eyes.

'Stop,' she whispered, her eyes wide and pleading, and he didn't feign innocence.

There was no point.

He knew his desire was stamped on his face and he wouldn't pretend it didn't exist. His reputation as a player was well-earned but he didn't engage in cat-and-mouse games. When he set his sights on a woman he pursued her without pretence. He wouldn't deny the truth, to Emily or to himself.

And the truth was, he wanted her.

She'd had too much champagne.

Emily put down her spoon and lowered her gaze from Ramon's. She couldn't watch his eyes stare at her mouth a moment longer. Not because she felt scandalised by the brazen interest in his heavy-lidded gaze, but rather because of the wild curiosity pulsing through her. The shocking temptation to lean across the table, part her lips and invite him to take what he wanted in spite of having just now implored him to *stop*.

Oh, yes. She'd had too much to drink.

And it was time to be sensible. Time to steer the conversation back to safer ground.

Except she'd tried that, hadn't she? And it hadn't worked. Worse, now she found herself not wanting to behave sensibly at all. Not yet, at any rate. She was dining in Paris in plush, exotic surroundings with a man who made her think about sex! She was, quite literally, miles removed from her normal, familiar world and she didn't feel like herself. She felt like Cinderella, and she wasn't ready for the ball to end.

She lifted her lashes and looked at him. 'Show me your club,' she said before good sense prevailed and spoiled her fun. What harm could prolonging the evening cause? Tipsy or not, she wouldn't do anything foolish. Thinking about kissing Ramon was one thing—acting on the impulse quite another.

He held her gaze, the look in those toffee-coloured eyes dark and deliciously potent.

Warmth blossomed in her stomach. Knowing he would kiss her if she let him filled her with a heady sense of feminine power she'd never experienced before.

He pushed his empty espresso cup aside. 'What would you like to see?'

'Everything.'

His lips spread in a slow smile. 'Then everything it is.'

Their tour of Saphir took almost a full hour. The club was enormous, far more extensive than Emily had imagined and utterly, unapologetically luxurious. They started with the recreation complex, where a full-service health spa and bathhouse operated twenty-four-seven alongside a yoga studio, squash courts, a huge swimming pool and a gymnasium. Despite the late hour, a handful of men and women were sweating it out on the state-of-the-art machines and the sight of their toned, sculpted physiques made Emily uncomfortably conscious of all the calorie-laden food she'd devoured at dinner.

Even more impressive than the recreation wing were the entertainment facilities. In addition to the restaurant where they'd dined, and two other eateries, the club boasted a champagne and caviar bar, a glamorous nightclub and the gorgeous Blue Lounge with its live jazz ensemble, sophisticated cocktail menu and cerulean silk-lined walls.

Emily tried to pay attention to what Ramon was telling her but she absorbed only half of what he said. She couldn't concentrate. The champagne still fizzed in her bloodstream and the sexual awareness that had shimmered like a desert heat wave across the dinner table all evening seemed only to grow more intense. By the time they stepped into another lift to travel to yet another floor, Emily felt as if she were caught in the grip of a blistering fever—one that was burning up her mind as much as it was her body.

She couldn't stop looking at him. Couldn't stop thinking that he really was the most beautiful man she'd ever seen. His bone structure was nothing short of magnificent, his face a perfect landscape of hard, contoured angles. And his mouth…

'Emily.'

The warning in Ramon's tone only vaguely registered. She felt giddy, drunk not on champagne but on the pheromones drenching her senses, and the speed of the lift shooting them skywards wasn't helping. She stumbled forward, and she couldn't honestly say if she'd done so by accident or on purpose. Ramon caught her, just as he had that day in her father's office, but this time she was prepared for the impact of hard muscle, the swathe of masculine heat, that instantly engulfed her. Their gazes tangled for breathless seconds, and when the lift doors whispered open neither of them moved.

'Are we getting out?' Her voice was husky. Alien. Not at all her own.

The doors started to close and Ramon reached his hand out to halt them, his other hand remaining on her hip. 'That's your call.'

'Why mine?'

'Because this is the penthouse.'

She blinked. The feverishness in her blood made the act of thinking a challenge. Or maybe it was the intimate press of her curves against his hard body, the hot imprint of his hand on her hip, that scrambled her brain. 'The penthouse?'

'A private suite.'

His gaze probed and she needed only a second to interpret the question blazing in his eyes. Only a second longer for the curiosity she'd failed to stem to flare brighter, wilder, in her veins. If she waited one more second, sanity would intervene and she'd be saved. Saved from doing something foolish, reckless and totally out of character.

And then she'd go home to London and never know how it felt to be kissed by a man as beautiful as Ramon.

She didn't wait. She rose up on tiptoes, the sweet lure of anticipation combined with a surge of heart-pounding adrenalin giving her the courage she needed to press her lips to his.

Her first impression was of warmth. Her second, of how firm and perfect his lips felt against hers. She pressed harder, heard a rough sound like a harsh, stifled exclamation climb his throat, and then his mouth opened over hers and suddenly they were kissing, really kissing and… *Lord*. It was everything she'd imagined and more. Passionate. Molten. Consuming.

One strong arm looped around her waist and suddenly her feet floated off the floor. Their mouths still fused, he walked them out of the lift. When her toes touched the floor again and his mouth slid off hers, a sound that was half-protest, half-plea fell from her parted lips. She opened her eyes and got a fleeting impression of plush surroundings and muted lighting before her gaze centred on Ramon. His other arm came around her, encircling her fully as he dragged her close, and she didn't flinch. Didn't try to escape despite the unfamiliarity of being held.

His gaze roved her face, settled on her mouth. 'Do you know how long I've thought about doing that?'

She stared up at him. Her lips tingled, aching for the return of his. 'Since Tuesday?'

He shook his head, one corner of his sexy mouth lifting. 'The first time we met.' He tugged her closer and coils of heat kindled in her belly. 'You were so cool. So superior.' He lifted a hand and brushed the pad of his thumb over her lower lip. 'I wanted to kiss the prim, haughty smile you gave me right off your beautiful face.'

Somehow, through the thick haze of desire shrouding her senses, her mind summoned a sliver of indignation. 'And I wanted to slap yours.'

He laughed, unabashed, and then as swiftly as it had arisen his amusement vanished and the dark, smouldering look that made her stomach swoop was back. He removed her clutch from her hand, her wrap from over her forearm, and dropped the items onto a sleek, red lounge chair. His jacket followed and then he returned to stand before her.

Heart racing, Emily pressed her palm to the centre of his chest. When she spoke her voice belonged to someone else. Someone she didn't recognise. 'What happens in Paris stays in Paris.'

Another of those slow, sensual smiles slanted his mouth. 'As the lady wishes,' he murmured, and wrapped his fingers around her wrist. He raised her hand to his mouth, kissed her knuckles then turned her palm up and bit the base of her thumb.

Emily's breath caught on a soft gasp. The sharp press

of his teeth followed by the velvet slide of his tongue was unexpected—and surprisingly erotic. Her spine loosened, her legs went weak, and then he was scooping her into his arms, holding her effortlessly against his broad chest, as he strode through the suite. Seconds later he set her feet down and she barely had time to register they were in a bedroom before he was kissing her again, the heat of his mouth on hers even more explosively potent than before. Wantonly, she slid her arms around his neck and revelled in the earthy scent of him, the hot, bold stroke of his tongue against hers and the branding heat of his palms through her dress as they took possession of her hips.

His hands slid downwards, cupped her buttocks, and a low groan rumbled up his throat. He pulled her against him hard, pelvis to pelvis, giving Emily her first taste of the sheer strength and size of his erection. Before she could acknowledge the dart of apprehension in her stomach, his fingers hooked into the soft, clingy fabric of her dress and tugged upwards. 'Lift your arms,' he commanded against her mouth.

Willingly she obeyed, stretching her arms above her head, and he dispensed with the dress with a speed and ease that suggested he was well-versed in the art of removing women's clothing—a thought Emily refused to dwell upon as she stood before him in nothing but her heels, her cream satin underwear and her pearl necklace. She reached for him, partly to disguise her self-consciousness, and partly because she craved the return of his heated body against hers.

But he took a step back. 'Patience, *mi belleza*,' he said throatily, his accent more pronounced now, and she dropped her arms helplessly back to her sides. His gaze trailed over her. Hot. Intense. 'I have seen you naked in my mind many times,' he said. 'I want to know if my imagination did you justice.' He started to move, walking around her in a slow, deliberate circle, his unhurried appraisal of her near-naked body setting fire to every inch of her exposed flesh.

Her legs trembled, barely supporting her. She closed her eyes. 'Ramon...'

'I like hearing you say my name.' His voice came from behind her and she felt the silk of his shirt brush her shoulder blades. Still he didn't touch her. 'Say it again.'

She swallowed. 'Ramon.'

'Yes, Emily?'

Excitement made her heart pound, the tension and build-up of anticipation proving unbearably sexy.

Without warning he drove his hands into her hair, his fingers spearing deep and tangling in the mass of soft curls. He tugged her head back against his shoulder and put his mouth against her ear. 'What do you want?' he rasped.

'I want you to touch me.'

'Where?' His voice was rough, laced with satisfaction and a dark note of carnality that made her insides quiver.

'Everywhere,' she whispered, and felt a deep shudder move through him.

His hands came around her waist and just the hot slide of his palms across her naked midriff triggered a rush of liquid heat between her legs. He pressed an open-mouthed kiss to her bare shoulder and she arched her back, her breasts aching with an instinctive need that he answered by cupping his hands under them and dragging his thumbs over their tips.

She moaned, luxuriating in the sensations his touch was evoking. But she wanted more. She wanted skin against skin. Blindly, she grabbed at the straps of her bra and yanked them down, knocking his hands away in the process.

'*Sí, mi belleza.*' His voice rumbled with approval. 'That's right. Show me what you want.'

She did. She seized his hands and moulded them to her

bare breasts, her back arching again as he rolled her hardened nipples between his thumbs and forefingers. A little cry of pleasure escaped her, then he was kissing her neck, and she could feel his erection nudging her bottom, teasing her curiosity until she could no longer bear to stand passive. With a boldness that ordinarily would've shocked her, she reached back and palmed his groin, and even through his trousers she could feel how thick he was. How hard. *For her.*

That heady sense of feminine power surged again, throbbing in her veins like a potent aphrodisiac. 'More,' she croaked. 'I want more.'

Shifting his weight, he swung her off her feet, took three long strides and set her down on the edge of an enormous bed dressed in soft, luxurious linens. His dark gaze locked on hers, he stepped back, tugged his shirt out of his waistband and began unbuttoning it.

Her mouth filled with moisture and she stared up at him, mesmerised by the prospect of watching him strip down to nothing right in front of her.

With deft hands he peeled off his shirt and dropped it on the floor, and Emily's eyes widened.

He was utter perfection, his torso lean and chiselled, his skin like golden satin over ridges of steel. She wanted just to sit there and look at him, take the time to indulge in a leisurely inspection, as he'd done with her. But he toed off his shoes, dropped to his knees in front of her and plunged one hand into her hair, tugging her forward so that her face was close to his.

'How much more?'

She licked her lips. 'All of it.'

Eyes gleaming, he leaned in and claimed her mouth with a searing kiss that promised her she would get exactly what she'd asked for. Then his lips travelled down her throat, trailing hot, open-mouthed kisses over her sensitised skin until he reached the hard tip of her right breast.

She arched towards him before he'd even taken her nipple into his mouth. And when he did…it was exquisite, the pleasure almost unbearable. Her hands flew to his head of their own accord, her fingers streaking into the thick, dark strands of his hair, holding him to her as he mercilessly sucked her nipple into a tight, ultra-sensitive point. And then he lavished the same attention on her other breast and she dropped her head back, wondering if she might die from the blistering heat she could feel building inside her like an out-of-control inferno.

Her bra was still strung around her ribs and he unhooked it, threw it aside then pushed her back on the bed and dragged her knickers off with such efficiency, she had no time to feel hesitant or shy. But when he grasped her knees, eased them apart and lowered his head, her body tensed.

Pausing, Ramon glanced up from between her legs, hunger, heat and a clear, white-hot intent burning in his eyes. 'You wanted it all,' he reminded her thickly.

Yes…but she hadn't been thinking about oral sex. She'd never gone there before. The ex-boyfriend with whom she'd had her one, uninspiring sexual relationship had never initiated it and neither had she. And, while she was guilty of having entertained X-rated thoughts about Ramon's hands and mouth, she hadn't considered how it might feel to have his mouth on her *there*.

But, heaven help her, she wanted to know.

She relaxed her muscles, inviting him to do as he pleased, and the first stroke of his tongue elicited a shocked gasp and sent a bolt of red-hot sensation through her that made her body jerk against his mouth. With a broad hand flattened over her stomach, he anchored her to the bed and her breath seesawed on another gasp as he gently parted her with his fingers, giving his tongue deeper, more intimate access.

Oh, God.

She'd never known anything like it before. Had never experienced this tight, quickening sensation in her body. Had never imagined she would enjoy being pleasured in this way. He slid a finger inside her, finding a spot with his fingertip that seemed to set off an electric current deep within her core. She felt taut, tingly, as if her body were a high-voltage wire coiling tighter and tighter around his finger. He pushed deeper, flicked his tongue, and before she understood what was happening she came, every muscle in her body tensing with surprise and the sudden, unexpected eruption of pleasure.

As her limbs went from rigid to limp, she panted his name, once, twice, and he raised himself over her, his smile a study in male satisfaction. 'That's right, *dulzura*,' he murmured, tracing a line between her breasts with the tip of one finger. 'Get used to saying my name. You are going to scream it many times before we are done.'

CHAPTER SIX

EMILY WOULD HAVE told him how cocky he sounded if her flesh wasn't already crying out again for his touch.

She'd never experienced an orgasm like that before, yet he'd coaxed her to that sensational, mind-shattering peak with seemingly little effort.

He dropped a kiss on her mouth then levered himself to his feet, unbuckled his belt and pulled his zipper down, his gaze all the while tracking her naked, climax-flushed body.

Suddenly conscious that she was sprawled on the bed like some open-legged, sacrificial offering, Emily quickly closed her thighs and clambered backwards until she encountered the pillows. For a moment she thought she saw amusement flicker over his handsome face, but then he pushed his trousers and underwear down, kicked them off and straightened.

The air deserted Emily's lungs in a rush. Ramon de la Vega was a big man in every conceivable way and, though she was inexperienced—her sexual history confined to one partner—she knew she was small down there. Tight. Her pelvic muscles clenching with just a touch of apprehension, she watched him extract a condom from the bedside drawer, tear open the foil and roll on the sheath.

He climbed onto the bed, pulled her beneath him and kissed her, and this time she took full advantage of the opportunity to touch him, sliding her hands across the smooth skin of his shoulders, over his chest with its light smattering of hair and down the hard, ridged muscles of his abdomen. Apprehension giving way to need and excitement, she reached lower, curled her hand around his hot, rigid length and felt him tense. She tightened her hold and he growled something in Spanish against her mouth.

His knee came between her legs, pushing her thighs apart, and when he disengaged her hand from his shaft and then touched her just as intimately she could tell she was slick by the way his finger easily slipped into her. He added a second finger, stretching her a little further, and she gasped as he found the same hypersensitive spot he had earlier. A moment later he withdrew his fingers and the head of his erection replaced his hand. He stilled, poised above her, eyes locked on hers. 'Say my name.'

A tiny shred of stubbornness pushed to the fore. 'Kiss me first.'

His eyes glinted, one corner of his mouth lifting in a 'two can play that game' smile. Deliberately avoiding her mouth, he kissed her neck, finding the soft, sensitive place with his tongue that made her back arch in response. Then he pushed inside her, a strong, steady thrust that went only so far before her body resisted.

'*Dios*...you're so tight.'

He pushed in a little further and she stiffened, her body demanding a moment to accustom itself to the intimate invasion. Eyes closed, she dug her hands into his shoulders and willed her internal muscles to relax.

'Emily?'

Hearing concern in his voice, she opened her eyes, looked at him and saw a stark mix of lust and uncertainty in his expression. 'It's been a long time,' she whispered and felt her cheeks redden at having revealed that small intimate truth. She shifted and drew her knees up and back, and suddenly her body yielded and he slid all the way in, so deep and so completely they both gasped aloud and shuddered.

Groaning, Ramon buried his face in her neck and ground out more words in Spanish.

And then he rode her hard, a sheen of sweat gathering

on his skin, his magnificent body rippling above hers as he drove them both towards climax with breathtaking skill.

Emily clung to him, each powerful thrust of his body into hers pushing her closer to the edge. She tried to hold on, sensing he was close, wanting him to come at the same time as her. But there was no stopping the intense burst of pleasure that hurtled her high into the stratosphere. White light splintered behind her eyelids and then she did what she'd refused to do before.

She cried out his name.

Again. And again. And again.

Ramon hit the 'end call' button on his phone and padded through to the bedroom. It was after one a.m. and, since Sleeping Beauty had appeared dead to the world, he'd decided to make some calls in the living room.

He studied her sleeping form. Emily was an outrageous bed hog and the discovery both surprised him and amused him. She was so contained most of the time, so controlled, he had assumed she would sleep in a similar fashion—either curled into a tight ball or flat on her back, hands folded neatly on her stomach. Instead, she lay sprawled across two-thirds of the mattress, her arms flung wide and her long legs half-in, half-out of the tangled covers. She was totally naked except for the silver chain and pearl that hung around her neck, and her tumble of golden curls, damp still from their shower, spilled across the pillow, begging him to bury his hands in them.

His body stirred, lust pooling with the memory of how many ways he'd enjoyed her body in the last two hours.

She'd blown his mind. Revealed a streak of passion and daring underneath her natural reserve that he'd relished exploring. Her inexperience had surprised him but pleased him too, satisfying some dark, proprietorial part of his male ego he hadn't realised existed. He'd planned to take his time with her and he had up to a point. But the second her body had accepted him, pulling him into the heart of her tight, satin heat, he'd lost control.

And then he'd lost control in the shower too. He'd carried her in with the intention of doing no more than soaping the sweat from their bodies, and instead he'd lifted her against the tiles and plunged into her, the roar of pleasure in his veins obliterating all thought until she'd whispered urgently in his ear, telling him not to come inside her. He'd withdrawn immediately, shocked that he'd forgotten to protect them—even more shocked that for one reckless, fleeting second he'd wanted to bury himself inside her again and say to hell with the risk.

He'd stood panting, torn between lust and good sense until, with a bold, saucy look that'd stopped his breath, Emily had dropped to her knees, wrapped her fingers around him and taken him in her mouth. He'd tried to summon a protest but his attempt had been half-hearted at best, and in a matter of seconds she'd brought him to the edge of completion.

Ramon had slept with countless women in countless places, but standing in that shower, with his hands braced against the walls, staring down at Emily's flushed, satisfied face, had been the single most erotic experience of his life.

Her words from earlier came back to him.

What happens in Paris stays in Paris.

At any other time, such an edict would have suited him down to the ground. What self-professed playboy wouldn't want to hear words that relinquished him of any unwanted strings or emotional commitments?

And relationships without strings were Ramon's golden rule. It was how he'd lived his life for the last twelve years and how he intended to carry on. Forming attachments was something he avoided for good reason. You couldn't hurt people if they didn't get close.

The thought of hurting Emily made him feel physically ill. She was tough, but he sensed her outer armour shielded an underlying vulnerability. Their conversations hadn't touched on family, but he recalled reading some tabloid bio on Maxwell that had talked of his wife having died in childbirth.

How must it feel, knowing the woman who'd given you life had lost her own while bringing you into the world? He couldn't imagine it, yet *he* knew a worse pain. The pain of knowing his actions, his choices, had led to another person's demise—not once, but twice.

His hand tightened around his phone. He had no business comparing Emily's life to his own. Unlike him, she had done nothing wrong. She wasn't responsible for her mother's death.

He thought of his mother, Elena, and her difficulties with conceiving and carrying a child to term. Having Ramon after adopting Xavier must have been quite the shock. To their credit, his parents had shown no favouritism, treating their sons with equal affection, but no doubt it'd been a great irony for them that Ramon—their own flesh and blood—was the one who'd proved a disappointment. Who had shamed the family. His mother was a good woman, but he wouldn't blame her if she never found it in her heart to forgive him.

He ran his gaze over Emily's face, wincing at the small patches of redness where his stubble had grazed her skin. He felt a tightness grip his chest. He'd known her for less than a week yet he knew she was strong and principled—a good woman, like his mother. Was that why she made allowances for her father? Or was it because she had no one else? Her grandfather was dead, she had no siblings and there didn't seem to be any extended family on the scene. Aside from Royce, who hardly qualified as a contender for Father of the Year, was Emily alone in the world?

The tightness intensified and with it came a vague sense of unease. Since when did he speculate on the personal lives of his lovers?

Yet he knew he couldn't class Emily as one of his casual flings. His relationship with her was primarily a professional one and tonight he'd crossed a line he shouldn't have crossed. He'd been reckless, allowing his base desires to govern him, and he knew he should be regretting it right now, but he wasn't. Instead, he was thinking about pulling the sheet away, easing her thighs apart and tasting her again. He was thinking that one night, a few brief hours, wasn't enough time to do all the things he wanted to do with her...*to* her. And he was thinking that, if their time together had to be confined to Paris, then perhaps this one night wasn't long enough. Perhaps they needed the whole weekend.

Her eyes opened and she blinked drowsily, stretched her gorgeous limbs and smiled up at him with lips pink and swollen from his kisses. 'Ramon?'

'*Sí, mi belleza?*'

'What time is it?'

'Late—or early, depending on your view.'

She rose onto her elbows. 'Do we need to go? Is the plane waiting for us?'

He put his phone on the nightstand. 'No. I've stood the pilot down for the night.'

A flicker of anxiety showed in her face. 'Will he be available to take us back first thing in the morning?'

Ramon climbed onto the bed. 'He's available when I want him to be available.' He pushed the tangled sheet off her and palmed the soft mound of honey-blonde curls at the apex of her thighs. Slowly, he ran a fingertip down her sensitive flesh and her soft gasp made his groin tighten. 'Tender?'

'Only a little.'

He gave a slow smile then moved his hand and made her gasp again. 'In that case, I'll be gentle.'

Bright morning sunlight streamed through the lounge windows of the penthouse and for the first time in Emily's life she truly appreciated the sentiment behind the expression 'the cold light of day'.

She pulled the belt of the fluffy white bathrobe tighter around her waist. 'No,' she said and felt an immediate rush of relief, because the other word she could have uttered— the big, fat, resounding *yes* that was even now attempting to crawl up her throat against her better judgement—could not, under any circumstances, be allowed to escape. 'I can't stay another night. I need to go home to London this morning.'

And I need you to put some clothes on, she almost added, although thankfully only his chest was on display. He wore his dark suit trousers from last night but they weren't belted or zipped properly and they sat too low on his hips. She knew if she let her gaze drop she'd see more of his flat, muscled stomach than her composure could handle at present.

Unaware of her internal struggles, he poured coffee from a silver pot into two china mugs. 'Is there something you need to return for today?'

'Yes,' she lied, accepting the coffee he handed her without meeting his eye. Her *sanity*. That was what she needed to return for. Because clearly she'd lost it somewhere between here and London and she could really do with getting it back before the wanton, needy creature he'd unleashed in her decided that staying in Paris with him was more appealing than returning home.

She took her coffee over to the big floor-to-ceiling window and stared out at the stunning view of the city.

Perhaps the light of day wouldn't have seemed so harsh right now if she hadn't emerged from the bedroom at just the wrong time. If the man who'd been wheeling a heavily laden breakfast trolley out of the lift hadn't glanced at her and she hadn't seen, in the moment before he blanked his expression, the speculative glint in his eyes. He'd been judging her, eyeing up the drowsy, bed-rumpled woman who'd slept with his boss—and, given she was guilty as charged, could she really blame the guy for looking at her as if she were a two-bit slut?

She swallowed, self-disgust rising in her throat like bile. She'd set aside all manner of caution and self-preservation and let curiosity and pure physical lust take control.

Oh, God.

All these years of despising her father's behaviour and now she couldn't even claim the moral high ground.

She gripped her mug between her hands. She couldn't spend another night in Paris with Ramon. Just thinking about the things they would do together made her skin flush with heat and her body tremble with a deep-seated longing she couldn't quash. He was like a dangerous, addictive narcotic. She'd had her first hit, experienced the ecstasy of the high, and now she was craving another.

Could addiction take root so quickly?

She shook her head. Crazy thinking. She was out of her element, her comfort zone, and she'd just done something completely out of character. Something that—even now with self-condemnation dragging at her stomach—had felt wrong and yet impossibly right at the same time.

Good grief. No wonder she was feeling disoriented.

'Emily…' Ramon's arms came around her from behind and she stiffened so suddenly her coffee spilt, the hot liquid scalding her thumb.

Cursing softly, he took the mug away and returned with a napkin.

She patted her hand dry. 'Sorry.'

'For what? For flinching when I touched you just now, or for what we did last night?'

Hearing an edge to his voice, she fisted the napkin in her hand. What could she say? That she wasn't used to having someone put their arms around her? She wasn't. She was more comfortable when people kept their distance, though not because she didn't crave human contact. Contrary to the nasty things her ex had said after she'd ended their relationship, her veins didn't run with ice water. But when you hadn't been hugged much as a child, when you had never experienced the physical manifestation of a parent's unconditional love, you were hardly going to blossom into a touchy, feely adult.

And as for last night…her and Ramon…that hadn't been about affection, or emotion. It had been about sex.

Nothing else.

She drew a deep breath. 'I think last night was a mistake.' His eyes rapidly narrowed and she hastened to add, 'I'd had too much champagne. I… I was tipsy.'

His face darkened. 'Are you saying I took advantage of you?'

'No! Of…of course not,' she stammered, instantly regretting her feeble excuse. 'But…my judgement was impaired.' She twisted the napkin between her hands and cringed inwardly. She was making a hash of this. 'I… I wasn't thinking straight.'

'Are you drunk now?'

She blinked. 'No.'

'Are you thinking straight?'

Hardly. How could she think straight with his bare, muscled chest and powerful shoulders dominating her field of vision? 'Yes.'

Moving with lightning speed, Ramon grabbed the belt of her robe and gave it a single hard yank.

Before Emily had time to react, the sides of the garment gaped open and exposed her naked breasts.

She made a small, startled sound and tried to tug the robe closed but his arm was already snaking under the soft terry towelling and circling her waist like a band of reinforced steel.

He hauled her against him, plunged his other hand into her loose, bed-tousled curls and cupped the back of her head.

Her breasts tingled, her nipples hardening into treacherous points of need. 'Ramon—'

His mouth came down on hers. Hot. Forceful. A teensy bit brutal. Somewhere in her reeling mind she wondered if she should struggle, try to bite him, perhaps. She didn't. Instead, she curled her hands over his shoulders, arched her body like the wanton creature he'd turned her into and opened her mouth under his. He backed her against the solid glass window, his kiss growing more fervent, more demanding, and she didn't notice he'd released her head until she felt his hand sliding between her legs. A single finger thrust inside her, right into the centre of her wet, pulsing heat, and she gasped against his mouth.

He lifted his head, withdrew his finger and, holding her gaze, very deliberately put it into his mouth. He sucked, extracting his finger slowly, and then licked his lips. His smile was utterly, wickedly shameless. 'That doesn't taste like a mistake to me.'

Outrage surged, instantly tempering the hot pulse of desire between her legs.

How dared he smash through her defences and mock her in a way that was so…so *erotic*?

She banged the heels of her hands against his chest, twisted out of his grip and yanked the robe closed. 'I'm going to get dressed,' she told him, holding her chin high, injecting a hard, chilly note into her voice. 'And then I'd like to go home please.' Her throat feeling tight all of a sudden, she secured the belt around her waist and strode towards the bedroom.

'Emily.'

Civility overriding the urge to ignore him completely, she stopped and turned, just as a brown paper package bound with string landed at her feet.

'Clothes,' he supplied before she could ask. 'So you don't have to worry about the 'walk of shame'.'

He turned away to the breakfast tray and Emily stared at his back. Then she picked up the package, blinked away the sharp sting of unexpected tears and shut herself in the bedroom.

By the time the London limo driver turned into her quiet neighbourhood street, a headache pounded in Emily's temples and she felt as if her nerve endings had been wrapped in razor wire.

Ramon sat beside her on the back seat, silent and brooding, as he had been for most of the journey. They were both angry. Both upset. Which only reinforced Emily's belief that they'd made a terrible mistake. Jeopardised their professional relationship for—*what?*—a bit of short-lived gratification?

She wiped a clammy palm over her thigh. The jeans she wore fit perfectly, as did the sleeveless, pale blue top and matching cardigan. Even the underwear was the right size. Every item she'd found in the neatly wrapped package had been new, the tags still attached. Emily was appreciative but she didn't want to think too hard about whomever had bought and delivered the clothing and what they must have thought of such a task. Or maybe they hadn't thought anything. Maybe they were used to running such errands for their boss.

The idea made her feel slightly ill.

The limo stopped. Ramon said nothing, so she quietly gathered up her things.

'Are you staying in London?'

He turned his head and looked at her and electricity arced between them, as red-hot and incandescent as ever. Anger, it seemed, had only intensified their chemistry.

'No. I'm returning to New York.'

'Good.' She prayed the word sounded more convincing to his ears than hers. 'I think it would be wise if you stayed away for a while. Gave us both some…space. We can conduct any business by email and phone.'

A muscle flickered in his jaw. 'I'll come to *our* club in person whenever I deem fit.'

Stiffening at his arrogant tone, she opened her mouth to offer a pithy retort and found she had nothing. 'Goodbye, Ramon,' she said instead, ignoring the sudden dull ache beneath her breastbone, and climbed out.

He said something but Emily didn't catch it, his words muffled by the thud of the limo door as she slammed it closed.

CHAPTER SEVEN

SIX WEEKS.

That was how long it was before Ramon finally returned to London, although it had taken considerably less time for him to conclude that his morning-after behaviour in Paris had been reprehensible.

Abominable.

He hadn't reacted well to rejection. Yes, Emily could have handled the situation with more grace than she had, but his own behaviour had lacked any degree of decorum. He wasn't unfamiliar with self-contempt and regret, but until that weekend those particular demons had not sat so heavily on his soul in a long time.

So he'd respected Emily's wishes and stayed away, keeping their communication to a minimum.

But six weeks was long enough. He was done with the polite, impersonal emails. The short, stilted phone calls. She still hadn't hired a replacement accountant and he wanted to know why. If she was keeping the position open in the hope that he would grant Turner a pardon and allow her to invite the man back, she was courting disappointment.

He walked down the carpeted corridor on the executive level of The Royce and saw Marsha sitting at her desk. At his approach, her eyes widened and she jumped up as if she'd been stuck with a cattle prod. 'Mr de la Vega! I didn't know we were expecting you.'

'You weren't.' He unleashed a good-humoured smile and gestured to the closed door of Emily's office. 'Is she in?'

'Er...no.'

'When will she be back?'

She blinked then stared at him.

'Marsha?' he prompted.

'I… I don't know.'

He frowned. 'What do you mean, you don't know?'

'I mean…she's not in today. She's sick…' Marsha bit her lip. 'At least, I think she's sick… She rang yesterday morning and said she was taking the day off—which is very unusual. And then today…she left a message on my phone early this morning, saying she'd be in before noon, but I haven't seen her yet.'

He glanced at his watch. 'It's after two p.m.'

Marsha wrung her hands. 'I know.'

'Have you tried calling her?' he demanded.

'Twice. I left her two messages. She hasn't called back.'

An icy sensation hollowed out his gut. That didn't sound like the dedicated, conscientious Emily Royce he knew.

'Call me if you hear from her,' he commanded and turned on his heel.

Emily opened her eyes.

Someone was pounding on her door. Or was it the pounding in her head that she hadn't been able to shake for two days that she could hear?

Her doorbell chimed, the sound piercing in the silence of her flat, and Emily groaned. It was a week day and her neighbours should all be at work, except for Mr Johnson, who was retired. But he had never climbed the stairs to visit her. Of course, he could have forgotten to lock the main entrance again, in which case the person banging on her door could be a stranger.

She groaned again, closed her eyes and snuggled deeper into the softness of the sofa.

'Emily!'

She froze, the sound of her name being barked on the other side of the door forcing its way into her stress-addled mind. She knew that voice. Deep, masculine…

'Emily!'

She sat up—too fast, apparently, because her stomach performed a sharp lurch and roll.

Ramon was at her door.

The knowledge sent a rush of heat over her skin followed closely by a cold wave of dread.

He knows.

She swallowed hard and fought down the flare of irrational panic with a forced dose of sanity.

Of course he doesn't know.

She'd only found out for herself a little over a day ago, though she'd had her suspicions for almost three weeks before visiting her doctor.

The doorbell pealed again, repeatedly, as if he were leaning on it, and she threw off the light cotton throw she'd curled under and urged her legs to move. When she opened the door a moment later, the thought came to her, much too late, that she looked a mess.

The fact that Ramon looked both powerful and sexy in his immaculate three-piece suit made her feel hot and unaccountably irritable at the same time.

She dragged her attention from his body, blotting out images in her head that she'd tried hard for the last six weeks to forget, and focused on his face. A deep frown marred his brow.

'Are you all right?'

'Yes.'

'I knocked for ages.'

'I was asleep.'

His gaze tracked over her grey tee shirt and black yoga pants then returned to her face. Her very pale, make-upless face. 'Are you unwell?'

'Yes—no…' She shook her head. Tried to bring some semblance of order to her thoughts. 'Why are you here?'

'I went to the club,' he said. 'Marsha thought you might be sick. You haven't returned her calls.'

Confusion descended. She glanced at her watch and her heart lurched. It couldn't be almost three o'clock! It'd been only ten a.m. when she had decided to take some pain-killers and lie down for half an hour before heading into work. She'd slept for almost five hours which, now that she thought about it, wasn't all that surprising given she hadn't slept a wink during the night.

She put her hand to her forehead, guilt surging. 'Oh, no. Poor Marsha.' She turned towards the hall table where she'd left her phone. 'I need to call her.'

Not waiting for an invitation, Ramon stepped inside and closed the door. 'That can wait,' he said, taking hold of her shoulders and turning her to face him.

Emily tensed. His touch had been seared into her memory ever since Paris, but memory was no match for the reality of having his hands on her body, even in a non-sexual way. Her heart raced and she felt warm, a little lightheaded.

His gaze scoured her face. 'Something's wrong,' he stated, his voice firm with certainty. 'What is it, Emily?'

Fear gripped her throat and for a moment she couldn't speak. Revealing her condition was something she had planned to do in her own time, when she had managed to come to terms with it herself. She'd wanted to put careful thought into how she would tell him, but now he was here and she no longer had that luxury. She had to tell him now, because the alternative was to lie, and she couldn't do that. Not about something so important, so potentially life-changing.

She swallowed, her throat painfully dry. 'I think you'd better come in.'

His hands dropped from her shoulders, and she knew a moment's regret, because their weight and warmth had felt oddly steadying in the midst of the tumult occurring in her body and mind.

But soon, *very* soon, he would share the tumult. And then he might not feel so inclined to offer support.

Her stomach churning, she led him through to her lounge. Like the rest of her flat, it was light and spacious, and decorated by her own hand, the palette of soft creams, pale lemons and blues intended to create an elegant, soothing space that invited one to relax. She loved this room, but she was conscious now that in less than nine months' time the cream carpet and pale colour scheme would be terribly impractical.

She stood by the sofa, thought about offering him tea or coffee—or something stronger—then decided against it. She doubted he would stay for long.

'I'm pregnant.' Saying the words out loud made her knees do a little wobble, but she stayed standing, even as a renewed bout of nausea rolled through her.

In the middle of the room, Ramon went as still as a statue, and his face... A small, detached part of her mind was fascinated by the way the colour slid right out from under his skin, leaving a pallor that made it look as if someone had tipped a bucket of whitewash over him.

Emily wrapped her arms around her middle. Waited for him to say the words she imagined most men came out with in this situation.

Is it mine?

The seconds ticked by in heavy silence, and she felt as if she were a character in some tacky scene from an overdramatic soap opera. The final line of dialogue had been delivered and the actors had paused for dramatic effect before the show cut to a commercial break. The random thought nearly tore a hysterical giggle from her before she caught herself. She closed her eyes. What was wrong with her? Nothing about this was funny.

'Have you confirmed it with a doctor?'

It took her a moment to realise it wasn't the question she'd expected. That he wasn't doubting that he was the father. Wasn't insulting her by suggesting there were other men to whom she could point the finger. 'Yesterday,' she said, her throat growing thick with something awfully like gratitude.

A glazed look entered his eyes and she knew he was processing. 'We used protection.'

Emily had said those same words to herself, over and over. It hadn't changed the outcome. She shrugged. 'Condoms aren't foolproof,' she offered. 'And maybe…the shower…?' Their gazes locked, the sudden, scalding intensity of his transmitting loud and clear that he hadn't forgotten the things they'd done to each other under the steaming water.

Ramon looked away, dragged his hand over his mouth and breathed in hard, his nostrils flaring. 'Give me a minute,' he said abruptly, and walked out of the room.

Emily stared after him, her breath locking in her chest as realisation struck and her stomach curled into a hard, familiar knot of resignation. Ramon was walking away, doing exactly what she'd expected him to do, exactly what she had known he would—so why was a silly sob pushing its way up her throat?

She slapped her hand over her mouth but she was too slow and the sob escaped, making a loud, choked, hiccupping sound. A *humiliating* sound.

Ramon appeared in the doorway, his brows clamped together. 'Emily?'

She jerked her hand down. 'Just go.' Somehow she managed to inject some backbone into her voice. 'I'm fine. I don't need you to stay. This is my problem to deal with.'

He stood looking at her for a long moment, then he stalked across the room and her heart surged into her throat. He looked angry but, as he drew closer, the hard lines bracketing his mouth resembled determination more than fury. He stopped in front of her, lifted his hands and framed her face. The warm pressure of his palms against her cheeks made her pulse skitter. 'I am not leaving,' he said. 'I am going downstairs to dismiss my driver and then I'm coming back here so we can talk.'

She stared at him in stunned silence.

'Do you understand me, Emily?'

Her brain told her a simple 'yes' would suffice, but her throat suddenly felt too tight to speak. So she simply nodded. And then she sank onto the sofa, watched him leave and waited for him to return.

Ramon braced his palms on the wall outside Emily's flat and sucked in one lungful of air after another.

He didn't need to go downstairs. A simple text message to his driver had done the job. But he'd needed an excuse to grab a moment alone, to get a handle on himself—on the turbulent emotions storming through him.

Dios.

He wanted to run. To somewhere. To anywhere. As fast and as far away as his legs would carry him.

How the hell had this happened?

Stupid question. He knew how it had happened. He'd been reckless. Unthinking. And now he was the father of an unborn child.

Another unborn child.

Another innocent life to destroy.

His breath shuddered out of him. He wasn't meant to be a father, or a husband. Husbands and fathers were supposed to protect the people close to them and Ramon had already failed that test on a spectacular scale. He kept people, his family included, at arm's length for a good reason: to protect them from *himself.*

He swallowed hard and straightened, a grim sense of determination rising in him, pushing through the turmoil, calming both his thoughts and his breathing. It was the same determination that had seen him do his family and friends a favour by walking away from them twelve years ago, except this time Ramon wouldn't be walking away. How could he? He'd been presented with an opportunity to protect his unborn child—an opportunity he'd been denied all those years ago. He'd barely processed Emily's revelation, but he had enough clarity of mind to recognise that he was being given a rare second chance. A chance to do something right...this time.

He pulled out his phone, called Marsha and told her Emily had the flu and wouldn't be back for at least two days.

When he re-entered the flat she was sitting on one end of the cream sofa where he'd left her. Her hands were clasped on her knees, her grey eyes big and unblinking. They grew even larger when she saw him as though, in spite of his assurances, she hadn't truly believed until that moment that he'd return. That she'd assumed he would desert her filled him with too many emotions to examine. He removed his suit jacket and draped it over the back of an armchair.

'It's yours,' she said.

He turned to her. 'Pardon?'

'The baby.' Her fingers fiddled with the pearl around her neck. 'It's yours.'

He sat beside her, clasped her chin and forced her gaze up when she tried to look away. 'I know.'

Her tongue came out to moisten her lips in a nervous gesture that he shouldn't have found arousing in the circumstances—but he had lain in bed and thought about those lips on many nights during the past six weeks of self-imposed celibacy, and they were just as lush and pretty as he remembered.

He dropped his hand. 'I'm sorry, Emily.'

'What for?'

'For the way I behaved in Paris. I wanted another night with you. When you refused, I didn't like it,' he confessed. 'I was out of order.'

She shrugged. 'I'm not proud of my behaviour, either. And, since we're making apologies...' colour seeped into her pale face '... I didn't sleep with you because I was drunk.'

He knew that, but the part of his male ego she'd wounded six weeks ago appreciated hearing it all the same. He lifted his hand again and traced the elegant arch of one cheekbone with his thumb. 'You look tired,' he remarked. 'And pale. Have you eaten today?'

She shook her head, her long, untethered curls tumbling about her shoulders. 'I've been a bit ill.'

'Are you drinking plenty of water?'

'Some...not as much as I should.' She stood up, her plain tee shirt and stretchy black leggings emphasising that she'd lost weight.

He frowned. Just how ill had she been?

'Actually, I could kill a cup of tea,' she said. 'I'll make us a pot.'

'Sit.' He rose to his feet. 'I'll do it.' Her eyes widened and he adopted an affronted air. 'You don't think I can make tea?' he challenged.

A faint smile crossed her features. 'I'm sure you're very capable. But it's my kitchen and I know where everything is. And I've done nothing all day... I need to move.'

He let her go without further protest, then sauntered to the window, thrust his hands in his pockets and studied the street below. He let his thoughts run to practical matters. The building wasn't wired with a security system and that bothered him. The neighbourhood seemed respectable but good neighbourhoods weren't immune to crime. The building's current security measures were flimsy and not helped by her downstairs neighbour who repeatedly left the main entry unlocked. Ramon had walked straight in today, just as he had six weeks ago.

And the stairs…three flights of them. Should pregnant women climb stairs every day?

He heard movement behind him and turned. Emily carried a wooden tray bearing a blue china teapot and matching cups. He waited for her to place the tray on the coffee table before he spoke. 'You can't stay here.'

She looked up, one hand gripping the handle of the teapot. She frowned as if he'd spouted something unintelligible. 'Excuse me?'

'Come and stay with me at Citrine.'

'Your West End club?'

'Yes. I'm using the penthouse. I can make it available for us long-term.'

Slowly, she put the teapot down and straightened. 'Why?'

'Because it's safer. And closer to work for you.' He paused. 'Not that you'll want to do that for much longer, of course.'

She stared at him. 'What are you talking about?'

He pulled his hands from his pockets and reminded himself that she was tired and stressed. Most likely not thinking straight. 'Emily,' he said patiently, walking towards her. 'Your life is about to change. Permanently. We need to consider what's best for you and the baby.'

'What's best for me,' she said, her voice rising a notch, 'is to stay in my own home.'

'It's not secure here.'

'This is a decent neighbourhood!'

He put his hands on her shoulders to calm her, but she shrugged him off and took a step back.

'Bad things happen in good neighbourhoods all the

time,' he said. 'And what about the stairs? How do you think you'll cope with those in six months' time?'

She put her palms to her cheeks. 'Ramon—just slow down for a minute. Please.'

'Emily. We need to talk about these things.'

She shook her head.

'Make some decisions,' he pressed. 'Think about the future.'

'Oh, my God.' She scrunched her eyes closed. 'Next you'll be suggesting we get married.'

Her tone was incredulous and Ramon clenched his jaw, jamming his hands back into his pockets. Marriage ranked right alongside fatherhood on his list of undesirable scenarios, but he'd be lying if he said the idea hadn't crossed his mind in the last twenty minutes.

When he remained silent, she opened her eyes and gave him a blunt look. 'I'm not marrying you.' She picked up the teapot and started pouring as if she hadn't just plunged a knife into the heart of his male pride. 'And besides...' She set the pot down and straightened again. 'Don't you think all these suggestions are a little premature? I'm only six weeks along and—' She hesitated, biting her lip for a moment, her gaze lowering. 'Miscarriages aren't uncommon in the first twelve weeks of pregnancy,' she finished quietly.

This time her words cut deeper than his pride and he felt their impact like a cold blade under his ribs. The sharp reminder of history only strengthened his resolve. 'I know,' he said, deciding then and there on a more ruthless approach. 'I've lost a child before.'

The look of shock on Emily's face was swift and complete. Her hand flew to her stomach. 'Oh, Ramon... I'm so sorry. That must've been awful.'

He picked up a cup and took a mouthful of black tea, welcoming the hit of warmth in his stomach. 'It's ancient history,' he said, replacing the cup. 'But, yes, the experience was difficult. My girlfriend miscarried and I was helpless to prevent it.' It wasn't the full story but hopefully enough to elicit Emily's sympathy. With a hand on her slender waist, he guided her to the sofa, handed her her tea as she sat and pressed home his advantage. 'You're clearly not well,' he observed. 'And you could have some challenging months ahead. Why stay here alone when there's an alternative?'

She shook her head, her jaw taking on a stubborn tilt. 'I'm fine.'

'You're pale and weak.'

'I'm in shock,' she defended. 'I haven't known about this for much longer than you have. And I have a bit of morning sickness, that's all.'

He sat down beside her. 'Your mother died in childbirth.' He delivered the words as gently as he could, but still her face drained of what little colour it possessed. Ramon himself wasn't unaffected by the statement. The thought of Emily dying evoked a dark, volatile emotion that tore through his chest.

Her hand rose to her throat and he saw her fingers tremble as they closed around the pearl. When her gaze met his, the naked appeal in her eyes reached into his gut like a fist and squeezed. 'Can we just slow this down?' she implored him. 'Take one day at a time? Please?'

He inhaled a deep breath. 'Slow' wasn't how he preferred to do things but he knew that pushing Emily too hard in her current state would be counterproductive. Which meant a change of tack was required. He expelled his breath, making a swift decision. 'Of course,' he said, then got to his feet and pulled out his phone.

She frowned. 'Who are you calling?'

'Someone who'll arrange to have my things packed and brought over.'

Her eyes rounded. 'I beg your pardon?'

'If you stay,' he said, 'then so do I.'

She stared at him and then she flopped against the sofa and slapped her hand over her forehead. 'Oh, my God.' Her laugh held a touch of hysteria. 'You're really *not* leaving.'

Calmly, he hit the number for the concierge at Citrine and put the phone to his ear.

Emily glowered at him.

He glowered back. 'Drink your tea, Emily.'

Emily awoke with a violent shiver. She felt cold. She lifted her head and saw she'd thrown the duvet and sheets off some time during the night. She'd had a hot flush, she suddenly remembered. Was that a symptom of early pregnancy? Or was it more to do with the man who was sleeping in the spare room across the hall?

She squinted at her clock. Four a.m.

Sighing, she dragged the duvet over her and stared at the ceiling. None of this felt real. The pregnancy. Ramon being in her home. A future looming that was nothing like the one she'd envisaged.

Not that she'd ever devoted much time to pondering her future beyond running The Royce. Marriage and children weren't things she'd allowed herself to dwell upon. Doing so had filled her with an unsettling yearning. A feeling of emptiness she could only banish by burying herself in work.

And there was nothing wrong with that. Nothing wrong with being a career woman. Not every girl got to marry the perfect man and have the perfect family, the perfect life. Look at her mother—she'd married a charming, handsome man who'd turned out to be a philandering pleasure-seeker and then died having his child.

A metallic taste surged in her mouth.

Oh, no. Was she going to be sick?

She tossed the covers off, sat up and waited for a moment to see if the nausea would pass. She should grab her robe or a sweatshirt, she thought. She and Ramon were sharing her only bathroom and she was wearing only knickers and a cotton...

She clapped her hand over her mouth, ran from her room and reached the toilet just in time.

Ugh. She hated this. *Hated* it.

She retched again and, as she tried to scrape her hair away from her face, felt a warm, firm hand touch her back.

Ramon didn't say a word. He just knelt behind her, relieved her hands of her hair and waited for her to finish.

'I'm done,' she croaked a long, humiliating minute later, and he helped her to her feet and gave her space to clean herself up at the basin.

When he scooped her up she acquiesced with a shameful lack of protest and, despite her mental exhaustion, she was acutely conscious of everything as he carried her back to her room. His strong, muscular arms. His clean, soapy scent. His hard, tee-shirt-covered chest under one of her hands.

She shouldn't have liked any of it.

She liked all of it.

He sat her on the edge of her bed and pressed a glass of water into her hand. 'Drink.'

'You're very bossy,' she muttered.

He crossed his arms over his chest. 'And you're very mouthy for someone who's just been hugging the toilet bowl.'

It was difficult to find a dignified response to that, so she sipped her water instead. Her throat hurt. And so did her head. Although she figured that wasn't from throwing up so much as it was a side-effect of the relentless racing of her mind over the past forty-eight hours.

She put the glass on the nightstand. Her hand trembled, but it was nothing compared to the uncontrollable shaking inside her. 'I'm not sure I can do this,' she said, fear and uncertainty crashing in like a fast-moving tidal wave she couldn't outrun.

He dropped to his haunches. 'Do what?'

'Have a baby,' she whispered.

His shoulders tensed, a stark expression descending over his features, and her heart clenched as she realised he'd misinterpreted her words. 'No,' she said hurriedly, cursing herself silently. 'I don't mean that. I don't want to get rid of this baby, Ramon.'

How could she have forgotten what he'd told her? That he had lost a child? The revelation not only shocked her but cast him in a different light. It was easy to look at Ramon and see only the confidence and charm. But he had suffered something devastating. That kind of loss had to leave a scar. She inhaled a deep breath. 'I mean… I don't know *how* I'm going to do this. I feel…'

'What?'

She shrugged, reluctant to articulate such a weak emotion. 'Scared,' she admitted, and glanced away.

Slipping a finger under her chin, he returned her gaze to his. 'I think you can do anything you set your mind to, Emily Royce.'

His tone was firm, his vote of confidence unexpected, and a burst of warmth blossomed in her chest.

But was he right?

She knew nothing about motherhood. Nothing about the bond between mother and child. She'd never had her own mother to bond with. No aunts or grandmothers or female role models. Just her strict teachers at boarding school and her grandfather's housekeeper, the humourless Mrs Thorne. Emily didn't doubt she would love her child—and she would do so fiercely—but would her child love *her*?

As a daughter she was hardly worth loving; her father had demonstrated that time and again through his rejection of any close bond with her. Who was to say she'd prove any more lovable as a parent?

And then, as if her insecurities weren't enough to unsettle her, there was her mother's death to consider. The frightening reminder of life's utter fragility.

What if childbirth put Emily at a similar risk?

She felt the prick of tears and mentally rolled her eyes. *Great.* Another symptom of pregnancy. She wondered if she could also blame her newly discovered condition for the heavy, achy sensation in her breasts or, like the hot flush, did that have more to do with the man hunkered beside the bed and the desire that flooded her body every time she looked at him?

'I'm tired,' she said, lowering her gaze before her eyes betrayed her. The man had just held her hair as she hurled up the last contents of her stomach. He was unlikely to find her attractive right now. 'Thanks for checking on me.' She curled onto her side and pulled the duvet up to her chin. 'I'm going to try to get some more sleep.'

Ramon stood up and she closed her eyes, listening for the tell-tale sounds of him leaving her room and going back to his. But the absolute silence told her he hadn't moved. Her heart thudded in her ears, and then she felt his hand brush gently over her hair. Felt his lips press a soft, feather-light kiss on her temple. 'We'll do this together, Emily,' he said, his breath fanning warmth across her cheek. 'You're not alone now.' And then he padded out of the room.

As the door closed Emily's chin wobbled dangerously and she tucked her face into the pillow. Yesterday, walking into her empty flat after visiting her doctor, she'd felt very alone but had told herself it didn't matter.

She was used to being alone.

You're not alone now.

She drifted off to sleep, that last conscious thought wrapping around her like a warm, comforting cocoon.

CHAPTER EIGHT

ON THURSDAY EMILY returned to work even though Ramon had wanted her to stay home and rest for the remainder of the week—a preference he'd expressed for the umpteenth time in her kitchen last night. She'd been preparing a simple meal for them and he'd not long been back from a meeting in the city. He'd loosened his tie and collar, rolled his shirt sleeves up his bronzed, muscular forearms and planted his palms on the kitchen island as arguments and counter-arguments had bandied back and forth.

For a brief time Emily had felt as if they were an ordinary couple in the midst of a minor domestic dispute. The thought had left her feeling slightly breathless and flustered, not because it was outlandish or repellent, but rather because it'd sent a flare of unfamiliar warmth through her chest.

No one had ever cared about her enough to argue with her over her choices before.

He cares about the baby. Not you.

The insidious thought elbowed its way into her head and she frowned at her computer screen.

Of course he cared about the baby. And that was all that mattered, she assured herself. He was accepting responsibility for the child they'd conceived and Emily wasn't hoping for anything more. Certainly not marriage or any long-term commitment beyond his being a loving, supportive father to their child. If her grandfather had been alive he would have demanded that she wed, but the eccentric, formidable Gordon Royce was no longer here, and not even the outrageous financial incentive laid out in his will could persuade Emily to consider a hasty, loveless marriage. No. She and Ramon would take a sensible, modern-day approach and work out some kind of shared custody arrangement. Ultimately they would lead separate lives while keeping things amicable for the sake of their child.

She clicked her mouse and opened a file on her computer. *Work*. That, if nothing else, would give her a sense of normality, of being in control. And, given that her home and her independence were being seriously encroached upon, she needed to feel in control. Right now she was humouring Ramon, allowing him to assert his dominance because she suspected that underneath all that machismo he, too, was afraid. Who wouldn't be after experiencing the devastating loss of an unborn child? It was why she was willing to tolerate his over-the-top concerns for her safety and wellbeing—for now.

But he couldn't camp in her spare room for the next seven and a half months. It wasn't practical for either of them. He had an office and a home in New York. Clubs and resorts around the world. A jet-setting lifestyle she couldn't imagine him curtailing for long. And she needed her space. Her equilibrium restored. She could barely think straight with all of that potent, simmering testosterone floating about her home.

Which was why she'd been so desperate to return to work. She needed some distance. Some perspective.

A knock sounded on her office door.

'Come in,' she called, glancing up with a twinge of guilt. A closed door sent a message to her staff that she was unavailable. In fact, it was only closed because she'd been making a list of gynaecologists to consider and hadn't got round to re-opening it.

She pasted on a smile that slid off her face the moment the door opened and Ramon stepped in. Exasperated, she glared at him.

He closed the door. 'If I didn't know you were secretly thrilled to see me, *querida*, I'd take offence at that scowl on your face.'

The endearment combined with his dry wit made her heart skip a beat. She sat back in her chair. 'I thought you had meetings all day at Citrine?' She eyed him in his dark pinstriped suit and wondered how many female mouths he'd left watering in his wake that morning. 'Don't you have other places to be besides checking up on me?'

One dark eyebrow lifted. 'Such as?'

'I don't know… New York? Paris? The Arctic Circle?'

He sauntered over and lowered his big frame into a chair in front of her desk. 'You know, you're cute when you're not throwing up.'

She sent him a withering look. 'That's not funny.'

The twitch of his lips suggested he thought otherwise. 'How are you feeling?'

'Fine. As fine as I was feeling an hour ago when you called and asked the same question.'

'Nausea?'

'Better.'

'No more vomiting?'

'Not since this morning.' When yet again he'd knelt on the bathroom floor and held her hair as she'd wretched into the toilet, then carried her back to bed before returning to the spare room. The fact she'd almost grabbed onto him at the last second and implored him to stay in her bed with her was something she'd deliberately avoided dwelling on today. 'Honestly,' she said. 'I'm fine.'

He frowned. '"Fine" is not a term I would apply to someone who is throwing up several times a day.'

'It's just morning sickness. It won't kill me.' She thought of her mother and ruthlessly quashed the inevitable surge of fear.

'Or it could be *hyperemesis gravidarum*.'

She blinked. 'Excuse me?'

'Severe morning sickness,' he said. 'Which could be harmful to both you and the baby.'

She stared at him. 'How do you even *know* that term?'

'It's in one of the booklets on your coffee table. The ones you said your doctor gave to you.' His eyes narrowed. 'You have read them, haven't you?'

She shifted in her chair. 'I'm working my way through them.' It was close to the truth. She'd made a start and then given up when she'd felt overwhelmed by the sheer volume of information. She'd educated herself on the basics—what she should and shouldn't eat, which supplements to take—and that was all she could cope with for now.

'Good.' He stood up. 'Let's go.'

She frowned. 'Where?'

'To lunch.'

She shook her head. 'I'm not hungry.'

'You have to eat, Emily.' His tone grew stern. 'For you and for the baby.'

The knowledge that he was right—she couldn't live entirely on crackers and herbal tea—grated against an instinctive urge to rail against the web of control he was slowly weaving around her. She wasn't accustomed to having her decisions made for her…and yet she understood that he had the best interests of their baby at heart.

And that, she reminded herself once again, was all that mattered right now.

Her baby.

Their baby.

She retrieved her handbag from a drawer and stood. 'Very well,' she said, the prospect of trying something other than crackers for lunch not as unappealing as she'd made out. She missed food. Missed her ordinarily healthy appetite.

Before Ramon opened the door, she placed her hand on

his forearm. 'I haven't told anyone yet,' she said. 'Not even Marsha. I'd prefer we keep the pregnancy a secret until I've passed the first trimester.'

'Of course.'

She felt the muscles in his arm tense under her hand and quickly let go. 'You haven't told anyone?'

'No.'

'Not even your family?'

His mouth tightened fractionally. 'No one, Emily.'

Sensing she'd ventured into sensitive territory, she left the subject alone, yet as they exited the club through a discreet side entrance she couldn't help wondering about his family. She'd assumed he would want to tell them almost straight away about the pregnancy but clearly that wasn't the case. For a moment she thought that was strange and then it occurred to her that she was the last person qualified to make that kind of determination.

What did *she* know about family?

Sadly, not a lot.

On Saturday morning Ramon flew to Paris to meet with a team of engineers at Saphir. Apparently there was some structural issue with the enormous swimming pool in the recreation centre and a dispute with the original installation company that was sufficiently serious for him to involve himself.

He'd urged Emily to go with him, but she'd refused. Returning to Paris, to the same place where they'd shared their one night of incredible, mind-blowing sex, would do neither of them any favours. Sharing her home with him, sleeping in separate rooms while every night she yearned for his touch, was challenging enough without stirring up memories safer left buried. Reluctant to leave her alone even for a single night, Ramon had argued, and their heated exchange had acted like lighter fluid on an already blazing fire, ramping up the sexual tension that'd simmered below the surface of their every interaction in the last five days.

Tired and irritable by the week's end, Emily had told herself she was looking forward to his absence.

Now, after twenty-four hours without his overwhelming, charismatic presence in her home, she had to admit the truth.

She missed him.

Which was lunacy. How could you miss someone who'd been a fixture in your life for less than a week?

She frowned into the bowl of brownie batter she was mixing by hand with a solid wooden spoon. Allowing herself to grow dependent on Ramon would be a mistake. Whatever form their relationship eventually took, he would be there for their child, not for her. And that suited Emily just fine. She needed him to step up and be a father—a better one, hopefully, than Maxwell had been to her—but she didn't need him to be anything else. Not in the long term.

Curbing her thoughts, she focused on her baking. This morning, for the first time in a week, her nausea had been short-lived and mild enough to avoid a sprint to the bathroom. Taking advantage of the unexpected reprieve, she'd gone for a walk in the autumn sunshine, picked up some fresh produce from a local market, indulged in an early-afternoon nap and then awoken with a fierce, irrepressible craving for chocolate.

She stopped stirring, dipped her finger into the batter for a taste test and closed her eyes as she let her taste buds reach a verdict. The balance of the dark chocolate and the vanilla was perfect. Sliding her finger out of her mouth, she hummed her approval.

'Dios.'

Emily almost screamed with fright at the deep, gruff

voice that echoed through her kitchen. She flattened her palm over her racing heart and turned.

Ramon stood in the doorway, one powerful shoulder propped against the frame, the compact leather holdall he travelled with sitting on the hardwood floor at his feet. In a casual open-necked shirt and thigh-hugging jeans, he looked rugged, gorgeous and a thousand times more mouthwatering than any brownie batter.

A rush of need tightened her belly. 'I thought you weren't getting back till later!'

His gaze slid over her, leaving a trail of heat in its wake. 'Why are you cooking in your underwear?'

Her cheeks burned and she silently cringed. Her pink knickers were the old, practical cotton ones she wore for comfort, and she knew without looking that her stretchy white camisole did little to conceal the fact she was bra-less. She resisted folding her arms over her breasts. 'I went for a nap.'

He straightened. 'Are you unwell?'

She stopped herself from executing an exasperated eye roll. 'No. I was just tired. When I woke up I was craving something sweet and... I was hot...' It was her only excuse for not having thrown her clothes back on after her nap. She cast him an accusing look. 'Why did you creep in?'

One corner of his mouth lifted. 'I didn't "creep". I came in quietly in case you were resting.' He pushed away from the door frame, his gaze trailing over her again, and there was something very deliberate about the way he looked at her. 'So you're feeling okay?'

She swallowed, her mouth gone dry. 'Yes.' Was her imagination running wild or was the gleam in his eyes almost predatory? She cleared her throat. 'Did you get the problem with the pool sorted?'

'*Sí.*'

He moved closer and her skin started to tingle. She pressed her back against the edge of the bench. 'Will you need to return next week?'

'No. Did you miss me, Emily?'

Struggling to keep her breathing even, she shrugged. 'Not really.'

One dark eyebrow rose. 'Not at all?'

He moved another inch closer and her limbs weakened. 'Maybe a tiny bit,' she relented.

He braced his hands on the counter either side of her. 'I missed you.'

His voice was low and gravel-rough, and a pulse of excitement flickered in Emily's throat. She sent her tongue out across her lower lip to alleviate its dryness and heard his breath catch. Raw desire flared in his eyes, and the look of intense arousal on his face, the palpable throb of leashed energy from his big body, was enthralling. Intoxicating. He wanted her, and his patent hunger called on some deep, primitive level to her own equally ravenous desire.

'What are you making?'

She saw his mouth move, saw those sensuous lips form the words, but couldn't comprehend the question. 'What?' she asked faintly.

He tipped her chin up, forcing her gaze to lift from his beautiful mouth. 'What are you making?' he repeated.

This close, she could see the tiny individual pinpricks of the dark stubble along his jaw, feel the impact of the raw heat radiating off him. It shimmered in the air, saturating her skin, slowing the blood in her veins to a sluggish, sensual beat.

She managed to articulate a response. 'Chocolate brownies.'

'Doesn't chocolate contain caffeine?'

As if drawn by the pull of a powerful magnet, her gaze returned to his mouth.

'Are you going to lecture me,' she challenged huskily, 'or kiss me?'

Ramon slid his mouth over Emily's and drank in her sweet taste like a man savouring his first sip of water after days trapped in a merciless desert.

Except his deprivation and thirst had lasted for weeks, not days, and this last week had proven by far the most torturous.

Four nights of sleeping in her spare room. Four nights of doing the right thing. Four nights of struggling to dampen the hot embers of desire that constantly threatened to burst into flame and incinerate his restraint, along with his questionable attempts at chivalry.

And the mornings… The mornings were their own special brand of hell. Each time she was sick, a gut-wrenching combination of powerlessness and disgust tore at him. *Self*-disgust because, even as he carried her back to bed after a bout of illness, his body stirred with an untimely lust he had no ability to switch off.

Last night in Paris had offered no reprieve. And not only because of the constant, gnawing concern about her welfare that he knew in some part of his brain was irrational and extreme. He'd stayed in the same suite they'd shared seven weeks before and realised too late his mistake. Every inch of the place, from the living room, to the bed, to the shower, had teased hot, erotic images from his memory until desire had pounded through him so relentlessly he'd had to rely on his hand to achieve a degree of release.

Flying back today, he'd been as grimly and ruthlessly determined as ever to keep his lust banked and his hands to himself—and then he'd walked in and found her standing in her underwear in the kitchen, with her glorious mane of hair flowing loose over her shoulders and her finger in her mouth like some provocative magazine centrefold.

God forgive him.

He was only human.

Her hands in his hair, her soft body moulded to his, she moaned against his lips, a low, needy sound that ramped up the heat in his body and assured him that she was a willing, enthusiastic participant. Reluctantly, he dragged his mouth from hers. If he didn't press pause he'd end up taking her right there against the kitchen bench, or on the floor. He gathered her into his arms, strode from the kitchen and halted in the hallway.

Intuiting his quandary, she whispered in his ear. 'My room.'

Seconds later he lowered her onto her bed and ripped off her scant attire in between pressing hot, urgent kisses to her mouth and throat. When he had her completely naked, he groaned. Her creamy skin was smooth and flawless, her breasts as perfect as he remembered, perhaps even a little fuller. He drew one of her rosy nipples into his mouth and she arched up, drove her hands into his hair and encouraged him with little mewls of delight that intensified the throb of his desire.

She tugged at his shirt, her fingers fumbling with a button. 'Not fair,' she panted. 'I'm the only one naked.'

To which he gave a low chuckle, reluctantly left her side and quickly dispensed with his clothing. Naked, he returned, straddling her legs so he could admire the view while tracing the curves of her body with his hands.

Her stomach was flat, no sign of the life growing inside her evident as yet. But knowing it was there—knowing they'd created it together—flooded him with a fierce sense of possessiveness far more potent than any fear he'd wrestled with in recent days.

The child inside her was his.

She was his.

He leaned over and kissed Emily's stomach, glancing up as she lifted her head. Their gazes locked and it seemed in those few seconds, with only the sounds of their breathing and the drum of his heartbeat filling his ears, as if something unspoken and powerful passed between them. He dragged his gaze from hers before the strange pressure in his chest could intensify, then went lower, down to the sweet, feminine centre of her body. Gently, he parted her and found her wet and swollen. He slipped his finger inside her, loving the way she panted and writhed.

'Come for me, *mi belleza*,' he commanded, then licked once, and she climaxed almost immediately.

'Ramon!'

Gasping his name, she dove her fingers into his hair, gripping his scalp as he sucked and licked, extending her orgasm until her keen cries of pleasure became soft whimpers and her whole body went limp. He rose up between her legs, his body taut with tension, his muscles trembling from the effort required to contain his need. He was afraid that, if he plunged into her now, he'd lose control and take her too hard and fast. *Dios*. Was it possible to hurt the baby?

He rolled onto his back and took her with him so that she sat astride him. Grasping her hips, he positioned her above his erection. This way she'd have control. She seemed to understand because she reached down, wrapped her fingers around his aching shaft and guided the tip to her entrance. For a second he tensed, automatically thinking, *Condom*, then realised they didn't need one. He closed his eyes and couldn't stop a rough cry ripping from his throat as she sank onto him, encasing him in a sheath of silken heat.

Teeth gritted, he kept his pelvis as still as possible, allowing Emily to set the pace and decide how deep to take him. She began to move, her tight, wet heat sliding up and down his shaft, and Ramon's consciousness narrowed until there was nothing but her sitting atop him, her face contorted with pleasure as she wantonly rode him.

Nothing else filled his head.

No concerns.

No fears.

Just their stunning, mind-blowing chemistry and the shattering pinnacle of a climax more powerful than any he'd ever experienced.

'I've made an appointment for us to see a gynaecologist on Tuesday.'

Emily's head rested on Ramon's chest. She blinked drowsily. His deep voice had registered but she had trouble processing his words. Possibly something to do with the post-coital haze shrouding her brain, she thought with a bloom of lazy satisfaction.

A smile pushed its way onto her mouth. She'd always thought the notion of multiple orgasms was a fallacy, just as she'd always believed she would never be someone who enjoyed sex very much.

Now she knew better.

On both counts.

She thought about the brownie batter, abandoned on the kitchen counter, and smiled again. Who needed chocolate when you could have…?

Suddenly her limbs went from languid to rigid. 'What did you say?' She tried to sit up but his arms tightened, keeping her locked against his side. 'Let me go,' she demanded.

'No.'

His abrupt refusal sent a pulse of anger through her. 'Why not?'

'Because you're about to get upset.'

'I'm already upset,' she snapped.

'All the more reason to stay here and calm down.'

Furious, she struggled against him, but he was too strong, his arms like bands of solid steel, his big, muscular thighs trapping one of her own. 'Fine,' she bit out after a moment of angry panting and mental cursing. 'At least let me look at you properly.'

He loosened his hold, just a fraction—enough for her to twist around. The movement brought her breasts into full contact with his chest, and she ignored the puckering of her nipples, the strum of heat in her belly. They were both naked still, the sheets tangled around their feet, the air heavily scented with sex. She looked at him expectantly, and he blew out a breath.

'You were taking too long to decide on a specialist,' he said. 'So I made the decision for us.'

'Us?'

'Yes, Emily. Us.' He propped a hand behind his head, his biceps bunching impressively, and stared down the length of his nose at her. The strong, proud quality of that particular appendage reminded her that many generations of Spanish aristocracy ran through his blood. 'It's my baby too.'

His tone chided, and she felt uncomfortably as if she'd been slapped on the wrist. 'But it's my body,' she countered. 'I should get to choose who looks after it.' The fact she hadn't done so yet was beside the point. Damn it, she was pregnant. She was allowed to be indecisive.

'And when were you planning to make your decision?'

'Soon,' she prevaricated.

'Well, now you don't need to. I've done you a favour.'

'No, you haven't. You've swooped in and taken control again as if—' She stopped and drew her bottom lip between her teeth.

'As if I'm the child's father?'

A tense silence descended. She couldn't argue with that simple truth. Then again, she wasn't in a terribly rational mood. She set her jaw. 'I'm not going.'

He scowled. 'You will.'

'I won't.'

'Now you're being childish.'

'What are you going to do?' She gave him an arch look. 'Spank me?'

He growled and moved so fast she was spread-eagled on her stomach before she'd taken her next breath. A large, heavy palm in the centre of her back kept her playfully pinioned to the mattress with her bottom helplessly bared.

She twisted her head to glare at him. 'Don't you dare!'

His grin was wicked and devastatingly sexy. He didn't spank her—she hadn't really thought he would—but he did hold her down, run his hand up the inside of her thigh and do things with his fingers, and later his tongue, that made her whimper, plead and promise to do absolutely anything he commanded.

Afterwards, they lay together again, Emily's cheek pressed to his chest, one arm flung over the hard, beautifully sculpted surface of his abdomen.

'Which gynaecologist?'

He told her the name and her eyes widened. He had chosen a Harley Street specialist. One she had struck from her list of potential private ob-gyns because the cost was too prohibitive and he was bound to have a waiting list.

Clearly, there were certain benefits to be reaped when the father of one's baby was a billionaire.

Her gaze drifted to the pearl necklace lying on the nightstand. Feeling hot and sticky earlier, she'd taken it off before her nap and forgotten to put it back on.

The pearl was the only possession she had of her mother's. Surprisingly, her father had given it to her. He'd left it in a small velvet box on her bedroom dressing table in her grandfather's mansion a few days before her sixteenth birthday, while she'd still been at boarding school. There'd been a handwritten note with it—nothing elaborate, just three short sentences in her father's untidy scrawl:

> *This belonged to your mother.*
> *She would have wanted you to have it.*
> *Happy Birthday.*
> *Maxwell*

Not *Love, Dad*.

Just *Maxwell*.

Her throat tightened. She'd heard people say you couldn't miss something you'd never had, but Emily knew that wasn't true. She'd never known her mother, but she had missed her desperately throughout her life. When Emily was ten, Mrs Thorne, in a rare moment of compassion, had given her two photographs of her mother and she had cherished them, looking at them often and longing to know more about the woman with the wild blonde curls and the pretty smile. But Mrs Thorne, when asked, had said she hadn't known Kathryn very well and had told Emily to ask her father.

It had taken Emily six months to work up the courage to broach the subject during one of his infrequent visits, and then Maxwell had brushed her curiosity aside.

Closing her eyes, she held her breath and listened to the sound of Ramon's heart beating. It was strong and powerful, much like the man himself. How had she ever drawn parallels between Ramon and her father? They weren't cut from the same cloth. She saw that now.

If her mother had had someone like Ramon by her side during her pregnancy, ensuring she received the proper care and attention, would she have lived?

Emily would never know the answer. She would never know her mother and she could do nothing to change that. But she could do everything within her power to ensure *her* child would grow up knowing its mother.

'I'll go to the appointment on Tuesday,' she said softly, and he kissed the top of her head.

'Gracias, mi belleza.'

CHAPTER NINE

MR LINDSAY, THE Harley Street specialist, was a mild-mannered, softly spoken man to whom Emily warmed at once despite the nerves jangling in her belly in the hours leading up to the appointment. As an expectant mother she felt as if she should be more excited about her first prenatal visit, but it simply made a situation she still grappled to cope with all the more stark and real.

Mr Lindsay smiled from the other side of his big desk in his big, plush medical suite. 'Do you have a rough idea of when you conceived?'

Emily felt her face flame. Was it normal to know the exact date you'd conceived? Or did that scream *one-night stand*?

Just as she opened her mouth to stammer out an answer, Ramon smoothly intervened, supplying the date and then adding, 'We think it was around then, at any rate.' From the chair beside hers, he gave her a warm, encouraging smile. 'It's hard to say exactly, isn't it, *querida*?'

She nodded, returned his smile and tried to transmit a 'thank you' with her eyes.

She was glad he was there—a turnaround from this morning, admittedly, when she'd told him she'd prefer to come alone. A waste of breath, of course. He'd been adamant about attending with her, and no argument had come close to changing his mind.

Mr Lindsay did a swift calculation and pronounced a due date, and Emily's breath locked in her lungs for a moment. In just under thirty-one weeks her baby would be born. Suddenly, it all felt very real.

And very frightening.

She tried to focus, answering Mr Lindsay's questions to the best of her ability. After a while her head spun. The checklist was exhaustive. Medications, supplements, health conditions…

'Any family history of miscarriages or complications with pregnancy?'

Emily froze. She'd anticipated the question, but now the time was here the words jammed in her throat. A chill rippled over her skin—a whisper of the fear she'd tried until now to ignore—and she shivered. The seconds stretched and her silence grew awkward, embarrassing, but still she couldn't unlock her voice. And then Ramon reached over and closed his fingers around hers, stilling their shaking. He squeezed, his touch firm. Reassuring. She looked down at their joined hands, the panic abating, then inhaled deeply. 'My mother died in childbirth,' she said.

Mr Lindsay looked up from his notes. 'Your birth?'

'Yes.'

His expression was grave. 'I'm very sorry,' he said. 'Do you know the details?'

'Not really. I think it might have been pre-eclampsia.'

He scribbled a note, then put his pen down and clasped his hands together on his desk. He stared directly into her eyes. 'Emily, it's perfectly natural given your history to feel some fear about your pregnancy,' he said, 'but I want to assure you both—' he glanced at Ramon, then back at Emily '—that you'll be receiving exceptional care throughout every stage of your journey. We'll take extra precautions, with frequent check-ups and regular testing, and keep a close watch on your blood pressure.' He smiled reassuringly. 'We'll do a physical exam and an ultrasound today to check everything is fine,' he continued. 'There won't be much to see, however. It will be another six weeks at least until we can determine your baby's sex.'

'Oh.' She blinked. Did she want to know her baby's sex

before it was born? She glanced uncertainly at Ramon. Would it matter to him if their child was a girl or a boy? It didn't matter to Emily. And the crazy clause in her grandfather's will certainly didn't sway her one way or another. Gordon Royce had been a fool to attach such an outrageous condition to a large part of his legacy. Even if she had a boy she wouldn't accept the money. It could go to charity for all she cared. 'I don't think I want to know that anyway,' she said. 'I mean—' she glanced again at Ramon '—I'd rather it was a surprise, if you don't mind.'

He shrugged. 'Of course.'

Half an hour later, her first prenatal check-up was over. Ramon had sat in the waiting room while she'd undergone the exam and the ultrasound. She emerged and smiled at him. His coming with her today had shifted something and their connection felt less tenuous, less fragile. It was something Emily hadn't experienced before—a close connection with another person. It gave her hope. Hope that her bond with her baby would be strong. That she'd be a good mother. *That her child would love her.*

Ramon held her hand as they stepped out into the warm autumn sunshine. Outside, they paused on the pristine Mayfair pavement, waiting for his driver to arrive. Emily looked up at him, at those gorgeous, perfectly landscaped features, and her heart performed a slow somersault in her chest. She opened her mouth, wanting to thank him, to tell him how much his support meant to her today, but a bright pop of light stopped her in her tracks.

'Mr de la Vega! Who's the lady? Is she knocked up? Is it yours?'

The lone paparazzo fired off another round of shutter clicks. Scowling, Ramon turned Emily into him, cupping the back of her head and pressing her face protectively into his shoulder.

'When's the kid due?'

Ramon swore under his breath, and then their car pulled up and he was bundling her into the back of the sleek black sedan. The second they were safely ensconced, the driver sped off. Heart pounding, Emily sucked in a shaky breath and cast a stricken look at Ramon.

His face was thunderous.

'You'll marry her, I assume.'

The statement carried a faint air of command. Ramon gritted his teeth. If he could have reached down the phone line and strangled his brother with his bare hands, he would have. There were never any grey areas with Xavier. Life was comprised of black and white.

Right and wrong.

Do or don't.

Right now Xav was urging him towards the 'do'. More specifically, the words 'I do'.

'I'll make that decision when I'm ready.'

A short silence. 'You *are* taking responsibility for the child?'

Ramon ground his teeth a little harder. Xav's opinion of him really did scrape the bottom of the barrel. 'Of course,' he bit out.

He curled his hand into a fist on the desk top and absently cast his gaze over the office that had belonged to Maxwell Royce. In recent days Ramon had staked a more permanent claim on the space, using it as his main base from which to work while in London. He leaned back in the chair, his mind working overtime as it had for the past twenty-four hours. Perhaps he should stake a more permanent claim on the man's daughter as well. It wasn't as if he hadn't already entertained the idea many times over.

'Mamá and Papá are upset they had to find out this way.'

Ramon couldn't help but hear the implicit criticism in his brother's voice. The unspoken words.

You've hurt them. Again.

'Why did you not tell us?' Xav demanded.

'We haven't told anyone. It's too soon. The pregnancy was only confirmed last week.'

'Did you not think the photos would surface?'

He'd thought, *hoped*, they would make a small, scarcely visible splash. Certainly here in England that had been the case, thanks to a minor royal and her very public skirmish with law enforcement dominating the tabloids. Spain was a different story, however. Every gossip site had picked up the photograph of him and Emily standing outside a Harley Street gynaecologist's clinic. In addition, the shot taken of them outside Saphir in Paris over seven weeks ago had surfaced.

'The photos are unfortunate,' he said tightly.

A heavy sigh came down the line. 'Hector's been on the phone. He's on his high horse again. He says the board will have some natural concerns about the potential for negative reaction from our more conservative shareholders.'

'Tell Hector he can go scr—'

'I did.'

Ramon leaned back in his chair. His cool, diplomatic brother had told Hector where to go? That was a conversation he would have liked to witness.

'But he has a point.' Xav's voice was weary. 'This kind of publicity could have a negative impact on both the business and the family.' He was silent. 'Marry the Royce woman and make this right, Ramon. It's what Mamá and Papá will expect. Make them happy. Don't bring disgrace on the family.'

He didn't add the word 'again', but he didn't need to.

The inference was loud and clear.

* * *

'I made you some tea.' Marsha walked across the office and placed a mug of steaming liquid on Emily's desk. 'It's ginger,' she said. 'For the nausea.'

Emily managed a grateful smile. 'Thanks.'

'Can I do anything else?'

'No. Thank you. You're doing plenty. Have there been many more calls?'

A scowl formed on Marsha's pretty face. 'Those tabloid journalists are scum,' she declared. 'Honestly, the things they have the nerve to ask—' She broke off, perhaps seeing Emily's silent wince. Quickly, she added, 'But they're not worth fretting over. And they're not getting anything from me but a "no comment".'

Emily nodded, gratitude surging again. From the moment her pregnancy had become fodder for the tabloids, her assistant had been a godsend. Seventy-two hours of online speculation and gossip had taken its toll, however, and it seemed even Marsha's sweet, patient disposition was being tested.

Emily waited until the younger woman had left before dropping her head in her hands. Humiliation swamped her. This was not how she'd wanted her pregnancy revealed to the world. It was embarrassing and intrusive, and she didn't want even to think about the impact it could have on The Royce. So often she'd swept her father's scandalous behaviour under the carpet, condemning him for his irresponsibility and lack of discretion. Not once had she ever imagined that *she* would cause a scandal.

At least they hadn't made the front page of the papers, although the online gossip sites were having a field day. Emily had fought her curiosity until a moment of weakness had struck. She'd regretted the impulse as soon as she'd clicked on the photo of her and Ramon standing outside the clinic. It made her want to crawl into a very deep hole and never come out. The paparazzo had snapped them just as she had looked up at Ramon, and the expression on her face…

Oh, God.

A fresh wave of humiliation struck. The photo made her look besotted. Infatuated. *In love.* Which was ridiculous. Yes, they were sleeping together—something she knew they'd have to stop doing eventually—but she wasn't in love with him. How could she be? She didn't know the first thing about love.

'Emily.'

She jerked her head up, an immediate shiver running down her spine. She mightn't love Ramon, but his deep voice nevertheless held the power to elicit a swift, visceral response. He moved from the doorway, a mouthwatering mix of raw masculinity and sharp, sophisticated style. He didn't own a single suit that didn't fit his broad frame to utter perfection. The casual look he sported in the evenings in her home was the one she'd come to prefer of late, however. Faded jeans, tee shirt and bare feet. Until recently, she hadn't realised how sexy a man's feet could be.

'Emily?'

She started. 'Sorry?'

'I asked if you're all right.'

'Of course.' A lie. She was a mass of tension and nerves.

'Do you have much more work to do?'

Bereft of her usual focus and energy, she looked at the report on her desk. The one she'd stared blankly at for the last hour. She glanced at her watch. It was only four o'clock. 'A bit,' she said.

'Finish up and come with me.'

She frowned at his commanding tone. 'Where?'

'It's a surprise.'

'You know I don't like surprises.'

His smile was gentle enough to melt her insides. And her resistance.

'Humour me,' he said.

An hour later Emily stood in the centre of an enormous living room on the lower floor of a beautiful late nineteenth-century mansion in Chelsea.

'What do you think?'

Slowly, she turned and looked at Ramon. He stood in front of the big window that overlooked the large fenced-in front garden, rays of late-afternoon sunshine highlighting the rich, glossy mahogany of his hair. His jacket was undone, his tie was loosened and his hands were thrust casually into his trouser pockets.

Emily wasn't fooled, however.

Every hard inch of him radiated tension.

She gazed up at the moulded ceiling and the beautiful, intricate glass chandelier above her head. 'It's stunning.' More than stunning, she thought. Even unfurnished, the three-storey, seven-bedroom residence was breathtaking.

Having grown up in her grandfather's mansion north of London, she wasn't unaccustomed to large houses. But, while the interior of her grandfather's home had been characterised by dark wood and heavy, oppressive furnishings, this house was light and airy, its preserved period features interspersed with touches of contemporary luxury that gave it an elegant, timeless appeal.

And the kitchen!

Emily had salivated over the walk-in pantry, the giant stove, the hand-crafted cabinetry with oodles of storage space and the massive custom-designed granite counter-tops offering plenty of room for culinary experimentation.

Her heart had soared with excitement, and then just as quickly had dropped.

This was a 'for ever' home. The kind where kids grew up

and couples grew old. Where families laughed and argued and loved and cried. Where children and grandchildren came back for Christmases and birthdays and boisterous reunions—the kind you saw in movies or read about in books that guaranteed you a happy ending.

It wasn't the sort of home a billionaire playboy considered buying.

Sadness weighted her down. 'Ramon,' she whispered, a wealth of feeling and helplessness pouring into that single utterance of his name.

His gaze held hers and she thought maybe he understood. Thought he might be experiencing some of the same turmoil she was. He crossed to where she stood and curled his hands over her shoulders. She wanted to press a finger against his lips so he couldn't say the words, but her limbs were frozen, her breath locked in her chest.

'Marry me.'

She closed her eyes. 'I can't.'

He was silent a moment. 'You're saying that because you're scared.'

She lifted her lids. 'Aren't you?'

A muscle worked in his jaw. 'Yes,' he confessed, the word seeming to drag from the depths of his throat. 'But fear isn't a reason to avoid doing the right thing.'

She drew a deep breath. 'Is that what we'd be doing? The right thing?'

His brows lowered. 'Of course.'

'How do you know it's the right thing?' she challenged softly.

His eyes hardened a fraction. 'Providing our child with a stable home with both parents isn't the right thing?'

She swallowed. He painted a nice picture. And, if she let herself, she could easily indulge the fantasy. Imagine them living here as husband and wife, raising their child in this beautiful home. 'Is this what you want, Ramon? A life of domesticity? Tied down with a wife and child?'

His jaw flexed. He dropped his hands from her shoulders. 'I'm thirty years old. Most men settle down eventually.'

Her chest grew heavier. 'I'm not asking what other men do. I'm asking if it's what *you* want. If Paris hadn't happened,' she pressed. 'If I wasn't pregnant, would you be thinking about giving up your bachelor lifestyle?'

'But you are pregnant, Emily.' His voice turned a shade cooler. 'With *my* child.' He paced away, turned back. 'Would you relegate me to the role of part-time father? Someone who breezes in and out of our child's life whenever the custody arrangement tells me I can?'

Emily felt her face blanch. That was exactly the kind of arrangement she'd assumed they would agree upon. But Ramon's description made her blood run cold. Made her think of all the times she'd curled up on her bed as a little girl and cried, believing her daddy didn't care enough to visit her.

A fluttery, panicky feeling worked its way up her throat. 'But what about us?'

He moved closer, eyes narrowing. 'What do you mean?'

'I mean…' she hesitated, colour seeping back into her face '…us—our relationship. You're talking about a long-term commitment. Or at least until our child has grown and left home. That could be twenty years, Ramon. Twenty years of commitment to our child…and me. Twenty years with no other…' She hesitated, her chest suddenly constricting.

'Women?' he supplied.

She lifted her chin. 'I won't tolerate that kind of relationship.'

'Marriage,' he corrected. 'We're talking about marriage, Emily. And, yes, I understand the full implications of such a commitment. For the record—' he grasped her chin and locked his gaze on hers '—I won't tolerate that kind of marriage either.'

She blinked. A part of her wanted to believe him. Another part of her said it didn't matter if she believed him or not, because all of this was hypothetical.

Besides, pledging his faithfulness now, when they were still burning up the sheets, was easy. How would his vows hold up when she was heavy and listless with his child, or exhausted from juggling the demands of motherhood and a job?

He clasped her shoulders again. 'We're good together, *querida*. Are you denying that?'

'Lust is hardly a foundation for marriage.'

The hard line of his mouth softened. 'But it's a good starting point, *si*?'

Love was supposed to be the starting point for marriage, she thought. But then what did she know?

She stepped back, forcing his hands to drop. 'It's a beautiful house,' she said, casting a final look around the room. 'But I... I just need some time to think.'

Emily didn't stop thinking. Not for a single waking minute. For the next forty-eight hours, her mind spun and her stomach churned and Ramon waited on her answer with barely leashed impatience.

At two a.m. on Sunday morning she sat on the cushioned window seat in her lounge, staring out at the moonlit night, her mother's pearl tucked in her hand. She laid her other hand over her stomach and knew instinctively the bond she had feared mightn't grow between her and her child was already there. She could feel it with each beat of her heart. A strong, deep connection unlike anything else she'd ever known. It filled her with a fierce resolve to nurture and protect. To do whatever was best for her child. To give it the best life possible and shield him or her from the same bitter hurts and disappointments she'd suffered as a child.

Breathing deeply, she rose and went back to bed. Ramon lay on his back, the white cotton sheet bunched around his waist, his bare chest rising and falling. The sound of his deep, steady breathing was familiar and somehow comforting. She slipped off her robe and climbed between the sheets.

Ramon stirred, his arm lifting so she could curl into his side. 'Emily?' His voice was a sexy, sleep-roughened rumble.

'I'm fine.' She snuggled close and leaned on her elbow. 'Ramon?'

He caressed her hip. *'Si?'*

'Yes,' she said softly.

He went still. And then he deftly turned her onto her back. He didn't say anything. He just stroked his fingers over her hair. Her cheek. Her mouth. And then he kissed her. Long, deep and hard.

CHAPTER TEN

'ARE YOU CLOSE with your brother?'

Ramon glanced up from his laptop. Emily sat in the seat opposite him in his private jet. In a pale blue trouser suit, with her hair caught loosely in a band over one shoulder, she looked beautiful and flawless in spite of the vomiting spell that had struck shortly before their departure for the airport. Ramon had regarded the sudden resurgence of her nausea as sufficient excuse to cancel their trip to Barcelona, but she had refused to let him postpone the weekend.

Five days had passed since she'd agreed to marry him, three days since he'd placed the enormous radiant-cut diamond on her finger. Two days ago he'd notified his family and afterwards released an announcement to the press. Yesterday, he'd closed the deal on the house in Chelsea.

With each step he'd waited for a sense of panic to set in. Instead, he felt a deep, unmitigated satisfaction. A growing certainty that he was doing the right thing.

He answered Emily's question. 'Not especially.'

'Oh.' She sounded surprised. 'Xavier's adopted, right?'

'Yes. But that's not a factor in our relationship. We have different personalities, that's all. Sometimes we clash.' He closed his laptop, noting Emily's hands fidgeting in her lap. 'You're nervous,' he observed.

'A bit. I'm afraid the whole family thing is rather alien to me.'

Little wonder, he thought. She'd grown up with an absentee father and no mother. By her own account, the closest thing she'd had to a maternal influence as a child had been her grandfather's housekeeper, who she described as an austere woman whose one saving grace had been teaching Emily to bake and cook.

'Have you heard from your father?'

She shook her head, her mouth turning down, and Ramon knew a fierce desire to find Maxwell Royce and hurt him. The man's daughter was pregnant and engaged and he hadn't bothered to return her calls. Out of courtesy, Ramon had left a message on his phone the day before the engagement was made official, but Royce hadn't responded.

'Why The Royce?' he asked, voicing a question that had been lodged in his brain like an annoying burr for weeks.

'What do you mean?'

'You're smart, dedicated, hard-working. You could have done anything,' he said. 'Chosen any number of professions. Why carve out your career there?'

Colour swept her cheeks. 'When I inherited half of the club, I had no choice but to step up.'

'But you devoted yourself to The Royce long before then.'

She frowned. 'It's my family's business.' A defensive edge crept into her voice. 'Why wouldn't I get involved?' Her expression became shuttered. Averting her face, she looked out of the window at a bank of solid cloud, effectively ending the conversation. But, slowly, her gaze came back to his. 'Actually, there's more to it than that...' She hesitated, her throat moving around a tight swallow. 'I think, in the beginning, I was looking for some kind of connection.'

'To your father?'

'Yes. And to my grandfather. I wasn't close to either one of them, but they were the only family I had. Working at The Royce gave us some common ground. I suppose I wanted to prove myself. To earn their respect. Their attention.'

Ramon felt a tugging deep in his chest. No young person

should have to earn attention from a parent. His dislike of Maxwell Royce strengthened.

'What about you?' she asked, swiftly diverting the focus from herself. 'You gave up an architectural career to join your family's business. Do you miss being an architect?'

'Yes and no,' he hedged. 'I often have a hand in the design and renovation of the clubs and properties under my purview, so I still get to dabble.'

'It must be amazing to have a creative talent.' Her voice was wistful.

'You don't see yourself as creative?'

'Not really.' She wrinkled her perfect nose. 'The most creative I get is baking.'

'I like it when you bake.'

She gave him a pert look. 'Correction. You like it when I bake in my underwear.'

He couldn't hold back a grin. On impulse, he reached for her left hand and pressed a kiss on her knuckles—just above the glittering diamond that proudly proclaimed to the world she was his. A smile softened her face and his mood lightened. Perhaps, with Emily by his side, he wouldn't find this weekend with his family too painful.

Emily sensed a dark storm of tension building within Ramon from the second the jet's wheels touched down in Barcelona. During the flight he'd been happy to talk and their conversation had distracted her from her nerves. Now, as they travelled in the back of a chauffeur-driven SUV to his parents' villa, he was silent and brooding.

Did he not get along with his family? The thought sent a shaft of dismay through her. If his relationship with them was strained, how would they receive *her*? Would they welcome her as a daughter-in-law? Or would she be the scarlet woman who'd trapped their son into marriage by getting herself pregnant?

She looked at the enormous rectangular diamond that glittered on her ring finger. Set in platinum and flanked by two sapphires and clusters of smaller diamonds on either side, it was a beautiful piece of artistry which had drawn a shocked gasp from her when he'd slipped it onto her finger. But after three days it still felt heavy and unfamiliar on her hand—as alien and disconcerting as the experience of meeting his family was going to be.

Her stomach threatening to rebel again, she rummaged in her handbag for a piece of crystallised ginger and popped it in her mouth.

Twenty minutes and three pieces of ginger later, their driver turned off the road and drove between two massive gated pillars. A long tree-lined driveway dappled with early-evening sunlight eventually opened onto lush, colourful gardens and led to a circular courtyard at the front of a magnificent two-storey villa. Before the vehicle had stopped, the villa's big front door swung open and a slender, casually dressed woman emerged.

She was beautiful. A generation older than Emily, but still trim and fit-looking in white trousers and a simple sleeveless burnt orange top. Dark chin-length hair streaked with the odd strand of grey was tucked behind her ears, revealing a stunning bone structure that bore such a striking resemblance to Ramon's, Emily knew at once that this was Elena de la Vega, his mother.

She smiled broadly as they exited the vehicle, then stepped towards her son, her arms extended. She spoke to him in Spanish and Emily didn't understand the words, but she heard affection in the older woman's voice, and saw the shimmer of restrained tears in her eyes. Her emotion, so visible and patently heartfelt, made Emily's chest squeeze. But when mother and son embraced, Ramon was stiff, the hug he gave his mother awkward-looking in spite of Elena's obvious delight at seeing her son.

Emily had no time to dwell on the odd dynamic. Elena turned, clasped Emily's hands in both of hers and squeezed. 'And you are Emily,' she declared, her English accented but perfect. Her eyes shone, a rich shade of caramel-brown like her son's. 'It is a great pleasure to meet you.'

'And you, Mrs de la Vega.'

'Elena,' she insisted. 'My goodness, you are beautiful.' She touched Emily's cheek, her eyes glistening again. 'Come.' She motioned them towards the villa. 'Vittorio has been feeling breathless today so he's resting in the salon before dinner. But he is looking forward to seeing you both.'

As they headed indoors, Ramon placed his palm in the small of Emily's back and murmured in her ear. 'My mother can get a little over-emotional.'

'It's fine,' she whispered, wondering why he felt the need to apologise. Elena de la Vega was delightful.

Vittorio de la Vega turned out to be a tall, commanding man who looked reasonably well, despite the heart problems Ramon had briefly mentioned on the plane. He greeted his son with a firm handshake, then welcomed his future daughter-in-law with an infusion of warmth similar to his wife's, if less effusive. After kissing Emily on both cheeks, he politely enquired about their journey, then offered her a choice of non-alcoholic beverages. The subtle deference to her pregnancy made her blush, but she saw no outward sign of judgement or disapproval.

'Have you set a wedding date?'

Elena posed the question the moment they were all settled on comfortable sofas in the beautiful, high-ceilinged salon.

'Elena,' Vittorio gently chided. He sent Emily an apologetic look. 'You must forgive my wife. She can be very excitable.'

Elena flicked an elegant hand, unperturbed. 'I've recently discovered I'm getting a daughter-in-law *and* a grandchild. I think a little excitement is perfectly acceptable.' Her warm smile encompassed both Emily and her son. 'You'll want to get married before the baby arrives, yes?'

'When we decide on a date, you'll be the first to know, Mamá,' Ramon said.

If Elena found her son's tone a little too sharp, she gave no indication. She addressed Emily. 'Your mother must be very excited.'

Emily stiffened, her gaze shifting to Ramon. Had he told his family nothing about her? He covered her hand with his and rubbed his thumb over her knuckles, his eyes offering a form of apology. To Elena, she said, 'My mother died when I was born. I never knew her.'

'Oh, my dear.' Dismay clouded the older woman's eyes. 'I'm so sorry.' She was silent, as though taking a moment to respect the depth of Emily's loss. Then, 'I would not wish to intrude but, if you need help with planning for the wedding or the baby, I would love nothing more. You may already know that Ramon and Xavier don't have a sister, so I've missed out on all the exciting girl things. I would have loved a daughter...' Her gaze flicked to her son. 'But when Ramon came along, he was our miracle. We couldn't have expected another.'

Ramon didn't say anything, but the slight tightening of his hand over hers betrayed the sudden flare of tension in his body. She glanced at him again, but his face was impassive. Unreadable. Hiding her confusion, she smiled at Elena. 'Thank you. I'd appreciate that. I think I'm going to need all the help I can get.' And then, because Ramon's ill humour was starting to unsettle her, she remarked on the splendour of the villa and asked Elena for a tour.

Less than an hour later, they sat down to dinner at one end of a long table in a sumptuous formal dining room.

'Xavier couldn't join us tonight,' Elena said, her tone apologetic. 'But he'll be here tomorrow.'

Vittorio poured wine for the table and a sparkling grape juice for Emily. 'Have you been to Barcelona before?'

'No. This is my first time in Spain.'

Elena clapped her hands together. 'Oh! That's very exciting. You have so much to see! Ramon, where will you take her first?'

For the first time since they'd walked off the plane, a relaxed smile curved his mouth. 'Barri Gòtic,' he said.

'Ah. Marvellous,' Elena enthused. 'The old city is magnificent.'

From then on the conversation remained light and flowed throughout the meal. With her nausea gone and the tension dissipated, Emily was able to enjoy the fabulous food served over three courses to the table by a trio of discreet, efficient waiting staff. As the evening grew late, however, she found herself stifling a series of yawns.

'I believe my fiancée needs to retire.'

Ramon's statement elicited a small start of surprise from Emily. Was he really so attuned to the subtleties of her body language? And there she'd been, thinking her efforts to hide her tiredness had been rather stellar.

'Of course.' Elena cast her a sympathetic look. 'You must go and rest. We will have plenty of time over the weekend to talk.'

Upstairs, the suite she and Ramon had been allocated was enormous and just as resplendent as the rest of the villa. Emily dropped onto the end of the majestic four-poster bed, sighed and kicked off her low-heeled sandals. 'Your parents are lovely, Ramon.'

He stripped off his shirt and she admired the impressive expanse of hard muscle and smooth skin. She didn't think she'd ever tire of gazing at his magnificent body. He was truly breathtaking. He toed off his shoes and unbuckled his belt. 'They're good people.'

Emily dragged her gaze away from his taut, flat stomach and that tantalising downward arrow of dark hair. 'But...?' she said softly.

He paused. 'But what?'

She hesitated. 'Did I just imagine the tension earlier?'

He shrugged. 'No family is perfect, Emily.'

Brows tugging together, she opened her mouth to ask why he was being cryptic, but he turned away, shed the rest of his clothing and then straightened to face her.

Emily's mouth dried.

Not only was he standing naked before her...he was erect. Proudly, gloriously erect. Liquid heat pooled between her legs.

Struggling to remember the gist of their conversation, she forced her gaze up. 'Is this your best attempt to avoid talking?'

One corner of his sinful mouth curled. He tipped her chin up. 'Sleep or sex, Emily?'

If she said sleep, he would leave her alone. Respect her need for rest. But suddenly rest seemed very overrated. And her nausea hadn't recurred in several hours. What was the expression? Make hay while the sun shines? She arched an eyebrow. 'Conversation isn't an option?'

'No.'

'Well, in that case...'

She reached out, curled her fingers around his hot, rigid length and took him into her mouth.

Showing Emily the sights of Barcelona proved a more pleasurable experience than Ramon had anticipated.

Rising early on Saturday, he borrowed one of his father's cars and took her on a scenic coastal drive before heading into the centre of the city. They parked up and strolled along grand boulevards and winding cobblestone streets, and he realised it'd been many years since he'd allowed himself to enjoy the energy and vibrancy of the city he'd loved as a boy. Whenever he returned for business he kept his visits as short as possible. Now, as he pointed out iconic landmarks and showed her some of the city's greatest architectural gems, he realised his designer's eye had missed the unrivalled beauty of Barcelona with its mix of contemporary, Gothic and mediaeval design.

Barri Gòtic, the Gothic quarter, was still a tangle of old, narrow stone alleyways and unique, interesting storefronts. Emily loved it and insisted they explore. When their stomachs growled for sustenance, he chose a traditional tapas bar with art nouveau murals on the walls, lively jazz music and a reputation for outstanding food.

Whether from pregnancy or the excitement of discovering a new city, Emily glowed. She was beautiful—and she had charmed his parents, as he hadn't doubted she would. His mother already adored her. More than that, her presence had been a balm of sorts, gradually easing the tension in him. The burning shame and brutal guilt he relived every time he saw his parents and which, even after twelve years, made looking his mother in the eye almost impossible.

He reached across the table and tucked a curl behind her ear as she bit into another savoury croquette. So far today, no nausea. In fact, her appetite was exceptionally healthy, not unlike her appetite in bed last night…

'Ramon?'

Jerked from the memory of her lush mouth on him, he smiled at her, but her attention was elsewhere.

She frowned, looking over his shoulder. 'There's a young man over there staring at you.'

Twisting round, he followed the line of her gaze.

And felt his stomach muscles clench into a sudden, violent spasm.

Jorge.

His spine turned to ice. He blinked, trying to shake the crazy notion from his head. It couldn't be Jorge. Jorge was dead. Ramon knew this. He had watched him die twelve years ago.

The lookalike stood up, started stalking towards their table and a swift bolt of recognition cleared the confusion from Ramon's head.

Slowly, he rose. 'Mateo.'

Mateo Mendoza glared at him with fierce, undiluted hatred blazing in his black eyes. He spoke in Spanish, his voice a low, belligerent snarl. 'You've got a nerve showing your face around here, de la Vega.'

Keeping his cool in the face of the younger man's hostility, Ramon tried to remember how old Jorge's brother had been when he'd last seen him. Twelve? Which would make him twenty-four now.

Another man, roughly the same age, appeared at Mateo's back. He put his hand on his friend's shoulder and murmured something, but Mateo shook him off.

Ramon threw a glance at Emily. A look of startled alarm had settled on her face.

Dios.

He didn't want her to witness this. Didn't want her in the middle of a situation he might not be able to control. Body tensed, alert, he focused his attention on Mateo. 'Whatever you want to get off your chest, Mateo,' he growled, 'this is not the place.'

The younger man drew his right arm back and Ramon knew he was about to put his weight behind a punch. He could have ducked, blocked the blow; he was bigger and stronger, so he could take the other man easily. Instead, he braced his shoulders and took the full impact of Mateo's fist on the left side of his jaw. It hurt like hell, making a cracking sound like a gunshot inside his skull.

Emily shot to her feet. 'Ramon!'

'Sit down, Emily,' he gritted out. He didn't want Mateo's attention on her.

'I will not sit down!' she cried. 'What on earth is going on?'

Eyes narrowed, chest heaving, Mateo trawled his gaze over her, a sneer twisting his lips.

Ramon fisted his hands. 'Did that make you feel better, Mateo?' he asked drawing the other man's attention.

Slicing another look at Emily, Mateo jabbed a finger in Ramon's direction. 'This man is a murderer,' he spat in English, and then his friend grabbed his arm and roughly dragged him out of the bar before the burly staff member who was weaving through the tables reached them.

His heart racing, Ramon apologised for the disturbance, paid the bill and added an extra-large gratuity, then took Emily by the elbow and walked her into the street.

In a high-pitched voice, she demanded, 'What on earth was that about?'

Retaining a firm hold on her arm, he headed in the direction of the car. 'Keep walking, Emily.'

'Why did you let him punch you?'

'Because he was angry and needed to vent.'

'By *hitting* you?'

'I deserved it.'

'What do you mean?'

He realised she was panting and slowed his stride a little. 'I'll explain later.'

'He said you were a murderer.'

Ramon clenched his teeth and winced as renewed pain shot through his jaw. 'I heard what he said.'

'Are you going to tell me what he meant?'

'Later,' he repeated.

She fell silent but he sensed her gaze darting back to him, again and again, questioning. Confused. In the car, a thick, heavy silence enveloped them, Emily's rigid posture telegraphing her anger.

He cursed under his breath.

Coming to Barcelona had been a mistake.

When they reached the villa, he stopped the car outside the front steps and kept the engine idling. 'Go inside, Emily.' He felt the weight of her gaze on him, but he looked straight ahead, his hands clenched on the steering wheel.

'Where are you going?'

He didn't know. But he needed some space. He couldn't deal with her questions right now. 'Go inside,' he said hoarsely. 'Please.'

She got out and slammed the door, and he gunned the engine and drove off.

Dinner that evening was a tense, awkward affair, the empty chair beside Emily a painful reminder of the awful incident at the tapas bar.

She still had no clue what the confrontation had been about, but she knew one thing with utter, unequivocal certainty.

Her baby's father was *not* a murderer.

She wished he would come back and tell her that himself. But she hadn't seen him since he'd sped off in a cloud of gravel and dust and brooding testosterone.

Anxiety gnawed at her, diminishing her appetite for the lovely meal in front of her. Question after question tumbled through her head. Where was he? Was he okay? Why hadn't he called? Had he been involved in an accident? Why hadn't he returned for dinner?

Had he abandoned her?

Reading her anxiety, Elena said gently, 'He'll be back.'

The man seated across from her gave a derisive snort. 'This is typical of him to run off.'

Xavier's voice vibrated with anger and Emily gripped

her knife and fork, everything within her rebelling against the notion that Ramon had 'run off'.

He wouldn't desert her. Not here. Like this. He could have run at any time in the last three weeks, starting from the moment she'd told him she was pregnant. He hadn't. And she refused to believe he'd done so now.

'I am sorry you had to witness what you did this afternoon.' Xavier spoke to her. 'My brother—'

'Xavier.' Vittorio interrupted his son. 'Emily deserves an explanation, but I think it must come from Ramon.'

Xavier's expression tightened, his intense, somewhat superior gaze flicking back to Emily.

Like his younger brother, he was devastatingly handsome, but far more formidable. Although they weren't genetically related, nature had graced them both with strong, broad-shouldered physiques and stunning facial structures. The most striking contrast Emily could see was their eyes. Where Ramon's were expressive and warm, Xavier's were a cold, hard grey. Not unlike her own, she supposed, though hers were several shades paler and a lot less piercing.

She suppressed a shiver.

Had she been wise to tell them what had happened? When she'd gone inside, bewildered and upset, Xavier had been there with his parents and Elena had seen her stricken expression and immediately put a comforting arm around her. Before Emily had thought better of it, she'd spilled the details of the entire incident.

Distracted, she toyed with the food on her plate.

And then the sound of a car engine and gravel crunching outside had everyone surging to their feet.

Xavier threw down his napkin and stormed out first, a fierce scowl on his face.

Vittorio strode after him.

Emily made to follow, but Elena placed a restraining hand on her arm. 'Give them a few minutes,' she advised.

'My boys have tempers. There might be some fireworks.'
She looped her arm through Emily's. 'Walk with me on
the terrace.'

Emily didn't want to walk. She wanted to go to Ramon.
She wanted to check with her own eyes that he was all right.
She wanted the explanation she was owed.

No sooner had they stepped onto the terrace than the
arguing commenced outside the front of the villa. Raised
male voices carried clearly on the still evening air and she
heard Xavier, then Ramon, and his deep, familiar bari-
tone made her heart clench in her chest. Vittorio wasn't as
loud—the mediator between his sons, she assumed. They
spoke in rapid-fire Spanish, frustrating her attempts to understand. And then their voices grew muffled, suggesting
they'd moved into the house and closeted themselves in a
room.

Emily's breath shuddered out, a deep sigh of despair. 'I
don't understand any of this.'

Elena hugged Emily's arm as they strolled. 'I'm afraid
things have been strained in our family for a long time.
Ramon has struggled to move on from the past—from the
mistakes he made as a boy—and he believes that, because
he hasn't done so, we haven't either.'

Emily looked at her. 'But you have?'

'Of course. I love my son. I always have. I never stopped
loving him—he simply stopped allowing himself to *be*
loved.'

Why? Because he believed he didn't deserve love? A
deep ache spread through Emily's chest.

Elena sat down on a cushioned rattan sofa and urged
Emily to sit beside her. 'Everything will be fine. You'll see.'

Emily wished she shared the older woman's optimism.
'What did Xavier mean—when he said it was typical of
Ramon to run off?'

Elena shook her head. 'Pay no attention to what Xavier

says. He is hard on people—himself included.' She wrapped her hands around Emily's. 'Ramon is a good man. He will be a good father. Already I see changes in him I never would have imagined.'

Her heart missed a beat. 'Really?'

Elena smiled. 'Really.' She squeezed Emily's hands. 'Sometimes all a man needs is the love of a good woman.'

Love.

Emily's heart began to race.

Did she love Ramon?

These last few days, she had started to think she might, and the idea overwhelmed her with a wild, conflicting mix of wonder and fear.

'I've only known you for twenty-four hours, Emily,' Elena continued, 'but I am a good judge of character. I believe you have a kind, forgiving soul. And I believe my son can learn from you.' She cupped Emily's cheek with her palm. 'He fears responsibility, but not for the reasons you might think.'

'Emily.'

Ramon's voice stopped her breath in her lungs. In unison, she and Elena rose and turned.

Rumpled, dishevelled and still breathtakingly handsome in the khaki trousers and black tee shirt he'd worn throughout the day, he strode across the terrace.

He held his hand out to her and, after a brief hesitation, she slipped her hand into his.

His grip was firm as he turned to his mother, his demeanour stiff. 'I apologise for my absence, Mamá.'

Elena reached up and kissed her son's cheek. 'Apology accepted. Now, go. Talk with Emily. You owe her an explanation.'

CHAPTER ELEVEN

KEEPING HER HAND firmly in his grip, Ramon led Emily into the gardens, along a lighted pathway and into a secluded alcove. Hedges and fragrant rose bushes provided privacy and, to one side, an ornate stone bench sat beneath a high, vine-covered arch.

His blood still beat furiously in his veins from his run-in with Xav.

His brother could be so sanctimonious. So self-righteous, at times.

He let go of Emily and she lifted her hand to his face.

'Ramon…your jaw.'

He seized her wrist and pulled her hand down before she could touch him. 'It's just bruised.'

Frowning, she jerked her wrist free, then hugged her arms around her middle. 'Where have you been?'

He heard the hurt in her voice and his self-hatred burned brighter. Deeper.

But he'd needed the time alone. Time to bring his emotions under control. Time to work out how to explain—how much to tell her.

All of it, his conscience cried.

'I hadn't planned to miss dinner,' he said. 'There was a road accident—' Her eyes widened and he quickly added, 'Not me. Tourists.' A group of three young Australian holidaymakers who'd run their camper van off the coastal road and flagged him down in distress. 'I stopped to help and waited until the emergency services arrived.'

Even upset and pale, Emily was beautiful. The mint-green knee-length dress she'd donned for dinner was fresh and feminine, showcasing a figure that was starting to show subtle signs of pregnancy. Her hair was captured loosely at her nape and he knew an overwhelming desire to sink his hands into those lustrous curls, bury his face in them and breathe deeply until her scent overtook his senses and his mind was filled with nothing but her.

He jammed his hands in his pockets and nodded towards the stone bench. 'Sit, Emily.'

Her chin came up, and for a moment he thought she might refuse. Then she sighed and sat down.

He took a deep breath. 'The young man in the tapas bar today was Mateo Mendoza,' he said. 'He's the younger brother of Jorge Mendoza, my best friend during my teens.' He drew another breath but his chest was so tight his lungs wouldn't expand properly. 'When we were eighteen Jorge drowned in a boating accident. Mateo blames me for his brother's death.'

Emily stared at him, wide-eyed. 'Why?'

'Because it was my fault.'

She shook her head. 'I don't understand.'

'It was a reckless teenage escapade. There was alcohol involved. And the boat wasn't seaworthy.' He clenched his jaw against the surge of hated memories. The vision of Jorge's pale, blue-lipped face as he slipped beneath the surface of the ocean, beyond Ramon's desperate reach.

Emily turned her palms up, imploring. 'Ramon. Please. I still don't understand.'

'I was the ringleader,' he bit out. 'And it wasn't the first time I'd led Jorge on some reckless pursuit. His parents had already spoken to mine, expressing their concern.'

She was silent. Then, 'Isn't that what all teenage boys do? Push boundaries? Do reckless things?'

Her attempt to minimise his culpability only fuelled his guilt. She'd heard only half the story. He doubted her sympathy would withstand the rest. He forced himself to go on. He just wanted it out now. Over with.

'I had a girlfriend at the time. Same age, eighteen. After Jorge's funeral, she tried to comfort me but I was in a bad place. I didn't want comfort, so I pushed her away, ended the relationship. I was blunt,' he confessed. 'Cruel, even.' He paused, emotion rising, threatening to engulf him. His throat felt hot and thick. 'She was upset. She went out with her friends and overdosed on a party drug. In the hospital, it was discovered she was five weeks' pregnant.' Shame burned his insides, hot and searing. 'She lost the child.'

'Oh… Ramon…' Emily stared up at him, her features illuminated by silvery moonlight. 'Did she know she was pregnant?'

'No.'

Emily stood up, took a step towards him. 'Which means you didn't, either.'

He frowned. 'That doesn't exonerate me.'

'Of what?' she challenged. 'Ending a relationship? That's not a crime, Ramon.'

He hardened his jaw. 'My actions were callous and irresponsible.'

'That doesn't make you a murderer.'

'I killed my best friend and my unborn child,' he grated.

She placed her hands on his shoulders. 'You don't really believe that. *I* don't believe that. You were just a teenager.'

'I was old enough to know better. I was reckless. Careless with the lives of the people I cared about. I hurt Jorge's family. I hurt my girlfriend's family. I hurt *my* family.'

Emily moved closer and he wanted to push her away. Urge her to protect herself. Protect their child.

From *him*.

'You're a good man, Ramon.'

'You don't know that.'

'Yes,' she argued, tilting her chin up. 'I do. When I told you I was pregnant, you could have run. You could have abandoned me. You didn't. You're standing by my side. By our child's side.'

'Don't paint me as a saint, Emily,' he warned. 'I'm not.'

'You're not a monster, either.'

He pinched the bridge of his nose and then remembered it was Xav's favourite gesture and dropped his hand.

'Come to bed,' she said, her voice soft. 'You look exhausted.'

Expelling a heavy breath, he lifted his hand and pushed a stray curl back from her face.

'That's my line,' he growled.

She smiled. Then she caught his hand, interlaced her fingers with his and led him back to the house.

The next day, by mutual agreement, they embarked on their return journey to London sooner than originally planned. Elena was disappointed, but she understood they both wanted to put Saturday's incident behind them and have some time alone to process it.

As their bags were loaded into the SUV that would take them to the airport, she drew Emily aside and embraced her in a tight hug. 'Whatever happens, you and your child—my grandchild—are now part of this family,' she said. 'You will always be welcome here.'

Emily fought hard to stem a rush of tears. In a different life, a make-believe life, she would have grown up with a kind, compassionate mother like Elena. She could only hope she'd be as good a mother to her own child. 'Thank you.'

Elena gripped Emily's arms and gave her a firm look. 'For what it's worth, I believe you and Ramon are going to be fine.'

Not wanting to burst the older woman's bubble, Emily forced a smile. Yesterday, wandering hand in hand with Ramon through the old city, talking and enjoying each other's company as they'd explored the intricate labyrinth of winding streets, she might have agreed. Today, doubt, fear and uncertainty had stripped away any fledgling sense of happiness and hope. Already she could feel an unsettling shift in Ramon, his mood when he'd woken this morning taciturn, remote.

She swallowed, her throat tight. 'How can you be so sure?'

Elena pressed her hand to Emily's cheek. 'Because my son has been running for twelve years,' she said. 'Now he has a reason to stop.'

The journey to the airport was dominated by silence, and as soon as they were in the air Ramon opened his laptop and Emily buried her nose in a magazine.

She didn't absorb a single word.

Instead, her mind replayed every line of every conversation she'd had over the weekend with Ramon and with his mother.

You have a kind, forgiving soul.

Did she? She'd never thought of herself as a particularly benevolent person before.

Her mind skipped to her father who'd been AWOL for weeks now and hadn't returned any of her calls.

Was he all right?

She snuck a glance at Ramon, still focused on his screen, and knew he'd be angry if he knew she was worrying over her father's welfare. Her tenuous relationship with Maxwell frustrated Ramon. He didn't understand why she didn't simply sever all connections with her father. She couldn't blame him. Most days she didn't understand it herself.

Where *was* Maxwell? Holed up with a woman somewhere? Deep in some gambling den, perhaps, losing whatever possessions and money he had left to his name?

A familiar feeling of despair washed over her. When it

came to winning her father's attention, she'd never stood a chance against the lure of the high life. For Maxwell, women and high-stakes poker games had proved far more appealing than the responsibilities of fatherhood.

Why had he never settled? Was he running from something? The way Ramon had been running for the last twelve years?

As soon as they'd landed and transferred from the plane to a chauffeured black sedan, Emily fished her phone from her bag. She hadn't checked for messages in more than twenty-four hours. She powered the phone on and held her breath, waiting. Praying.

Seconds later, the air left her lungs on a little exhalation of surprise.

On the screen was a text from Maxwell.

Ramon sent her a questioning look. 'Is something wrong?'

She shook her head. 'No,' she said, and slid her phone back into her bag.

Emily chose a small, quaint restaurant nestled in one of Mayfair's quiet side streets, just a few blocks from The Royce, in which to meet her father. Their phone call, three days previously, had been brief, just long enough for Maxwell to ask if she'd be willing to meet with him and for Emily to agree. He'd turned the choice of time and place over to her and told her to text him the details.

She paused outside the restaurant.

Would he turn up?

She stepped inside and Maxwell rose from a table in the rear corner, gesturing to catch her attention.

A dart of surprise shot beneath Emily's ribs. She was ten minutes early, yet he was here waiting for her.

Dry-mouthed, her hands clammy, she propelled her legs forward and made her way over.

Maxwell stayed on his feet, hands by his sides, waiting until Emily had seated herself before taking his chair again.

'You look well, Emily.'

'So do you.'

She couldn't hide her surprise. There were no hollows carved into his cheeks, no dark shadows beneath his eyes. His complexion was healthy, and the whites of his eyes weren't bloodshot. He looked as if he'd spent a month at an exclusive health spa.

'I've been in Switzerland,' he said, as if her expression had broadcasted her thoughts.

'For two months?' The query came out more sharply than she'd intended. But she'd not had a scrap of communication from him until his recent message. It wasn't unusual for him to disappear for weeks on end, but two months was the longest he'd ever gone incommunicado.

'Yes,' he said quietly. 'I was at a private rehab clinic. For gambling and...other addictions.'

Shock suspended Emily's breath. Her gaze went automatically to the table top. There was no whisky tumbler, she realised. No bottle of expensive wine. Just a carafe of water and two glasses.

A waiter approached and Maxwell raised a hand. 'Could we have ten minutes, please?'

When they were alone again, she said, 'I don't know what to say, Maxwell.'

He shook his head. 'There isn't anything you need to say. But, if you're prepared to listen, there are some things I'd like to say to you.'

Emily nodded; she didn't trust herself to speak. Her mouth was too dry, her throat too tight all of a sudden.

'I'm sorry, Emily. I know those words are inadequate,' he said, his voice thick, a little uneven. 'But I want you to know that I am sorry. For everything. You deserved better than me for a father.'

His gaze held hers and she felt as if it was the first time her father had ever looked at her.

Really looked at her.

The ache in her throat intensified. She *had* deserved better.

Silence cloaked them for a long moment.

Finally, her voice barely above a whisper, she said, 'Why? Why was it so hard to love me?'

A wretched look crossed his face. 'I wanted to. More than you'll ever know. And I thought maybe I could…after those first few years had passed. But then you started to look so much like her.' His gaze moved slowly over her face, her hair. His look of anguish deepened. 'I couldn't let myself do it. I couldn't risk that kind of pain all over again. If anything had ever happened to you…it would have been like losing Kathryn a second time.'

Her lungs locked again. 'You loved her?'

'More than anything else in this world.' His voice was raw. 'Losing her was the worst thing that's ever happened to me.'

Emily stared at him. The revelation tore through every belief she'd had about her father. 'I… I had no idea.'

A deep frown etched his brow. 'That I loved your mother?'

'How could I have known? You always refused to talk about her.'

'Because it was too painful.'

She rubbed her forehead. 'But…all the women…'

His face reddened. 'When your mother was alive, I was faithful to her, Emily. She was my soul mate. She was irreplaceable… So, after she was gone, I didn't try. I just…'

He let the sentence hang, and Emily thought she understood. He'd resigned himself to casual, meaningless flings because he didn't believe he could love again—or was too afraid to try.

She sucked in a deep breath. Then asked the question she was most afraid to ask. 'Did you blame me for her death?'

Maxwell's chin dropped, agony and shame driving his gaze away from his daughter's. 'Yes.'

The stark admission felt like an all-over body blow, as if someone had dropped her straight into the path of a speeding truck. A part of her understood the psychology of it. Grief could make people irrational. Warp their view of things. Still, it hurt. 'Do you still feel that way?'

His gaze jerked up. 'My God…no. Emily…' He shook his head. 'The fact you look so much like her is still…difficult. But no. It wasn't your fault.'

Her eyes stung, and she blinked back the tears. 'You made me feel unlovable.'

His expression was bleak. 'I don't know how to make that up to you. But I'd like a chance to try.'

'Will you tell me about her?'

'If that's what you'd like.'

Emily thought she'd like that very much.

She took a long sip of water, soothing the burn in her throat. Then she put the glass down and gave him a shaky smile. 'You're going to be a grandfather.'

Maxwell swallowed. 'So I understand. Congratulations, Emily.' He reached across the table and covered her hand briefly with his.

Emily's heart contracted.

The gesture was a long way from a hug.

But it was a start.

When Emily left the restaurant over an hour later, the black sedan and driver that Ramon had insisted she have at her disposal waited on the other side of the street for her.

The driver emerged and opened her door and she sank gratefully into the soft leather.

'Home, Ms Royce?'

'Yes. Thank you.'

Closing her eyes, she let her head fall back against the seat. Her father's unexpected attempt to connect had left her feeling quietly optimistic, but it also heightened the sense that her life was changing at a more dramatic pace than she could handle.

She looked at her watch and sighed. It was barely eight o'clock and she already craved the comfort of her bed.

A comfort she'd soon relinquish, she reminded herself with another flare of unease.

Tomorrow at ten a.m. she would meet with an interior designer at the house in Chelsea to discuss colour schemes and furnishings. Within the month, she and Ramon would be living in their new home and her beloved Wimbledon flat would be rented out to strangers.

Ramon wanted her to sell it.

Emily had refused, then enquired pointedly if he planned to sell his penthouse in Manhattan.

The stand-off had only sharpened the tension between them these last few days.

After thanking and dismissing her driver, she dragged her feet up the stairs and opened the door to her flat, relieved to be home, but also aware of a flutter of trepidation.

Ramon had been deeply unhappy about her meeting with her father and his mood before they'd left for work this morning had been dark and intractable.

Much like his mood every day since their return from Spain, she thought gloomily.

She flipped on a light and put her bag and keys on the hall table before walking through to the lounge. Darkness blanketed the room and suddenly she remembered Ramon had said he was entertaining a business associate at Citrine this evening. Her mind moving to thoughts of hot chocolate and bed, she turned on a lamp—and felt her heart lunge into her throat.

'My God! Ramon!' She clapped her hand over her breast, staring at him as he turned from the window. 'You scared me half to death. Why are you standing in the dark?'

He moved into the lamplight and Emily saw from his face that his mood had not improved from this morning. He still wore his work attire, although his tie and suit jacket had been discarded, and his shirt collar loosened. 'How was dinner with your father?'

His tone was clipped and Emily stifled a sigh. She was exhausted, her emotions drained; she couldn't talk about her conversation with her father, not right this minute, standing here in the middle of the lounge. 'Interesting,' she said, turning towards the kitchen. 'I'm making hot chocolate. Would you like some?'

'I had an interesting meeting, too.'

Reluctantly, she stopped.

'I ran into Carter,' he said.

She frowned. 'Carter…?'

'Ray.' His voice carried an edge of impatience, as though he thought she were being deliberately obtuse. 'Your lawyer.'

'Oh.'

'He offered his congratulations on our engagement and the baby.'

'That's…nice,' she said, the skin at her nape beginning to prickle.

'Asked if we knew yet if it's a boy or a girl.'

The prickling spread into her throat, then her chest, making it difficult to breathe. 'Ramon…'

'Said if we're expecting a boy,' he barrelled on, as if she hadn't spoken, 'you should notify him so he can prepare to activate your inheritance as soon as the child is born.'

Her breath stopped altogether. *Oh, God.*

He stepped forward, his jaw clenching. When he spoke again, his voice was soft. Dangerous. 'What did he mean, Emily?'

She forced herself to breathe. Told herself it wasn't a big deal. Not to her. Surely it wouldn't be to Ramon?

'There was a…a clause in my grandfather's will. A ridiculous clause,' she added. 'It bequeathed a sum of money to me if certain…stipulations were met.'

His eyes narrowed. 'What kind of stipulations?'

She swallowed, embarrassed. 'If I marry and produce a male heir by the age of thirty.'

She heard his sharp inhale.

'How much?'

'S…sorry?'

'How much money, Emily?' he snapped, and she jumped, unaccustomed to him raising his voice.

'Two million pounds,' she croaked.

'Dios.' For a second, incredulity wiped the anger from his face. 'And if you don't?'

'I forfeit the inheritance. The money goes to charity.' She shifted her feet under his hardening stare. 'I'm sorry I didn't tell you about it sooner, but it's not important to me, Ramon. It was my grandfather's eccentric attempt to ensure his legacy eventually passes to a male heir. I couldn't care less about that money.'

The hard gleam in his eyes remained. 'Does your father know about the clause?'

She hesitated. 'Yes.'

'And what did he want tonight?' The cynical twist of his lips made his implication shockingly clear.

She took a step back from him, her insides wrenching. *'No.'* The word burst from her, almost a shout. She gave her head a vigorous shake. 'You're wrong.'

He grasped her wrist, halting her retreat. 'Don't be naive, Emily,' he said tersely.

'I'm not being naive. You're being twisted and cynical. And unfair!' She tried to pull free but he held fast. 'You have no idea what happened between my father and me tonight.'

'Then tell me.' He tugged her close and cupped his other hand under her jaw, forcing her gaze up to his. 'Convince me he hasn't crawled out of the woodwork after two months hoping to benefit from your potential windfall.'

'That accusation is disgusting.' Her voice trembled with outrage. His scepticism cast an icy pall over her optimism. Worse, it filled her head with horrible, stomach-shredding doubts. 'My father has been in a rehab clinic for the last two months, if you must know. He's getting himself together. And yes—' she stared at him defiantly '—he wants to reconcile.'

He gave a low, grating laugh. 'Like I said, *querida*. Naive.'

His mocking tone drove a dagger of hurt into her thundering heart.

Ramon never spoke to her like this.

Not the Ramon she knew.

Not the Ramon she loved.

But he'd not been the same man since Spain, had he? The awful incident with his friend's brother had affected him on some deep level, somewhere far beyond the limit of her reach.

'I don't think this...this *mood* of yours is about my father at all,' she challenged. 'I think it's about you.'

As though she were suddenly radioactive, he released her and stepped back. 'What the hell does that mean?'

'It means you don't believe you're worthy of forgiveness, so you don't think anyone else is either.'

A savage frown furrowed his brow. 'Forgiveness must be earned, Emily.'

'Is that what you've been doing, Ramon? Earning forgiveness these last twelve years?' His expression darkened but she forged on. 'Is that why you gave up your architectural career to join the family business? Why you set your sights on The Royce? Is it all about earning brownie points so your family forgives you?'

'Emily.' His voice was a low growl.

She ignored the warning. 'Do you know what the crazy thing is? You have amazing parents who love you, but you're so busy keeping them at arm's length you haven't noticed they forgave you a long time ago.'

'Enough!' He slashed his hand through the air. 'This *is* about your father. And I forbid you to see him.'

Disbelieving laughter tore from her throat. 'You can't stop me seeing my father, Ramon.' Before he said anything else that further shredded her heart, she spun on her heel and stormed into the kitchen.

Ten seconds later, she heard the front door slam. The sound echoed through the empty flat and through her chest like the final, crippling thrust of his knife into her heart.

Ramon found a pub in the local village, wedged himself into a dimly lit corner and nursed a glass of single malt until his temper had cooled.

Dios. Why was she so stubborn? So blind? So willing to give her father yet another chance?

Maxwell was a gambler. Was it not obvious to her that he was playing an angle? Playing *her*?

Protectiveness surged, fierce and overwhelming. He believed her about the money not mattering to her. If it had, she would have wanted to know their child's sex as soon as possible, yet she had told the specialist she'd prefer to wait until the birth.

But not to question the timing of Maxwell's desire to reconcile was insanity.

Perhaps they *should* find out the baby's gender. It would

put the matter to rest. If it was a girl, and Maxwell's enthusiasm for connecting with his daughter suddenly waned, it would dispel any illusions.

And break Emily's heart at the same time.

He pushed his empty glass away and rose, regret scything through him.

He'd seen the look on her face when he had questioned Maxwell's motives. He knew the sour mood he hadn't shaken off since their disastrous weekend in Barcelona had lent his tongue a harsh, uncharacteristic edge. He'd hurt her. Which went against the grain of everything he was trying to achieve.

And then she'd lashed back.

I think it's about you.

His feet pounded the pavement, frustration congealing in his gut as he stalked the streets back to the flat. She'd seen him with his family for all of thirty-six hours and thought she understood him.

She understood nothing.

Nothing.

When he arrived, she was waiting up, sitting in the window seat she favoured for quiet reflection. Her glorious golden hair flowed loose and a pair of flannel pyjamas swamped her delectable curves. He suspected the attire was a deliberate attempt to discourage him from intimacy. It didn't work. He wanted to bundle her into his arms. Carry her to bed and make passionate love to her until the hurt and anger on her face dissolved into something else.

His desire only deepened his frustration. Intensified the sense he was waging a losing battle within himself. Every part of him felt at odds. His emotions. His instincts. His desires.

He wanted to protect her. From her father. From the world. From anything and anyone who dared to threaten the wellbeing of her and their child. But he also wanted to distance himself from her. Protect her from himself. From his inherent ability to hurt the people he loved.

And Ramon had come to suspect that what he felt for this woman was raw, terrifying, unadulterated love.

'I can't marry you, Ramon.'

He blinked, her statement skating over his thoughts, taking a moment to register. 'What?'

She uncurled from the cushions, stood and faced him. 'You told me I wouldn't have to do this alone.'

He shook his head, confused. 'You don't. I'm here, Emily.'

'Are you?' She stared at him, her eyes gigantic pools of anguished grey in her pale face. 'Because these last few days, it's felt as if you've been somewhere else. As if you've erected a wall I can't see over, or through.'

'That's not true.' His denial was abrupt. Hoarse.

'It is,' she disputed. 'And this business with my father— with the inheritance—it's all just a smokescreen for the deeper issue.'

Exasperation had him throwing up his hands. 'Not this again.'

'Yes, Ramon. *This* again. You have to forgive yourself and move on.' She took a deep breath. 'I learned something about my father tonight. He's been running for a long time. Choosing the lifestyle he has because he's afraid to love and lose again, the way he lost my mother. I think you're running too, Ramon.'

Her comparison with him to Maxwell cut to the bone. His nostrils flared. 'I'm here, Emily,' he repeated. 'I haven't run since the day you told me you were pregnant.'

'Not physically.' She stepped forward, pressing her hand against the centre of his chest. 'But in here…you're afraid. Afraid to get too close to people in case you hurt them.'

'You're talking nonsense,' he gritted out.

The look of utter sadness crossing her face sliced a

sharp, unbearable pain through his chest. She dropped her hand. 'I'm in love with you, Ramon,' she said, and the words robbed his lungs of breath. 'You're the father of my baby and you're a good man. I want to marry you, share a home, raise our child together. But I can't be with you if you're going to be emotionally distant, the way you are with your family. I—we—' she placed her hand over the gentle swell of her belly '—deserve better.'

She twisted the diamond and sapphire engagement ring off her left hand.

'Emily…'

'I've put your things in the spare room. You can stay to-night—or not. Up to you. But I want you to leave tomorrow. Take some time and decide if you're ready to stop running. Until then—' she put the ring on the coffee table '—I think you should hold onto this.'

CHAPTER TWELVE

So far Emily had waited five days, and they'd been the longest, most misery-filled days of her life.

She missed Ramon. Every hour. Every minute. Every second of every day.

The weekend had been the worst. The home she usually adored had felt cold and soulless, and even an afternoon of baking had failed to stir any joy.

And now, back in the office, seated at her desk and staring listlessly at her screen, work wasn't proving the distraction she'd hoped for either.

Her stomach churned with doubt and fear.

She'd taken an enormous risk by confessing her love to her baby's father then sending him away.

Had she made a terrible mistake?

She hadn't wanted him to stay away. She'd wanted him to go and take a long, hard look inside himself and then come back to her.

And tell her he loved her.

Because she wouldn't settle for less. For too many years she had pined for love. She couldn't waste the rest of her life pining for his. He'd always have a place in their child's life—she'd never deny her child its father—but she could not marry a man who didn't love her.

Emily's phone pinged. Shutting off her thoughts, she delved into her bag and pulled out her phone.

And froze.

Her heart climbed into her throat.

Ramon.

His message was short.

A car is waiting outside for you. See Marsha on your way out.

She frowned at the screen. He'd made her wait five days and these were the words with which he'd chosen to communicate with her first? Hands shaking, she texted back.

It's 3.30 p.m. on a Monday. I'm working.

His response was immediate.

Finish early.

Heart pounding, she chewed her lip, then forced her thumbs to work again.

Where am I going?

It's a surprise.

I don't like surprises.

Humour me.

She stared at the screen for a long moment, her tummy taut with indecision. When the phone pinged again, she jumped.

Please.

She hesitated, but her resistance was already melting, her desire to see him too powerful, too overwhelming. Releasing a pent-up breath, she fired back an 'OK'.

Outside the office, Marsha rose from her desk, her cheeks flushing pink. 'I'm sorry,' she said, holding out Emily's passport. 'He said I wasn't to warn you.'

A flicker of excitement and hope skimmed through Emily's stomach before she quickly dampened the hazardous feelings. She had no idea what he'd say to her when she saw him. She'd be a fool to allow hope to soar only then to find her heart painfully crushed.

Still, the fluttering in her stomach grew more intense during the ride to the airport. Not even the short, sharp jab of disappointment she felt when she boarded Ramon's plane and saw he wasn't there could diminish the jittery feeling of anticipation for very long.

The male flight attendant brought her an orange juice. 'It's nice to see you again, Ms Royce.'

She managed a smile. 'And you. Umm… Could you tell me where we're going, please?'

His polite expression didn't alter. 'Paris,' he said. 'We should be there in fifty-five minutes.'

By the time Emily climbed out of the back of a shiny limo in front of Saphir, her mouth was bone-dry and her palms so damp she had to repeatedly wipe them down the front of her simple black dress. A smiling concierge greeted her, escorted her inside and led her to the same lift she'd ridden with Ramon three months earlier.

She stepped in and gripped the handrail.

Only three months?

It felt like a lifetime ago.

The lift bore her swiftly upwards and when she stepped out into the penthouse, feeling breathless and a little light-headed, he was there.

Her feet stumbled to a stop.

Clean-shaven and wearing dark trousers and a pale blue open-necked shirt, he looked as vital and bone-meltingly beautiful as he had on that fateful late summer night when he'd brought her here.

Their gazes locked and she began to tremble, desire and

nervous excitement pin-wheeling through her in a potent, knee-weakening mix.

Then, abruptly, he pulled his hands from his pockets and strode towards her, his steps long and purposeful. He halted in front of her and cradled her face in his hands, and just that simple touch catapulted her senses into overdrive.

'Did you miss me, Emily?'

Oh, so much. She feigned a shrug of indifference. 'Not really.'

His eyes gleamed. 'Not at all?'

'Maybe a little bit,' she whispered.

They both faintly smiled. It was the same exchange they'd had in her kitchen more than three weeks ago when he'd returned from Paris—moments before they'd had scorching hot sex in her room.

'I missed you.' He drew his thumbs across her cheeks, lowered his forehead to hers.

Emily felt her insides melting. Felt little tendrils of hope weaving around her heart. She dropped her bag, lifted her hands and curled them over his strong, masculine wrists. 'Where have you been?'

He raised his head. 'I went back to Spain.'

'What for?'

His hands lowered, settling around her waist, drawing her close. 'I had some ghosts to lay to rest. Some people to visit.'

'Including your parents?'

'Including my parents.'

Emily's thoughts flickered to Elena and her heart swelled with gladness for the other woman. 'And did you make any discoveries?'

'A few.'

His heart pumping at a fierce pace, Ramon studied the exquisite features of the woman who had boldly declared her love for him, then sent him packing and told him not to return until he'd figured himself out.

She'd shocked him to his core. Flipped him into a brutal tailspin of anger and disbelief.

And fear. Mind-bending, gut-wrenching fear—because he'd known he couldn't lose her.

'I learned,' he said, 'that sometimes a man must confront his past before he can put it behind him.'

Soft grey eyes searched his. 'And have you?'

'*Sí, querida.* I have.'

Tears filled her eyes then and, though he had no wish to see her cry, he took them as a good sign.

'Who else did you visit?'

'Many people,' he confessed.

He had started with his old girlfriend, with whom, once he'd tracked her down, he'd had the conversation they should've had twelve years ago before he'd fled Spain. He'd found Ana in a stylish home in Madrid, married with two small children, and happy. She'd moved on and she bore Ramon no ill will. Next he'd visited Jorge's parents in Barcelona, whom he'd not seen since the funeral, and discovered they didn't share their youngest son's antipathy towards Ramon. Jorge's mother had hugged him, cried for a moment, then invited him in. Matteo, they'd said, was a troubled young man, and they'd been appalled to hear of the incident in the tapas bar.

The next day he'd gone to see his brother, and then he'd returned to his parents' villa, where, for the first time in a long time, he'd looked his mother in the eye and embraced her in a hug that had lifted her feet clean off the ground.

Finally, he'd come back to London and had a long, frank conversation with Maxwell Royce.

It'd been an intense, cathartic five days, and at some point he'd tell it all to Emily, but not now. That was the past. Right now his interest lay only in the future.

'Want to know what else I learned, *querida*?' he asked softly.

She nodded, and he reached into his pocket, pulling out the black velvet box containing her engagement ring.

'I learned that I'm tired of running...' He plucked the ring from its bed, lifted her left hand and slid the cool platinum band with its striking setting of diamonds and sapphires onto her finger. 'And that I want to be the man—the *only* man—who loves you for the rest of his life.' He pressed his lips to her knuckles. 'I love you, *mi belleza*. Will you do me the honour of becoming my wife?'

Eyes glistening, she wound her arms around his neck, her delicious curves pressing into his body. 'Yes,' she said, and a groan of relief mingled with desire tore from Ramon's throat.

Gathering her close, he claimed her mouth in a kiss that was almost savage in its intensity.

Long minutes later, when their breath-deprived lungs cried out for air, they broke apart.

Surrendering to the feverish need to stamp his possession on her in every way possible, he swung her into his arms and headed for the bedroom.

As he lowered her onto the bed, she captured his jaw in her hand and murmured, 'Why Paris?'

He laid his hand over her stomach, the small bump which he couldn't wait to see grow filling his palm. 'This is where we began. Where we created our child.' He trailed his lips along her jaw, down her neck. 'It will be a special place for us always, *sí*?'

Her eyes filled again. 'I love you, Ramon.'

Fierce emotion flooded him. 'Say it again,' he demanded roughly against her throat.

Her laughter was pure. Sweet. 'I love you.' Insistent hands tugged his shirt tails from his trousers. 'Your turn,' she whispered.

He slid his hand under her dress, his questing fingers moving over heated, quivering skin. 'I love you, *mi belleza.*'

She arched under his touch.

'Show me,' she urged.

And he did.

EPILOGUE

WITH A GLASS of chilled Prosecco in her hand, Marsha slipped away from the lively gathering taking place in the big, sunny back garden of Emily and Ramon's Chelsea home and crossed the bright green lawn towards the house.

She stepped into the kitchen and her gaze fell on the home-made custard tart over which Emily was grating fresh nutmeg. 'Yum! That looks delicious.' She shifted her attention to the large kitchen table where Emily and Ramon often shared their meals instead of in the formal dining room. This afternoon, savouries and cakes and slices and tarts crowded the table's surface. 'I can't believe you did all of this yourself.'

'I had some help from my housekeeper,' Emily confided.

Marsha's eyebrows rose. 'You have a housekeeper?'

'A part-time one,' she said. 'Ramon insisted. It was either that or a nanny and I refused the latter.'

Marsha put her glass down on the bench and cast her gaze around the gorgeous designer kitchen. 'I miss you at work but I can't blame you for not rushing back.' She gave a wistful smile. 'Do you think you'll ever return?'

Emily's shrug was non-committal. 'I haven't decided yet,' she admitted, her feelings on the matter mixed. The club and her role there had been her life for so many years, and she'd expected to miss it, but she had other priorities now. Priorities that filled a void she hadn't realised existed and which meant a great deal more to her than The Royce.

A small, plaintive wail pierced the air and Emily's maternal instincts went on instant alert.

Elena de la Vega entered the kitchen, making shushing, soothing sounds to the tiny bundle in her arms. 'I think my granddaughter has already tired of her christening party,' she said to Emily, her lovely face awash with pride and pleasure as she handed over her grandchild.

Emily smiled her thanks. 'I'll feed her and settle her for a nap and then I'll be out.' She glanced at Marsha. 'Would you do me a favour and let everyone know they can help themselves to food?'

She climbed the elegant curved staircase and made her way to the light-filled nursery, an intense joy ballooning in her chest as she gazed down at her daughter.

Kathryn Georgina de la Vega—Katie, to her parents— had arrived ten weeks ago, exactly three months from the day her parents had wed in a beautiful church in Barcelona. The wedding and reception, attended by hundreds of guests, had been a larger, more elaborate affair than Emily had wanted, but the de la Vegas were a prominent family in Spain, and she'd quickly understood her hopes for a small, private ceremony were unrealistic. Plus, Elena's enthusiasm for the planning had been both irrepressible and contagious. Emily hadn't had the heart to restrain her.

She'd invited Marsha and her management team to the wedding and, to her surprise, they'd all come, but the person whose presence had mattered to Emily the most had been her father's. He'd given her away and as he'd walked her down the aisle in her stunning gown of ivory silk and French lace, cleverly styled to hide her baby bump, she'd been fairly sure she'd seen a tear shining in his eye.

Of course her relationship with her father remained a work in progress. Twenty-eight years of hurt wouldn't heal overnight. But they were moving in the right direction and even Ramon was thawing towards him, especially now the inheritance issue had been temporarily sidelined.

Emily finished nursing then drifted to the window with Katie nestled in her arms, humming the tune of the Spanish lullaby Ramon crooned to his daughter every night.

Chatter and laughter floated up from the garden, along with the squeals and shouts of their neighbours' children—Joshua and Maddie—who chased each other through the trees at the rear of the property. Amidst the clusters of people Marsha chatted with Maddie and Joshua's mother, Tamsin, who'd become a friend to Emily, while Elena, a natural-born conversationalist, talked with Marsha's boyfriend and Tamsin's husband. Seated in the shade of a large oak tree, Vittorio and her father conversed and, further away beneath a different tree, Ramon and his brother appeared deep in conversation.

Whatever they spoke about it must have been serious, for the expressions on their faces were intense.

Emily still marvelled that Xavier, an incurable workaholic, had taken time out of his demanding schedule to visit London.

Suddenly Ramon looked up and caught her eye through the glass and her breath hitched. Her husband seemed to possess a sixth sense where she was concerned; rarely did she get to observe him without his noticing.

She watched him grip his brother's shoulder, say something and then stride across the lawn towards the house. By the time he walked into the nursery, she'd settled their daughter down to sleep and returned to the window. He leaned over the cot, kissed a rosy little cheek and then moved behind his wife, sliding his arms around her middle.

She leaned her head against his shoulder, her gaze focused on the figure of his handsome, enigmatic brother, standing alone beneath the tree now. 'Is everything all right with Xav?'

Ramon kissed the top of her head. 'He's fine.'

'He doesn't look fine,' she said. 'He looks…lonely.'

Ramon gave a soft snort. 'My brother isn't lonely.'

'How do you know?'

He turned her in his arms and looked down at her. 'How

about more focus on your husband and less on his brother?' he growled.

Emily hid a smile. Her husband's occasional displays of jealousy always amused her. 'Fine,' she whispered, conscious of their daughter sleeping. 'Let's join our guests, then.'

She went to move but his arms tightened, locking her in his hold. He dropped a kiss on her mouth that stole her breath with its tenderness, then raised his head. 'Happy?' he queried softly.

This time she let her smile show. How could she be anything else? She had a family, people she loved, people who loved *her*. And she had this beautiful home that was already filling with love, laughter and joy.

Their 'for ever' home.

She wrapped her arms around his neck and kissed him. 'Blissfully.'

* * * * *

SURRENDER TO HER
SPANISH HUSBAND

MAGGIE COX

With grateful thanks to my lovely editor
Sally Williamson.
Her gentle guidance and support help
make my part of the deal a joy!

CHAPTER ONE

AN EAR-SPLITTING bolt of lightning shrieked through the air, lighting up the interior of the house's cosy hallway and outlining in threatening shadow the figure that loomed up behind the door's decorative stained glass panels. Her foot on the first tread of the stairs, on her way up to the hot scented bath that promised to be the perfect antidote to the day's accumulated stresses and strains, Jenny came to a sudden shocked standstill.

It was almost ten in the evening. There had been no phone call to tell her of the imminent arrival of a guest, and there were no other occupants in the entire place but her. Bearing in mind Raven Cottage's remote, some might say wild location—miles from anywhere—she had to quickly rid herself of the nightmarish scenario that her mind unhelpfully and frighteningly presented her with. But deepening dread paralysed her for long seconds before she could shake it off.

Installed as temporary caretaker of the charming thatched-roof guesthouse for nearly three full months now, courtesy of her friend Lily, who had gone to visit her parents in Australia, in all that time Jenny had not once chafed against her isolated surroundings at all. If anything, its lonely proximity to the Atlantic Ocean had given her a chance to properly take stock of all that had happened. Bit by bit she'd been rebuilding her esteem.

Divorce was never easy, but hers had been reluctant and sorrowful. She still ached for what might have been if her ex-husband hadn't rent her heart in two by deciding he could no longer continue with the marriage. Even though that had been years ago, from time to time Jenny still reeled from it. Standing out at the water's edge sometimes, she'd stare at the colossal waves sweeping into the shore and they seemed to symbolise the emotional battering she had taken. And If the divorce hadn't been traumatic enough fate had then delivered another blow—one that that had been particularly cruel.

But maybe it was because it was such a stormy 'end of the world' kind of night that her imagination seemed intent on putting her centre stage into a scene straight out of a horror movie…the kind that made her wonder if the people who watched them were altogether sane.

The shadowy figure outside lifted the brass knocker, banging it loudly. The discordant sound was like nerve-jangling rifle-shot, intent on drilling a hole through her skull. Biting her lip, Jenny breathed in deeply.

'Just a minute. I'm coming!' Having raised her voice above the din of a growling roll of thunder she fleetingly wished she'd pretended she wasn't home. Her caller would hopefully have just gone away and she could have enjoyed her longed-for bath in peace. But, knowing Lily needed the business, she plastered on a smile then opened the door.

'Dios mio! Could there be a more remote inhospitable place in the world?'

The darkly clothed male figure who, even after only the short sprint from his car, looked as if he'd been swimming in a roiling wild river, immediately vented his frustration.

Eyes the colour of silken jet pierced Jenny like dangerously sharpened dagger-points. Her determinedly upbeat smile vanished. It had been on the tip of her tongue to burst out *Well, if it's so inhospitable, and you'd rather be somewhere else, why have you bothered to knock on my door?* But the words died in her throat—because her visitor was shockingly familiar.

Eyes widening, she pressed her hand to her chest. 'Rodrigo. What are you doing here?' Her body shivered hard from the blast of freezing air that the opened door brought with it.

Her ex-husband stepped inside, causing Jenny to back up nervously. Shaking his mane of sleekly dark hair, then staring at her with a gaze that deluged her with a sea of haunting memories, he wiped the back of his hand across his damply glistening face. 'I might ask you the same question.'

'I'm looking after the place for Lily while she's away in Australia.' Clearly Jenny's presence was as much a surprise to him as his was to her. The ridiculous hope that he'd sought her out because he wanted to reconcile was cruelly and devastatingly snatched away. Despite her sorrow, she forced herself to carry on speaking. 'Now it's your turn. What brings you to the wilds of Cornwall? I wouldn't have thought it could hold much appeal—especially in the winter. The Mediterranean is much more your style.'

He sighed, as though it pained him to even consider some suitably witty repartee. 'I'm in the area because I have a meeting tomorrow. Have you a room? For pity's sake don't turn me out into that—that violent monsoon again!'

'I'd take pity on anyone who was in danger of being swept away by such wild weather…even *you*, Rodrigo. It's pretty grim out there tonight. Anyway… you're in luck. We're not fully booked. We're actually very quiet at the moment.'

Best not tell him he's the only guest just the same… Unconsciously grimacing, Jenny skirted round her formidably built ex-husband to hastily shut the door against the raging storm.

'Thanks.' Reaching out a hand, he squeezed her shoulder as his well-cut lips formed a lopsided smile. 'It is gratifying to know that you don't hate me enough to leave me to my fate.'

Parrying the nervous heat that flooded her, she backed up again.

'I expect you'd like to go straight to your room? You must be dying to get out of those soaking wet clothes.'

Another inconvenient wave of heat suffused Jenny at the remark she'd made. But she'd been referring to the imminent shedding of Rodrigo's clothes, so it hardly came as a surprise.

'I am. But first I will have to make a dash back to the car to collect my luggage.'

No sooner was this said than done, and once again Jenny was treated to a perfectly icy blast of arctic cold as she waited for Rodrigo to return with his suitcase, and an expensive calf leather shoulder bag that she knew contained a laptop.

'You'd better give me your coat,' she said, making herself wait patiently as he removed his damp trench-coat and then held it out to her. She desperately wanted to present an appearance of composure, even though inside her feelings easily mirrored the violent chaos of the storm.

A fleeting rueful smile touched Rodrigo's lips. 'I don't want to ruin Lily's polished wooden floor-boards,' he remarked.

Hanging the garment on a peg at the back of the door, she saw droplets of icy water from the hem drip rhythmically onto the raffia doormat. 'I'll hang it in the utility room in a little while,' she told him.

The spicy cologne that clung to the material of his

coat made a direct assay into her already besieged senses, causing another disturbing skirmish low in her belly. She frowned, hugging her arms over the lilac wool sweater that she'd teamed with well-worn faded blue jeans. 'So…where's this meeting you've got tomorrow?'

'Penzance. I was booked into a hotel there, but the roads were treacherous in this storm, and my sat nav stopped working. As I was driving I remembered that Lily had a guesthouse somewhere close by. I didn't even have to look for it—that was the crazy thing. Believe it or not somehow the place just loomed up before me… It's a total surprise to find *you* here.'

He hesitated, as if he was going to add something, and Jenny deliberately smothered the persistent ridiculous hope that doggedly had hold of her heart with a pincer grip.

'So you only need a room for the one night?'

'That's right. And what you said earlier was right too…the Mediterranean *is* more to my taste.'

'Then God forbid that you should suffer more than you have to!' she answered waspishly, turning away. Her insides went crazy when Rodrigo caught hold of her hand.

'Do you want to make me suffer, Jenny?' His dark eyes glittered.

Pulling her hand free from his icy cold palm, she dismissively tossed her head. 'I can assure you that I've got far more important things to do with my time. The room's this way.'

She led him upstairs to the luxurious accommodation at the front of the house, knowing that it was the best room in the building. No matter what had transpired between them as a couple, she knew he had faultless good taste—and she didn't want him to find flaws in her friend's much loved business. In the morning he would be treated to something pretty spectacular. When the landscape wasn't shrouded in mist and dark, or sheeted with blinding incessant rain, he'd find a view that couldn't fail to stir the senses and feed the soul. Again—despite her personal feelings—Jenny hoped Rodrigo would appreciate it.

Artists, writers, honeymooning couples and folk recovering from illness, divorce or bereavement—they had all stayed in that room, Lily had told her. With its unparalleled vista reflecting the Atlantic Ocean's dramatically beautiful unpredictability, it was a firm favourite with everyone. And, going by the comments in the visitors' book, they all swore that the bewitching and haunting wild scenery had definitely worked its magic, making them devotees for life by the time it came for them to leave.

Now, surveying the exotically handsome looks of the man who had once been her husband as he deposited his stylish suitcase and bag on top of the lovingly created silk patchwork quilt on the bed, Jenny saw him glance round the room with little evidence of pleasure or satisfaction on his face. Didn't he like it? There was a brooding, disenchanted air about him that reminded her that he had seen and done it all, more or less, and since there wasn't much that could impress him it was probably a waste of time even trying.

On her friend's behalf, Jenny was affronted. The beautifully presented room, with its plush velvet curtains and matching swags, tasteful designer wallpaper that had cost an arm and a leg, immaculate antique Davenport and sumptuous king-sized bed, complete with bespoke iron bedstead, had taken a large chunk of her friend's savings to perfect. It was a luxurious and relaxing atmosphere, yet at the same time Lily had managed to retain the old-fashioned English charm that the tourists expected and loved. And, being in the business of interior design, Jenny had been happy to advise her.

After the devastating death of Lily's sister and her husband in a car crash, Lily had found herself sole owner of Raven Cottage, and she had become absolutely determined to rise above the terrible tragedy she'd suffered and make the guesthouse a resounding success in their memory.

Like Jenny, Lily was no stranger to the bitter and jolting twists of fate that could cut a person off at the knees. That was why the bond between them that had begun all those years ago at school had deepened even more over the last couple of years.

Just before they had entered the room Jenny had flicked a switch to turn on two small antique table lamps either side of the bed, bathing the room in a softly inviting amber glow. As the rain whipped at the old-fashioned windows, and the crashing thunder overhead literally shook the rafters, she thought it would be hard to find a cosier place to shelter from such primitive violent weather. But again she found herself wondering if her jaded ex-husband even had the capacity to appreciate it.

'So…how come you've got a meeting in Cornwall?' Summoning a determinedly neutral tone, Jenny focused her apprehensive gaze on Rodrigo Martinez—billionaire owner of a chain of spa/hotels that were some of the most exclusive in the world. His carved handsome face, with its deep-set black eyes and spiked ebony lashes still damp from the rain, gave her his full attention. In return, her hungry glance moved helplessly over his arrestingly fit body. A body that suggested a disturbing physicality for which the outer garb of black sweater and jeans was only a thin shield. Rodrigo's simmering sexuality had fascinated and thrilled Jenny right from the beginning.

'I'm opening one of my hotels in Penzance,' he replied, his accent underlined by the husky gravel of his voice. 'Research tells me it's a popular area.'

'So naturally you want to capitalise on it?'

Unoffended, he shrugged. 'I'm a businessman in the hotel trade…what did you expect?'

Jenny's mouth dried with hurt. 'Nothing. I expect nothing of you, Rodrigo. Except maybe for you to act like you've always acted. I learned that lesson a long time ago, remember?'

'And you still bear a grudge towards me for it, by the sound of things.' Sighing, he drove his fingers irritably though his rain-damp hair. 'I need to get out of these wet things and take a hot shower. Unless you're feeling reckless and want to join me, I suggest it's time you vacated my room.'

'Go to hell!' Jenny reacted instantly, her heart suffused with indignant anger as well as painful regret.

'You think I haven't been there before, *querida*?' Shaking his head, his voice low, Rodrigo ruefully dropped his hands to his hips.

'When was that? When you failed to secure some million-dollar deal to make you even richer? That must have been a real low point!'

'What a flattering not to mention *damning* opinion you have of me, Jenny. You think all I'm interested in in life is making money?'

'I don't think that at all.' Her hand curved round the doorknob, Jenny met his disturbing gaze with unflinching steadiness. 'I *know* it.' She would have slammed out through the door there and then if her innate good nature hadn't got the better of her. 'I'll make you some coffee and get you a bite to eat. I expect you're hungry after your long drive. It'll be in the kitchen when you're ready.'

'Jenny?'

'Yes?'

'Nothing…it will keep. We can talk later.'

Bereft of a handy reply, and hardly trusting herself

to speak without becoming emotional, Jenny left the room. In the corridor her footsteps slowed. It had been over two years since she'd seen Rodrigo. She'd foolishly kept hoping he'd ring or get in touch, but he never had. In her mind she'd imagined him saying he'd made a mistake—he'd only asked her for a divorce because he was stressed—he'd been working too hard and hadn't been thinking straight. *No such event had occurred.* When she'd returned to the UK from Barcelona, where they had lived together, Jenny's friends had advised her not to waste any more precious time thinking about him. If he couldn't see the gift he had so easily let go then he just wasn't worth it. Why didn't she just spend the money he'd insisted she take as a divorce settlement, have a good time, and forget him?

As if she was going to wake up one morning and forget how to breathe. Day and night Rodrigo's memory haunted her. Her thoughts seemed incapable of dwelling on much else. But she wasn't happy that he still had the power to affect her so profoundly. She wanted to show him that she'd moved on…made a new and satisfying life without him. But after the pain and mayhem her brother Tim had caused when Jenny had returned to the family home 'new and satisfying' would have been a lie.

Her teeth clamping painfully down on her lip, Jenny headed back downstairs to the kitchen. A violent shudder rolled through her as a flash of lightning eerily illuminated the house's interior. The hall lights flickered wildly. To add to the sticky, uncomfortable tension in the air that shrouded her like a fine cloying mist—despite the arctic temperature outside—she nearly jumped out of her skin when a slightly over-weight, well-fed tabby weaved her way awkwardly round her legs and almost sent her sprawling.

'Cozette, you naughty girl!' Jenny scolded, scoop-ing the purring feline up from the floor and then holding the generous bundle of warm soft fur close into her chest.

She didn't mind admitting that Lily's pet cat had become a very welcome companion during her so-journ in the wilds of Cornwall.

'How many times have I told you not to do that? Never mind, are you scared of the storm? Is that what's bothering you? Poor little kitty…don't worry. I'll take you into the kitchen and find you a nice tasty bite to eat to help take your mind off this terrible racket!'

Upstairs in his room, in the act of retrieving his laptop from its leather holdall and wondering if this Cornish wilderness had even *heard* of the internet, Rodrigo paused. The voice that drifted up to him from downstairs riveted him. *It always had.* Now he stood perfectly still, listening. The lady had a voice as alluringly velvet as a warm midsummer's night, and it wrapped itself round his senses like a soft Andalucian breeze, full of the scents of jasmine, orange and honeysuckle and other exotic flowers that could render one hypnotised by their scent alone.

Hearing Jenny's voice again after being denied the sound for over two years... The effect it had always had on him ricocheted hotly through Rodrigo's brain. *Not to mention other sensitive parts of his body.* As he listened to her croon now, to what he quickly deduced must be Lily's pet cat, the napped velvet tones and cultured British accent were enough to raise goosebumps up and down his forearms and unquestionably to arouse him. He blew out a breath. *Steady, Rodrigo...*he ruefully warned himself. She was still pretty mad at him, and had every right to be.

They'd been married for just over a year when he'd declared that they must part. Even now he could hardly believe he'd said the words—never mind seen them through. He should definitely rein in the almost instantaneous lust that had all but exploded through him at the sight of her tonight. Those luminous cornflower-blue eyes in a stunning oval face framed by a gilded curtain of shoulder-length blonde hair had always hit him where it hurt. He had never set out to wound her so badly. But—that aside—he had travelled to this spectacularly haunting part of the country for the purposes of business, *not* pleasure. And of all the startling scenarios he might have envisaged on this trip, having his beautiful ex-wife open the door to him on arrival at her friend's guesthouse was not one of them—though he had to admit his spur-of-the-moment plan had been influenced by the hope of hearing news of her.

His heavy sigh was laden with equal parts of frustration and tension. He kicked off his Italian-made shoes and tore off his socks, allowing his long tanned feet to sink gratefully into the luxurious carpet, before stripping off his clothes and heading for the shower...

'Do you have access to the internet here?'

'What? Oh, yes...but the signal's a bit dodgy. I mean, it comes and goes...especially in a storm like this.'

'I feared as much.'

'We'll probably get connected again tomorrow, when things have calmed down a bit. You may as well resign yourself to a night of not working. Think you can cope?'

'Very funny. Is this my coffee?'

'Yes. Sit down and help yourself. I presume you still take sugar? At any rate I've added two.'

'It's still the one pleasure I cannot give up,' Rodrigo joked. Seeing the glimpse of hurt that flitted across Jenny's face, he could have bitten out his tongue. The truth was that *she* had been the hardest pleasure of all to give up. Going by the ache in his ribs and low down in his belly, she still was.

As he arranged himself at the table, a generous mug of coffee steaming invitingly before him alongside a neat round plate piled high with sandwiches fashioned out of thick-cut wholemeal bread, Rodrigo tried to smother the swift stab of longing that filled him as he stared at Jenny.

Pulling his gaze reluctantly away, he made a leisurely inventory of the homely, country-style kitchen that surrounded him. With its mismatched stand-alone oak and pine furniture, old-fashioned cooking range and long wooden shelves lined with quaint but fashionable china it was a million miles from the state-of-the-art bespoke modern interiors that his exclusive holiday resorts prided themselves on featuring. But its homespun charm was seductive and inviting all the same. In fact it reminded Rodrigo very much of the simple Andalucian farmhouse high in the Serrania de Ronda hills he had grown up in. He experienced a fierce pang of longing as the not very often explored memory unexpectedly gripped him.

'This looks very good,' he muttered, taking a swig of the burning coffee and a hungry bite of a ham and English mustard sandwich.

'If you'd arrived earlier you could have had dinner…I cooked a cottage pie, but I've put what was left of it in the freezer now. Will this snack be enough for you? I've some fruitcake you can have afterwards with your coffee, if you like.'

As she talked, Jenny brought a decorative round tin to the table and opened it. Inside nestled a clearly homemade fruitcake that smelled mouthwateringly of cloves, cinnamon and nutmeg.

Rodrigo nodded approvingly. 'I might have to take you up on that offer. You know how fond I am of homemade cake.' His well-cut lips curved in a smile. '*Is* it one of yours?'

'I made it, yes.'

'Still the little home-maker, I see, Jenny Wren.' The nickname he had settled on from the very first time they were together came out before he could halt it. The flawless alabaster skin bloomed hotly with what he guessed must be embarrassed heat. Checking his apology, he lazily watched to see what she would do next.

Outside, a flurry of stormy wind crashed against the windows, bringing with it a sleeting rush of hammering rain. Jenny's clearly affected gaze locked with his.

'Don't call me that,' she said brokenly, the volume of her voice descending almost to a whisper.

Beneath his black cashmere sweater, Rodrigo sensed tension grip his spine. 'Why not?'

'You forfeited the right when you told me our marriage was over…that's why.'

'Then I won't use it again.'

'Thank you. Besides…I told you it's the name my father always called me, and he really loved me. Eat your food, Rodrigo, you must be hungry.'

Miserable with regret, he knew that any comment he made would likely pour petrol on an already simmering fire, and automatically crammed another bite of bread and ham into his mouth. It might as well have been sawdust for all the enjoyment he received from it.

Jenny moved away across the unadorned warm brick floor to one of the many immaculately clean pine worktops that filled the room. Presenting her back to him, she started slicing up more bread from the generous-sized loaf on the breadboard, her hurried, quick movements telling him that mentioning her father had definitely made her even more upset than she was already.

'I know how much you loved him too. He raised you and your brother single-handedly after your mother died,' he remarked. 'I would have liked to have met him. I too lost my parents when I was young... remember? My father first, and then my mother.' Carrying his mug of coffee with him, Rodrigo went to join her at the counter.

Clearly startled, Jenny glanced up, her hands stilling on the knife and bread. 'Yes, I remember.'

'Their deaths spurred me on to make my own way in life...so although it was tough for a while without them I am grateful.'

'Would you—do you need that coffee topped up? The water in the kettle should still be hot,' Jenny said, anxious to move the conversation away from the dangerously personal direction it had taken.

'No, thanks. It is fine just as it is.'

'Are you sure? It's no trouble.'

Warmth spread through Rodrigo's entire being as he stared down into the lovely face before him. How he resisted the almost overwhelming urge to pull Jenny into his arms, he didn't know. Except that— as she'd told him earlier about using the pet name he had for her—he had *forfeited the right.* But the warmth that had invaded him remained, making him he realise it had been a long time since a woman had taken care of him so thoughtfully. *Not since Jenny had left, in fact.*

For the past two years he had been travelling and working abroad almost continually, and it shocked him to learn that a part of him missed that treatment. From the very first time he'd met her Rodrigo had received the impression that it was Jenny's nature to be helpful, kind and thoughtful of others. All this was coupled with an extraordinary beauty—and she had been a blessing he had hardly been able to believe had come his way.

CHAPTER TWO

'WHY don't you make yourself a drink and come and talk to me while I eat?' Rodrigo suggested, his steady dark gaze making Jenny feel as though he was putting her under a powerful microscope.

For a little while she was utterly hypnotised by his compelling examination. He was staring at her as if he honestly craved her company, and she couldn't help but feel all at sea about that. What were his motives? she wondered. It was natural to be suspicious after two years without a word. And if she was honest she was also afraid of hearing the other reasons why he'd let her go, besides the fact that he couldn't properly commit to their union because of his dedication to work. More than once at the back of her mind she'd entertained the possibility that he'd been having an affair. If that was the case then she definitely didn't want to hear about it. Rodrigo had already broken her heart, and she had no desire to have it shattered again.

'I don't have time to talk to you now,' Jenny answered nervously, tucking some corn-gold strands behind her ear. 'Besides…you've had ample time to contact me if you wanted to talk, and the mere fact that you haven't clearly illustrates what I've always known to be true: your work is much more important than any relationship. What's to be gained by digging over old ground? I picked up the pieces after our farcical marriage and made a new life, and you just returned to the one you liked best as a bachelor.'

A muscle jerked visibly in Rodrigo's high-angled cheekbone. 'What a pretty picture you paint of my conduct.'

'I'm only telling the truth. Our marriage *was* a mistake, was it not?' Her breath was so tight Jenny felt dizzy. 'I'm as much at fault as you. I had no business accepting your proposal when we'd only known each other for three short months, but I quickly learned that your work was priority number one and always would be.'

Returning to the table, Rodrigo dropped down into the chair he had vacated. Linking his hands, he lifted his dark eyes to observe Jenny. 'Why have you never spent any of the settlement I made on you?' he asked.

'Because I didn't want your damn money in the first place!' Her heart pounding fit to burst, she willed the threatening tears that were backed up behind her lids to freeze over. 'I thought I was marrying the man I loved…not entering into a lucrative business deal.'

'You have every right to the money.' Shaking his head wearily, Rodrigo surprised Jenny with a lost look that made her insides turn over. 'I let you down—made you a promise I couldn't keep. It was only fair that I compensated you for that.'

'I didn't want compensation. After the divorce I just wanted to rebuild my life and start over. I wanted to forget about you, Rodrigo.'

'And did you?'

The question hung in the air between them like a detonated grenade. Not trusting him enough to voice the truth, Jenny moved away from the pine counter and assumed a businesslike air. 'There are a few things I have to do before I turn in for the night, and I have to get on.'

'Conscientious as ever, I see. Lily has a good friend in you, Jenny.'

'She's been a good friend to me too…a real support the past two years especially.'

'She must despise me for what I did to you.' Rodrigo's mouth twisted wryly.

'On the contrary. The truth is you rarely even come into our conversation. Now, I've got to empty the rubbish and check over the house before I lock up for the night.'

'How long is Lily away?'

'She's been gone nearly three months now. She's due back in a fortnight.'

'I see. And what about the interior design consultancy that you intended to resurrect when you returned to the UK? Are you not involved with that any more?'

'I'm still running it, though business has been a bit slow throughout the summer months. That's why I was able to come here and help Lily out.'

'And how are things with your brother Tim? Are you still paying the mortgage on the family home you shared with him? I remember he had a particular talent for avoiding work and paying his own share.'

Rodrigo's question, along with his sardonic remark, made Jenny feel queasy. Of course Rodrigo had no idea what had happened when she'd returned...how sour things had turned between her and Tim—culminating in a most shocking event that she would never forget...

'Tim met somebody and moved to Scotland after I bought out his share of the house.'

'So you're still living there?'

Feeling her face throb with uncomfortable heat beneath Rodrigo's razor-sharp scrutiny, Jenny glanced away. 'I'd better go and see to those bins.'

She was still wary of further probing questions as she lifted out the recycling bag from its plastic container beneath the double butler sink that Lily had excitedly sourced from a local reclamation yard, and prayed Rodrigo would cease quizzing her.

Heading for the door opening into the utility room, she threw over her shoulder, 'Why don't you just relax and enjoy your refreshments in peace?'

'Jenny?'

Turning, she found to her astonishment that he was right behind her, his half-drunk mug of coffee left on the table. Her heart foolishly hammered at his unexpected nearness. 'What is it?'

'Let me do that for you…it sounds like a war zone out there and I don't like the idea of you coming under fire on your own.'

Even as he uttered the words a thunderous crash resounded above them, its threatening echoes rumbling like some disgruntled giant disturbed from his sleep. Once again all the lights buzzed precariously on and off, as though the whole place might be plunged into darkness at any second.

Clutching the recycling bag tightly between her fingers, Jenny shook her head. 'I'm not afraid of the storm. I'll only be gone a couple of minutes.'

Not hanging around to see if he would try to persuade her, she rushed out through the door into the utility room. Once there, she opened the back door to the part of the garden where a paved pathway led towards a sturdy iron gate, beyond which was the road. *Or where she knew there should be a road.* Switching on the night light, all she could see through the grey shroud of misty, heavily falling rain was an uprooted tree lying drunkenly across the path. The ferocious wind was tossing everything around as though it were the flimsy furniture in a child's dolls' house. Lily's beloved greenhouse was ominously shaking and shuddering. It was definitely under threat of losing its moorings as the rain viciously pelted the thin glass panes, Jenny saw. Dangerously, just a few feet away a slim-stemmed birch was being all but battered to kingdom come. If it came crashing down on top of Lily's beloved greenhouse the several almost ripened tomato plants that she'd been tending like a broody mother hen would certainly be demolished—as would every other plant and vegetable in there.

The idea of being the one who was responsible for losing them galvanised Jenny into action. Determinedly she headed for the shed at the bottom of the garden, the wind's eerie elemental power making her stumble more than once as she negotiated her way round the fallen tree that lay across the path. A while ago, whilst searching for a particular garden tool, she'd spotted what looked like a fairly robust rolled up tarpaulin inside the shed, which could now be put to good use.

The large tarpaulin clutched against her sodden chest, along with some tent pegs she'd found, Jenny shook her drenched hair from her eyes and then steeled herself to walk back to the other side of the garden where the greenhouse stood. Grimacing as another bolt of silver lightning lit up the sky, she uncurled the tarp, shaking it out as best as she could.

It didn't take long for her to realise she was fighting a losing battle. Every time she managed to get one corner straightened out the wind all but ripped it out of her now freezing hands and she had to fight to uncurl it again. The rain was like a grey blindfold over her eyes as she worked, making her curse out loud because she hadn't thought about the implications of such a storm earlier, when she'd first seen the darkening clouds appear in the sky.

'What are you trying to do?'

A voice to the side of her lifted to make itself heard above the storm. Already drenched to the skin from his dash from the back door to reach Jenny's side, Rodrigo was staring at her as though she was quite mad.

'The greenhouse!' she shouted, pointing. 'I need to secure it so it won't get flattened by the storm. I was going to throw the tarp over it and then fasten it to the ground to hold it.'

Comprehending, Rodrigo unceremoniously relieved her of the wildly blowing tarpaulin and then shoved one corner back into her hands. 'Move back and we will shake it out together,' he instructed. 'Do you have anything to secure it?'

'Yes.' She quickly stooped to retrieve the long tent pegs she'd left by her feet. 'These.' She handed them over.

'We need a hammer to bang them into the ground.' Momentarily he shifted his gaze down to her feet, as if expecting to see the necessary tool lying there.

'Oh, God.' Biting her lip, Jenny stared back at Rodrigo with an apologetic shrug. 'I forgot to bring the mallet with me. It's still in the shed.'

'I'll get it. Stay here.'

'It's at the other end of the garden. Can you see it?'

'Yes, I see it.' Before he left, Rodrigo furnished her

with a wry look. 'And do your best not to get blown away by the wind while I am gone…I am looking forward to my full English breakfast in the morning, and that's not going to happen without a cook!'

No sooner had he left than he was back again, a large wooden mallet clutched tightly in his hand, as if the storm and the fallen tree had been but mere annoying trifles that had not even vaguely threatened his mission. Taking charge with reassuring confidence, he yelled instructions to Jenny, helping them both negotiate the best way of working in the increasingly untamed weather.

By the time they had the tarp over the greenhouse roof and the sides rolled down securely over the glass walls—Rodrigo having deftly banged in the tent pegs through the loops to fasten it to the ground—Jenny felt as if she'd been packed in ice and left to freeze. *Thank God her ex had been around to help her.* That was all she could think as she took one last glance through the drowning rain at the secured tarp covering Lily's treasured greenhouse. She'd never have managed it on her own, she realised.

Gratefully dashing into the house again, she knew she must look half-drowned, with her sodden clothing and dripping hair. Next to the efficient DIY expert, who still managed to look nothing less than gorgeous even though he was also wet through, Jenny felt like something the cat had dragged in. It wasn't a picture she wanted to project to anyone…least of all the man that had broken her heart. But her hands were so chilled that she could barely even make a fist, and she had no choice but to leave the locking of the door behind them to Rodrigo too.

Dark hair was plastered to his well-shaped head, and Jenny watched an icy rivulet of water streak down his face over high-sculpted cheekbones and a clean-cut jaw that didn't have so much as a smidgeon of spare flesh detracting from its perfect symmetry. On its way, the pearl of moisture flirted briefly with a corner of his mouth, making her dangerously aware of how full and sensual his upper lip was—just like one of those Italian sculptures that art-lovers gasped at because they were so beautiful.

'Tomorrow morning I'm going to cook you the best breakfast you've ever had.' She took a nervous swallow. 'I owe you big-time for what you just did. Lily has worked so hard to grow her own vegetables, and—'

The lips that had so riveted her attention were suddenly laid over hers as gently as a butterfly wing. Shocked rigid, Jenny was nonetheless *compos mentis* enough to register the erotic warmth of the breath that came with it, as well as the burning heat hovering beguilingly beneath the rough velvet skin that had been rendered arctic cold from his rescue mission outside.

As soon as Rodrigo lifted his mouth away from hers her body throbbed with insistent hunger for a second helping of that incredibly arousing fleeting contact. The idea of having a properly passionate kiss from her one-time husband again made her feel dizzy with want…quite primitively crazy with it.

Fearing her gaze must easily reflect her torrid feelings, Jenny stepped away, her hands fiddling with the drenched ends of her shoulder-length hair, praying he wouldn't guess how violently his brief kiss had affected her. 'What was that for?' she breathed.

He shrugged, as though amused. 'Regard it as a thank-you from the absent Lily. No doubt she would be quite moved to learn that you care so much about her greenhouse that you were willing to venture outside in a violent storm to protect it.' Rodrigo smiled. 'Now…I think we both need to rid ourselves of these wet clothes before we succumb to pneumonia, don't you?'

The suggestion sounded like something X-rated articulated in that sexy Spanish voice. So much so that Jenny felt as if a fire had been lit beneath her blood. But, with his hands on his hips, Rodrigo's next words quickly brought her disturbing fantasies to an abrupt if regretful end.

'We'd better not stand here talking all night. We need to get back to our rooms, change into dry clothing and then return downstairs for a hot drink to warm us up…*sí*?'

'Good idea,' Jenny muttered, wrenching her gaze determinedly away from his. Ascending the staircase, she hurried as though being chased by some dogged pursuer up to no good. But in her heart of hearts she knew it was her own tumultuous feelings that she was really hoping to distance herself from...

In the shower, as he stood beneath the needle-sharp scalding spray, Rodrigo stared through the curtain of water, filled with disbelief at what had just happened between him and his pretty ex-wife.

Recalling the incident with more intent, he remembered that her sweet-lipped cupid's bow pink mouth had suddenly become like the most sensuous narcotic. A longing to still the tantalising little quiver he had glimpsed, to taste the heat as well as the rain-cold damp he knew he would find there, had spontaneously driven him to press his mouth against hers. What Rodrigo had not been expecting was that kissing Jenny's soft little mouth would feel so instantly essential to him the moment he made contact.

Reliving the experience made his insides dance wildly. How could he have forgotten that she could make him feel like that? His mind moved on to a far more disturbing thought. How many lovers had she taken to her bed since they had parted? She was young and beautiful, and these dark cold nights stuck out here on her own would undoubtedly get lonely. He had no right to feel so jealous and angrily affronted by the idea. Jenny was free to do as she liked. They were divorced. But if she had *not* taken a lover was it because she still thought of him?

The idea sent a burning arrow of explosive heat

straight to Rodrigo's loins and he murmured an expletive in Spanish. How long since he had had a woman? He traced the outline of a circle in the collected steam on the shower stall's glass, added a downturned mouth and scowled. *Clearly long enough for it to seriously start to bother him.*

It wasn't that there was ever a lack of opportunity. Females of all ages had taken a profound interest in him ever since he'd started to hit puberty at around thirteen. But he had done nothing about more recent opportunities because he had allowed work to gobble up his free time like an insatiable termite instead. Before he'd realised it the days and weeks in his diary had suddenly revealed that a whole year had gone by—a year during which he could practically equal a Franciscan monk for lack of sexual activity. Not to mention the complete dearth of a social life or even anything remotely related to relaxation.

He was beginning to feel a little like an automated machine—going here, going there, and hardly even noticing his surroundings. It scarcely mattered whether it was some sensual eastern paradise or one of the glamorous foreign playgrounds of the rich and famous—private playgrounds to which gradually, through his single-minded dedication to his goal, Rodrigo had at last gained membership. But the successful business he'd been so focused on achieving from such a young age had gradually turned into a monster, intent on gorging every ounce of energy and life force he possessed in return for the rewards he'd once deemed so essential to his self-esteem and his life.

Frighteningly, he had experienced periods of late when his body had threatened to barely get him through the day at all. More frightening still was the fact that very little in his life—either some achievement or something material—managed to give him pleasure any more. It appeared as though he was numb to the sensation. Even this new project, installing one of his exclusive resorts in this scenic, wild and—as research informed him—*desirable* corner of south-west England was quickly starting to lose the excitement and appeal it had initially held. But the last thing his shareholders wanted to hear was that he had lost that lucrative, moneymaking killer instinct that had helped so spectacularly to line their pockets too.

Sighing, Rodrigo stepped out of the shower onto the aquamarine tiled floor. Reaching for a voluminous white towel that had been left warming on the radiator, he dried himself vigorously, dressed in clean jeans and a sweatshirt, combed his fingers through his still damp hair and then turned to view his scowling reflection in the steamy mirror.

He didn't like what he saw. The confirmation of his thoughts about the lack of relaxation in any form was written clear in the dullness of his eyes, in the new lines he spied round his mouth and gouged into his forehead. Even through the steam they mercilessly confronted him.

A picture came into his mind of his angelic-looking ex-wife. Would a hot night of unconstrained lust in her bed, with soft sighs, mutually hungry needs passionately met, cure him of the dullness in his eyes? Would it help him regain some of the strength and vitality that lately he sensed he had lost?

Grimacing as another wave of erotic heat seized his body, Rodrigo didn't doubt it would. But after the way he had treated her would Jenny even consider it?

As he turned to leave the room he silently acknowledged that it wasn't just the promise of a warming nighttime drink he was hoping for...

She was standing by the stove, watching over a simmering pan of milk. Somehow knowing he was there, she turned towards him and, surprisingly, gifted him with a smile. Her lovely face was scrubbed clean as a child's and her huge china-blue eyes set up such a violent longing in Rodrigo that he barely knew how to handle it. It wasn't just the natural healthy longing of a sexually aroused male at the sight of an attractive woman either. It was the totally contradictory yearning for an impossible dream that he usually dismissed as viciously as swatting an annoying fly—a dream that he had had within his grasp but had incredibly let go. But sometimes—like now—it broke through his insatiable need for success and acceptance by the world and almost throttled those desires by the throat. *Yet its tantalising promise could never be for him.* He was a pragmatist, a realist…a man a million miles away from ever putting his faith in such an impossibly unattainable idea. *No doubt his lovely ex-wife would back him up on that.*

Wearing a full-length cream dressing gown, its lapels patterned with tiny sprigged red roses, little Jenny Wren radiated the kind of innocence and purity that made Rodrigo briefly mourn for the hopefulness and joy of his early youth. *Before* he had discovered that in his ardent pursuit of success the world would extract every ounce of that hopefulness and joy and pay him back with constant growing tension and a vague unease that all was not right.

Rubbing his hand over his chest in a bid to ease the sudden clutch of discomfort that had collected there, he appreciatively registered that Jenny's golden hair had been left to dry naturally, in almost too tempting to touch blonde ringlets. Finding himself in a trance, he paused in the doorway just to gaze at her…enjoying the stirring sight she made as if paying homage to an exquisite work of art in a gallery.

'I'm making hot chocolate. Is that okay?'

'It is more than just okay. I could not think of a more perfect ending to a night like this.'

Liar, his silent inner voice mocked as he easily thought of a far more exciting and alluring alternative. But, as if to illustrate his comment, a violent blast of furious thunder overhead made the whole house feel as though the very walls were about to disintegrate into a pile of rubble.

'Sit down. I'll bring it over to you when it's ready.'

'I get the feeling that there's no one around tonight but us. Am I right in thinking I'm the only guest staying here?'

'You are. Like I said…' she whipped up the milk in the pan with a tiny whisk as if she was no stranger to the task '…we're pretty quiet at the moment. The summer holidays are long over, and it probably won't get busy again until nearly Christmas.'

'And will you still be here then, helping Lily out?'

Jenny's slender shoulders visibly stilled. 'No. I won't. I told you…she's due back in a couple of weeks and I'll be returning to London.'

'To the house you grew up in as a child.'

'Yes.'

'Yet you seem more at home here than anywhere I've seen you before.'

'What makes you say that?'

'Because this rural environment suits you… In fact, it wouldn't require a great stretch of the imagination to see you as a country girl, Jenny. Yes, I can visualise you sitting in your cosy little stone cottage each evening as the sun goes down, the tantalising smell of the day's fruitful baking lingering in the air.'

'And in this tantalising little scenario am I on my own?' The catch in her voice had Rodrigo frowning deeply.

'I don't know.' He shrugged. 'You tell *me*.' Even though his voice was calm, it felt as if an icy boulder had taken up residence inside his belly.

'You know I've always wanted a family.'

'Yes.' He shifted uncomfortably in his chair. 'I do know that.'

'But you never wanted children, did you?'

'No. I didn't.'

'Then it was just as well you decided our marriage wouldn't work, wasn't it?'

Lifting the pan off the stove, Jenny poured the steaming milk into two waiting ceramic mugs, then gave the contents a brief stir. Bringing their drinks to the table, where Rodrigo sat silently and broodingly waiting, she lowered herself into the chair opposite him. Straight away he scented the soap she'd used to wash herself with. It smelled like newly laundered linen. Once again it lit a fire in his blood that made him feel more alive and intensely aware than he had in ages.

Sighing softly, she focused her shimmering cornflower-blue eyes on his. 'One day you might meet someone you really care for, Rodrigo, and change your mind about having children.'

'I don't think so.'

'How can you be so sure?'

'Because I know exactly what I want and what I don't want. There's no confusion about that.' His mouth set uncompromisingly.

'It must be marvellous to be so certain of things… to be so sure that you're right.'

Jenny turned her face away. When she glanced back Rodrigo couldn't pretend he didn't see the avalanche of hurt in her eyes. It all but sliced him in two, knowing he was the cause of it.

'It doesn't feel so marvellous when you put it like that,' he replied drolly.

'Then let's change the subject. Let's not talk about us—what we want or don't want—let's stick to safer topics. Your shower…was the water hot enough?'

Shrugging, Rodrigo warmed his still chilled hands round his mug of hot chocolate. 'It was fine.'

'Good.'

'You worry too much about others, Jenny.'

'I suppose I do. At least I worry that Lily's guests have everything that they need and are comfortable. It's a big responsibility, taking care of someone else's house and business, and I want to do a good job for her while I'm here.'

'Trust me…you do such a good job of taking care of your guests that you would put a top hotel to shame.'

'I suppose you'd know about that, wouldn't you?'

'I suppose I would.' Regarding her from beneath the sweeping black lashes that any female would envy, Rodrigo edged a corner of his mouth towards a smile. 'Anyway, I've always believed in acknowledging effort and good work where I see it.'

'Your staff must love you for that. As well as being paid well, everyone wants to feel valued.'

He raised an eyebrow. 'I agree. Sometimes employers can forget that.'

In his mind Rodrigo made a quick inventory of some of the people who worked for him... Were they happy? Did they consider him a good employer? Certainly his management team seemed to think so. After all, in fifteen years he had had very few complaints. From that he had to deduce that all must be well. For their loyalty and hard work he rewarded his staff with regular bonuses and luxury breaks at different foreign resorts from the ones they worked in, as well as seeing to it that they all had good pensions and private healthcare. He also knew that despite his strict adherence to high standards, he was well liked.

'So, you still enjoy your work?' Jenny enquired, dark blonde brows lifting a little.

'Yes, I do,' Rodrigo replied.

Now it was *his* turn to guard and protect his feelings. The stormy night, this warm cosy house and its unexpected pretty and familiar hostess might have lulled him into relaxing far more than he had in ages, but he was not about to confess to Jenny that lately he had fallen a little bit out of love with his chosen career.

'I suppose that was a bit of a stupid question.'

'It wasn't.'

'I mean…your work is your life, right? Of course you must still enjoy it.'

Taking a brief sip of her drink, Jenny licked the chocolate-coloured froth from her lips with the tip of her elegant pink tongue. Already feeling the disturbingly sensual effects of her alluring sweet company, Rodrigo felt the taut muscles in his belly constrict even more.

'My dad was only a plumber, but he really enjoyed his work too.' Her gaze roamed from Rodrigo's features down to his Ralph Lauren sweatshirt. 'Of course he didn't dress nearly as stylishly or expensively as you. Truth is he never made a lot of money, even though he worked hard. If he thought a customer would struggle to pay his bill he'd only charge them half the price. He wasn't a natural businessman, I'm afraid. But he was the very best father you could wish for.'

'You clearly admired and loved him very much.'

'I did. After all, what could be more important than being a good parent, and supporting, loving and adoring your children so that they don't ever doubt they mean everything to you? Being good at business is nothing in comparison to that.'

CHAPTER THREE

RODRIGO'S expression suggested an iron portcullis had slammed down over his emotions—as if everything in him, every feeling and sense, had been incontrovertibly closed and shielded against anything Jenny cared to throw at him.

She hadn't deliberately intended to make a jibe about his preference for work as opposed to having children, but she supposed it was inevitable it should come out like that. The fact was she had loved being married to him. Had prayed he would change his mind about them having a family together, and hoped his love affair with work would one day dim when it was replaced by the joys of fatherhood... But her prayers and hopes had been cruelly shattered the day he'd come home and announced their marriage was over.

It had been like listening to an icily aloof stranger, Jenny remembered with a shudder. Here in the kitchen, where the heat from the cooking range lent an air of cosiness and security as the storm rampaged outside, she wished the sense of safety and warmth she felt went beyond creature comforts. *She wished it were created by mutual love between her and Rodrigo.*

The force of her yearning made her want to weep. But she was wasting her time, dwelling on such futile things. Better that she remembered that her handsome ex-husband was just a visiting guest in the house, staying for one night only because circumstances dictated it...*not* because he'd intended them to meet and be alone together.

As soon as Lily had asked her to stand in for her for three months Jenny had vowed she'd be utterly professional and considerate at all times, and that was how she meant to proceed for the remainder of the time Rodrigo was there. She would treat him just like any other guest. She could manage that for twenty-four hours, couldn't she?

Her head swam for a moment.

'I'm going to check the house, then go to bed,' she announced, rising to her feet.

'Why do I get the distinct feeling that you're running away?' Rodrigo asked lazily.

'I'm not running away! If anyone knows how to do that it's *you*, not me.'

'You sound as though you've missed me, *querida*. Could that be the truth behind this petulant temper of yours?'

'I'm not petulant. And I haven't missed you. I'm merely getting on with my life without you and relieved that I'm not sitting up late every night waiting for a phone call to tell me you'll be home late or have to fly off somewhere for two weeks without me.'

'Then I've done you a favour.'

'If the idea helps you to believe what you did was right, then go ahead and think that. At any rate, I'm too tired to stand here and argue with you about it. By the way, what time do you want breakfast in the morning?'

'I'm an early riser, as you know. Seven-thirty okay with you?'

Jenny briefly met his mocking glance and forced herself not to react to it.

'Seven-thirty's fine.'

'Then I'll bid you goodnight, Jenny,' he said, taking her hint that the evening was at a close and he was most certainly going to bed alone. 'Sleep well. I hope the storm doesn't disturb you too much.'

'Goodnight,' she muttered, determinedly heading for the door.

The storm contributed to a practically sleepless night for Rodrigo. Yet he couldn't blame the turbulent display of thunder and lightning for his wakefulness entirely. The truth was he was tortured by how callously he'd ended his marriage, even though he'd genuinely believed at the time that he was doing it for the right reasons. For two years he'd held his disturbing feelings at bay, but now, being with Jenny again, they were uncomfortably surfacing.

Her words about sitting up late every night waiting

for a call to say he was coming home or flying off somewhere played over and over in his mind, driving him almost to madness. Several times he got up and walked the floor, wondering if she too was awake, like him, remembering that painful final scene between them when Rodrigo had sounded the death knell on their marriage.

At some point during the early hours, with no lessening of the fury of the storm, he crawled back into bed. A splitting headache knifing through his head, he determinedly closed his eyes, willing sleep to free him from the disturbing litany of guilt-ridden thoughts that plagued him.

When Rodrigo didn't show for breakfast at seven-thirty, Jenny put the generous plate of bacon and eggs she'd cooked in the oven, to keep them warm, then made a second fresh pot of coffee. Grimacing at the arc of furious lightning splintering overhead in the distance as she glanced out of the window, she shivered, pulling the edges of her cardigan closer over her chest to keep warm.

What was keeping Rodrigo? He was, as he'd said, an early riser.

As she continued to stare out the window through the driving rain at the reluctant dawn appearing on the horizon, she wondered if he could risk travelling anywhere in weather like this. A horrible vision of the tyres of his car skidding uncontrollably in the wet, causing the vehicle to crash violently into a tree and injure him, insinuated its way into her mind and wouldn't go away. Before she'd realised her intentions Jenny found herself apprehensively making her way upstairs. Gingerly, she knocked on Rodrigo's door.

'Rodrigo?' she called. 'Are you up yet? It's almost a quarter to eight.'

No reply. Again she rapped her knuckles against the door, her heart thudding hard under her ribs.

'Rodrigo, are you all right?'

From inside the room came a sound like a heavy book crashing to the floor. It was followed by some indecipherable low-voiced muttering. The door swung open before she had the chance to step back and Rodrigo stood there, rubbing at his eyes, his black hair more unruly than she'd ever seen it, his body encased in nothing but navy-blue silk pyjama bottoms clinging sexily low round his arrow-straight hips. The provocative sight made Jenny's mouth go dry.

Quickly pulling herself together, she folded her arms over her chest. 'Overslept, did you? That must be a first.'

'Who the hell could sleep with that din going on all night?' he retorted irritably, 'It sounded like a bombing raid!'

'It's just as wild this morning,' Jenny replied, serious-voiced, 'I don't think you should attempt to drive anywhere for a while yet...at least until things calm down.'

'Scared I might get swept off the road and end up in a ditch somewhere, *querida*?'

'That's not funny. I know male pride might convince you that you're invincible, but you'd be crazy not to listen to what I say. I've been here nearly three months now, and even in the summer the weather can get pretty scary.'

'Well, I'm neither crazy nor ignorant, and I thank you for your concern. Perhaps I'll put my meeting off for one more day and go tomorrow instead.'

Feeling a little stunned that he would even consider such an option, Jenny widened her blue eyes. 'Anyway...' she started to retreat '...your breakfast's keeping warm in the oven and I've made a fresh pot of coffee because the first one went cold. I've been up since six-thirty myself. Maybe some hot food and something to drink will revive you after your sleepless night?'

Rodrigo's suddenly amused gaze swept disturbingly up and down Jenny's figure. 'Maybe it will. Or maybe the fact that you look so wide awake and beautiful this morning will revive me even more? But that coffee sounds good too. Give me a few minutes and I'll come downstairs and join you.'

'Okay.'

Even though he'd ostensibly taken the day off, to Jenny's utmost surprise Rodrigo insisted on making himself useful, and she couldn't find it in her heart to refuse his help. At least if he was undertaking a couple of necessary DIY jobs around the house they wouldn't be at loggerheads, she reasoned. But it was disconcerting to see how impressively practical and handy he was.

Who would guess he was one of the wealthiest hoteliers in the world, much more at home in Armani tailoring and working behind a king-sized desk than getting his hands dirty in jeans and a plain black T-shirt, as he rolled up rain-damaged linoleum in the utility room and repaired some no longer properly functioning blinds in a bedroom?

The rain was still thundering against the roof when Jenny called to him upstairs to come and eat lunch. Was this relentlessly stormy weather never going to end?

Rodrigo witnessed her shiver as he came through the door into the kitchen. Immediately he frowned. 'Are you okay?'

'I'm fine. Somebody just walked over my grave, that's all.'

'What do you mean?' He was studying her with alarm.

'It's just an expression.' She smiled awkwardly. 'Nothing to worry about. Sit down—you must be starving. It's only chilli con carne on a baked potato, but it's hot and nourishing.'

'Trust me...it's very welcome'

'I never realised you had such talent for DIY.'

'I spent a lot of time with my uncle when I was young. He was a carpenter. He taught me that there is

honour in a man being able to put his hands to work.'
He pulled out a chair at the table and sat down.

'But your father wanted you to go into business?'
Jenny remembered.

'Sí he did.'

'And you never yearned to be a carpenter
instead?'

A forkful of food on its way to his lips, Rodrigo
paused to answer her. 'Maybe I did for a while…
But then I got more realistic—in terms of earning a
living, at least.'

Sitting down opposite him, Jenny made a start on
her own meal. Every now and then her gaze flicked
to the tight bronzed biceps displayed by his T-shirt
and her stomach rolled over.

They ate in an oddly companionable silence for
a while, until he glanced across at her and asked,
'Do you miss your brother since he moved to
Scotland?'

'No, I don't. You remember how difficult he could
be sometimes? Well, things got worse when I returned to the house. He felt I should just sign it over
to him completely…give him everything. He was
badly in debt because of one thing and another and
he blamed me.'

'That sounds about right—but why did he blame
you?'

'Because I'd looked out for him ever since our
parents died and he was jealous that I was getting
on well with my career and he couldn't seem to stick

at anything for long without getting into trouble. Anyway…in the end I bought him out and he moved to Scotland to live with some besotted girl he met.'

'You haven't heard from him?'

'No.' She didn't particularly *want* to hear from him either. Truth to tell, she needed more time to get over the hell he'd put her through.

His disturbing dark eyes roaming her face, Rodrigo put down his fork and stopped eating. 'You could have bought a place of your own with the settlement I made you. Then you could have just let him have the house and forgotten about him.'

Her heart racing, Jenny stared. 'I didn't want to touch a penny of that money. In fact now that we've met up again you must take it back. Do you think you're the only one who has any pride? I didn't want anything of yours after you heartlessly told me our marriage was finished. Don't you understand that? I told that solicitor of yours when he rang me about the settlement. If you wanted to cut the ties between us then we should have cut them completely! I want to make my own way in the world—just like I did before I met you.'

Could she make it any more clear how little she wanted to do with him? Each word flayed him.

Taking a long draught of the water she had poured him, Rodrigo returned the glass to the table, wiped his napkin over his lips and got up, before quietly saying. 'I should get back to what I was doing. There's still quite a bit to do. Thanks for the meal.'

She ached to say something to make him linger, but sheer hurt at the fact they were no longer together overwhelmed Jenny and she sat in silence as he walked across the floor and went out.

That evening, as they sat across the table from each other finishing their evening meal, Jenny began to realise how unwell she was feeling. Not just a tad on the warm side either. Her skin was fever-hot.

Resisting the urge to touch her hand to her head to gauge her temperature, she tugged the sides of the dressing gown she'd donned after her bath more securely over her chest. 'If this rain continues to fall we'll have to build an ark.' She smiled. 'Your carpentry skills will certainly come in handy.'

The timbre of her own voice took her aback. It sounded as if she regularly smoked cigarettes and downed whisky. *Damn!* She hoped she wasn't developing a cold. That was the *last* thing she needed when she was in a position of responsibility while her friend was away.

'Are you all right?' Rodrigo enquired, black eyes sweeping what she now knew must be her fever-bright reflection.

'I'm sorry…' Jenny mumbled. The drugging fatigue that washed over her was making her suddenly long for her bed. She pushed to her feet. 'I'm afraid I'm not feeling too good all of a sudden. I'll have to go to bed. Take your time finishing your food. There's no hurry. I mean of course it's up to you when you want to call it a day, it's just that…well…can I ask you a favour?'

'Ask away.' His dark gaze continuing to mirror concern, Rodrigo also stood up.

'Do you think you could turn off the lights for me and make sure that Cozette is in her basket before you go up to your room? She's probably hiding somewhere again because of the storm. The thunder and lightning really spook her.'

'I'll do everything you ask, but will you be okay? Studying you now, I can see that you look quite feverish. Shall I call a doctor?'

'Heavens, no. I'm just getting a bit of a cold after being in and out of the rain, that's all. I'm sure it won't hang around long.' But all the same Jenny put her hand up to her head. Her fingers almost sizzled at the burning heat that emanated from her skin. 'I'll—I'll get a good night's sleep and I'm sure I'll be feeling back to my normal self in the morning. What time do you think you'd like your breakfast?'

'Any time that you—Jenny? Are you sure you are all right?'

'I'm fine. I just need to—' To accompany her sky-high temperature, a wave of sickness arose inside her stomach. Her sight was going worryingly hazy, and Jenny sensed the strength in her legs frighteningly desert her. In the next surreal moment her knees crumpled like paper and the warm bricked floor rushed towards her.

The last thing she remembered before she blacked

out was Rodrigo catching her as she fell. His arms were strong as iron bars as he swept her up close to his chest. There was a faint scent of some arrestingly exotic cologne on the air just before darkness closed in on her and she surrendered to unconsciousness with impunity…

Having found Jenny's bedroom by glimpsing some feminine clothing thrown over a chair beside a bed through a slightly ajar door on the same landing as his, Rodrigo kicked the door further open and carried her limp body across to it.

Bending a little to yank down the freshly laundered covers, he carefully lowered his charge onto smoothly ironed white sheets. As soon as he had done so she turned onto her side, clearly shivering despite the warm woollen dressing gown she wore. His heart all but missed a beat at the sound of her softly ragged breath.

Muttering a soft, 'Gracias a Dios,' that she had regained consciousness, he drew the embroidered covers carefully over her shoulders, then sat on the edge of the bed to touch the flat of his hand against her forehead. 'Maldita sea!' She was burning fiercer than the hotplate on the stove downstairs. It did not bode well. He had to act fast to help bring that temperature down, but first he had to find the telephone number for an emergency doctor.

After murmuring some consoling words in Jenny's ear, Rodrigo leapt to his feet and ran downstairs. The telephone was on the small chestnut bureau in the hallway. Picking up the receiver, he rifled through an alphabetised leather-bound address book, managing to quickly locate the number of her friend's GP. Greeted by an answer-machine message that gave him a number for emergencies only, he hissed out his frustration. Seconds later he spoke to a weary sounding male voice in person.

Explaining the reason for his call, Rodrigo was taken aback when the doctor swiftly pronounced that he couldn't possibly come out to Raven Cottage on a 'filthy night such as this'. He already had several patients to visit in the local vicinity, and unless it was a case of life or death Rodrigo would just have to take the medical advice he was about to dispense and look after Ms Renfrew himself. If her temperature did not go down within the next twenty-four hours then he should by all means ring again.

Accustomed to only having to snap his fingers and get what he needed, Rodrigo was appalled at the doctor's seemingly cavalier attitude. Wrestling the strongest urge to call the man an uncaring imbecile, he corralled his temper and quickly scribbled down the ensuing medical instructions. In any case, he had already made up his mind to ring his own personal physician in Barcelona for help should the advice he'd been given take too long to effect a change.

Back upstairs in Jenny's bedroom, he touched his hand to her forehead again. Her skin still felt hotter than a radiator with the dial turned to maximum. As if to echo the fear that bolted through him, a deafening explosion of thunder burst violently overhead. Refusing to believe that her condition would worsen, Rodrigo urgently tugged down the quilt that covered her. The warm woollen dressing gown would have to go too.

Half lifting Jenny's limp slender form towards him, he tried to be as quick and as deft as he could. But his heartbeat accelerated as he observed her unnaturally rose-tinted cheeks and fluttering lashes, her body jerking now and then as if in acute pain. Out of the blue a partially remembered Spanish lullaby came to him. Softly, beneath his breath, he began to sing. *'Duerme, niña Chiquita sleep my little babe Duerme, mi alma sleep my precious soul.'*

Lifting his hand, he smoothed some delicate golden tendrils back from the pale fevered brow before him. Then, with the dressing-gown cast aside, he gently lowered Jenny back down into the bed. The nightdress she wore underneath was a sleeveless cotton affair in white, with a chain of tiny pink rosebuds dancing across the demure round-necked bodice. In the innocent gown she looked like some fairy tale princess waiting to be woken from a dream with a kiss from a handsome enraptured hero.

Grimacing ruefully, Rodrigo levered himself to his feet. First the lullaby he had not heard since his grandmother had crooned it to him as a child, then an observation that was too whimsical for words! Ever since he had stepped over the threshold of

Raven Cottage he'd been feeling as if he was under some kind of enchantment. But there was no time to waste reflecting on the strangeness of his reactions. Not when he had to urgently bring down that temperature.

Hurriedly seeking out the adjoining bathroom, he filled a decorative ceramic bowl with tepid water, grabbed a washcloth off the towel-rail and returned to his patient's bedside. Steeping the washcloth in the water, he carefully squeezed it out again. Pressing it against Jenny's forehead, then at the sides of her neck, he murmured, 'You will be better very soon sweetheart...I promise.'

Where did he get such confidence in his healing powers? he wondered. Especially when the tight little knot of anxiety that had taken up residence inside his chest had to be a far truer indication of how he was feeling.

'So...so hot...' she murmured, moving her head from side to side. 'Need some...water...'

'Here.' Sliding his arm round Jenny's shoulders, Rodrigo helped raise her head, then reached for the carafe of water on the nightstand. Pouring some into the matching glass, he touched the cup to her lips. She sipped thirstily, some of the liquid escaping to streak down her chin onto her gown.

'Please...let me lie down again.' Her sky-blue eyes opened wide to stare up at him. 'You—you shouldn't be doing this.'

'Why?' Rodrigo smiled, lifting an eyebrow at the

flash of lightning outside the window that for electrifying moments dwarfed the dim glow of the lamp. 'What else should I be doing on a night like this? You are ill, Jenny, and I am the only one around to take care of you.'

'But you—you're not responsible for me any more.' As she bit down anxiously on her quivering lower lip her feverishly bright blue gaze was shrouded in tears.

'Do not talk further…you will only distress yourself. Rest. That is what you must do now. It's all you *can* do.'

Moving back to the bathroom, Rodrigo searched through the mahogany cabinet for some of the regular medication that was recommended for flu and fever. The doctor had advised him to give some to Jenny just as soon as he could. It would settle her and help her have a more comfortable night. Discovering an unopened packet near the back of the cabinet, he scooped it up in triumph and not a little gratitude.

It wasn't the easiest task to get her to take the two capsules he placed in her hand. She was trembling so violently with fever. Fear slashed through Rodrigo's insides that she might take a turn for the worst after all. If she did then that singularly unhelpful doctor would rue the day he had refused to come out to her, he vowed passionately.

Biting back his apprehension and doubt, he persuaded Jenny to swallow the pills with a slurp of water. With her eyes closed again, she turned onto her side. A couple of minutes later she displayed all the signs of sleeping deeply.

Freeing a relieved sigh, Rodrigo scraped a hand round his stubbled jaw, studying her closely, with microscopic thoroughness. *It was no hardship to watch her...not when she resembled some slumbering angel lying there.*

Downstairs in the kitchen, a gratingly anxious *meow* greeted him. Smiling, he dropped to his haunches to gather up the softly striped ball of fur that had instantly pressed against his ankles, as though desperate for reassurance. The feline was clearly jittery about the storm, and he took a few moments to pet and make a fuss of her before popping the animal back onto the woolly plaid blanket in her basket beside the range.

Making a swift inspection of his surroundings and spying the uncovered cake of which he'd enjoyed a slice earlier, he replaced the lid on the tin so it wouldn't dry out. Satisfied that all was as it should be, he flicked off the lights and headed back upstairs. Dropping by his bedroom first, Rodrigo grabbed some paperwork relating to the meeting rearranged for the following day, dragged the satin quilt off the bed and returned to Jenny, unable to suppress the concern that had been building inside him ever since she'd fainted into his arms earlier. He was anxious to ascertain how she was doing.

He saw at once that she was still asleep, but even so he laid his cheek briefly against her chest to reassure himself that the soft rise and fall of her breathing was progressing normally. The action sent a spasm of volcanic need jackknifing through his body that almost tore his breath from his lungs. The sweetly intoxicating scent of her flesh combined with the touch of her soft breast beneath his cheekbone almost made him forget she was ill and made him long to be able to lie down beside her instead.

He glanced ruefully across at the rattan-cushioned chair he planned to spend the night in to watch over her, and his sigh was stoic. He didn't suppose he would get much sleep at all tonight, no matter *where* he slept. Not when he needed to keep his wits sharply about him to take care of Jenny. In four hours' time he would get her to take another dose of flu medication. Before that he would be sponging her down with tepid water again, to cool her temperature.

Moving across to the chair, Rodrigo stared down at the sheaf of papers in his hand. His reluctance to give the words on the page the proper attention hardly surprised him. Not when every sense and faculty he possessed was completely given over to the welfare of the lovely young woman sleeping fitfully in the bed before him. His unexpectedly dedicated commitment to his former wife left him with little desire for anything else right now.

If Jenny were well, no doubt she'd find it quite ironic. She firmly believed he had no inclination to care for anyone but himself. Many times during the brief year they'd been together she'd bemoaned the fact that he was too wrapped up in his work to spend proper time with her. Eventually Rodrigo had had to face up to the fact that he was poor husband material because it was true…he *was* married more to his work than Jenny. And that was ironic too, really, when he considered the simplicity of his mother's long-ago hope for him. Her heartfelt desire had been that her only son would find a warm, loving partner for life, father a healthy brood of children and then settle down somewhere he could be happy—preferably somewhere in Andalucia—and be content for the rest of his existence.

It was his *father* who had conditioned and programmed him from an early age to seek the lucrative rewards of a successful career in business. Benito Martinez had all but banged the idea into Rodrigo's head with a sledgehammer, giving him no choice to explore the alternatives. As a young man Benito had tried and failed to make his fortune from a housebuilding business. He had made some poor financial decisions and—to his shame—had lost everything. If Rodrigo achieved success in business then he, Benito, would truly be able to hold his head up in their village at last, and show them that the Martinez name meant something.

The implication had been that until such a time he would remain disappointed. And in pursuing an idea that hadn't even originated from him Rodrigo had learned that sometimes children were expected to fulfil the frustrated dreams of their parents instead of following their own…

The most disturbing images and feelings had been running through Jenny's brain. Nearly all of them involved a man who looked as if he'd stepped out of a Renaissance painting. Such endlessly dark soulful eyes he had, such glossy black hair and a heavenly shaped mouth. *His beautiful face haunted her.* His warm accented voice took her to a land of hot sun, cool Mediterranean waters and the echo of an ancient drumbeat that had been the heart of its people for centuries. Her Renaissance man also had powerful muscular arms that could carry her anywhere he wanted if Jenny allowed it, and those arms seemed to represent security and safety and something else— something essential that she'd longed for. It didn't matter right then that her fevered mind struggled to put a name to it.

A choking cough suddenly seized her. Each breathless convulsion was like a scythe slicing through her brain, it hurt so much. The arms she had dreamed of were suddenly holding her up, lifting a glass of water to her parched lips, patiently supporting and encouraging her as she gulped thirstily. Sensing her hand tremble where it circled the glass, Jenny gripped it a bit too tightly to still the tremors and accidentally tipped half the contents over her nightgown. The icy water that connected with her heated skin was akin to the touch of the coldest steel blade, and she gasped in shock.

'Oh, how stupid! What have I done?'

'It's nothing to be anxious about, *querida*, and nothing that cannot be put right in a moment. Here…I will help you remove this, then get you a towel and a clean gown.'

Before Jenny could find the strength even to protest, Rodrigo was lifting up her nightgown, bunching it into a ball, and heading off into the bathroom. Too sick to mind that he'd just seen her naked, she crossed her arms over her chest, shivering violently from a combination of fever, cold, and pure distress that she was too weak to help herself. He returned quickly, to drape a large bathtowel round her shoulders. The floral smell of lavender-scented washing detergent as well as the disturbingly sensual whiff of her ex-husband's aftershave permeated her fogged brain to cause a faint skirmish of acute awareness deep in her belly.

'Thanks.' She couldn't bring herself to raise her eyes to look at him.

'Where do you keep your clean nightgowns? In that chest of drawers over there?'

'The second one down.'

As deftly as he'd removed the wet nightgown, Rodrigo slid a fresh one down over Jenny's head and shoulders, with the same pragmatic ease. Outside the bedroom window another starburst of vivid white lightning followed by another rumble of thunder reminded her that the persistent storm had not yet exorcised its rage.

A sense of feeling safely cocooned here inside, whilst the elements caused mayhem around them, rippled beguilingly through her. It was no good feeling resentful or embarrassed about needing Rodrigo's help tonight, she concluded wearily. All she could do was surrender to the deep malaise that dragged at her limbs and made her head feel as though it was stuffed with cloth and pray and hope that when the morning came she would be over the worst and finally able to care for herself. Till then, she had no choice but to leave Rodrigo in charge.

Lowering her head resignedly against the pillows once more, Jenny shut her eyes to the surprising and hypnotic sound of his husky velvet tones softly singing what sounded very much like a lullaby in Spanish.

CHAPTER FOUR

IN THE space of a heartbeat a lovely consoling dream—a dream about a man who had a healing touch and a honeyed voice to match—turned into a nightmare of a passage in darkness, with flames licking under the only door. Jenny's pulses were wild with terror. Suddenly it was impossible to breathe. Consumed with fear that she would die there, she let words tumble from her lips incoherent and terrified as she pleaded to be rescued—pleaded for her very life.

Strong hands imprisoned her wrists and implored her to calm down in case she hurt herself. It was all right, the disembodied voice soothingly promised. Nothing was going to harm her—he would make sure of that.

As awareness of her true surroundings returned, Jenny stared frantically at the lean, high-cheek-boned face that stared back at her with rock-like steadiness in his depthless black eyes, as if whatever troubled her—however big or small—he would handle it. Her heart continued to thump crazily beneath her ribs until bit by agonising bit she recognised Rodrigo.

'It's all right,' he soothed again and the kindness mirrored back to her from his glance and his voice was like being in receipt of a warm woollen blanket on a raw winter's night. Slowly her terror started to recede. 'You were having a nightmare, baby…but you were here all the time, safe in your bed. You're burning up with fever. You're going to have to let me do what I can to help make you more comfortable.'

'A nightmare…' she mumbled through the tousled skeins of spun-gold hair that in her urgency to be free had spilled across her face.

'Don't move,' Rodrigo told her firmly. 'I'll be straight back.'

True to his word, he was, bringing with him the ceramic bowl refilled with fresh tepid water and a newly rinsed washcloth. Without words he began to apply the cloth to Jenny's face, neck and shoulders, tugging down the thin straps of her nightgown to do so, smiling directly into her eyes when her gaze dazedly fell into his.

After a while he said, 'You were screaming, "Fire!"' Neither his expression nor the tone of his voice changed as he stated this. Calmly and methodically he continued to cool her heated skin with the gently wrung-out cloth.

'I haven't had that nightmare in ages.' A violent shiver bounced up Jenny's spine like tumbleweed tossed around by strong winds. Desperately she tried to push away the cloying dark remnants of the stark cold horror that had visited her. She felt so weak and ill. But even more than the longing to be free of her sickness she craved the comfort and reassurance of someone who cared about her.

What did it say about her life that in her time of need she had to depend on the man who had left her? Was she destined to pay the price of the poor choices she had made for the rest of her days? She was so tired of being afraid, so weary of waiting for some new disaster to yet again destroy everything she'd once depended upon, leaving her with the sense that she was nervously walking a precipice that at any second she might plunge off.

'So…what makes you have such disturbing nightmares? Do you know?'

As Rodrigo touched the cool washcloth to the area just below her throat, Jenny shivered again. 'The house burned down. I—I lost everything… my parents' photos, the mementoes of mine and Tim's childhood, all our furniture and belongings… everything.'

'You were not there at the time? You didn't get hurt?'

'No. I was away when it happened, thank God. But every time I dream about it somehow I'm there in the middle of it all and I can't get out.'

'Why did you not let me know about this?' Her ex-husband's voice sounded fierce for a moment.

'We'd parted. We were no longer together and it was up to me to handle it.'

Rodrigo breathed in deeply. 'So what caused this fire?'

'The police investigation concluded it was an electrical fault.'

'That was the most incredible bad luck. But we won't talk about such distressing matters right now. It won't help. I'm going to give you some more medication to help lower your temperature and then you will sleep again.'

Letting the cloth drop back into the bowl, Rodrigo moved the items onto the nightstand then turned back to Jenny to lightly curl his hand round her delicately made wrist. Adjusting his palm, he thoughtfully stroked the pad of his thumb across the finer skin at the base of her fingers.

'And this time it will be a healing, dreamless sleep, I am certain…no more nightmares.'

'You sound so sure.'

'I *am* sure.'

'Why?'

'Because my intuition tells me so.'

'You believe in that?'

'I do.'

After swallowing down the two capsules that Rodrigo gave her with a few sips of water, Jenny smiled shakily. 'You should have been a doctor.'

'What? And deprive the hotel business of my incredible flair and superb know-how?'

'You'd be superb at whatever career you chose, Rodrigo. You would have made the best carpenter too.'

Unable to ignore the weariness that was like a powerful warm wave taking her under, Jenny slid back down into the bed, her eyelids closing even before her head touched the pillow. She'd happily accept the idea of a dreamless sleep, she silently admitted. But she'd equally welcome another dream of a man with sable eyes deep enough to swim in and a gentle sure touch that was far more healing than any medicine...

For a long time after Jenny had returned to the land of sleep Rodrigo sat in the rattan chair, listening to the rain lash furiously against the windows, soberly mulling over what she'd told him about her family home burning down and losing everything.

He had been drifting off himself when her anguished cry had rent the air and sent him bolting out of his seat as if an explosion had just ripped through the room. But even though his heartbeat had thundered in alarm, he'd still had the presence of mind to stay calm, so that when she emerged more fully from whatever nighttime horrors had visited her he could reassure her that it was only a dream. Those incandescent blue eyes of hers definitely didn't lack courage, but he'd sensed early on in their acquaintance that there was some fragility in her make-up too.

It had made it all the harder for him to end a

marriage that should never have happened in the first place. But Rodrigo had been so head over heels in love with Jenny from the instant he'd seen her chatting to a friend, one of the receptionists at the hotel he'd been staying at in London, that for a while he hadn't been thinking straight.

Now, after witnessing the distress caused by her nightmare, Rodrigo willingly resigned himself to the fact that he would be getting no sleep for the rest of the night. How could he risk even dozing if that fever of hers got worse? It was vital to stay alert in case he had to make an emergency dash in his car to the nearest hospital. But even the idea of negotiating a safe path through this hostile storm in the pitch-dark, in an area he wasn't even familiar with, keeping one eye on his possibly dangerously ill passenger as he drove, filled him with dread. Yet there was no question that he would do what had to be done and deliver Jenny safely into the competent medical hands she deserved...

Grimly firming his mouth, he beat his fingers in a soft, restless tattoo on the arms of his chair. It was best not to concentrate on the worst-case scenario, he decided. If Jenny woke suddenly he would not want her to sense that he was rattled by the situation in any way.

Needing a distraction, he reached for the sheaf of papers he had brought from his room, resolving to concentrate.

Two hours later the thunder and lightning was at

last a spent force, the storm having subsided to the ghostly sound of the wind rushing pell-mell through the trees and faintly rattling the windows. Judging by the hushed rhythmic breaths that had softly accompanied the reading of his documents Jenny was still sleeping peacefully, and a welcome atmosphere of calm had descended on the room.

His eyes feeling as if he'd rinsed them out with gravel, Rodrigo laid down his papers and stood up. Yawning and stretching, he moved barefoot to Jenny's bedside. Glancing down at her angelic profile—at the curling dark blonde lashes brushing the tip of her velvet cheekbone, the slim, elegant nose and lips as serene as those of the blessed Madonna herself—he felt a rush of forceful commanding need rock him to his soul.

After helping her change her gown during the night and seeing her naked once again it was hard to get the arresting image of her bewitching perfection to leave his mind. *She was so lovely that Rodrigo had to force away the idea of her being with someone else.* It made him feel jealous and suddenly possessive. If he had a second chance with her then he would definitely *not* spend all his time at work. Even *he* must learn from the lessons of the past.

Suddenly realizing the road his hypnotized thoughts were taking him down, Rodrigo shook his head. For heaven's sake, was he going mad? His marriage to Jenny was finished—over. He'd made his choice and he was destined to live by it. Dedication and hard work had helped him become the owner and head of one of the most successful luxury spa hotel empires in the world, and he wasn't about to ease off the gas for anything—least of all a precarious rekindling of a relationship that he'd really known from the first could never work. The only real solace and satisfaction to be had in life was in his work. No woman, no matter how soft, feminine and lovely, could bring him more happiness and fulfilment than that. He might indulge his need for sex and companionship from time to time, but that was all.

Moving away from where Jenny lay peacefully sleeping, in case he was tempted to meander into the realms of such pointless fantasy again, he rubbed his palm round his unshaven jaw with a scowl. Reaching the window, he swept the curtain aside to see the faint pink and gold light of dawn edging the horizon. Hovering over the smooth glass of the sea, it was a sublime sight. *A sight surely worth missing out on a night's sleep for...* It didn't happen very often that he did that. The strict routine he adhered to didn't factor in long, soulful glances at charming scenery.

'Rodrigo?'

'*Sí?*'

He spun round with a jolt to find Jenny throwing back the covers and lifting her legs out of the bed.

'What time is it?'

'Just after seven a.m. Where do you think you're going?'

Reaching her side, Rodrigo frowned deeply. To

his surprise she kept her head bowed and he sensed she was embarrassed.

'I—I need the bathroom.'

'Let me help you.'

'I can manage.'

But even as she strove to rise to her feet he saw that she was trembling like some fragile birch leaf in the wind. It was clear she was still feverish, and far from recovered.

'I disagree.' His tone strongly disapproving, Rodrigo had no hesitation in scooping her up into his arms and marching into the bathroom. Through the paper-thin cotton of her nightgown her body heat all but scorched him. There was no way on earth that she'd be fit enough to run her friend's guesethouse for a good few days yet. He also knew he wouldn't or *couldn't* leave her stranded. His scheduled business meeting would just have to be postponed again. No doubt his contractors would be relieved to have the extra time to get things ready for the boss's inspection.

Switching on the light, Rodrigo carefully stood Jenny down in the middle of the floor. And, because he couldn't resist, he gently moved a few tousled strands of corn-gold silk back from her face. 'I will be waiting right outside the door to help you back to bed,' he told her. The unsullied crystal of her huge blue eyes reminded him of an Andalucian mountain lake, caressed by sunlight. His stomach rolled over at the sight.

'Okay…'

When she emerged from the room a few minutes later Rodrigo once again swept her up into his arms to carry her back to bed. As she settled back under the covers Jenny's expression was forlorn. 'I'm so embarrassed that I've let you do all this for me that I almost don't know what to say to you.'

'Were you well last night?'

'No, but—'

'Are you feeling any better today?'

'No… But I still—'

'Is there someone—some friend, family member or even a neighbour I can ring—who will come and take care of you for the next few days?'

Rodrigo didn't miss the flash of despair in her eyes. 'Not that I can think of…no…'

'Then there is nothing else for you to do but go back to sleep. I am here, and will remain so until such time as you are able to get back on your feet and go about your business as normal. If anyone rings to make a reservation then I'll simply tell them we are closed until you are better.'

'But what about your work? You came down here for a meeting, didn't you?'

'It is easy enough to delay for another day or two.'

'You would do that for me?'

'I know you find that hard to believe but, yes, Jenny…I *would.*'

'Even so, I can't let you, Rodrigo.'

'You have no say in the matter. It's my own decision. No one is forcing me to do anything I don't want to do—least of all you.'

'I feel so useless.' Her pretty mouth struggling with emotion, she looked as if she might cry.

Still feeling appalled that there was no one Jenny could ask to help but him—his own past neglect of her not withstanding—Rodrigo gave her a gentle shove so that her spun-gold head fell back onto the creamy white pillows.

'Since I have already complimented you on your ability to make guests feel more than at home here, and have seen how dedicated you are to running things for Lily in her absence, that's clearly not true. Go back to sleep. When you wake I'll make you a cup of tea, if that's your preference. But I warn you that my tea-making skills would hardly earn me a job working here.'

Chuckling, he reached out to lay his palm flat against Jenny's forehead. She was still unnaturally warm, but thankfully not as dangerously hot as last night. Cautiously, he prayed that meant her fever had broken and she was over the worst.

'You're a long way from recovered, *querida*, but hopefully you are on the mend. Right now I need a shower and a shave—then I'll see what has to be done downstairs. Do as I say and get some more rest… I'll return in a while to make sure everything is okay.'

Settling back against the bank of pillows she'd just about mustered the strength to arrange behind her,

Jenny swept her gaze round the sunlit bedroom with frustrated resignation and felt a little jab of fear piercing her. It was perfectly true that she felt weaker than a newborn foal, and twice as vulnerable, but to have allowed Rodrigo, her work-obsessed ex-husband, to postpone his business meeting to help take care of her... Well, it hadn't featured in even her *wildest* dreams. *And why had she trusted him so easily when his past record of considering her needs was so abysmal?* It was inexplicable.

She'd had similar issues with Tim. Jenny knew her brother wasn't the type of man who could take care of anything much. He certainly wouldn't have been able to even look after their home if she should have fallen ill. In truth, he would have simply gone out and left her. His attitude to any sort of responsibility was casual, to say the least. When she'd returned to live in her old home after she and Rodrigo had split up, the beautiful Victorian semi she'd grown up in had been an absolute *tip*. It had taken several weeks of diligent home-making application on Jenny's part to restore it to anywhere near its former beauty and comfort.

Then, after months of growing suspicion of her brother's irresponsible behaviour, she'd discovered the real reason he was inclined to let things slide— and that included work. It was because he despised any demands that came between him and his increasing dependence on drugs.

A flutter of pain tightened her chest. *Dark times...*

Not the kind of thing Jenny wanted to recall when she was feeling so poorly.

In stark contrast, the vibrant and charismatic Rodrigo had taken on the mantle of carer so gallantly and effortlessly that she was already half bewitched by him all over again. *Dangerous.* Her temperature had soared even higher when he'd swept her up into his arms to take her to the bathroom and back to bed when she came out. There was no disputing the man's strength, or the beguiling warmth of his body at close quarters, or the fine and expensive way he smelled. But the situation couldn't continue for much longer, Jenny vowed. Somehow she had to get better quickly to resume her stewardship of Lily's guesthouse. It was kind of Rodrigo to say he would tell people they were closed until she was recovered, but it was her friend's precious income she was denying if she allowed that.

'How are you feeling?'

The man himself stood in the doorway, carrying a tray with a cup of tea on it. The sight of him had the same effect as a shot of dizzying adrenaline in the arm. He was wearing a fitted coal-black T-shirt and faded light blue denims that hugged his muscular thighs like a glove. The deceptively ordinary clothing must *love* being so close to his smooth bronzed skin, Jenny thought wildly, because the things they did for that mouthwateringly fit body surely shouldn't be allowed in a defenceless woman's bedroom.

Flustered, she sat up a bit straighter against her

pillows. 'I thought about lying to you and telling you that I felt much better, but if I got up and fell flat on my face I realised you'd pretty soon get the picture that perhaps I should have made a will…just in case.'

'At least you've got your sense of humour back. That's got to be a good sign. And you're not going to die…not on *my* watch.'

Moving towards the bed, Rodrigo deposited her cup of tea on the nightstand.

'Room service as well?' Jenny quipped, wishing it wasn't so hard to breathe whenever he came near. 'Did you master that when you were starting out in the hotel business too?'

CHAPTER FIVE

'IF YOU want to learn how a business works from the ground up then you have to familiarise yourself with everything.'

'I agree. When I first started doing interior design I found there were so many dimensions to it that I hadn't realised. It made the work even more interesting, though.'

'And how's business these days?' Rodrigo asked.

'It's been a bit up and down, which is why I could come here and help Lily out. But I've got a couple of good commissions coming up.'

Her plump lower lip was receiving some unfair treatment from her teeth as she chewed on it, he observed.

'Anyway…from what you say about the way you approach things it's obvious that you've become a success because you're so…thorough.'

The corners of his mouth edged into a sardonic smile. 'I am, as you say thorough. That applies to whatever I might be engaged in, if you recall.'

Jenny lapsed into a self-conscious and pink-cheeked silence. Had the same stimulating scenario gone through *her* mind as had just flashed through his? *Rodrigo certainly hoped so.*

'Thanks for the tea. You've made it exactly the way I like it.'

'Muchas gracias, señorita.' He made a mock bow. 'I aim to please. Here.' Carefully he passed her the cup and saucer, noting immediately that her hands shook a little as she accepted it. 'And after you drink it you are to stay put for the rest of the day. I'll see to everything else that needs to be done.'

'I'll have to pay you for your help, Rodrigo.'

'What?'

'It's only right. If you're working for me I'll have to pay you…especially as I'm delaying your return to your own job.'

'That's crazy talk. You need do no such thing.' A spasm of anger shot through him that she would think for even a second that he expected to be paid for helping take care of her when she was ill. 'Now that the rain's stopped I'm going into the garden to check on the greenhouse. I'll remove the tarpaulin we put up the other night and look over any damage that the storm might have caused. For lunch I'll make us a simple soup—my cooking skills do actually exceed my tea-making ones, though I confess I didn't demonstrate them when we were together. You were clearly a bit rundown for this fever to have occurred and no doubt your immune system needs building up again with good food.'

'Right now I couldn't contemplate eating any-thing—not when my sense of taste is probably non-existent.' Taking the tiniest sip of the hot tea he'd made, Jenny passed him back the delicate blue and white cup with its matching saucer almost immedi-ately. 'I don't mean to sound ungrateful, but I feel so stupidly weak that I—' Touching her hand to her head, she grimaced.

'Does something hurt?' Rodrigo demanded, examining her flushed pretty face with renewed concern.

'My head feels like a re-enactment of the Battle of Waterloo is going on inside it,' she answered. 'I really need to shut my eyes again. Do you mind?'

'Of course not… It's clear that you are nowhere near recovered.' After returning her cup and saucer to the nightstand, when next Rodrigo looked she'd slid back down into the bed and buried herself beneath the plump feather duvet like a small animal going into hibernation.

'Rest, then, *querida*,' he said with a smile, and although he would have been quite happy to stand and gaze at her for a while longer, he wrestled the desire to the ground and headed back downstairs.

During the following three days it honestly went through Jenny's mind more than once that if she slipped away into the afterlife one fever-racked night it might be a blessing. Never before had her constitution been under such miserable threat. But she held onto the vehement assurance that Rodrigo had given her— 'You're not going to die...not on *my* watch.'

Had she ever slept this much in the whole of her twenty-seven years? Her dad had told her once that even as an infant she had only slept six hours out of every twenty-four. *Not much rest to be had then for her long-suffering parents.*

But during those memorable three days while she was ill Jenny heard Rodrigo moving reassuringly round the house, doing this and that, and at one point forced opened her heavy lids to see a smart-suited stranger urging her to 'just relax' whilst he placed a cold thermometer under her arm to take her temperature. Whatever the doctor concluded it had caused Rodrigo to move into her bedroom permanently, it seemed—because whenever Jenny did manage to open her eyes he was there in the rattan chair next to her bed, either scribbling away on a notepad with his pen or tapping away at the keys on his laptop. A couple of times she registered him speaking on the phone too...once in mellifluous Spanish.

But, as much as his continued presence reassured her, Jenny had mixed emotions about it. Her tired brain could hardly credit why he would stay with her for so long and not simply leave... It was nothing like his old behaviour, when work had always come first.

On the fourth day of her illness she woke up

feeling less likely to die and longing for a bath. Her teeth were also in dire need of the brushing of a lifetime, because frankly her mouth tasted as though some small creature had crept inside and died in it. It was after eight in the morning, and the rattan chair beside her was empty of her handsome dark-haired guard. With a little jolt of unease in her stomach at the fresh realisation of just how much she had been relying on Rodrigo she swung her legs over the side of the bed and stood up.

Wrong move, Jenny... The room spun alarmingly, as though she'd just stepped off a manically twirling carousel

'What are you doing?'

'I need a bath. If I don't have one soon you'll have to report me to the health and safety department.'

Moving away from the doorway, his face unsmiling, Rodrigo walked right up to her. Recently showered and shaved, and wearing a fresh white T-shirt and black corded jeans, the man smelled *gorgeous*. It made Jenny all the more flustered and aware of her own less than scented condition after lying ill in bed for three days.

'Are you up to having a bath, *querida*? Perhaps I could bring a basin of warm water and you could have a bed-bath instead?'

'With you playing nurse?' Her eyebrows flew up to her scalp. 'I don't think so!'

'This is hardly the time for false modesty, Jenny Wren. Besides...' a teasing spark of heat ignited in his soulful dark eyes '...I've seen you naked, remember? And not just when I helped you change into a fresh nightgown.'

She'd been praying she'd dreamt that. Learning that wasn't the case, she felt her heart skip an embarrassed beat. 'It's hardly gentlemanly of you to remind me about that.'

He chuckled—a husky, compelling sound that made her legs feel weaker than water. 'Sometimes I am a gentleman and others *not*. I don't have to leave it to your imagination to wonder about the times I am not...do I?'

Clutching the front of her nightgown a little desperately, Jenny tipped up her chin. 'I have to have a bath. In fact I insist. Just leave me alone for a while, would you? I'm quite capable of sorting it out for myself.'

But he'd already stalked into the bathroom and turned on the taps. Stepping back into the bedroom, he dropped his hands to his hips, grinning with a distinct air of amused defiance at her disbelieving look. 'Which bubble bath shall I pour in? You have several.'

'I—I...' Flustered, she bit heavily down on her lip again. It might appear ridiculous to Rodrigo to quibble about such an innocuous thing, but somehow pouring in her bath fragrance seemed like the ultimate in intimate acts when she was already feeling disconcertingly fragile. 'I'll do that.'

Moving into the already steam-filled bathroom on

legs that felt like cotton-wool, Jenny shouldn't have been a bit surprised to find Rodrigo right behind her, but she was.

'This is no time to be petulant,' he told her, stern-voiced. He stepped in front of her, his black eyes roving her face as if he would know the secrets of her very soul. 'Which fragrance shall I use? If you won't tell me then I will put in the rose...especially since you reminded me of one from the moment I saw you in the reception area of the Savoy Hotel.'

Stoically resisting a huge urge to cry, Jenny scanned the array of prettily shaped bottles on the shelf above the bath and sniffed. 'That's the most ridiculous thing I've ever heard.'

Rodrigo took hold of her elbows and impelled her towards him, so that she had no choice but to make him the sole focus of her attention. 'You didn't always throw my compliments back in my face, Jenny... No,' he added lazily, 'sometimes they could make you blush, and other times make you extremely affectionate as I recall.'

Now, as heat cascaded through her like a rampaging river, Jenny's legs really *did* feel as if they might not hold her up for very much longer. There was a heaviness and a heat between her thighs she couldn't deny.

'That was when I trusted and loved you,' she burst out irritably, pulling free of Rodrigo's loose hold on her—suddenly terrified of the need that made her want to surrender to his arms and give him everything. 'And I don't any more. Now I'm much more careful about who I give my affection to.'

'Is that your way of telling me you've found someone else?'

'Are you joking?' she answered scathingly. 'After the way my brother behaved as well, I don't think I'll ever trust another man again.'

'Not now, perhaps… But when enough time has passed you might learn that not all men are so despicable.' Tenderly Rodrigo smoothed back her hair, standing his ground as Jenny's body stiffened with tension

'If I ever make the mistake of trusting a man again, then I deserve everything I get!'

'Yet you *did* trust me again.' His tone was gentle but firm. 'You trusted me to take care of you while you were ill.'

'I didn't have much choice, did I?'

'Do you want to vent your anger at me Jenny? Is that it?'

'All I want is my bath,' she said weakly. Frighteningly, she sensed that the full flood of grief and pain over what had happened between them hovered dangerously close now that she'd opened the lid on it again. It must be because she was sick she reasoned. Usually she managed to contain her hurt and rage much better.

'Then that's exactly what you shall have.' Reaching up to the shelf for the crystal bottle labelled 'English Rose,' Rodrigo gave her an unperturbed smile. After liberally applying it to the splashing hot water, he returned the bottle to the shelf. 'I'll leave you to get into the tub by yourself, but if you need me I'll be just outside the door,' he told her.

'Thanks,' she murmured. And as soon as the closed door was a barrier between them she dropped down onto the loo seat and allowed herself to listen to the sound of her heart breaking again...

That was when I trusted and loved you, she'd said. He could drive himself mad with regret and pain because she'd never say she loved and trusted him again. And it wasn't easy for Rodrigo to leave Jenny to cry. He'd sensed the hurt she normally held in strict check had just catapulted to the surface and spilled over. Every heaving sob was like a knife slicing through his heart, and it disturbed him to discover that he could be so affected by this woman's tears.

Why had it not been that way before? The more she had cried, the more he had been furious with what he saw as typically female behaviour employed to manipulate his emotions. He sat in the rattan chair and dropped his head in his hands. Listening to Jenny's distress was nothing less than pure torture.

A few moments later, the sound of her crying ceased. Resisting the strongest urge to knock on the door and ask if she felt better, he heard the relieved groan she released as she settled herself back into the hot water. About five minutes later, lost in his own thoughts, Rodrigo jolted when he heard her call out his name. He was at the door in a second.

'What is it? Are you okay?'

'Can you—can you come in?'

Surprised, he didn't hesitate. Such a picture she made, lying there amidst the fragrant pink bubbles, her big blue eyes staring back at him like a crestfallen child's, that Rodrigo's heart slammed hard against his ribs.

'Do you want me to scrub your back?' he joked, although the idea of sliding his hands over that gleaming wet satin skin was definitely no cause for amusement. Even as he stood looking down at her his body throbbed with equal measures of pleasure and pain.

'Could you help me wash my hair?' Jenny asked softly, her expression clearly nervous in case he should refuse.

'Of course... Where is your shampoo?'

'Here.' She handed him a tube-shaped bottle.

Dropping to his knees behind her, Rodrigo breathed her in, stealing a vital couple of moments to contain the lava-flow of desire that rocked through him and stay clear-headed enough to do the job in hand. But every sense he had was already saturated with her essence, even before he touched her.

Applying some shampoo to her already dampened hair, he could hardly attest to breathing as he began to move his palms slowly over her scalp. Nobody had ever told him that washing a woman's hair could be so immensely satisfying and erotic. Over one satiny-smooth shoulder he glimpsed the delicate swell of her breast, disappearing provocatively down into a sea of pink foam.

'Rodrigo?'

'Yes?' His voice sounded as if it scraped over gravel, he was so aroused.

'I'm sorry I acted like such an idiot just now. Perhaps we can call a truce?'

'I'm not at war with you, Jenny. I never was.'

'What do you mean?'

Jenny turned her head to glance at him, and he painfully observed the tiny collection of moisture bubbles clinging to the delicate furrow above her top lip. He yearned to lick away every one.

'I've never thought of you as my enemy…that's all.'

'So you want us to be friends? Is that what you're saying?'

'*Dios!* I know you are ill, but I don't want you to delude yourself that it's friendship I'm interested in! Pass me that jug so I can rinse your hair, would you?' He clicked his fingers, scarcely able to contain his impatience and—it had to be admitted—his *annoyance*. Suddenly he was in no mood for playing games. Not when it was all but killing him to wash her hair.

'Are you mad at me for asking you to do this?' When Rodrigo had finished rinsing, Jenny hurriedly scraped her fingers through her damp shoulder-length locks to move them out of her face, her gaze anxiously tracking him as he stood up and moved round the tub to survey her.

'No. I'm not mad at you at all. But don't fool yourself that all I want to do is take care of you while you're ill. Trust me…I'm not as selfless or gallant as you may imagine. Neither am I made of stone.'

'Oh.'

'Is that all you can say?'

'Rodrigo, I didn't ask you to stay and take care of me. Are you saying that I should sleep with you as some kind of thank-you?'

'Dios!'

His handsome face looked so thunderous that Jenny shrank back as far as she could in the tub, her heart beating hard.

'That you even *dare* make such a crass remark is beyond belief. Admitting that I desire you does not mean I'm suggesting you give me your body for services rendered! I know perfectly well that you're not immune or unaware of the attraction flaring between us again. I was merely being honest about my intention.'

'And that is?'

He curled his lip in a sardonic smile, then folded his arms across his chest. His action drew Jenny's heated gaze to the ripple of toned hard muscle in his bronzed biceps and taut torso, and she felt the hot sting of arousal burning in the tips of her breasts.

'I am definitely going to make love to you very

soon, Jenny,' he drawled. 'I will, of course, wait until you are fully recovered, but make no mistake that it will happen. Now… Do you need my help getting out of that tub?'

'No!' she answered quickly, disconcerted to see him nod with a little mocking smile.

'Okay, then. If you think you can manage on your own then I'll go downstairs and prepare some breakfast for us. You are hungry this morning, yes?'

Hungry? Suddenly the word had all kinds of dangerous connotations for Jenny.

CHAPTER SIX

CURLED up on the living room couch with a cosy woollen blanket, Jenny watched Rodrigo rise from where he'd been stoking the burning logs in the woodstove, then smooth his long artistic hands down his jeans. Although she was still feeling frustratingly tired and achy, it was impossible not to notice how strong, well made and fit he was. He might work in the hotel trade on the business side of things, but he wasn't a man who shied away from hard physical work either.

Earlier, she'd glanced out of the kitchen window to see just how hard he'd been working in the storm-tossed garden. It looked as if it had been given a serious face-lift. Even the fallen tree had been moved to lie safely against the fence, and without its temporary tarpaulin Lily's beloved greenhouse appeared intact and sturdy as ever.

'You'll be wanting to head off soon, now that I'm feeling better.' Suddenly, the thoughts that had been buzzing round inside Jenny's head were out in the open.

Remaining quiet, Rodrigo strode across to lay his palm against her forehead. A hot current of awareness hummed right down to the very edges of her toes.

'You are still a little warm.' He frowned, his ebony gaze sweeping over her like an arresting searchlight.

'Yes, but I really am feeling so much better.'

'But hardly well enough to get back to work and run Lily's business efficiently. Today is Friday…I'll stay until Monday at least, to make sure you are well on your way back to being fighting fit before I go.'

'You don't have to.'

In answer to that comment, he merely raised an eyebrow.

'By the way, I've been meaning to ask you… Have we had any enquiries about bookings over the last few days?'

'*Sí*…we have.'

'And?' Jenny's hands twisted anxiously in the folds of the woollen blanket.

'And I made the required reservations, of course. They were both for the end of the month, when your friend returns from Australia. A married couple from Jersey and a single woman from Edinburgh. All the details are in the reservations book.'

'She'll be pleased about that. Thanks for seeing to things. You've been working hard in the garden too, I noticed. I can't let you do all this for nothing.'

'We have already put that subject to bed, have we not?'

'Okay…I'll drop it. But as soon as I feel able I'll cook you something nice.'

Cozette chose that particular moment to stroll into the room and make a beeline for Jenny's lap.

She grinned in delight as she stroked her hand over the deliciously soft striped fur. 'Cozette, my angel! How have you been, baby? Have you missed me?' The cat rubbed its face against Jenny's arm, then settled into the blanket against her middle to purr contentedly.

'Little traitor.' Rodrigo grinned, dropping easily down to his haunches to fondly pet the animal.

'A traitor… Why?'

'Because since you've been ill she's behaved like I am the sun, moon and stars—playing up to me, wanting me to pamper and pet her whenever she gets the chance…just as if she lives for nobody's attention but mine. Now she's with you I see that she was merely toying with my affections, like the typically mercenary little female she is!'

'All females aren't mercenary, Rodrigo.' Imbuing her tone with a teacher-like scold, Jenny bravely met his mocking glance. Almost instantly the humour in his eyes vanished, leaving her with the strangest sensation that she was falling through space—plummeting at frightening speed—with no sense or idea of when or *if* she would land safely on earth again. A gasp caught and died in her throat as he reached for her hand to place it firmly against his rough-velvet cheek.

'I find myself intensely jealous of the attention that you're paying Cozette, *querida*…I'm wondering if you have any left to spare for me.' Moving her palm to his lips, he pressed a warm kiss into the centre.

'I expect you've been missing the routine and demands of your work.' Keeping her voice deliberately light, so that he wouldn't see how affected she was, Jenny retrieved her hand to lay it over Cozette again. She prayed Rodrigo wouldn't see that it was trembling. 'Your friends are probably missing you too. I feel slightly guilty that I've monopolised your time because of this stupid illness.'

'So you expect never to get ill? You are infallible?'

'I didn't mean that. All I meant was that it was inconvenient.'

'You know my lifestyle. I travel too much to be concerned with friends.'

Shrugging, Rodrigo rose to his feet, briefly rubbing his hands together.

'You don't always have to isolate yourself from people, Rodrigo.'

'I am perfectly happy with the way things are.'

'Really?' It hurt Jenny to hear that.

'I find it works better for me if I keep a little distance.'

'But still…don't you get a bit lonely, doing all that travelling and never really being close to anyone?'

'My work is my life. You of all people know that.

Now, I've got some phone calls to make that have been backing up. Are you okay by yourself for a while?'

'Yes, I'm fine.' Her heart thudding heavily, because Rodrigo suddenly seemed to be clearly illustrating his preference for a little distance, Jenny sighed.

'At least you have Cozette for company, no?'

'I told you—I'm fine. I don't need a babysitter... Just go and make your phone calls and forget about me.'

'I'll make my phone calls...but I won't forget about you, Jenny Wren.'

Because he'd taken the wind out of her sails, Jenny glared at him. 'Just go!'

'Okay, okay, I'm going.' Having the audacity to chuckle at her petulant tone, he held up his hands in a gesture of surrender and backed slowly out of the room.

As soon as he was gone, Jenny was appalled to find hot tears boiling up behind her eyes. Suddenly the prospect of him leaving made her stomach lurch with sadness. What was the matter with her, for goodness' sake? She was over him, wasn't she? What on earth was she doing, attaching herself to the idea that somewhere deep inside he perhaps still held a torch for her? They'd parted a long time ago now. Why couldn't she just accept that and get on with her life as she'd been doing before he'd shown up?

Lifting her hand up to her face, she stared at the

spot that his lips had so spine-tinglingly caressed. It throbbed like a brand. Did he still not need anyone at all…ever?

In the afternoon, after the light lunch he'd prepared for them both, Rodrigo absented himself again, leaving Jenny with a stack of DVDs to choose from to keep her entertained. It appeared she was in no mood for conversation.

Seeing definite signs of her recovery, even though her complexion was still marble-pale, he took the opportunity to return to his room to work. Yet from time to time, as he studied his paperwork and made his phone calls, he couldn't help remembering how they'd been captured by each other's gazes just before he'd kissed her palm. It caused a flutter of mayhem in his stomach to recall it. Irritable, but not wanting to explore why, he diverted his attention to his most pressing phone call.

It had been just as he'd thought at the site in Penzance—the building schedule had indeed fallen behind, and even more so with all the rain. Although Rodrigo had had to delay the meeting because of Jenny, he now wanted to get to the root of the hold-up. There were several things he wanted the manager to keep him up to speed with, in fact, which meant that the afternoon flew by in a long, detailed discussion until Rodrigo had thoroughly satisfied himself that all was now proceeding as it should be.

Rising from behind the antique desk in his room,

he rolled his shoulders to unlock the cramps in his muscles. Sighing, he strolled across to the window. In the far distance the sun-kissed silver Atlantic lapped the sand-covered shore, the white foam rolling in and out again as it had done since time immemorial but no-less mesmerising. Narrowing his gaze, he observed the seagulls cutting cleanly across the winter blue sky that would soon turn to dusk, dipping gracefully every now and then into the ocean in avid search of their supper. An urgent need suddenly arose inside him to breathe in some of that wild sea air.

Jenny was dozing on the couch when he looked in on her and so, deciding to follow his impulse, Rodrigo drove down to the beach.

She was definitely over the worst, he assured himself, so he could risk leaving her to sleep for a while. He tucked his rich burgundy cashmere scarf deep into the neckline of his leather jacket and strode across the sand, wincing but enjoying the bracing air. On Monday, when he left this place, his usual routine would be quickly reinstated, he reflected. Jenny would no longer need his help, so work would once again take precedence.

A sharp twist low down in his belly protested at the idea with a painful jolt. It was merely frustration, Rodrigo thought impatiently—frustration at not being able to satisfy his lustful desire for his pretty ex-wife. He knew he'd sworn that he would make love to her soon, but the more he thought about it, the more he guessed that wouldn't be wise. Jenny still had dreams

in her eyes, he realized, and if he got involved with
her even briefly and then left again it would no doubt
reinforce her angry belief that cruelty was indeed
inherent in his character.

No... He just had to put any further thoughts of
bedding her right out of his mind. Instead, as soon
as his business meeting was over, he would return
to London where he could hook up with a Spanish
actress he knew. He occasionally took her to dinner—
and more often than not to bed. She was a real Latin
firecracker, and knew all kinds of stimulating ways
to entertain and relax a hard-working man.

But the thought of the red-lipped fiery *señorita*
left Rodrigo cold when he compared her charms to
the warm and beguiling Jenny.

Biting back a ripe curse, he saluted an old man
who was walking a terrier, then—with his head down
against the strong gusting wind—retraced his steps
back to the car.

'Where did you go?'

'I took a walk on the beach. You were sleeping
when I left.'

'I sensed you weren't in the house when I woke
up.'

'So you missed me, then?'

'I didn't say that. I just didn't want you to leave
without saying goodbye.'

'I would not have left without telling you I intended to go...nor would I have absconded without paying my bill.'

Her mouth dropping open, Jenny stared at Rodrigo in amazement. 'You don't think I'm going to charge you for your stay when all you've done since you walked in here is look after me?'

'That was hardly your fault. Besides...' his hand scraped through his windblown black hair, then down over his jacket '...it's a business your friend is running here, *querida*—not a charity.'

At the apt reminder Jenny's heart sank. *Some helpful caretaker she'd turned out to be!* Her own business was struggling, and she had an inkling it was because her heart wasn't really in it. When she returned to London she would throw herself into things a bit more determinedly, but what if she just wasn't cut out to run a business at all? Ostensibly her talents lay in her creativity, not making money.

Thinking back over what she'd had to deal with in the past as far as her relationships were concerned, she wished she could have been stronger. But her trust had been shattered both by her brother and Rodrigo, and she'd defy anyone to cope with that and be full of confidence.

Glancing across at the flickering television screen, Rodrigo slipped off his jacket and threw it onto a cream pin-tucked armchair. Even at a distance Jenny scented the tang of the sea that clung to him from his walk. She wished she'd been well enough to accompany him.

'What are you watching?' he asked interestedly.

'Pride and Prejudice.' She swallowed down the regret that washed over her. All she'd ever really desired was a kind, loving husband, children of her own and a lovely home. A wistful sigh escaped her at the story unfolding on the screen, where she knew the heroine Lizzie *would* get the man and the house she dreamed of. 'I love period dramas…the clothes, the beauty of the architecture, the manners…and the simmering unspoken passions underneath all that buttoned-up corsetry and politeness.'

The phrase 'buttoned-up corsetry' made Rodrigo wince. He was having trouble enough trying to keep his desire for Jenny under tight control without being taunted by images of her in an old-fashioned virginal white corset—that he, of course, would be only too eager to divest her of…

'And is Mr Darcy your idea of the perfect man, Jenny?'

Her blue eyes looked dreamy for a moment, but then she shook her head. 'Not really.' Her fingers plucked restlessly at the plaid wool blanket. 'After all, he's just a character in a book. If you really lived with a man like that I'd bet it wouldn't be long before his true colours emerged. He'd probably prove to be exactly what she originally thinks him to be—an egomaniac who believes it is his God-given right to have exactly what he wants including a wife who reflects his pompous vision of himself! It's been my experience that men are selfish creatures, on the whole. They only really want what *they* want…no matter how much it may hurt the women who care for them.'

Rodrigo winced. He knew instantly this wasn't just about the fictional Mr Darcy. 'I'm sorry your experience of men has been so negative,' he murmured.

Tugging the blanket up around her chest, she visibly shivered. 'I'm not just referring to you. My brother Tim was an addict… You didn't know that, did you? You name it, he was hooked on it. Pot, cocaine, heroin, alcohol, gambling—everything. And when his own money wasn't enough to pay for it all, he thought it his right to demand mine. Especially after you and I parted and he thought I was rich.'

'I had my reservations about your brother, but I had no idea he was as you say. I wish you could have shared that with me when we were together.'

'Why? You couldn't have changed him. If you'd got to know him he'd only have ended up using you for what he could get…just like he did with me. It didn't matter that we were brother and sister.'

'What happened before he went to Scotland, Jenny? I want to know.'

She stared at him with a haunted look. 'He put me through hell, trying to get our family house from me.' She dropped her head onto her raised knees. Glancing up again, she pushed back her hair. 'When I finally agreed to buy him out, that and the legal costs almost bankrupted me. The court case was horrendous. He persuaded a besotted rich girlfriend to pay for some whiz-bang lawyer, and the lies he told about me to plead his case were vile...such vindictive, terrible lies that I wanted to die. Anyway, when I was worn out with fighting I agreed to a settlement. I only did it because I knew if he won the case everything my parents had worked so hard for would have been sold for a song to pay for his out-of-control lifestyle. Ironic that not long after he'd been paid out the house caught fire and burned down and it all went anyway.'

'My God! If I had had any idea that that was the situation you were returning to when we broke up I would have—'

'You would have what, Rodrigo? Taken me back?' Her eyes glittering, Jenny shook her head. 'I don't think so. Besides...I can fight my own battles.'

'You are strong, that is true... But it grieves me to hear you went through that alone.'

Switching off the television, Rodrigo lowered himself onto the end of the couch. His glance alighted on Jenny's lovely face as fervently as a ship looked for the lodestar—and he saw that her gaze shimmered with tears.

'The truth is I don't know if I have the heart to continue with my business' she confessed. 'I worked so hard at it—and for what? The thing I wanted most in the world was a family and a home of my own. You and I only lasted a year, my parents are gone, and my relationship with my brother is non-existent because of what happened. I never envisaged spending the rest of my life alone.'

'And neither will you be alone for ever, Jenny. It simply is not possible. One day everything will change for the better and you will have your dream.'

'Does your famous intuition tell you that Rodrigo?'

Fielding the swathe of pain that cut through him at the despondency in her voice, Rodrigo struggled to find the words to convince her life would improve. It didn't help that he had played a big part in making her mistrust her future.

'It's no surprise that you got ill. There is too much hurt and unhappiness weighing down your heart, and I honestly regret that.'

Jenny stared at him. 'I think you do. But, like me, you can't help how you're made. Your past has shaped you too, and you've grown to believe that work is the most important thing. I don't like the idea of you being alone for the rest of your life either.'

'Maybe I deserve to? Anyway, I will just have to live with my mistakes, if that's what they are.'

'Sometimes you're far too hard on yourself—do you know that?'

When she leaned over and squeezed his arm, Rodrigo sensed such a tide of heat and longing sweep over him that all he could do was stare down at that small perfect palm circling his wrist without any words at all. Then his brain engaged properly.

'I'm a man who goes for what he wants and gets it, Jenny. To get on in this life you have to cultivate some steel. To this day I've never allowed sentiment to get in the way of making the decisions that suit *me* best—whether that's in my private life or my work. You know that to your cost. So please don't waste your time thinking I need kindness and forgiveness.'

CHAPTER SEVEN

RODRIGO was on his feet before Jenny had a chance to respond. 'It's getting late, and I should see to our meal. Finish watching your DVD…relax and enjoy it.'

Without glancing back to gauge her expression, he strode out through the door into the hallway. The cat followed him. In the kitchen, he automatically located the ingredients he needed for their meal from the fridge and the larder, pausing briefly to fill a dish of food for Cozette when her pitiful mewing became too loud to ignore. Straightening, he leant his hip against the counter, pressing his fingers deeply into his brow.

It was about time Jenny fully realised that he couldn't pursue a relationship with her for a second time. Even if that meant that next time he met her eyes they would be even more wary and sad around him.

If he hadn't been married to her before would he have stayed and played nursemaid as he had done? It was an uncomfortable thought, but a truthful one at least. He'd stayed purely because it was Jenny. On Monday he was leaving, all being well, and right now he needed to employ some of that distance he spoke about. God knew it should be second nature to him when it came to relationships—especially when someone threatened to get too close. But twice now Jenny had almost made him forget that. If he employed his usual strategy it would make it less hard for him to go and easier for Jenny to let him.

A long time ago his father had warned him not to let his focus stray from his ambition. 'Play by all means,' he had advised his son. 'But do not allow yourself to become too involved.' Having made the error once before of thinking he could have it all— marriage *and* a successful business—Rodrigo intended to steer well clear of such a dangerous and misleading temptation again.

In the charmingly decorated living room, with its gently ticking French antique clock, Jenny was asleep. About to shake her, Rodrigo saw that she slumbered as deeply and peacefully as an untroubled child— just as if she'd laid all her worries and cares aside. Her angelic features were slightly flushed, and her glorious hair tumbled round her shoulders in shining ringlets the hue of golden summer sunshine.

It seemed heartless to wake her to tell her that a meal was ready. Instead he divested her of the blanket tucked round her, then lifted her carefully into his arms. She barely even stirred. Just disconcertingly rested her head against his chest and gently sighed.

Clenching his jaw, because her soft, pliant body was exquisitely, painfully arousing him, Rodrigo carried her upstairs to bed. Leaving the door slightly ajar, to let the light flood in from the landing, he didn't bother to switch on the lamp. The rose scent from her skin sneaked captivatingly under his radar. It stormed his senses as he laid her down under the covers. With great care he removed her already opened dressing gown, then dropped it onto a nearby chair.

As he leaned over to tuck the covers up round her shoulders, Jenny's stunning blue eyes fluttered open. 'Mmm…' she breathed, coiling her arms round his neck. 'You smell so nice.'

He froze. She must be dreaming he thought. But then she laid her hand across his cheek, tenderly stroking it.

'You're such a good man, really…and sometimes… sometimes so hard to resist.'

'Do you know what you are saying?' he demanded huskily.

'Yes, I do. I'm wide awake, Rodrigo.'

'This is a dangerous game you're playing, Jenny Wren.'

'Don't you want to kiss me?' she whispered, her hand moving gracefully from his cheek into his hair.

His blood heating violently, Rodrigo gripped her shoulder. Self-control was suddenly frighteningly thin. 'I want much more than just a sweet, drowsy little kiss, my angel. Unless you are prepared for that, then we will stop this right here, right now.'

In answer, Jenny gazed up at him with her bewitching light eyes full of longing. Then, with a fleeting bold smile, she slanted her petal-soft lips against his.

Kissing her back fully on the mouth was like coming home at last. His fantasy of tasting her like this again was like a pastel watercolour compared to vividly sensuous passionate reality. With a rough groan, Rodrigo let his hard, sensually aching body fall against the inviting feminine curves beneath him. His lips clashed urgently with Jenny's for a short-lived second before his tongue hungrily invaded the hot purse of the sweetest silken mouth he'd ever tasted. He devoured it like a pauper at a banquet.

Arching her body to get closer, she feathered soft little gasps of pleasure over him, and as he pressed her deep down into the mattress she matched every groan and feverish demand he was meting out with equal ardour. Her small hands urgently pushed at his sweater, in search of the warm hard flesh underneath, and she tangled her long bare legs with his still jean-clad ones.

Rodrigo was left in no doubt that they were of a single mind. Sweeping the counterpane aside so he could join her in bed, he shucked off his expensive Italian loafers, jettisoned his sweater, and repositioned himself on top of her. Then he feverishly manoeuvred Jenny's simple white nightgown up over her pale thighs until his palms located her firmly defined satin hipbones. Stilling for just a moment, he unzipped his fly.

It was as if he'd left his mind at the door. Pure, undiluted primal desire was what was driving him— desire sharpened into dizzying focus by Jenny's seductive hot mouth brushing against his over and over. Her hands were moulding themselves to his jean-clad rear as she impelled him urgently towards her.

'You have bewitched me without even trying,' he breathed against her ear, and then, freeing himself, he inserted his hard aching shaft deeply between her slender thighs in a long shattering thrust. Secluded by the semi-dark, they stared back at each other in mutual wonderment.

If this was a dream then Jenny wanted it to go on for ever... It was true she *had* been lost in the most delicious sensual fantasy about Rodrigo when she'd sensed him lift her up from the couch. The warm, woody scent of him along with the colossal strength in his arms had made that fantasy blossom into the most vividly detailed erotic sequence she could have imagined.

Then she had opened her eyes, felt his warm breath on her face, and been so transfixed by the most tempting magnetic sea of ebony silk that she hadn't had a prayer of resisting.

She could fool herself by pretending she was

delirious because of her illness, or that as a result of her fever she wasn't yet in her right mind—but both would be a lie. Jenny knew *exactly* what she was doing—and why. She wanted Rodrigo more than she'd ever wanted him. Two years apart hadn't quelled that desire.

The Spaniard had intoxicated her senses from the moment he'd stepped up to her at the Savoy and so charmingly asked to know her name and if she'd like to have dinner with him. And when he'd stepped into Lily's guesthouse from out of the rain and then come to her rescue when she'd fallen ill—well…she was so *drunk* on whatever magic he'd conjured up that she could barely think straight. Even in the throes of raging fever she'd ached to be loved by him once more. *Now she had her wish.*

Although Rodrigo's kisses were greedily burning, he gulped at her as if he was drinking from the rejuvenating crystal waters of a life-giving well—as if every taste of her was too precious to spill even a drop. Moving deeply inside her, his magnificently taut male body rocked Jenny to the furthest reaches of her soul. He'd helped take care of her when illness had struck her down, even postponing his meeting. *He had never done that before.* Now, incredibly, he was meeting another great need. A need to be held and loved by him once again—a need that she'd feared would never be met again.

Rodrigo had talked about maintaining distance as friends… Surely he couldn't want to put distance between them a second time after a union as profoundly magnetic and unforgettable as this?

Cupping her hands round his arrow-straight hips, Jenny took him even deeper, locking her legs round his hard-muscled back. 'Is this good for you?' she breathed, catching a glimmer of surprise in his eyes.

'Is this *good*? You underestimate your powers of seduction, my angel. Right now my body, my heart, my soul—they are all lost to you.'

Although his words touched Jenny deeply, his smile was as sinfully delicious as a taste of decadent chocolate ice cream in the middle of a strict diet. *The kind a girl would willingly put on a couple of pounds for...*

He began to thrust harder and deeper, making Jenny cry out as he bent his head to nip the hotly tingling tips of her breasts with the edges of his teeth, then soothed them with the heat from his hot damp mouth. The dammed up feelings building inside her burst violently free. Surely the barrier restraining them had been guarded only by the slimmest of gossamer threads? As soon as she had wound her arms round Rodrigo's neck she had started to come undone...the incredibly seductive scent of his body was enough to do that alone.

A ragged cry left her throat as wave after wave of rapturous sensation bombarded her. Her heart hammering, Rodrigo's name was suddenly a heartfelt mantra of unimagined joy on her lips. Shockingly, twin rivulets of tears seeped from the corners of her eyes, mingling with the joy and pleasure. The sheer magnitude of her emotions overwhelmed her—as if every deep wound and fear she'd stored away inside her heart had suddenly surfaced at once. But Jenny scarcely had time to dwell on that as Rodrigo shivered in her arms and convulsed. Holding onto the broad, magnificent slopes of his hard male shoulders, she registered the scalding spurt of his vigorous male seed seeking its home inside her.

What have you done, Jenny? It simply wasn't like her not to think about something as vital as protection. But right then, with her body feeling so loved and languorous and her head still a little woozy from her bout of sickness, she somehow didn't care.

Resting his head on her shoulder, Rodrigo murmured something vehement in Spanish. Judging by the tone, it sounded pretty much as if he was berating himself for the same thing.

He propped himself up on an elbow, his dark gaze serious. 'I would be lying if I said I didn't know what got into me to make love with you without taking precautions, Jenny... But I want you to know I'm profoundly sorry for compromising you like this.'

'Is that all you have to say about what we just shared, Rodrigo?' Lightly, Jenny wove her fingers through the glossy sable strands of his hair.

'No.' He caught her hand, then brushed his lips across her knuckles, his expression intense. 'It is not all I have to say at all. What we just shared was incredible, wonderful…*beyond* wonderful. You are a lovely, generous, sexy woman, Jenny. Already you've made sure that I'll never forget you.'

Her heartbeat jumped in dismay. 'If you're talking about leaving then please don't. What I want right now is just to savour these precious moments we've got together without thinking about anything that makes me sad.'

'You were crying. I saw tears in your eyes.' Tracing the outline of her mouth with his forefinger, he dragged her plump lower lip downwards for a moment.

'It was overwhelming…the way you loved me. You touched feelings that I'd suppressed for a long time. Something inside me broke open, Rodrigo…something that I've held back for far too long. I feel—' Suddenly self-conscious, Jenny turned away from his intense ebony glance. 'I feel cleansed, somehow.'

'So you will sleep much better tonight. No bad dreams will come to visit you again, hmm?' Rolling over onto his side he laid his bare arm protectively across her middle.

'You'll keep them away for me,' she agreed.

Just hearing him say that the bad dreams wouldn't come made Jenny feel safe. But with her head still feeling achy and hot she sensed her body succumbing to another helpless wave of tiredness. Sighing, she snuggled down deeper into the bed. Under the covers, Rodrigo's hand moved possessively over her bare hip.

Registering the sensuous tug in her solar plexus, along with the surge of heat in her breasts, Jenny smiled. 'That's nice.'

'I have even more nice things to show you if you want.'

'You do?' *Just the anticipation made her feel boneless.*

'But there is something I need to do first.'

'What's that?'

'Sit up for me a minute.'

'Why?'

'So many questions... Have you never heard that sometimes you just need to go with the flow?'

Jenny obediently scooted up, and without pre-amble found her nightdress expertly pulled up over her head and flung to the side. Her skin prickled with goosebumps at the hot appreciative glance Rodrigo shamelessly submitted her to. His slow burning gaze all but devoured her.

'You are like an exquisite painting of a fairy queen come to life,' he said huskily. 'Perhaps I have dreamed you up?'

'I'm no dream, Rodrigo. I'm fallible flesh and blood, just like you. If I was a dream then I couldn't be hurt, could I?' She heard the catch in her voice.

Unperturbed by her comment, Rodrigo shrugged his shoulders and smiled. 'I don't care what you say. You'll always be my favourite fantasy...the one I'll summon when I'm alone in my bed at night after a hard day and need reminding of something beautiful.'

Not liking his reference to being alone, and the scene it conjured up of him being back in Barcelona without her, Jenny shivered. Desolate, she folded her arms over her chest. 'I'm cold, Rodrigo.'

'Then lie down with me, *querida*, and let me put the heat back into your blood to keep you warm...'

'Maldita sea!' He could hardly credit his clumsiness. That was the second mug he'd managed to break that morning. Sweeping the broken remnants into a dustpan, Rodrigo impatiently deposited them into the bin. Then he reached up to the overhead pine cupboard with its meticulously arranged shelves of bright painted crockery for another one.

He groaned as a tight muscle in his back stretched a little too abruptly. Strenuous exercise never fazed him. When all was said and done he was a man in the peak of fitness—even if lately his body *had* sometimes felt fustratingly fatigued. But last night he'd been making love to Jenny until the early hours of the morning. *And the more he'd demanded of her body, the more he'd craved.* It seemed as if his impossible desire was never sated.

His hand stilled on the coffee percolator's handle. It pricked his conscience that he might have selfishly taken advantage of her when she was not totally well, but she had more than matched his passion, he recalled. The memory of her soft inner thighs clamped round his middle instantly hardened him. He hissed out a ragged breath. The sooner he returned to work the better. He was quickly realising that the longer he stayed, the more this white-hot lust and longing for Jenny would consume him...no doubt to the detriment of his ability to think straight, concentrate on his work and all he had set out to uphold and achieve. *Just as his father had warned him it would.*

'Is there any of that coffee going begging? I can't tell you how good it smells.'

Rodrigo spun round. Jenny stood in the doorway, dressed in light blue denims and a sweatshirt that was just a shade darker than her eyes. The picture she made was stunning and fragile at the same time.

Rodrigo's heart lurched. 'What are you doing up? I told you to rest.'

'I'm sick of resting. I need to be up and about again or I'll go mad. Let me pour the coffee. I can do that much at least.'

Seeing her hand tremble as she reached for the coffee jug, he tutted. 'You are your own worst enemy—you know that? I'd almost forgotten how impatient you are.'

'I've lots of faults, that's true.'

'Come here.'

'Why?' She blinked owlishly at him.

He let her finish pouring the coffee, then pulled her into his arms. Everything about her delighted him...her slim compact body, sunshine gold hair, flawless blue eyes and pale satin skin.

Outside, a light rain fell onto the greenhouse roof and the neat flowerbeds alongside it. The air had a real crisp, cold bite to it. In an attempt to cool his ardour—as well as help distract a mind that seemed intent on dwelling on one thing and one thing only—Rodrigo had already been out walking, and the icy temperature had made him glad to return inside. It had also made him ache momentarily for the sunshine of Barcelona. But standing here with his arms wrapped round a sweetly scented Jenny he felt warm as toast and—not surprisingly—*aroused*.

'I want to kiss you good morning,' he murmured, lowering his face to hers.

Jenny ducked her head out of the way. 'You've already kissed me a hundred times this morning.' She grinned, her cheeks turning charmingly pink. 'I just hope you don't catch what I've had—then you'll be sorry!'

'Never.' He feigned a disapproving look. 'I would never be sorry for kissing you. It would be worth being struck down for a few days just to have had the chance to sample your irresistible charms again, my angel.'

'But then you wouldn't be able to go to your meeting and I'd have to look after you.'

'How tedious for you.' Rodrigo tried to hide his automatic resistance to the idea but failed.

'Why do you think that would be tedious for me?' A tiny concerned crease appeared between Jenny's neatly arched brows, 'I would relish every minute of it, Rodrigo.'

'And you would do it just because you have a naturally caring instinct, and not for any gain?'

'What gain? What are you talking about?'

'Wanting more of me than I can give.'

Unable to hide her alarm, Jenny stiffened in his arms.

CHAPTER EIGHT

'If I took care of you while you were ill it wouldn't be for any ulterior motive, Rodrigo. It would merely be because I care about you. Do you have a problem with that?'

All desire for coffee had fled. Jenny felt as if her stomach had a dead weight inside it at the suspicion and pain mirrored in her ex-husband's silky dark eyes.

Abruptly removing his arms from round her waist, he moved away, leaving her feeling as if she'd gone from summer to winter in one fell swoop.

'I don't want you to care about me.' A muscle flinched at the side of his jaw. 'I'd like us to part as friends, of course, but—'

'What?'

'When I leave it's best if you just forget about me. The commitment I have to my work is heavy. As I explained, that's why our marriage couldn't work. At least I was honest with you. A man like me hasn't the right to pursue a serious relationship when he knows that because of his dedication to business there's a high probability it will fail.'

'You must have been hurt very badly somewhere along the line to make you believe that—to believe that any attempt at a committed relationship would fail.'

'No!'

His denial was fierce. Jenny stepped back in alarm.

'Just because I happen to prefer concentrating my time and energy on making a success of my work doesn't mean that someone hurt me. The reality is that I'm aware of the false promises a relationship can breed...the false hope. Look around you—how many relationships do you see that even survive? I prefer to focus on something with a higher rate of success... something that does deliver on its promise.'

'And work can fulfil every hope, every dream of happiness, can it?'

'For me, right now, it gives me exactly what I want.'

'That sounds to me like somebody *did* hurt you, Rodrigo—or at least poisoned your mind about what can be possible as far as relationships go.'

'*Dios mio!* How have we got onto this tedious subject?'

Moving restlessly, as if his skin was suddenly too tight to contain whatever emotions were flooding him, the handsome Spaniard fixed her with a cold glare. Jenny held her ground.

'I know that we broke up and things didn't work out, but it wasn't because I didn't at least *try* to make it a success! But you- you decided not to try at all. What we had was really beautiful…have you forgotten that? And you just threw it away as if it meant nothing at all. I've thought about things a lot, lying ill in bed, and I know that for me life would be pretty meaningless if there was never anyone else to share it with.'

'To look after, you mean?'

'To take care of your husband and family isn't something to be ashamed of.' Inside her chest, Jenny's heart thudded hard. 'You talk as if it is.'

'You are right.' His expression surprisingly softening, Rodrigo nodded. 'Just because I have some issues about relationships, it doesn't mean that I think *you* shouldn't go for what you want, Jenny. A woman like you was not created to be alone. I know that instinctively.'

Stepping closer, he reached out to circle her waist again. Then, dipping his head, he gently brushed his mouth against hers. More than any of the passionate kisses she had received from him, that tender little kiss made Jenny's heart ache as if it had been cut in two…all the more because she tasted *goodbye* in it.

'How could I not wish anything but that all your dreams come true? I'm already envious of the man you'll eventually marry. When he gets a taste of your love and care he'll know what an angel he's fallen in love with.'

'And you, Rodrigo?' Tenderly laying her palm against his bronzed sculpted cheek, Jenny felt the pain in her heart constrict her voice to barely above a whisper. 'You're absolutely sure that you don't want my love and care?'

'I don't deserve it. And that's not because I'm feeling sorry for myself. I'm purely being realistic. And at the end of the day I'm too selfish to put someone else's welfare before myself, as you do. I tried to make our relationship work, but something in my make-up just wouldn't let me make it the priority it should have been. I've hurt you once already, Jenny... don't let me hurt you again.'

Sensing his stubbornness in clinging to such a damaging conviction, she swallowed hard. 'I can hardly equate what you're saying with how you've been towards me since you've been here. Now that we've been able to spend some proper time together without your work getting in the way, I can't imagine a man more thoughtful and caring...and, yes, unselfish. You could have left at any time, but you didn't. It's just not true that you're too self-obsessed to put someone else before yourself. I've seen a different side to you these past few days, Rodrigo...a side that really makes me hopeful.'

'Well, you should guard against that, because you'll only end up disappointed again.'

Fielding the huge swell of distress that welled up inside her, Jenny broke free of Rodrigo's hold. Reaching for her mug of coffee, she carried it across to the table. As she sat down she immediately sensed Cozette brush up against her ankles. Because she was so upset, she didn't gather the purring cat onto her lap as usual. Instead her glance alighted earnestly on Rodrigo's handsome yet troubled face, and it struck her hard that there were more shadows etched into those sublime angles and features than happiness.

'You claim the man I've spent the past few days with is too selfish to care for others? We're talking about the man who postponed an important business meeting to take care of his ex-wife—a man who sat beside her sickbed all night in a hard chair in preference to going to his own comfortable bed—a man who cooked for her and washed her hair. The same man who's so convinced only his work can bring him the happiness he craves. I think I need enlightening here, Rodrigo, because I'm honestly confused.'

Even before he opened his mouth Rodrigo despised himself for what he was about to say. Behind his hammering heart a small voice mocked: *You know what you're about to throw away again don't you?*

'To start with, I think you're deluding yourself about what I could potentially be like. This is a unique situation. We were brought together by the storm and by your sudden illness. In normal circumstances I *would* have put the demands of my business first. I'm not going to lie to you about that. I run a multi-million-pound international hotel chain that demands my input to ensure its continued success. I've worked extremely hard to get where I am—to enjoy the rewards it brings—and my aim is to continue to work hard. And, secondly, do you think I would have stayed on to take care of you if that old attraction between us hadn't flared up again? I'm only human, Jenny…even *I* can't resist the potent allure of sex.'

With her hands folded on the table, Jenny raised her stunned blue gaze to his. 'Is that all this meant to you…? A convenient opportunity to assuage your lust? I can hardly believe you could be so cruel.'

'I just want you to know the truth.'

'The truth… Yes, I realise that must be a real priority with you—especially when you stood beside me in front of the registrar and repeated your marriage vows as if they meant something. Clearly now I know they meant nothing to you at all. You should have told me from the beginning you were only here under duress. It would have been better if you'd just braved the roads and driven away to find another place to stay. It certainly would have been better for *me*!'

Feeling as if his words had hammered nails into his own coffin, Rodrigo grimaced. 'When I said my marriage vows I meant them. But sadly time and a large dose of reality proved me wrong,' he murmured. 'I should never have asked you to marry me in the first place. That *was* selfish of me.'

'Yes, it was, Rodrigo. It was selfish and cruel when probably all you wanted to do was have a brief sexual liaison without any inconvenient emotional strings attached.' Rising to her feet, Jenny hugged herself, as though fending off any more potentially hurtful blows. 'Well…in the light of all you've just told me I think it would be best if you just packed your things and left. You're probably itching to get back to work anyway. There's no need for you to stay here until Monday. I certainly don't want you staying out of any sense of obligation. In any case, I'm feeling more or less back to my normal self now, and I can't stay in bed indefinitely…not when I've a million and one things to do to get this place shipshape before Lily comes home.'

'Jenny—'

'What?'

She was withdrawing…shutting herself off from him with devastating intention, Rodrigo saw. The realisation put him in turmoil, even though he knew he was the cause.

'I promised I'd stay until Monday, and you are not right yet—I can see that. To reassure you, I'm not staying out of a sense of obligation or duty. It makes sense for you to take the next couple of days to fully get your strength back before you throw yourself into work again.'

'And you're suggesting that out of the goodness of your heart, are you? Forgive me if I can't quite believe that.'

At the door, her glance was scathing. Yet within the bitterness of her tone Rodrigo thought he heard sorrow, and regret too. His chest was so tight that he unconsciously rubbed his palm across it.

'You should just go on your way, Rodrigo, and do whatever's best for you. Put this whole inconvenient episode behind you and get back to the world you're clearly much more comfortable with. That's my advice to you.'

With her head held high, Jenny left him alone with his own morose thoughts…

Throwing herself back into taking care of things was what she had decided to do. If her body ached, or her head suddenly swam with heat, Jenny determinedly ignored it. She couldn't afford to be ill any longer.

Rodrigo had wounded her with his cruel words and the candid admission that the only reason he'd stayed to take care of her was because of the sexual attraction that had brought them together in the first place and his hope of having his lust fulfilled. Well, she had definitely contributed to helping him achieve *that* ambition. But—even though she was disappointed in him, as well as mad at herself for falling so hard for him again—Jenny found she couldn't regret the making love part. *It had been the realisation of a dream she had long held to hold him in her arms again.*

Now that he was leaving it would be all she had to console her over the harsh winter months back in London. Winter months during which she would try hard to keep her spirits up even as she worked at a career she'd lost heart in pursuing with any conviction, living in a small, cheerless rented flat because she'd lost the home she'd taken such pride in to a malevolent fire.

Seeking to drown out her despairing thoughts, she switched on the vacuum cleaner, running the machine up and down the hall carpet as if her life depended on it. Poor Cozette ran for cover at the frenetic, noisy activity, disappearing upstairs as swiftly as a bullet from a gun.

A short while later Rodrigo passed her in the hallway while she was working. But he barely glanced at her before he too ascended the staircase, presumably going up to his room to pack. Biting her lip, Jenny blinked back the scalding tears that surged into her eyes.

She was busy dusting the heavy oak sideboard in the living room when he appeared again. Sensing the aloof air that cloaked him, Jenny shivered. She saw that he was wearing his expensive raincoat—the one that had dripped onto the raffia mat that end-of-the-world stormy night—and knew with a heavy heart that nothing but sorrow lay ahead of her.

'So you're leaving, then?'

Pursing his well-cut lips, he nodded. 'It's not the way I would have liked to say goodbye, Jenny… whether you believe me or not. But it seems I have no choice, seeing as you've more or less told me to go. Can I settle my bill?'

You could say you refuse to leave me this way!
You could say you've changed your mind. Do you
think I wouldn't forgive you?

'Of course.' She made herself walk across the
carpet and out through the door ahead of him. But
she felt like an automaton because her senses were
so numbed by grief.

Pausing by the chestnut bureau in the hall that
accommodated the telephone and the reservations
book, she glanced up at Rodrigo with a frown.

'What am I doing? I said I wouldn't charge you.
You don't have to pay anything.'

'And I told you how I felt about that.' He proffered
a gold Mastercard.

Staring at it dumbly for a few seconds, she registered the reminder that he owned a multi-million-
pound business.

'Just because you've got money it doesn't mean
you should always pay. You looked after me when
I was sick and I'm very grateful. This is my way of
saying thank you.'

'I've had shelter here too, as well as eaten your
food!' His velvet-dark gaze flashed unrestrained
impatience.

Distress welling up inside her at his antagonis-
tic tone, Jenny smoothed a shaky hand across her
ponytail. 'I don't want to argue about this. Please…
just accept your stay here as a gift. I'm sure you're
impatient to be on your way and get back to work.
Here's a map of the area in case you need it.' She

returned the credit card, along with a slim folded map. 'Where will you go after your meeting here?'

'Back to Barcelona.'

After shoving both items she'd given him carelessly into his coat pocket, to Jenny's surprise he captured her hand. Her heart began to race wildly.

'It's been incredible, seeing you again. I'll never forget it. Looking after you…being in this peaceful place… It provided a rest I badly needed—even though there were a couple of nights when I must have aged about a hundred years because your fever was bad. I know I said that I only stayed because of my attraction for you, Jenny, but I promise you…there was not one second when I wished I was somewhere else.'

Her long-lashed summer-blue eyes regarded him gravely. 'At one point you told me your body, heart and soul were lost to me. I know you only said it in the throes of passion, so was that a lie too?'

It took Rodrigo a couple of moments to field the anguish that deluged him and regain his composure. 'It was no lie. When I said it, I meant it. I've never said such things to any other woman before or since you. I also meant our wedding vows when I made them, and truly regret that I couldn't keep them.'

'And yet now you can leave so easily? Without even the merest suggestion that we might see each other again?'

'I would willingly see you again, but whether it would be a good idea or not is debatable. My schedule is so crazy, and you know how much I have to travel. I wouldn't want to make you any promises I couldn't keep. I wouldn't want to let you down a second time.'

'Don't worry about it. It's okay. We had a nice time together, even though I was ill, and we'll part as friends… Is that what you want to hear?'

In answer, Rodrigo pressed a light kiss to her scented cheek and let go of her hand. He stooped to pick up his laptop case and slipped the leather strap over his shoulder. 'I hope you won't stay angry with me for ever. I hope one day you can forgive me. Don't overdo things. Please take my advice and get some more rest. *Adios*, my beautiful Jenny Wren.'

He hardly knew where he was driving—just followed the instructions to take him to Penzance from the now functioning satellite navigation system which had gone askew in the storm. It was as if he was on automatic pilot.

Verdant fields, hills, quaint Cornish villages and breathtaking beaches that were a Mecca for devoted surfers passed him by in a barely registered blur. In his mind all Rodrigo saw was Jenny's dazzling tear-washed blue gaze and the slight rosy flush to her cheeks that her illness had left behind. She was the most incredible woman…*too* incredible for a lost cause like him to even imagine having a meaningful relationship with. He could see her again, yes, and for a few short weeks, months—even a year—things might go well. But sooner or later Rodrigo's addiction to his work plus his insatiable desire for greater and greater success would bear down on him *and* Jenny, and then she would despair of him, start to mistrust him, and finally declare she had had enough and leave.

Slamming the heel of his hand against the steering wheel, he spared himself nothing with his vehement curse. Then, blinking dazedly at the map flashing on the sat nav, he saw that it showed he was now entering Penzance.

CHAPTER NINE

JENNY bade an affectionate goodbye to her reju-
venated friend Lily, then returned to London and
unexpected good news. There was a cheque in the
post from the insurers in answer to her claim for her
house.

Having waited a long time for the situation to be
resolved, she now found the amount exceeded all her
hopes. It meant she had a real chance to start again—
to maybe buy another property, expand her business,
or do whatever she wanted for a while without stress-
ing about income.

*However, nothing could make up for Rodrigo
walking away.* She knew that. Not when every
morning she woke to the stark possibility that she
might never see him again. Just the thought was like
a dagger in her breast. Her senses had been in a state
of frozen animation since he'd left. Before when she'd
been with him she'd felt everything so *intensely*. Now
she felt nothing.

The one small light on the horizon was that the
money she'd received would give her some much-

needed options to help improve her future. She still refused to consider spending any of the settlement Rodrigo had given her, and one day if she had the chance she would see that he got back every penny. But now that she was home again her three months in Cornwall seemed like a distant dream...especially the part where on a stormy October night Rodrigo had appeared.

Suddenly her small rented flat, with its impersonal air and lack of love, seemed too small to contain her increasing restlessness, and it was in this agitated state of mind that one dismal rainy evening she did a pregnancy test because her period was overdue. When the result showed positive Jenny dropped down onto the edge of the bath in stupefied shock. Staring down at the test, she finally registered the enormity of what she was seeing. *She was carrying Rodrigo's baby inside her.* The one event she'd believed would never happen had astoundingly occurred. But what was she going to do about it? Of course he would have to know—even if he decided absolutely he wanted nothing further to do with her *or* the child. She prayed that wouldn't be so. Hadn't he more than amply demonstrated that he wasn't exactly immune to her when they were together in Cornwall?

The following afternoon she took a break from work to visit a travel agent's. With thumping heart and a dry mouth she booked flights and hotel accommodation for Barcelona. What was to stop her? she argued silently as she handed over her credit card.

Thanks to her claim, she had the funds. Only yesterday she'd wrapped up the job she'd been working on so she was perfectly free to go. And her reasons were perfectly legitimate. Not only would she benefit from the warmer climate, but she would be able to see Rodrigo again and break the news that she scarcely believed was true herself.

He was going to be a father. Their re-ignited passion in Cornwall had made a baby...

'Buenos dias, señorita... What can I get you?'

'Just a glass of orange juice please...*gràciis.*'

When the smiling young waiter disappeared back inside the busy café, with its hypnotic salsa music drifting out onto the Moorish-style terrace, Jenny leaned back in her chair and flipped through her Catalan phrasebook, vowing to familiarise herself with the language she had started to learn when she was last there. But then a trickle of perspiration slid down her back inside her cotton sleeveless shirt and she shut her eyes to bask in the idyllic aromatic sunshine as the ebb and flow of other diners' conversations sounded on the air around her.

'Excuse me...but aren't you staying at our hotel?'

Jenny's eyes opened with a start at the sound of the unfamiliar American voice. A beaming masculine face with a row of impossibly white teeth beneath a neatly trimmed greying moustache loomed back at her. An enthusiastic hand was stuck out to shake hers.

'I'm Dean Lovitch and this is my wife Margaret. We arrived three days ago, same as you. We saw you at Reception but you looked a little distracted, if you don't mind me saying, and it didn't seem right to bother you just then. We've just been to visit the Sagrada Familia. Have you seen it yet?'

'You mean the unfinished cathedral? I visited it once two years ago, when I was last here, but I fully intend to go again. I've been mainly taking it easy for the past few days rather than visit the tourist spots, to tell you the truth. I was rather under the weather before I came out here.'

'I'm real sorry to hear that. But it seems like a good place to come to if you're in need of a pick-me-up, don't you think? Mind if we join you? All the other tables seem to be taken.'

'Go ahead. I'm Jenny Renfrew, by the way.'

'It's good to meet you, Jenny.'

The couple sat themselves down opposite her—the tall, spaghetti-thin husband and his plump, diminutive sandy-haired wife. Straightening in her chair, Jenny vowed to be sociable. She was here for a fortnight, after all. No doubt there would be plenty of other warm sunny afternoons in which to ponder her life over a cool drink on a terrace somewhere. Besides... Dean and Margaret had the kind of faces that immediately instilled trust, she decided. Their manner was warmly considerate, and she wasn't surprised to learn that they had three grown-up children who had all 'fled the nest'—which was why they'd decided a long overdue holiday in Europe was called for to help them adjust.

'Are you here all by yourself, Jenny?' Margaret softly enquired as the waiter placed the glass of juice she'd ordered in front of her.

'I am.'

'You seem so young. Isn't there someone special who could have come with you?'

'You mean like a boyfriend?' Fielding the arresting vision of Rodrigo that swarmed into her mind, making her tummy flip over, Jenny wrapped her hands tightly round her glass. 'There's no one special in my life, I'm afraid.'

'Well, there seems to be no shortage of good-looking boys around, that's for sure.' Dean grinned. 'It's a wonder a pretty English Rose like you hasn't got at least a dozen of them lining up to ask you for a date. Perhaps you do, but you're just not telling? I'm sure your parents told you that you gotta be careful. I'm glad that I've got sons, quite frankly. I would have been prematurely grey if I'd had a daughter! Especially one that looked like you.'

'Dean, you're embarrassing Jenny.'

'Sorry, sweetheart.' He instantly apologized. 'Hey, I've just had a great idea. We were going to check out this supposedly incredible spa hotel this afternoon. Margaret thought she might book herself a massage,

and I hear the grounds are spectacular. Want to come
with us?'

'A spa hotel you said?' Inside her chest, Jenny's
heart seemed to ricochet against her ribs.

'Yeah… It's owned by some local billionaire, so
we hear, and just a few streets over. How do you feel
about seeing how the other half lives for a while,
Jenny?'

In the end she couldn't resist accompanying the sociable Americans. Despite choosing her accommodation because of its proximity to his star hotel, she'd
put off confronting Rodrigo with her news for three
days now, while she nervously rehearsed how to tell
him about it in her head, but sooner or later she would
have to see him.

But as soon as Jenny stepped out of the sultry heat
into the air-conditioned foyer of the dazzling chrome
and glass hotel and onto the sleek marble floor, with
its chic contemporary furniture and coolly stylish
décor, her heart started to thump and her legs turned
to marshmallow.

Rodrigo was the owner of all this, she reminded
herself.

Faced with the reality of his wealth again after
two long years, she found it was almost too much to
take in. The man who had sat by her sickbed on a
hard rattan chair without so much as even one small
complaint, the man who had made himself so at home
in Lily's humble, quaint guesthouse was the owner

of this incredibly chic, ultra-modern luxurious hotel and several others like it. It was indeed a sobering thought.

'Shall we have the grand tour?' Dean smiled, already walking towards a formidably smart receptionist who looked more like a catwalk model for some elite designer label than a hotel employee.

'You're very quiet, Jenny,' the diminutive Margaret whispered to the younger woman as they followed another stylishly uniformed receptionist up the sweeping marble staircase to the first floor, the soothing sound of water spilling gently into an indoor fountain accompanying them. 'I think I can guess how you feel… The scent of money is practically oozing out of the walls. It's a little bit overwhelming, isn't it?'

Her gaze on the modern sculpture and eye-catching art, Jenny was still struggling to articulate something conversational when she noticed twin doors opening at the end of the walkway they were traveling down. A tall, dark-haired, designer-suited male figure emerged ahead of a group of similarly attired people. *Rodrigo!* She would recognise him in a veritable *sea* of strangers.

Suddenly there was no audible sound at all apart from the loud roaring of blood rushing at a hundred miles an hour through Jenny's head. *Oh, God…don't let him see me… Please don't let him see me.* What was he going to think if he should catch sight of her? That she'd deliberately tracked him down, expecting something from him? She'd *die* if he thought that—even though she was expecting his baby.

He was holding open the door for his board members, or whoever they were. She saw that now. Seeing him glance casually towards their little group, she momentarily froze. In the same instant a sickening sense of nausea gripped her insides. What a moment for morning sickness to hit! Her intention had been to walk swiftly back down the marble staircase, hopefully unseen, and try to meet Rodrigo at some later date. But now, disconcerted by the nausea, she turned on her heel too quickly and a searing pain shot through her ankle. It made her stumble awkwardly and, unable to right herself, she completely lost her balance.

'Oh, God.' Suddenly she was in a humiliating heap on the floor, with every pair of eyes in the vicinity on *her*.

'Are you okay, honey? Are you hurt?' Margaret's American husband dropped to his haunches, his avuncular features genuinely concerned as he put a comforting arm round Jenny's shoulders.

'I think I've twisted my ankle. I turned on it too suddenly... That's just typical of me, I'm afraid.'

On the periphery of her consciousness she saw a striking-looking dark-suited male issue an urgent command and, glancing up, watched an almost choreographed seam appear down the middle of the small group of people that had quickly gathered round her, allowing the man to step to the front.

He stared down at Jenny with utter disbelief in his ebony dark gaze. 'Is it really you?' he husked.

'Yes, Rodrigo.' She sighed heavily, pushing a swathe of tumbling blonde hair out of her eyes, her humiliation and embarrassment total. 'It's me.'

'What have you done to yourself?'

'It's unbelievable, I know, but I think I've twisted my ankle.'

'Does it hurt?' He crouched to gently circle the slim joint with his hand.

Jenny immediately flinched at the dizzying sensation of pain, though she was not unaware of the intoxicating warmth emanating from his large smooth palm either.

'Yes, it hurts.' She despaired of the quaver in her voice—was terrified Rodrigo might judge her as feeble and clumsy. To be frank, she'd have quite liked a handy magic spell to make her disappear.

But now the handsome Spaniard was at ground level too, and Dean Lovitch was assessing him with definite suspicion in his eyes.

'Do you know this lady?' he demanded.

'Yes, I do. And you are?'

As if sensing the other man's authority, Dean slowly withdrew his arm from round Jenny's shoulders. 'I'm Dean Lovitch. My wife and I are staying at the same hotel as Jenny and we all came here together.'

'She will be all right now, Señor Lovitch. *I* will take care of her.'

'And your name is?'

'Rodrigo Martinez. This is my hotel.'

'Oh.' Getting swiftly to his feet, his face a little red, Dean placed his arm round his wife's shoulders, as if needing to bolster himself after the shock of learning Rodrigo's identity.

'Please…' Jenny whispered, her blue eyes imploring as she glanced into the hypnotic beam of Rodrigo's. 'Don't be concerned about me. I'll be okay in a minute. My friends will help me… As Mr Lovitch told you, I'm staying at the same hotel as them. Go back to your meeting, or whatever it is you were doing, Rodrigo. I'll catch up with you at a more convenient time.'

'You're in no position to tell me to do anything, Jenny. Not when you have been injured in my own hotel and I don't even know what you are doing here. I have a personal suite in the building. I'll take you there and then call our resident doctor to take a look at your ankle.'

Just as he'd done at Lily's, Rodrigo slid his arm beneath Jenny to lift her bodily against him. Registering a mixture of surprise and respect in the interested glances watching them so avidly, she tried to rouse herself to protest. But it wasn't easy when the sensation of being held once more in front of Rodrigo's wonderful chest, along with the warmth of his hard body, was besieging her without mercy.

'You shouldn't be taking me anywhere! Put me down, Rodrigo…please.'

'Not on your life, *querida*. Stop fighting me and just relax.'

'Want us to wait for you, Jenny?' Dean asked anxiously.

Jenny shook her head, attempting a reassuring smile in her new friends' direction. 'Don't let this spoil your visit, you two. I—I expect I'll see you later, back at the hotel.'

What would the couple make of Rodrigo's possessive 'take charge' stance when she'd categorically told them there was no one special in her life? she fretted.

Issuing some crisp instructions to a well-dressed hovering male colleague, Rodrigo swept past the gathered throng of curious onlookers with a purposeful stride towards the elevator, his strong arms supporting Jenny as though she weighed no more than the smallest child...

Lying Jenny down on the plush leather couch in the suite's sitting room, Rodrigo propped her injured ankle carefully up on some satin cushions. Carrying her from the hall downstairs to the elevator, then up to the suite, had been like an exquisite form of masochism. He had felt every sweet contour of her body beneath her simple summer clothes, breathed in her heat and rose-tinted scent a thousand times magnified, and whenever she'd gazed up at him with those crystalline blue eyes all he'd been able to do was fall into silence. He had missed her more than he had dreamed possible, but it wasn't something that reassured him.

What was she doing in Barcelona? Had she come to look for him? The idea all but stalled his heart, even though he knew such an undertaking was fruitless. Hadn't he made it clear enough back in Cornwall that there could be no future for them? Jenny's unexpected enchanting presence definitely raised the spectre of a familiar old fear he hardly felt equipped to deal with again.

'I'll get you a glass of water. The doctor should be with us any minute now.'

'You're always coming to my rescue.'

'Did you think I would leave you lying there in the middle of the floor? Perhaps you were hoping that some other man would come to your rescue instead?'

'What are you talking about?'

Rodrigo shrugged, not liking the dizzying surge of jealousy that gripped his guts in a vice at the idea she might even *look* at another man, let alone hope for one to rescue her. 'Did you come to Barcelona on your own, or do you have a companion? And how is it that you are here?'

She glanced at him with a distressed look. 'Yes, I came to Barcelona on my own, and no, I don't have a companion. And I'm here because I—I...'

'Yes?'

'I'm here because something has happened that I need to tell you about.'

'Did your brother come back from Scotland? Has he been bothering you again?'

'No.' Jenny sighed. 'It's not that.'

'Why did you come to the hotel instead of my apartment?'

'I didn't intentionally come here today to find you. The American couple I was with downstairs wanted to visit the hotel because they'd heard it was something special. Margaret wanted a massage, and they asked me to join them to have a look round. Now I wish I hadn't.'

'Why? Because you didn't want to see me again?'

'I didn't even know you were here! How could I know when you haven't even been in touch?' In her agitation, Jenny restlessly moved her leg off the satin cushion, grimacing as the pain in her ankle obviously registered with a vengeance.

'*Maldita`sea!* Where is that doctor?'

'I don't want to see your doctor, Rodrigo. I'd much rather you rang me a taxi so I can go back to my own hotel. I probably just need to pack some ice round my ankle and it'll be fine.'

'Don't be ridiculous.'

'I'm not being ridiculous,' she protested, huffing and folding her arms over her candy-pink shirt. 'I'm being sensible. You don't want me here—I know that. You're clearly embarrassed that I've shown up, and to top it all off in such a stupidly dramatic way too. I'm not trying to compromise you, Rodrigo, whatever you may privately think. Our meeting up again like this at your hotel is pure coincidence. Now I just want to go.'

Profoundly disturbed by the idea that Jenny would refuse any further help from him, as well as leave on bad terms, Rodrigo dropped down onto the couch beside her. Before he knew what he intended, he'd reached for her hand and brought it up to his lips. Once again the subtle but lethal rose-tinted fragrance that clung to her invaded him. Heady desire infiltrated his blood with a vengeance, searing him hotter than any desert wind might. Inside, a quiet desperation clamored to have that desire once again fulfilled. 'I didn't realise until now that I've been suffering from a faulty memory, Jenny Wren.' The smile he delivered to her widened blue eyes was unapologetically provocative.

'Meaning?'

'I thought my recollection of your beauty was unimpeachable. But now I see it was not. You're far lovelier than even *I,* who has examined you closely, could recall. When I saw you standing there with your friends I honestly believed I must be dreaming.'

Someone rapped loudly on the outer door. Biting back his intense frustration, Rodrigo rose swiftly to go and greet the resident hotel doctor.

CHAPTER TEN

THE doctor's verdict was that Jenny had suffered only a slight sprain. During the whole time that she was being examined by the smart-suited professional her mind was racing.

The startling evidence of Rodrigo's wealth and status was all around her. From the chic contemporary furniture in the fabulously designed flower-filled air-conditioned suite to the stunning art on the walls and even the timelessly elegant way he was dressed. Every tanned, whipcord-lean, hard-muscled inch of him screamed success beyond the wildest of dreams.

Even though making her mark in business had never been her main priority Jenny still felt a little insecure that she hadn't made a better go of her own venture. But the reality was that her brother's addiction and sometimes cruel conduct had sapped her energy and her emotions down to the marrow—especially when he'd instigated the court case to try and take the family home away from her. All that had been coupled with her distress at her marriage ending, and Jenny was amazed she'd been able to continue working and functioning normally at all.

As Rodrigo politely thanked the urbane doctor and then showed him out, she determinedly swung her legs to the floor. Her injured ankle had a very neat professional bandage applied round it now, but it still throbbed like merry hell. Gingerly she slid her bare foot into her flat, brown-strapped leather sandal. It didn't exactly help her confidence to feel so physically vulnerable in front of Rodrigo once more. Especially knowing she still had to tell him about her pregnancy.

'What do you think you're doing?'

The rich-accented voice at the door made her jump.

'I'm putting my sandal back on. Thanks very much for getting the doctor to see me, but I'm not intending on taking up much more of your time.'

'You said earlier that you had something to tell me?'

'I do.'

'And that is?'

As he stood there in front of Jenny, with his arms folded across the front of that elegant suit, Rodrigo's sable eyes were admonishing and yet somehow wickedly teasing too. His black hair had a burnished shine on it fierce enough to dazzle an Alps skier. Frankly, he looked like the drop-dead gorgeous cover model of an *haute couture* fashion magazine for men, and just as intimidating. When he'd helped her throw the tarpaulin over Lily's storm-threatened greenhouse he had somehow seemed far more approachable and a little less out of her league.

'I'm pregnant.'

'What?'

Jenny was glad she was sitting down. Rodrigo's stunned expression was already making her anxious. 'I did a pregnancy test when my period was late and it was positive.'

'My God.' He crossed the room to the couch where she sat. 'Why didn't you ring me straight away?'

'It's not really the kind of news you should convey over the phone, is it?' It was hard to hear herself across the sound of her galloping heart. 'I thought it was best if I came out here to see you and tell you to your face. I know you never wanted children, and the fact is we're no longer married either...but I hoped that when you heard you were going to be a father you might—you might consider the possibility of us trying again.'

Did she really have the temerity to risk suggesting such a thing? Jenny thought in disbelief. And suddenly she found herself more vulnerable in front of Rodrigo than any illness or injury could ever render her.

When he dropped down onto the end of the couch she longed to know what thoughts were dwelling behind that serious dark gaze, but she feared hearing them revealed too.

'Jenny, *querida*, I—'

She laid her hand across his. 'Don't say no straight away... Please just think about it for a while. Do you think you could do that?'

To her surprise, he moved her hand and tucked it possessively inside his.

'*Sí*... I can do that. But you have to understand what a great shock this news is to me.'

Hearing doubt and apprehension in his voice, instead of the elation she imagined most soon-to-be fathers might express, Jenny felt the hurt ebb through her, making her want to tug her hand free. However, sheer hope made her keep it where it was, resting in the delicious warmth of Rodrigo's palm.

'But not a terrible one, I hope? To have a child is the most wonderful thing, Rodrigo... I know you've always resisted the idea, but given time you might come round to seeing that it can be the most amazing blessing.'

'One thing I do know is that we cannot have you remaining at your hotel. Clearly you should stay at the apartment. I'll drive you back there myself. You can stay there with me at least until you need to go back home. That will give us plenty of time to discuss things. We can pick up your luggage on the way.'

Now she did tug her hand free. He was talking about her going home, and that wasn't what she wanted to hear at all. Telling herself that he needed time to fully absorb her news before he reached a decision about renewing their relationship, Jenny realised she had no choice but to be patient. As much as her heart ached to have Rodrigo genuinely care for her, just as she cared for him, as well as yearning for him to embrace the idea of them having a child, she would simply have to bide her time.

But it was hard when she was so in love that the depth of her feelings was like a gnawing physical ache inside her.

Her breathing hitched. Staring back into Rodrigo's sculpted handsome face, it was as though she was looking at him for the very first time. The echo of her thudding heart reverberated round her brain. 'Do you really want me to come back with you now to the apartment?' she questioned quietly. 'What about your work?'

'Did you hear me say that work was my priority today, *querida*?' His lips formed a surprisingly tender smile, the charismatic gesture charging the space and making it thrillingly intimate. Looping his arm round her shoulders, he tipped up Jenny's chin so that she was forced to meet his disturbing gaze head-on. 'Whatever else is going on, Jenny Wren…it is good to have you here.'

His warm lips brushed gently and beguilingly against hers. Jenny heard her last defence crash to the ground in a pile of rubble and smoke. Her senses were so intoxicated by him, her heart so full, how could it do anything else?

But a kiss that had started out as an affectionate caress quickly flared into something more urgent and primal as his tongue dived commandingly inside her mouth and his strong arms circled her waist to crush her to him. His hand palmed her breast. The exquisite pressure against the already throbbing sensitive tip made Jenny emit a softly ragged sigh.

Tensing, Rodrigo immediately removed his lips to stare down at her with a rueful smile. 'My apologies for taking advantage of you yet again, *querida*... especially when you're injured and hurting. But it's clear I have a tendency to temporarily lose my mind whenever I'm around you.'

She wanted to tell him it didn't matter...that he could lose his mind around her whenever he liked. But the nausea that had gripped her downstairs suddenly returned in a debilitating wave.

'Jenny?' There was definitely alarm in Rodrigo's examining ebony gaze. 'What's the matter?'

When she didn't immediately answer, because she was concentrating all her attention on not disgracing herself, he jumped to his feet and swore.

'*Maldita sea!* Clearly you are in shock after your accident. The doctor should have foreseen this... How could he have been so remiss? What was he thinking of? Let me get you some water.'

He was back in a trice, proffering a tall crystal glass. Jenny gulped down the cool, clear mineral water it contained as though it were a lifeline. A few seconds later the sickness that had so uncomfortably invaded her thankfully abated.

'It's all right. It's not shock, Rodrigo. It's just a touch of morning sickness. I'm getting used to it.'

'Oh.' He appeared to mull this over. 'The sooner I get you back to the apartment in La Ribera the better,' he announced decisively. 'Then you can rest as much as you like until you feel better.' Delving into his inside jacket pocket for his mobile, he reeled off some urgent-sounding instructions in Spanish to the person he'd called. 'My car will be at the front entrance in five minutes,' he informed her.

He'd left Jenny relaxing on the terrace beneath an umbrella, her injured ankle elevated on a chair, a fresh glass of juice and a light snack at her elbow, and returned to work. Rodrigo's plan was to finish as early as he could to rejoin her. She'd been worryingly quiet when they'd left the hotel to drive to the apartment in La Ribera—the apartment they'd once shared. Something told him it was because he hadn't acted as if he welcomed her surprising and unexpected news about the baby.

He truly regretted that, but truth to tell he'd been knocked sideways by it—as well as by Jenny showing up at his hotel as she had. The idea of becoming a father still reverberated through him like the aftershocks of a quake. Understandably, he was feeling a little dazed. Yet after their passionate night together in Cornwall he *had* worried about the possibility of such an event happening after so thoughtlessly making love to Jenny without protection. There was no question he wouldn't do the right thing by her. Their child would have everything an infant could need and more. But the impact of a child on his up-until-now independent lifestyle certainly gave him pause.

And if he'd been a bit heavy-handed about insisting Jenny stay with him at the apartment while they thrashed things out he made no apology for it. *How else could he keep an eye on her and make sure all was well?* Her complexion was still far too pale for his total peace of mind. Was the pregnancy already taking its toll on her?

Not for the first time Rodrigo found himself regretting that he'd left her that day, when she'd only just started to recover from the fever that had afflicted her. Thoughts and memories of their time together had relentlessly assailed him ever since. And sometimes during business meetings at work Rodrigo had found his attention wandering from the agenda with worrying frequency. *His father would roll over in his grave!*

Each time it had happened it had been without a doubt because he was thinking about Jenny... He was usually recalling her enchanting blonde looks, the way she always smelled so good, the way she moved her hands so gracefully to illustrate what she was saying, and most of all the way her enticingly beautiful body had felt under his again...*sublime*.

That particular stirring memory had disrupted many a good night's sleep. And the next day Rodrigo was inevitably grouchy and ill-tempered due to lack of rest.

* * *

The Barcelona apartment was situated in an impressive eighteenth century building in an area that had formerly been the preserve of the traditional fishing industry. Now it was an ultra-modern destination, packed with boutiques, chic restaurants and bars. Rodrigo himself had had a large say in the innovative interiors that occupied the building, and a couple of prestigious awards had come his way because of it. *But right now all that seemed irrelevant somehow.* The only thing that really concerned him was Jenny.

She wasn't out on the terrace where he'd left her. Cursing his inability to leave work when he'd said he would in order to be with her, he quickened his stride, thinking maybe she'd got fed up with waiting and phoned for a cab to go back to her hotel.

As he flung open all the doors in the apartment his anxiety grew. But when at last he peered into the stylish contemporary living room it was to discover Jenny, dozing lightly on one of the sumptuous white couches.

'You're back,' she said huskily, opening her eyes.

The strangest sensation seized Rodrigo… It was a heartfelt impulse to know what it might be like to come home to Jenny *every* day when he finished work…to have her say 'You're back' and not be able to hide her pleasure or joy. For a second his throat was too dry to speak.

'Did you see the sunset?' she added softly, when

he remained mute. She briefly glanced out through the opened French windows that led onto another pretty balcony. 'It's so beautiful. I can even see the spires of Gaudi's cathedral. I'd forgotten just how incredible it is.'

The dazzling amber and gold rays that flooded onto the room's burnished wood floor were *nothing* compared to the incandescent loveliness of the girl in front of him, Rodrigo thought hungrily.

Before he could stop himself he promised to take her to see the work that had been done on the cathedral since she'd last been there, before adding, 'How's your ankle?'

'A lot less painful since I took one of the painkillers your doctor left.'

'Perhaps you shouldn't take any more. You're pregnant, remember?'

'I did check with the doctor when you briefly left the room to answer the phone.' Jenny frowned. 'But of course I would be sensible about things like that.'

'I'm glad to hear it. And it's good to see that you have some colour back in your cheeks too,' he observed, unbuttoning his jacket as he moved towards her.

'Did you have another long meeting?' Drawing her legs up to the side, Jenny curved her mouth into a sympathetic smile as he sat down beside her.

'There are *always* long meetings and equally long unsocial hours when you run a business. I'm sure you remember that, since it was one of the reasons I knew it wasn't fair to you to carry on with our marriage.' He shrugged, impatiently tugging his royal blue silk tie free from his shirt collar. 'But just the same I'm sorry I didn't get back as early as I promised.'

'There's no need to apologise...I do understand.'

'You do?'

Rodrigo couldn't quite believe she meant that. He'd always been acutely aware of just how much time he spent away from home when he was working, and had been uneasy about it when he'd been married to Jenny.

'Yes, I do. You must be hungry,' she commented lightly, her summer-blue gaze dipping for a moment when he glanced steadily back at her.

'I am, but I've got into the habit of eating out most evenings when I'm here. You must also be hungry, *querida*. Shall we go out to dinner? Are you up to it?'

'I'll be fine. I've got to start putting my weight on my ankle again if I want it to get better.'

'I wasn't particularly meaning your injured ankle. I was referring to the fact that you're with child.'

Their eyes met and locked. Jenny gave Rodrigo a slow smile. 'It's not some illness, you know. I'm not going to suddenly retire from the world just because I'm pregnant!'

CHAPTER ELEVEN

'I CAN still hardly believe it.'

In one fluid, easy motion, Rodrigo got to his feet. A little anxious, Jenny watched him move to the centre of the room and then turn to face her. The last spectacular amber gold rays of the sunset turned to fiery orange before dying away completely. In its wake the room became dim and silent. Uncurling her legs, she gingerly put both feet to the floor, trying not to wince as she experimentally put some of her weight onto her bandaged ankle.

But the pain of her injury was nothing compared to the sense of desolation that was rapidly growing inside her at the idea of Rodrigo rejecting her pregnancy or thinking she was trying to manipulate him back into marriage.

'I want this baby,' Jenny said dully, folding her arms protectively across her stomach. 'I want to keep it and I will. No matter what you decide to do.'

Her throat was suddenly so tight and painful that tears were a scant breath away. But any weeping she did she resolved to do in private. It was already humiliating enough to have the father of her expected child look at her as though he'd just heard the worst news he'd ever received, without humiliating herself further by breaking her heart in front of him.

'To raise a child...' levelling his gaze, Rodrigo wiped his hand over his cheekbone '...it's best that the parents are in a stable relationship...no?'

'Ideally, I think, yes. But I know we don't live in a perfect world. People make mistakes, and sometimes it's just not possible to have a stable relationship. In that case one might decide to raise a child on one's own. I'm willing to do that, Rodrigo. If you really can't contemplate us being together any more, don't worry that I'm going to demand you support me.'

'Is this how you were with your feckless brother?'

'What do you mean?'

'I mean he demands money to feed his addictions and you simply give it to him without a fight...without standing up for yourself?'

Jenny's stomach plummeted to the ground, as though she were travelling in an out-of-control elevator. 'I didn't just *give* him the money! You have no idea how he could be. He was manipulative and cruel, and he had ways of getting what he wanted no matter how much I resisted his demands or said what I thought.' Shuddering at the memories that mercilessly flooded back, Jenny felt her eyes burn as she stared at Rodrigo. 'He used to taunt me that I wasn't a "real woman" because my marriage had failed. The fault obviously must lie with me. When insults illustrating how useless I was both as your wife and a businesswoman didn't work he used fits of pure rage to intimidate me. When that kind of thing happens more times than you care to remember your confidence in your ability to do anything can very quickly desert you, and for a while my business got into trouble because I felt so overwhelmed. I'm not proud of that. But I *am* proud of the fact that one day I woke up and took steps to end the misery—despite the horrible threats that came my way. I fought to keep the house in court, then gave Tim a more than generous price for his share of it when I won so that he could move on somewhere else. You may not know this about me, Rodrigo, but I *am* strong. Strong enough to face whatever challenges might lie ahead and not be defeated…even challenges like raising a child on my own.'

'Your worthless brother shouted at you repeatedly?'

'Yes.'

'*Cabrón!* You are well rid of him. If I had known you were returning to such a situation I would have stepped in and dealt with it once and for all.'

'I know,' Jenny sighed. 'That's why I never told you the truth about how Tim could be.'

'In any case…understand that you will *not* be raising our child on your own.'

Immediately Jenny sensed the steely resolve in his voice.

'Do you really think I would stand aside and let you do that? I may not have planned on starting a family, but that doesn't mean that I won't face up to my responsibilities. I most definitely *will*.'

A single hard-to-contain tear slid down Jenny's check. 'Is that the only way you view this, Rodrigo? As a kind of duty you have to fulfil?'

'My head is spinning at what you've just told me about the situation with your brother—the fact that I unknowingly let you return to such abuse. It makes me furious. But I'm sorry...I don't mean to sound so cold.' The tension in his shoulders visibly relaxing, he sat down beside her and cupped her chilled hands between his palms. 'We will reach the best solution for both the child and us—of that I am certain. Will you just allow me a little time to think things through?'

'Take as long as you want.' Too distressed to want to notice how emphatically his touch warmed her, Jenny sniffed, tugging back her hands. 'I'll give you my home phone number in England before I leave. When you've had enough time to think things over you can ring me.'

It was almost *unbearable* to be so close to the man she loved and yet feel a distance wider than the most yawning chasm. Intent on escaping to deal with her tormenting emotions in private, Jenny surged to her feet. The pain that jackknifed through her ankle almost made her cry out, but she stoically ignored it.

Before she had the chance to move away, Rodrigo

stood up beside her. Firmly turning her round to face him, he settled his hands either side of her waist. 'You are not running back to England. We'll work things out together, Jenny. Don't turn away from me…please. I don't think I could bear it.'

The desolation she saw etched in the sublime angles and planes of his beautiful face almost made Jenny catch her breath. Somewhere inside her hope leapt like a rekindled flame in a burned-low candle. 'Oh, Rodrigo…' Touching her hand to his hollowed cheek, she suddenly couldn't prevent the steady flow of scalding tears that seeped from her eyes.

Murmuring something low, Rodrigo lifted her high in his arms against his chest and stalked with her into his bedroom. In the dim half-light of the balmy evening he urgently covered Jenny with his body on the king-sized bed as though the world might end if he didn't. Then he claimed her lips again and again with hot, open-mouthed kisses as passion-driven hands tore at her clothes—removing hers, then his own, before holding her arms high above her head and linking their fingers.

As their gazes locked in the subdued evening light, with the sensual, drugging scent of late-in-the-season exotic blooms drifting up to them from the lovely gardens below, he drove himself hard into her body, his soulful dark eyes burning like the sparks of fiery embers into the walls of her heart and capturing it.

His highly charged possession registered right down to the very corners of Jenny's soul. Meeting her lover's kisses with equal mindless hunger, she felt Rodrigo's fingers press deep into her buttocks to make their bodies fit even more closely. Her senses were already drowning in the musky heat of his slick, hard-muscled male form when they were seized by her violent climax. She barely knew where the feral cry that left her lips came from, but the sea of powerful sensual release was so profoundly intense and shocking that it rocked through her like an earthquake.

Glancing up, she looked, stunned, into Rodrigo's scorching gaze. As he rose above her she recognised blazing intent as he bucked, renting the sultry air with a primeval shout of his own. And as the echoes of that heart-jolting shout died away to mere shadows he laid his dark head between Jenny's breasts, the ragged deep breaths that left his lips gradually slowing.

Letting her lids flutter closed, Jenny played softly with his hair. The dark strands were incredibly soft and silky in her hand and cried out to be touched. *If only he loved me*, she thought fervently. If only he loved our baby and me with no holds barred, as if we were the most important things in the whole world to him. Then how perfect these stunning moments would be.

But he had asked her to give him time, she recalled. And she would...she *would*.

Stirring, Rodrigo lifted his head to contemplate her with a wicked lascivious grin, before pressing his lips to her still flat, smooth-skinned stomach, deliberately letting them linger so that his heat felt like a brand. Then he glanced back at her again, and the expression in his long-lashed sable eyes made Jenny's insides cartwheel.

'It is incredible that you carry the fruit of our loving deep inside you,' he murmured, and his rich voice had a definite catch in it. 'And now you have intoxicated me like a drug, and I am indeed… addicted.'

Moving upwards again, he bent his head to suckle her rose-tipped breasts in turn, and Jenny realised that the fire which had blazed between them had embers that were all too ready to be stoked again. As he smiled into her eyes, Rodrigo's gaze was again hungry and hot.

'I'm not trying to trap you, Rodrigo…with the baby, I mean' she said softly.

'Angel, you trapped me the first moment I saw you. I have never had such a violent reaction to the mere sight of a beautiful woman before. And when I found Lily's place, on that cold and rainy night, I could hardly believe that the storm had steered me back into your presence again. But let's not talk right now…I'm too impatient for words when all I really want to do is enjoy you. Come, sit astride me, so that I can savour every beautiful inch of you.'

His big hands were careful to help her avoid hurting her ankle as they swapped positions. Then it was Jenny's turn to feast her eyes on the taut, bronzed-skinned body beneath her, with a gentle riot of curling black hair dusting his nipples, disappearing in a slim, sensual column down to his narrow-hipped pelvis. Adjusting her thighs over his, she hungrily accepted him inside her. His penetration was deep and smooth, and she moaned low and tossed her head back with the sheer wild pleasure of it. Then she started to rock a little…

'I'd like us to take a shower together before we go out to dinner,' Rodrigo told her huskily.

'What about my bandaged ankle?'

He lifted a shoulder. 'What about it? There are infinite ways we can accommodate whatever is needed, my angel.' His expression glazed with passion, he cupped Jenny's hips to rock her even harder against him. 'You can lean against me the whole time…' His breath was ragged again as he watched her move over him, her blonde hair an enticing tousled mass of corn-gold against her pale slim shoulders. 'And I can wash your hair for you, just like I did once before. I'm an expert now, remember? Then you can wash mine. Afterwards, I will redo the dressing for you.'

'Rodrigo?'

'What is it, beautiful?'

'Didn't you—?' Another helpless moan left Jenny's lips as he pushed upwards and high inside her. 'Didn't you say something about not talking?'

'*Sí*. I did. I guess you'll just have to kiss me passionately to make me stop.'

* * *

His black silk pyjama bottoms riding low on his hips, his chest bare, Rodrigo returned to the bedroom with the two cups of coffee he'd made. Last night they had agreed to give going out to dinner a miss. Instead he had ordered some food from a favourite local restaurant to be delivered, and they'd enjoyed it sitting in their robes at the huge glass table in the dining room.

Now, the sun-kissed morning light was drifting in through the large plate-glass windows, and the undrawn coffee-coloured silk curtains were moving gently either side of the frames in the breeze.

The delicate light outlined Jenny's still sleeping form. Her slim pale arms were down by her sides as she slept on her stomach in the middle of the huge canopied bed, her golden hair a riot of silk over her shoulders and her exquisitely shaped back bare to the waist.

Leaving the coffee on a bedside cabinet, Rodrigo simply stood at the side of the bed to gaze at her. Just the sight of her made the blood pound hard in his veins. And last night…last night he had been so close to confessing that he loved and adored her. *What had held him back?* She was carrying his baby, for goodness' sake!

The thought was like a small explosion inside him. Prevalent in his emotions was pride, possessiveness and joy…ecstasy, even. It hardly made sense that he couldn't voice his feelings to Jenny. But unfortunately, given his past, it *did* make sense.

Even now Rodrigo sensed his father's austere ghost looming over him—his disapproving gaze and the countless warnings he'd drummed into him about the dangers of losing his focus making him shudder. Then he thought about how his dedication to the business and his long hours away from home had doubtless contributed the unhappiness he'd seen in Jenny when they were together. Could he risk hurting her a second time? He was crazy about her. It would hurt so much more this time if things between them didn't work out…all the more because they would have a child together.

In the bed, Jenny drew her knees up under the covers, rolling over onto her side, facing Rodrigo. Her dazzling eyes opened like precious sapphires winking back at him. His blood heated as if molten honey were being siphoned through his veins.

'*Buenos días*, beautiful…I've brought you some coffee.'

Grabbing the silk counterpane in front of her as she sat up against her pillow, she made a face. 'Not coffee. I can't stomach it at the moment, I'm afraid. But you go ahead.'

'This is because you are pregnant?' Again the immense enormity of the situation facing him hit Rodrigo.

'Yes. I haven't visited my doctor yet to confirm it, but when I return to the UK I will.'

'There's no need to wait until you return to the UK to do that. I can arrange an appointment for you to see a top obstetrician at any time, Jenny. In fact I'll get onto it as soon as we've had breakfast.'

'But don't get an appointment for today, will you?'

'Why not?' Rodrigo frowned. *Was she hiding the fact that something might be wrong?*

'Because you promised we'd visit the cathedral together today, remember? When I was here last I visited it on my own, but it wasn't the same without you.'

Her sweet dimpled smile eased his fears, and he climbed across the bed so he could join her. 'Then a promise is a promise, is it not? So we'll get ready soon and go to the cathedral. The earlier the better, as the lines of tourists form quickly. And afterwards we'll have lunch at a great restaurant I know that does fine dining.'

'We could have cheese sandwiches and a bottle of squash in the park…I really wouldn't care, Rodrigo. You don't have to impress me with fine dining.'

'I've never met another woman who was so easily satisfied.'

'Did I say anything about being easily satisfied, Señor Martinez?'

Rodrigo's stomach muscles clenched hard as iron when Jenny tugged at the drawstring on his pyjamas and then, with a warm, seductive glint in her summer-blue eyes, deliberately loosened them.

'So, you want me to show you how good I am in bed, Jenny Wren?'

She met his lowering mouth with a hungry little groan. 'Yes, please!'

CHAPTER TWELVE

IT WAS like a fairytale castle, and quite wonderful to have the chance to see it again—even more so because Rodrigo accompanied her.

As she leaned on the walking stick he'd provided Jenny gazed up at the collection of imbedded seashells in the cathedral walls, squinting in the warm early-morning sunshine to marvel at the tapering spires and curved walls, as well as the astonishing un-cathedral-like mounds of fruit that looked as if they were fashioned out of wax.

Gaudi had been a lover of nature, Rodrigo explained to her—he'd wanted to incorporate as much of nature as he could into his cathedral. Everywhere Jenny glanced was a quirky little gem, like a waterspout coming out of the mouth of a salamander or frog, and delight and awe were prevalent as she looked avidly around her. Inside, the cavernous interior was like a huge carcass that had been abandoned. But as they gazed from the walkway down at the tall cranes that were still very much part of the construction they saw that work on the Cathedral was still undoubtedly in progress. Even though the building would not be finished until around 2030 Jenny could easily imagine it filled with tall flickering pillar candles and a stunning altarpiece that the great and the good could marvel at and pay their respects.

Beside her on the walkway, Rodrigo stayed protectively close. A warm little buzz of pleasure assailed her every time she realised it. He might have experienced the cathedral many times before, but he clearly didn't take its beauty and magnificence for granted, and Jenny was certain she spent just as much time stealing furtive glances at his wonderful strong-boned profile as she did examining the stunning construction.

Leaning towards her, he whispered, 'I think it's time you took the weight off that ankle for a while. Come…we'll go back down and find a seat somewhere.'

Eschewing Jenny's idea of a simple picnic in the park, Rodrigo took her to a fabulous restaurant for lunch, which had a fleet of gleaming and expensive cars parked outside. It seemed he knew the manager well, because he was enthusiastically greeted like a long-lost friend and attention was danced upon him from the moment he and Jenny walked through the door.

Awed by the elaborate crystal chandelier twinkling above them, and the generous-sized table laid immaculately with sparkling silver cutlery overlooking a stunning white terrace, Jenny glanced down at her simple white short-sleeved blouse and aubergine-coloured skirt, praying she wasn't underdressed.

If Rodrigo's teasing sensual smile was anything to go by, she needn't have worried. Every glance he sent her way touched her like an intimate caress—as if to remind her of the passionate loving they had shared and *would* share again. And, although there were several amazing-looking women close by, having lunch with their partners or friends, it seemed he had eyes only for Jenny.

Yet as she tackled her deliciously light starter she began to feel queasy again. *This time it wasn't due to her hormones.* Why did he seem to be deliberately avoiding the topic of her pregnancy? He had asked her to give him time, but was that fair? What if he decided that he still didn't want to be with her, despite the fact they were going to have a child together? Now she didn't know if she *could* wait to have his verdict. It seemed that she'd already waited a long time for what she wanted in life.

Somewhere outside, the sound of a child's distressed crying highlighted her apprehension about the fact that her own baby's father had still not made a decision about their future.

'Rodrigo?'

'Yes, *querida*?'

'I need to talk about our situation…about what's going to happen?'

His fingers twirled the stem of his wine glass.

With a brooding expression, he lifted his gaze. 'I asked you to give me some time, did I not?'

'We don't have to get married again, if that's what you're worried about. We can still raise a child together unwed.'

But even as the words left her lips Jenny's acute sense of distress pressed in on her, like a claustrophobic bubble about to swallow her up. More than anything she'd always yearned for a family of her own. She'd waited so long to have her dream come true—had endured enough disappointment and hurt to last a lifetime. From across the table she observed Rodrigo's shuttered expression, and she couldn't help wondering if she was about to endure *more*.

'This is not easy for me,' he breathed.

'I can see that.'

His mobile phone rang. Reaching into his jacket pocket, he didn't ignore it, as Jenny had hoped he might. He spoke entirely in Spanish to the caller. She was completely excluded from the animated conversation.

When it came to an end Rodrigo leaned towards her, his air definitely distracted. 'I apologise for interrupting our meal with that call, but something has come up at the hotel that needs my attention. In fact...' he glanced down at the solid gold diver's watch that so expensively circled his tanned wrist '...I'm going to have to leave you for a while, I'm afraid. Would you mind very much if I arranged for my driver to take you back to the apartment when you've finished eating? All your needs will be catered for—you only have to ask. It's vital that I get back to the hotel for a meeting as quickly as possible.'

'You mean you're not even going to have lunch with me?'

'I'm sorry, Jenny. But this is very important.'

'And what we were just discussing *isn't*?' Crushed that he was proposing to abandon her in the restaurant to finish her lunch alone, Jenny picked up her linen napkin and threw it onto her side-plate. Searing colour scorched her cheeks as she faced him.

'Of course it's important.' Scowling in frustration, Rodrigo drummed his fingers on the table. 'But I have responsibilities—'

'Don't we all? I understand you're committed and dedicated to your job, Rodrigo—you wouldn't be such a resounding success at it if you weren't. But sometimes we have to balance our priorities, don't you think? Sometimes there are other forms of success besides work. And if the fact that in a few months' time you're going to be a father isn't a priority, then I honestly don't know what is!'

She pushed to her feet, forgetting about her still bandaged ankle, and almost lost her footing. Immediately Rodrigo came round to her side. But when he circled Jenny's waist with his arm she angrily threw him off. Right then she didn't even care if they had an audience.

'If you're leaving to go back to the hotel then I'll leave now too,' she told him, mentally garnering every bit of resolve not to cry. 'To tell you the truth, Rodrigo, I don't think I'm so keen to stay with a man who'll always put work before his personal life anyway—especially when he has a child to consider. What if our baby was ill and I needed you with me as his father, to be supportive? Would you say *Sorry, but I've got to get back to work?* Don't bother with a reply... Going by past experience I think I already know your answer.'

The Black Mercedes drew up in the private car park of the spectacular glass and chrome hotel. In the elegant, luxurious confines that separated them from the driver, Rodrigo tugged Jenny's pale slim hand onto his lap. His expression was racked and conflicted, she saw.

'Do you know how bad I feel about leaving you like this?'

'If you feel so bad then you'll postpone your meeting...at least for a couple of hours...so we can talk,' Jenny returned reasonably.

Scraping his fingers through his ebony mane, Rodrigo emitted a long frustrated sigh. 'I'm afraid that's impossible.'

'Impossible meaning you can't postpone it, or you *won't*?'

'*Dios mio!* An extraordinary meeting has been urgently called, with half a dozen shareholders waiting on my decision about a considerable financial undertaking for the hotel, and I absolutely *cannot* postpone it. Initially I instructed my second-in-command to stand in for me, but when I spoke to him at lunch I realised he was not as fully informed about the deal as I am. I'm genuinely sorry about this, *querida*, but we will talk as long as you want when I return. I promise you.'

With a quick kiss on her cheek, and the drift of his tantalising cologne lingering in the space he'd left behind, Rodrigo knocked on the glass partition to give some instructions to his driver and in a flash… was gone.

Never before had he endured such hard-to-bear impatience. It was like torture. As his driver weaved the car through the converging traffic, with furious horns being honked loudly and drivers gesticulating wildly, Rodrigo almost…*almost* wanted to get out and walk back to the apartment.

For about the hundredth time he checked the time on his watch. Leaving his delighted shareholders toasting him with champagne after the mutually satisfying outcome of the meeting—as well as the extremely healthy financial report his accountant had given them—he'd all but knocked them over to get out of the boardroom.

Dragging his tie away from his shirt collar, he glanced out of the tinted car windows and gritted his teeth. *All he wanted to do now was get back to Jenny.* He should have postponed the meeting. His portfolio and kudos were such that he could have easily put it off until it was more convenient. Now, remembering Jenny's disbelieving face and angry declaration that she wasn't so keen any more to be with a man who put his work first, Rodrigo wished he *had*. Oh, why had he messed up again when he'd been given an incredible second chance to make things right?

A sight suddenly transfixed him. The car had purred to a stop to let a small family cross the road in front of them. There was an older woman, with a red tint in her hair, and a pretty young couple with a baby. All three of them were fussing and cooing over the infant, until Rodrigo's driver beeped on his horn to indicate to them that they could safely cross, and suddenly Rodrigo was deluged by his need to hold Jenny close and confess his adoration and love for her—to make her see how sorry he was for being such an idiot.

Why on earth had it taken him so long to realise what a precious jewel he had in his grasp? Had he been blind? What if after this new disappointment she completely gave up on him and left him for good? Although it was totally his own fault, he didn't think he could bear it. She was carrying his baby, and— given the chance—he *would* be the supportive father she yearned for him to be. Never again would he put some damn board meeting before *her*. Somewhere along the line he'd lost perspective. Being a success in business had become like a runaway train.

Rapping on the glass partition, he spoke rapidly to his driver, opened the passenger door and leapt out.

With his heart pounding and the sweat sticking his shirt like glue to his back in the sultry afternoon sun he sprinted hard all the way back to the apartment.

She was gone. With mounting shock Rodrigo found the bedroom empty of all her baggage and belongings. The luxurious apartment had never felt so lonely or so empty—apart from the first time Jenny had left, that was.

With a despairing oath he prowled the rooms, searching for clues that might tell him where she'd gone. There wasn't even a note. However, he did find a scrap of paper with her address and telephone number back in the UK written hastily on it, left poignantly on his pillow.

Hardly daring even to mentally articulate the conclusion that was rapidly forming in his mind, he rang the concierge to have his worst fears confirmed: Jenny had indeed ordered a cab to take her to the airport...

Thankfully the airport manager had been a fantastic help. He'd had to waive quite a few airport regulations to get Rodrigo as far as the passenger lounge where customers waited before boarding their flights. Now, with his impatient gaze scanning the sea of heads, he felt his heartbeat almost careen to a standstill when he spied Jenny on a seat at the back, in deep conversation with a young, curly-haired youth dressed very casually in baggy denims and an equally baggy sweatshirt.

Rodrigo straightened his silk tie and stole a couple of moments in which to compose himself. His heart was still pounding. Suddenly, as if she'd sensed his presence, Jenny glanced up, her gaze colliding in astonishment with his.

Moving to stand in front of her, he felt the words he so desperately wanted to say die on his lips as he glanced avidly into her stunning summer-blue eyes.

'Forgive me,' he finally breathed. 'I've been such an idiot! I should never have gone to that meeting instead of staying and talking to you.'

'What are you—what are you doing here, Rodrigo?'

He grimaced. 'More to the point, *mi angel*...what are *you* doing here?'

She dipped her head. 'I'm flying home. I would willingly walk through fire for you, Rodrigo, but I won't stay around where I'm not wanted. When I saw that you were quite willing to leave me alone at lunch and go to a meeting, I realised that it was no different from the first time we were together. It's your business that means the world to you...not me or our baby. I'm afraid that Barcelona suddenly lost its charm.' She swallowed hard. 'When I get home we can discuss things on the phone. I left my number on your pillow.'

'You would walk through fire for me, you said?'

'I love you. Didn't you know that?'

With a racing heart, Rodrigo dropped down into the shiny hard chair next to her. When the curly-haired young man Jenny had been talking to openly stared at him he pierced him with a steely gaze and said, 'Do you mind? I'm having a private conversation with my fiancée.'

Jenny gulped, pressing her hand against her heart. 'What did you say?'

'Wait a moment. I want to do this properly, Jenny Wren.'

To her utter amazement, Rodrigo dropped down onto his bended knee in front of her. Several heads in the lounge's vicinity swivelled interestedly. Reaching for her hand, he raised it to his lips. The warmth of his mouth made her insides dissolve as surely as ice cream beneath a blazing sun. 'Will you marry me Jenny—and this time for good? Marry me and make me happier than I'm sure I deserve.' Removing the solid gold signet ring from the little finger on his left hand, he slid it onto Jenny's wedding finger.

'Are you serious, Rodrigo?' She couldn't help the husky catch in her voice. The whole scenario was overwhelming...*surreal*, even.

'More serious than I've ever been about anything in my life,' he answered, grinning. 'The business has always meant a lot to me...I don't deny that. My father drummed it into me from a young age that I should strive to make a name for myself in business...

that I should work hard and not be distracted from my focus. Not even if I fell in love. But the dream of success he sold to me was *his*, not mine. My mother was the wise one, but it took me until today to realize just *how* wise. She wanted me to have a family, Jenny. She told me it was the most important thing and she was right. And even though her relationship with my father was not exactly made in heaven she believed in the legacy of a loving family with all her heart. Now my own feelings echo that. You and our baby mean the world to me and I will always endeavour to put you both first...I swear it.'

'Do you mean that?' As she bent down to whisper the question, Jenny found her lips captured eagerly and hungrily, and for long moments she forgot everything but the sensation of the delicious pressure of Rodrigo's passionate mouth on hers.

Drawing away from him after a while, she was shocked to hear the steady resounding echo of applause in her ears. Several people were on their feet in support, and when Rodrigo also got to his feet he winked at Jenny, then turned to give their audience a highly theatrical bow.

As he pulled her back into his arms she gazed up eagerly into his loving dark eyes and smiled. 'I reckon that wild storm *did* bring you to me that night, Rodrigo. It took me a while to believe that fate had brought you back...given us a second chance...but now I don't doubt it. I'm just so grateful, my love.'

'And I echo the words I told you then… My body, my heart and my soul are yours for ever, my bewitching Jenny Wren. I pray you never have cause to doubt it, but I swear I will spend the rest of my life showing you how ardent I am!'

LET'S TALK

Romance

For exclusive extracts, competitions
and special offers, find us online:

 facebook.com/millsandboon

 @MillsandBoon

 @MillsandBoonUK

Get in touch on 01413 063232

For all the latest titles coming soon, visit
millsandboon.co.uk/nextmonth